Dayworld Breakup

Tor books by Philip José Farmer

The Cache
Dayworld Breakup
Father to the Stars
Greatheart Silver
The Other Log of Phileas Fogg
The Purple Book
Stations of the Nightmare
Time's Last Gift
Traitor to the Living

DAYWORLD
BREAKUP

Philip José Farmer

A TOM DOHERTY ASSOCIATES BOOK
NEW YORK

DAYWORLD BREAKUP

Copyright © 1990 by Philip José Farmer

A Tor Book
Published by Tom Doherty Associates, Inc.
49 West 24th Street
New York, N.Y. 10010

Printed in the United States of America

ISBN 0-312-85035-2

First edition: June 1990

0 9 8 7 6 5 4 3 2 1

To my first great-grandchild, Zachary Joel Gittrich,
born September 6, 1988

A Foreword Which Is also an Afterword
by Ariel Cairdsdaughter

My father used to introduce me as *my daughter, the historian*.

Jefferson Cervantes Caird never dreamed that, some day, he would be a prominent person in videobooks and rank with Robin Hood, William Tell, George Washington, and many other fictional, semi-fictional, and very real characters in legends and history. Nor did he anticipate that his daughter would be researching his life.

Why should I, his child, have to research him? Don't I know him through and through, have at my fingertips all the facts of his life from birth to now?

No, I do not. For one thing, I seldom saw him after I got out of high school.

For another thing, I no more knew that he had many lives, not just one life, than anybody else.

As for his very early life, what he knew about it was a lie. Only his parents knew the truth. After they died, no one knew. My father was ignorant of the truth, though it may have kept itself hidden deep in his memory, inaccessible to any callup code.

Another thing about his story. It would not have happened

before the middle of the 1st century N.E., what the ancients called the 21st century A.D. And what he did took place over two thousand years later.

Two thousand obyears, that is. That's a term, obyears, no longer used in official calculations or in everyday conversation. There is no longer a distinction between obtime and subtime. That is, between objective time and subjective time. We're back to the system of the ancients when we talk of time. All things return, but they're not what they were.

In the old days, which we then called the New Era, we grew up in what was called the Dayworld. We were accustomed to it from the time we became old enough to have understanding. It seemed quite natural.

Now, schoolchildren have to be taught about the Dayworld: stoners for people, the division of the living into sevenths, and the difference between obtime and subtime. To the children, it's fascinating history, though I suppose they're still like schoolchildren everywhere and any time. They'd rather be out playing.

Still, the world before they were born must seem as strange to them as the pre-New Era world was to me when I was a child. Now that I'm fifty years old, physiologically, that is, but actually three hundred and fifty years old as the Earth circles the sun, the post-New Era seems strange to me.

They learn that the world was once divided nationally, that there were many states each of which had its own government. Then they learn that, after a long and bloody struggle, there was a world government. Even after all the deaths from this war, eight billion people lived on this planet. In another hundred years, obtime, there would be ten billion. Maybe eleven. The planet could not support this many, especially since the pollution and ravaging of forests was swiftly poisoning all life.

But the invention popularly called the stoner was brought into practical use. The suspension of molecular movement in living bodies by the application of electrical power changed society enormously and changed the face of the Earth. For the better, in most respects. In other respects, no.

The world population was divided into sevenths, and each seventh would live one day of the week. The other six days it would be in the stoner containers, its life in a sort of suspended animation, though it really was not suspended. It was frozen. Tuesday's people, for example, would have to enter these coffinlike containers sometime before midnight. They would be "stoned," and shortly thereafter, Wednesday's people would be unstoned. And so on. The following Tuesday, that day's citizens would be "unstoned" and would take up their interrupted living.

There you were. Every day, only 1.1 billion would be eating and drinking food and water resources, emptying only 1.1 billion people's wastes, and so on.

But eight billion overall was still too much. So the world government imposed an almost inescapable birth control, and the population began dwindling toward the number the government thought that the planet could handle without ill effects. Even today, despite our many freedoms, parents know they cannot have more than two children unless the government lifts the limits temporarily in certain areas. But the most any couple can have is three.

The Dayworld was not Utopia. Utopia is impossible because innate human nature is non-Utopian. The majority of people accepted the system, though there was a certain amount of resentment and grumbling. Also, there was much fraud, lying, and struggle for power in the government hierarchy. No getting away from that. I do not doubt at all that it's still going on. The government, like all governments throughout history, needs to be watched carefully and to be checked, straightened out. In that respect, things have not changed at all. The governed must govern the governors.

In those days, there were "daybreakers," the discontented and the outright criminal persons who slipped away from the confines of the once-a-week living. Few of them escaped the police, euphemistically called the organics and referred to by the citizens as "ganks." When caught, a daybreaker was sent to a rehabilitation institution. If he could not be rehabbed, he was stoned permanently.

Among these daybreakers was my father. But he differed from the others. He had a powerful, though secret, organization to help him, to give him a different identity for each day of the week, and to maintain these IDs. Long before Jeff Caird was born, a Tuesday citizen, a scientist named Immerman had discovered a means for slowing down aging. With this, a person whose normal lifespan was one hundred years could live seven hundred years. But since the stoner system allowed a person to live seven times his normal lifespan, Immerman could use his ASF (age-slowing factor) to live fourteen hundred years.

He kept the ASF to himself and some family members. Later, the ASF was given to members of his expanding secret organization, the "immers." Jeff Caird, his grandson and great-grandson, was a courier for the immers. He "broke day," assuming an ID for each day so that he could carry messages the immers did not want to go through any electronic channels. He also performed certain duties for the immer chiefs, duties which they did not want the lesser immers to know about.

Eventually, my father *became* these seven personae. Then Panthea Snick, a detective, accidentally got on his trail. While tracking him, she was captured by the immers.

Immerman was now a World Councillor with the fake ID of David Jimson Ananda. His grandson, Jeff Caird, had become involved with Snick and was now a danger to the immers. Immerman ordered that his grandson be killed.

So much for family feeling and loyalty.

At the same time, Caird's seven personae were battling for control of his body. The immers, aware of this, deemed him to be a double danger to them.

Though Caird was caught, he could tell his captors nothing about his previous activities. Even the irresistible truth drug used could not make him reveal his illegal activities. He had suffered a psychic breakdown and had a new persona which had no memory of the previous seven personae. Then he got out of the supposedly escape-proof prison and fled to Los Angeles State from Manhattan State.

During his long odyssey, he rescued Snick from a stoner warehouse. She had been stoned and placed there after being railroaded in a secret illegal trial by the government. This was done at the circuitous instigation of Immerman (now the World Councillor Ananda). He was afraid that she would not be able to keep quiet about her knowledge of the immers.

My father (now calling himself Duncan), Snick, and a companion were captured by Ananda in Los Angeles. But my father and Snick killed Ananda's bodyguards and overpowered him. Using a drug, TM, Caird extracted from Ananda a secret override command. This enabled him to broadcast a TV message all over the world without being cut off by the government. He revealed some of the truth about the world government's misuse of its power, its lies, and the existence of the age-slowing factor.

Duncan (that is, my father, Jeff Caird) and Snick fled from Ananda's suite on the top floor of one of Los Angeles's city-towers. By then the police, the ganks, were hurrying to the tower.

The following is an account of his and Snick's adventures from that moment. As you will see, much of it has had to be reconstructed. We don't know what Caird was thinking during this time. Nor did we know why he fell into his final persona (we thought it was his final).

In a way, it was his final. But from then on, he grew into an adult, mentally speaking. And the scientists have good reason to believe that his character traits are those of his original persona, Jefferson Caird. But, as you will see, that was not his original character.

My father still does not remember the strange sea change into the genuinely original persona. However, long after the events described below, the scientists used a new and highly advanced technique which enabled them to reach back and display the brain waves of that period. It is not really thought-reading. It's a long and expensive and, for the subject, painful process. But the mental activity shown on the CRTs enabled the scientists to interpret more or less exactly what happened during that extremely crucial event in my father's life.

Thus, they can be given herein with a great deal of assurance that this is what actually happened.

NOTE: The events leading up to *Dayworld Breakup* are described fully in *Dayworld* and its sequel, *Dayworld Rebel*, by Philip José Farmer.

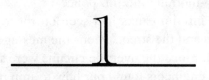

Running away was also running toward.

Duncan, sprinting across the rooftop of the tower, thought of how true that old Chinese proverb was. Wherever he went in his flight from the organic police, the "ganks," he would find others. They were a horde of locusts. He and Panthea Snick, his fellow refugee, were the crops the locusts meant to devour.

"Not if I can help it!" he said, gasping.

"What?" she said close behind him.

He did not reply. He had to save his breath. But his anger was not a thing to need conserving. It had long been a red tide building up in him, pulled by the moon of the injustices he had suffered. His wrath beat at his reason and discretion and threatened to smash them.

The low night clouds pulsed with the light reflected from the towers of Los Angeles. In all of the twenty monoliths rising from the waters of the L.A. basin, lights were flashing on and off and sirens were screaming like animals caught in traps. These were the last warning for Monday's citizens to go into their stoners. There they became as hard as diamonds, unconscious until next Monday. At eight minutes to midnight, only a handful of today's citizens would not be in their cylinders. These were the Monday-interim ganks who stayed at their posts until relieved shortly after midnight by the Tuesday-morning interim police.

Today's interim ganks had seen on the wallscreens in the precinct stations and the streetscreens the messages which Duncan had transmitted. Since the override circuits were still working (and would until the engineers found out how to stop them), Tuesday's interim ganks would also see the screen messages and the printouts. And so would Tuesday's citizens when they stepped out of their stoners.

Citizens of the World!
Your government has kept secret from you a formula for slowing aging by a factor of seven. If you had this, you could live seven times longer. The World Council and other high officials are using this to prolong their own lives. They are denying you this formula. Here is the formula.

Below this were the chemical formulae and the instructions for making the age-slowing factor.

The second message:

Citizens of the World!
Your government has lied to you for a thousand obyears. The world population is not eight billion. It is only two billion. Repeat: two billion. This artificial division of humankind into seven days is not necessary. Demand the truth. Demand that you be allowed to return to the natural system of life. If the government resists, revolt! Do not be satisfied with the lies of the government. Revolt!

Authorized message by David Jimson Ananda. A.k.a. Gilbert Ching Immerman. Also authorized and transmitted by Jefferson Cervantes Caird.

Duncan and Snick ran across the rooftop toward an access structure at the east end of the tower. It was over two hundred yards to the structure from the hatchway out of which they had climbed. They had to get there before organic airboats landed on the rooftop or the ganks who had stormed the suite on the floor below the rooftop came up the ladder.

Duncan stopped, breathing heavily, at the metal cube which was the access housing to the staircase. Snick joined him; she was breathing less heavily. They stood with their right shoulders against the door of the access house. He pointed up and out into the darkness westward. Whirling orange lights, faintly illuminating a dark form below them, were speeding through the air toward the rooftop.

"They'll land near the open hatch," he said. "They'll talk to the ganks in Ananda's apartment. Then they'll look in all the access houses. They know we came up to the roof."

She said, "They'll order the lights turned on up here. We'll have to get an airboat. It's our only chance."

He knew what she was thinking. If they opened the door now, they would be revealed in the light that would stream from the access-house interior. When the airboat ganks came, they would see them and would radio to those in the apartment on the level below to get to the staircase.

Duncan said, "Get behind here," even as he was walking to the blind side of the structure. She followed him just in time to avoid being revealed by the lights springing into being from the huge round kliegs set along the four-foot-high walls around the rooftop.

He looked eastward over the parapet. So far, there were no lights indicating gank airboats coming from the other towers. But Snick, peeking around the access house toward the west, said, "One's on its way. It'll land in a few minutes. Maybe sooner."

A moment later, she said, "They're quicker than I thought. One boat, landing by the hangar-room hatchway. Two ganks."

He visualized the officers getting out of the canoe-shaped aircraft. The light from the half-open hatch would beam upward, a beacon for all the other boats soon to come. The hatch slid horizontally into recesses in the rooftop. Below it was the hangar room from which he and Snick had climbed by means of a ladder. The room led to the huge apartment suite of his grandfather, World Councillor Ananda, whose real identity was Gilbert Ching Immerman. Ananda and his underling Carebara were unconscious and the only ones left living in the suite.

He and Snick had been unable to leave the apartment by the door that opened onto the corridor outside it. The ganks in the hall outside the apartment had barred their exit and were destroying the door so that they could get in. For all he knew, they might by now have gotten to the hangar room. He had to do something. Snick had the same thought. She put her mouth to his ear and said, "Now or never."

She had her proton-accelerator weapon in her hand, its bulbous tip pointed upward.

"You look around that side," he said, tipping his head to indicate the corner around which they had come. "I'll take this side."

She went to the southeastern corner of the access house, and he went to the northeastern. When he got there, he glanced upwards again to make sure that no second boat was approaching from the west.

What to do?

As the ancient Roman, Seneca, once said, *The gladiator plans his strategy in the arena.*

Where did that thought come from? Certainly not from the persona known as Duncan.

He stuck his head halfway around the corner. An airboat had landed six feet from the edge of the hatchway. A green-uniformed and green-helmeted gank was standing by the hatchway. The top of another helmet was sinking below its opening. One gank was going down the ladder to investigate; the other was standing guard. His back was to Duncan.

Duncan withdrew his head and looked behind him. Snick was walking toward him.

"You saw?" he said.

She nodded.

When she was by his side, he said, "We have to try to take him"—meaning the man standing by the hatchway—"and do it without his partner knowing it. When I say *go* . . ."

He closed his mouth. A man very near him was saying something in a low voice, though it was much louder than Duncan's. Ganks had come up the stairs from the 125th level. Snick whirled, crouching, her weapon leveled.

Duncan's heart bumped in the night of his body, but he did not panic. He tapped Snick's shoulder. She did not look behind her; nothing was going to take her gaze away from the corner.

He whispered, "I'm going around the other side."

She nodded.

He walked away very swiftly, his gun ready. He was thankful that his ankle-high boots had soft soles. The gank by the hatchway was bent over, his hands on his knees, apparently saying something to his partner in the room below. Duncan hoped that he would stay occupied. Before Duncan went around the next corner, he put his head around it just enough to see along the length of the access house. A woman's voice had, meanwhile, joined the man's.

The officer by the hatchway was still looking down into its opening. Duncan walked very quickly to the next corner of the structure, stopped, listened, then jumped around the corner.

Snick had come around her corner a second earlier. The ganks were facing her, their arms held high. Both had guns in their hands pointed upwards. Nobody had said anything, though Duncan had heard a loud gasp just before he had rounded his corner.

Snick, speaking softly, told the two to walk to the blind side of the access structure. She said, "If you're thinking of starting something, my partner is right behind you."

"That's right," Duncan said from behind them, startling them.

When all were behind the structure, Duncan reached up behind the man and the woman and took their weapons. Snick told the two to face the wall and lean toward it with their palms against it and to spread their legs. They did so, their faces grim and their lips squeezed with fury.

Both Duncan and Snick had spoken softly because it was possible that the ganks' helmet radios had been open to the precinct station operator. However, the man and the woman had obviously been talking to each other, not to the radio. Duncan touched a fingertip to his lips to signal that they should keep silent. Then he went behind them and turned off the R-T dials on the outside of their helmets.

Despite the chilly air, the ganks were sweating. Fear was mingled with the odor rising from their bodies.

"Take off your helmets and uniforms," he said softly. "Down to the underwear."

"Quickly!" Snick said. "Or we'll take them off your bodies!"

The ganks hastened to obey. When they were done, they stood shivering. Duncan held his gun on them while Snick donned the woman's uniform and helmet. The female organic was larger than Snick, but the uniform material shrank or expanded to fit the wearer. Snick then held her gun on the two ganks while Duncan put the man's weapon in the belt inside his jacket. He handed Snick the woman's gun before putting on the man's uniform. Before he was half-dressed, Snick, her gun set at MED STUN, shot the two prisoners in the back of the head. The violet-colored rays spat from the bulb at the end of the weapon, and the couple fell. The woman's head bounced off the floor; the man's, from the wall of the access structure. When they awoke, probably half an hour from now, they would have several broken blood vessels in their brains and severe headaches.

Duncan quivered, startled because a man's voice had come out of the earpieces in his helmet.

"Abie, report!"

No. AB, a code for the man propped against the wall.

Duncan turned the dial on the helmet's cheekpiece, and said, "AB here." He hoped that his acknowledgment was properly stated.

He looked at the big white location code painted on the side of the structure.

"No sign of the suspects," he said. "We're looking across the rooftop from staircase access-house entrance Number Q1, 15. An organic airboat is located by an open hatchway . . ."

"We have that report, AB," the voice said. "Note this. Keep your posts by the access. Tuesday is on the way to relieve you. When they get there, report the situation to them, then proceed immediately to the precinct station. Do not go to your apartments. Report to the precinct via wallscreen. Then go immediately to the emergency stoners there. Repeat. You must be stoned at the precinct station. Clear?"

"Clear."

"O and O, AB."

"O and O," Duncan said, and he turned the dial on his cheekpiece to OFF.

Panthea Snick said, "I heard it all."

He looked at his wristwatch. "One minute after midnight. Maybe the relief won't get here right away. They'll have their orders by now, but it'll take them at least ten to fifteen minutes. They have to get dressed, and so on."

Snick jerked a thumb to indicate the man on the other side of the structure, the man who had been standing by the open hatchway.

"He and his buddy will be relieved, too."

"We'll take him right now," Duncan said. "Set your gun for EP, tight-beam. I'll use STUN. When we approach him, he shouldn't get suspicious. If he does suspect us while we're still out of STUN range, drill him."

2

The gank by the hatchway was now pacing back and forth, probably wondering when he would be relieved. When he saw Duncan and Snick, he looked briefly at them from two hundred feet distance. Then he went to the edge of the opening and leaned over, his lips moving.

Now the gank had straightened up and was facing them as they approached. He was sixty feet away. Duncan raised the gun, which he had slipped out of his holster and concealed behind his leg while the man was looking down into the hangar. The man looked startled, and his hand flew down to his holstered gun. The pale violet beam from Duncan's gun struck the gank in the chest. His mouth open but silent, the gank staggered back and fell on his buttocks. Duncan shot him again, this time just below the chinstrap of his helmet. The man threw up his arms and fell onto his back, his helmeted head bouncing a little at the impact. His eyes were open and glazed when Duncan got to him. Snick had run past Duncan to the edge of the hatchway and was looking down into the glaring light of the hangar. She straightened up swiftly. "No one there. His buddy must've gone into the suite."

Duncan had put the unconscious man's gun powerpaks in his jacket pocket.

"Let's go," he said. He stepped inside the airboat cockpit and sat down in the pilot's seat. Snick was seated behind him by the time he had placed the safety webbing around him and snapped its lock. He pulled the canopy shut over him, then pressed the illuminated POWER button to ON. The LP (levitating power) READY lights came on as soon as Snick had locked her webbing. He pressed the LP ON button and scanned the instrument panel to assure that all systems were ready to operate. After pushing in the FL ON button, he lifted the wheel before him, and his left foot pressed down on the acceleration pedal.

The airboat rose slowly and pointed toward the northern edge of the tower. Snick said, "Oh, oh! Ganks coming out of the staircases! A dozen places!"

He did not look behind him. He sent the airboat to the north toward the wall rising four feet above the rooftop. When it was cleared, he moved the control wheel forward. The boat turned at a steep angle as swiftly as he dared to take it. Though he had not turned on the craft's running lights or searchlights, he could see the pale surface of the Los Angeles basin. Its water shimmered in the reflected lights of the towers. Then he straightened the boat out, but it still dropped. The only evidence of the sudden and large power output that slowed its fall was the glow on the ERG screen. The hull smashed into the water with a jarring crack. It felt as if its back had been broken. His back, too. There was silence except for his harsh breathing. But no water was pouring from the floor into the cockpit.

"Jesus!" Snick said. "I think my spine's sticking two inches out of my ass!"

His fingers flew, dimming the instrument panel illumination until he could barely make out their designations. Deciding that even this was too bright, he turned it off completely. He sent the boat down into the water until only the canopy was above the surface.

Six airboats, their signal lights flashing white, orange, and green, rode in formation from the west. They must have taken off from the central tower, where most of the organic airboats were headquartered. Very quickly, the looming wall of the mile-high tower hid the boats. They were landing on the rooftop.

"They'll be looking for us in a few minutes," she said. "Just as soon as they can talk to the gank you knocked out and find out what happened."

"He won't have the slightest idea what direction we took."

His throat was dry. His voice grated like gears running out of lubrication.

"Well?" Snick said.

He twisted around so that he could look at her. There was not enough illumination reflected from the clouds for him to discern her face. Those big brown eyes, the delicate skull structure, small nose, wide but perhaps too thin lips, and rounded chin were hidden. The helmet covered her black straight hair.

"The electrical power distribution tower is southwest," he said.

"I know. I was there when you called up the region maps," she said. "That was . . . what? . . . three days ago? You said . . ."

"I said it was where the ancient Baldwin Hills area used to be, before it was leveled and the power distribution tower was built on it. Let's go there."

"Why?"

He told her.

She said, "You're crazy! But I like it. Why not try it? It's desperate, but . . ."

"It might work. Anyway, what have we to lose? They'd never anticipate we'd do anything like that."

"What's one more crime against the state?" she said. "Against the criminal state?"

Her voice, not quite as hoarse as his, sounded eager.

11

"The cannon'll come in handy," she added. Her tone showed that she savored the thought.

He turned the boat to go around the base of the tower. The water lapped over the front of the canopy as the craft slid along at five miles an hour. Overhead, the flashing lights of more airboats sped toward the tower. When he saw the lights of a surface boat approaching at high speed, its wake white, he lowered the boat until only two inches of the canopy remained above the surface. When the boat got closer, he could see that it was an organic vessel. Its siren was screaming.

Waiting until it was well past, he raised his craft slightly and proceeded at six miles an hour. Ten minutes later, impatient with his slow pace, he brought the boat up to a few inches above the water. Then he accelerated to forty miles an hour. The University Tower to his right was passed; ten minutes later, the Great Congress of Earth Tower fell behind him. Ahead, ringed near its top by bright lights, was the squat bulk of the Baldwin Hills power-distribution tower. Unlike the other towers, its daily population was very small, only five hundred men, women, and children. One hundred were engineers and technicians. About half of this number would be up and about. The rest would have gone to bed after coming out of their stoners. All lived on the top level.

The boat flitted in the night, waves occasionally slapping against the underside of the hull. Below the black surface was fifty or so feet of water and then the deep mud. Under that lay the remains of ancient Los Angeles, drowned over two thousand obyears ago by the melting of the polar icecaps. The wood and the paper had dissolved into molecules, and the salt, like weak mice, was nibbling away at the tumbled stones.

Duncan burned with a rage that, if it could be seen, would make him a human firefly, a beacon, a bull's-eye for his hunters. He did not wish to be so fury-full. It blinded his reason, and he could not afford that. At the moment, he did not care. If discretion was the better part of valor, he had the worst part. He was charging in with a bull's brainlessness and recklessness at the matador's cape.

No, he was not. The matador, the people in the tower, did not know he was coming. And he would control his wrath. He would bend its force to fuel but not overpower his reason. He hoped.

Now, the quarter-mile wide and five-hundred-feet high black tower cut off all vision straight ahead. He stopped the boat for a moment. A hundred yards away was a dock complex extending from a huge arched entrance at the base of the building. A low-powered light streamed from the huge room, illuminating ghostily the sail and power craft anchored outside the docks and lying alongside slips. These belonged to the upperclass administrative officials and engineers. No one was in sight.

He lifted the boat up and moved it through the archway into the large room. Near its end was a bank of elevators. Beyond it was a door leading to a long high corridor according to the diagram he had studied a few days before. Dripping water on the cement floor two feet below, the airboat slid forward until it was near the door. The door was ten feet square and was moved sidewise out of a wall recess. It now closed the entrance.

The gray walls of the room must be activated monitor screens. He doubted that anyone was watching the monitors at the control center of the tower. Otherwise, the alarm signals would be ringing throughout the plant. But when he tried to get through that door, he would hear the hysterical clanging and whooping of the alarms.

He punched some buttons. The upper part of the nose of the craft split in two as longitudinal sections rose up. Then a cannon lifted up from the mechanism inside the nose. It was a Class III model, only two feet long but a foot thick, and the bulb at its firing end was as large as his head. After jockeying the craft so that the cannon pointed straight at an area halfway up on the right side of the door, he turned the CN PWR RDY dial. Next to it was the CONT FIRE button, which he pressed.

From the bulb sprang a violet-colored beam which disintegrated the thin plastic of the door, making a hole. Immediately, he lifted the boat two feet, the beam slicing out a vertical line four inches wide. Smoke poured from the edges, but the air-conditioning whisked it away. By moving the boat up, across, down, and then across to the right, Caird made a square three feet wide. Meanwhile, he could dimly hear the frenzied alarms through the canopy.

Snick said, "I have to open my canopy. I may have to use my gun."

He said, "O.K." He had turned off the cannon and moved the boat forward until its nose fitted inside the hole. Then he made the boat move to the left, and it shoved the door into the wall recess. He brought the boat back to the center of the doorway and shot it down the long and high-ceilinged corridor. Snick had also opened his canopy.

The airboat slowed when it came to the intersection of a hall running perpendicular to it. By just a few inches, the boat had room enough to round the corner to the right. Far down the hall —its walls blazed with colorful moving icons and designs—a man stepped out of a door. His eyes were wide, and his mouth was open. A woman's head popped out of the doorway behind him. She looked once, then her head snapped back out of sight. The man sprang back and disappeared.

Duncan sent the boat past the doorway down the hall until it was near the large windows of the control center office. When it stopped, Snick leaped out onto the floor, a progun in each hand. Duncan turned the boat leftward, its stern and nose scraping against the two walls. But it got by and was aimed straight at a window. Through it, he could see the big room with its many wall displays and the fifty or so work desks. The operators were running out of the three exits.

Snick, standing in the doorway of the hall entrance to the office, shot a woman in the leg before she could get to the door. The woman screamed and fell, tried to get up but could not make it.

Duncan pressed once on the CN MAN FIRE button. The

beam pierced the window and bored a hole through the wall just above a doorway jammed with struggling and shouting operators.

That beam had been shot only to increase the fright of the office people, and it certainly succeeded.

Snick ran into the office to pounce on the wounded woman.

By now, orange words: EMERGENCY, UNAUTHOR-IZED ENTRY were flashing on the walls. The alarms were still screaming.

He rotated the airboat until it faced the direction from which it had come. After putting the controls on HOLD, he climbed swiftly out of the craft and ran into the office.

3

Each wallscreen indicated the current time. It was exactly 12:31. He and Snick should be out of here in five minutes, which he hoped was enough for them to get out before ganks from other towers got here. The local ganks would have to be catch-as-catch-can.

Snick was dragging the still-screaming woman toward a workdesk and shouting, "Shut up! I won't kill you if you do what I tell you to do!"

The woman began whimpering, her face pale, her eyes wide and rolling. Duncan helped Snick to carry the woman to the chair and sit her in it. Her right leg had been pierced through the back of the thigh and out the front. But the beam had cauterized both wounds.

"Turn off the alarms!" he roared.

The woman, gasping, spoke a code word into the screen before her, and the sirens and flashing warnings stopped.

A man's head stuck out from one of the exit doorways.

Duncan shot a beam at it; the side of the doorway puffed smoke. The head withdrew. Duncan ran to the doorway to make sure that the man had gone. Behind him, Snick was yelling more orders, and the woman was shrilling, "I can't do that! They'll punish me!"

"No, they won't!" Snick said. "You're being forced! Anyway, I'll kill you if you don't! Take your choice!"

Duncan stopped just short of the door and crouched down and peered around the side of the doorway. No one was in the long hall, but the man could have gone into any of the open doorways along it. Never mind.

By the time he had returned to the desk, the operator had issued the command Snick had demanded.

The wallscreens now flashed with the codes the operator had so reluctantly—but quickly—inputted. And, for the first time in the history of the New Era, everybody in a city had been destoned at the same time.

Except for the Baldwin Hills power-distribution tower, every one of the twenty-one towers contained a million living people on any one day and six million in the stoners.

The codes had caused a simultaneous input of electrical power to all the cylinders holding the gorgonized citizens. The destoned would think that this morning was their scheduled day to live. The Tuesday, Wednesday, Thursday, Friday, Saturday, Sunday, and Monday citizens would be thoroughly confused when they found that the other days were also awake.

He could imagine the shock and the chaos now in every one of the twenty-one towers. Over one hundred and forty million would be jammed into a space which could comfortably fit only twenty million on any day.

That would be only the first shock. The second would be when they saw Duncan's messages on the wallscreens.

Snick set her gun to MED STUN, and it spat a violet beam against the back of the woman operator's head. She slumped forward onto the desktop.

Ten seconds later, Duncan and Snick were in the airboat,

and it was accelerating down the corridor. It slowed at the first intersection and turned right. Its nose and stern missed the walls by a few inches. Then it shot down a long hall until it came to an unusually large doorway. It stopped and rotated ninety degrees, facing the doorway.

Beyond was an enormous circular well-lit room, two hundred and fifty feet in diameter, soaring to a hundred feet, and ringed with galleries. In the center was a shimmering light-purple cylinder half the diameter of the room and rising seventy-five feet. Below its floor, Duncan knew, was a cable forty-five feet thick entering the cylinder base. It was connected to a smaller cylinder inside the larger, and from the sides of this cylinder twenty-one cables, each ten feet thick, sprouted downward and into the base along the wall of the outside covering. The large cable carried the power transmitted from the gigantic complex in the Mojave Desert. The center of that complex was the shaft that had been burned by proton accelerators down to the distance needed to feed off the heat from the metal core of Earth. A thermionic converter changed the heat to electricity, and part of this was sent to the Baldwin Hills plant in the state of Los Angeles.

All monitor screens in this tower had also been cut off. The tenants, including the local ganks, did not know where the airboat was.

He set the cannon for full-power continuous firing.

The bulbous nose of the cannon spat a violet beam, four inches thick, against the purplish cylinder. For a few seconds, the purple spot against which the beam was ravening was unchanged except for a darkening. Then the wall opened, and the beam struck through the hole to the inner cylinder. For another few seconds, there was only the silence of a thousand megawatts concentrated in a six-inch-thick beam and the eye-watering and nose-burning ozone-heavy air.

Snick had gotten out of the airboat and was crouching by the doorway, two proton handguns ready. Duncan kept glancing to both sides of him, alert if anyone should appear at either end of the hallway. He held a handgun, and another lay on the seat by his side.

Suddenly, Snick shouted, "Ganks on the galleries!"—he could not see them, they must be on the higher ones—and flame and smoke and white-hot sparks and a roaring as of a hundred Niagara Falls shot out of the hole in the side of the cylinder. Duncan was deafened, and he was quickly surrounded by a blinding stinking cloud that scraped his eyes raw and seemed to burn his nostril hairs and squeezed his lungs with fiery fingers. He coughed and coughed, and he heard Snick's deep tearing sounds while she climbed into the seat behind his.

She could not talk, but she tapped his right shoulder in a signal to get going.

He turned the boat around. So thick was the smoke, it hid the brilliant violet beam of the cannon. Then he shot the boat forward and also pressed the OFF button of the cannon. Suddenly the cloud was behind them, though still rolling down the hall, and the air was sweet and pure. But the hallway was no longer illuminated, and he knew by that that the power distribution cables were a torn-up and melted mess. At any other time, he would have shouted with joy. But he could only cough violently. The boat scraped along the sides of the wall, bounced off, and dragged its other side against the opposite wall. Then it was shot out of the archway and over the Los Angeles basin waters like a spat-out seed, and he was trying to see with eyes buried in tears and pain.

There were no lights from the rooftops and the bridges connecting some towers. The glow cast back by the low-lying clouds was gone. Only the firefly glowworm twinkles of the running lights of a few surface craft and airboats showed that this great city-state existed here.

Then, as his eyes ceased watering and became somewhat less painful, he could make out the pale sheen on the underside of the clouds above the Burbank Tower beyond the Hollywood Hills.

Still coughing, he brought the canopy up out of the hull.

There were at least a dozen gank craft, searchlights on, heading for the tower he had just left. Their occupants must be very puzzled and disturbed. They would be radioing their headquarters, asking what had caused this complete blackout.

His boat, now in the water, almost completely submerged, moved slowly toward the northwest.

Between spasms of coughing, Duncan hoarsely told Snick what he planned to do next. He ended, "O.K. with you?"

"It's more insane than what we just did. But I like it."

He took the airboat, its lights now on, up the side of the University Tower, his first stop. Any ganks seeing it would assume that it was one of theirs. When they found out different, they would be too late to do anything about it.

He found a huge arched opening on the tenth level and landed in it. There were two boats there and no one in sight. Further in, he knew, there would be at least one gank on duty, unable to leave his post because his orders would demand that he stay there. He should have a mobile emergency lantern to light his office.

After a fit of coughing—it was less violent now—he and Snick went down the hallway leading from the port and walked into the room where a lone woman, a sergeant second-class, sat at a desk. The lantern, klieg-bright, hung on a hook from the center of the ceiling. She stood up, smiling, though somewhat strainedly, and said, "Good to see you. I'm lonely. How's the situation out there? Found out anything?"

Snick took her gun from its holster, pointed it at the woman, and said, "Hands up."

The woman turned pale, her mouth open, but she obeyed. Her voice shaking, she said, "What *is* this?"

"Anyone else around?" Duncan said.

She shook her head. "You won't . . ." And she closed her mouth.

". . . get away with this?" Snick said.

The woman did not reply.

"Are you expecting anyone soon?" Duncan said. He coughed mildly.

Again, she shook her head.

Snick came around behind her, relieved her of her gun, and stuck it in her own belt. Then Snick went to a cabinet mounted to the wall and opened it. After looking its contents over, she took two cans of TM and four powerpaks for proton handguns. These she jammed into her jacket pockets. She went to a fountain in a corner and drank deeply. After she was done, she held her gun on the woman while Duncan drank.

"We want food," he said. "Show us where it's stored."

Still with her hands above her head, the woman conducted them down the hall to the precinct HQ kitchen. Duncan held the heavy lantern with one hand while they walked there. They returned a moment later with a box full of cans and two codekey can openers. He would have liked to have brought some delicacies, but these were stoned.

Snick handcuffed the woman to a deskleg, and they walked out with the lantern and her gun, powerpaks, and two flashlights while she protested about being left in the dark. Before they had left the office, she was cursing and threatening them.

When they got to the port, they checked out the two organic airboats there. The three-seater was not only faster but had fully charged powerpaks for both the motor and the cannon, which was a very powerful Class V. After storing the food, extra guns, and lantern in the rear section, they climbed into the cockpits. He called up a display of the map of the basin and of the contiguous areas which he needed. The boat, without running lights and close to the surface of the water, flew to the great reservoir in the northeast corner of the basin. Here the craft rose along the concrete dam, shot across the big lake, and then followed the course of the Los Angeles River. When it got to a large body of water called Lake Pang, once named Lake Hughes, Duncan turned the boat to the right and followed a three-laned plastic road to Boron. This was a small village and fuel station for the surface vehicles traveling between the Mojave Thermionic Power Complex and Los Angeles. Duncan turned off the lights well before reaching it, detoured into the desert for ten miles, then returned to the road.

Rain began to fall heavily, and lightning and thunder raised hell westward behind the boat.

As they whizzed above the highway, heading for the complex sixty miles distant, Duncan envisioned the babel and bedlam of Los Angeles. By now, the ganks must have figured out who had caused it. They would, however, have to try to restore order before they could spare many personnel to track him and Snick. Not until the wrecked power distributor was replaced would they be able to begin bringing order out of chaos. Nor would they know where the fugitives were.

It was good for him and Snick that the area was cloud-covered. The stationary satellites monitoring this area could not see through the clouds. Their infrared equipment would be operating, but his boat was not emitting enough of that kind of energy to be detectible. The Gernhardt-drive motor in the boat caused an electromagnetic disturbance which the satellites could sense. But the approaching electrical storm would soon interfere with that capability.

He grinned savagely. What he and Snick had done at Los Angeles was small potatoes compared to what they would do at the Mojave power site. If things worked out the way he planned, that is.

Then the storm caught up with them and netted them with rain, thunder and lightning. Duncan turned on the ultraviolet headlights to help him on the terrain. The lightning streaks were, however, frequent enough and close enough for him to make his way from point to point. Fifteen minutes later, the boat was on the edge of a hole. And humankind's mightiest work lay below them.

One of them, anyway. There were fifty of them on the five continents, and all were of equal size.

The boat rested on the lip of a circular depression twenty

miles across and one thousand feet below sea level. This had been dug out of the rock two obmillenia ago. The lights radiating from its buildings and ground shone so brightly through the driving rain that Duncan and Snick could discern the white cylindrical tower in its center and the structures arranged in a circle around it. The tower was two miles wide and five hundred feet high. Its walls were made of twenty-inch-thick cardboard subjected to stoning power and, thus, invulnerable to any heat except perhaps that at the center of a star.

The tower covered the half-mile wide shaft that plunged 1700 miles into the earth. The walls of the shaft were lined with stoned cardboard. The end of the pipe in its center was near the border of the Earth's mantle and liquid outer core. The heat conducted up it was passed out of the tower through dozens of pipes that passed horizontally to other huge cylinders stationed around the central tower. These contained thermionic converters, tremendous devices that changed heat to electricity.

From these, electrical conduits fifty feet thick went to the structures arranged in a third circle. These were transformers, and from them underground conduits relayed the power to transformers and then to power-distribution centers in ten western departments, also called states.

Duncan's target was the building housing the Number 6 transformer. This was on the western side of the outer circle, and it was made of steel. Hence, its walls could not resist the proton-accelerator Class V cannon in the nose of the boat.

Dimly, the lights from the residential buildings at the base of the Brobdingnagian hole wavered through the rain. There were no vehicle lights on the roads connecting the inner structures and the personnel housing.

"In and out," Duncan said loudly. "Like Finnegan. If their radar doesn't pick us up at once, we can do it. It's not likely in this rain, and we'll keep close to the surface."

He was sure that radar towers were placed along the edge of the hole and at its bottom. So far, he had seen none. It was also possible that they were not operating. No one in the history of the New Era had ever tried to assault a thermionic-generator complex. Security could be rather lax, especially on such a storm-ridden and pluvial night.

He slipped the boat over the edge. When the sky was clear and the sun had poured heat into the deep well, it would have caused an updraft day or night. But the rain had cooled off the air, and this was winter. Now the boat was caught in the downdraft of the strong western wind behind it, and hurled along the face of the cliff toward the bottom. He applied lifting energy to counteract somewhat the down-pushing air and descended at thirty miles an hour. Nearing the bottom, he slowed the vessel and then sent it in a curve which straightened out a few feet above the ground. The boat accelerated, reaching a hundred miles an hour velocity until it was two miles from the target.

He slowed the craft then because, at this rate, its momentum was not easily stopped within a short space.

A few minutes later, he brought the boat to a standstill. It was fifty feet above the ground, its nose pointed at the shell around the great converter.

So far, no alarms had sounded or flashed.

The cannon spat its violet. Smoke poured out of the shell, but the rain kept it from spreading far.

A minute passed. Two minutes.

The cannon charge-indicator on the instrument panel showed that two-thirds of the powerpak's energy was gone.

He cut the cannon off. Sirens began wailing and orange lights began flashing on the shell and on the fronts of the far off buildings. Squares of light suddenly blazed along the base of the hole. Garage and hangar doors were opening to loose surface cars and airboats.

Duncan took the boat up and away, accelerating it until it shot over the edge of the hole at two hundred miles an hour. He had the boat's radar on then but if a radar tower was just ahead of him, the scope did not show it.

After leveling off at a hundred feet above the surface of the Mojave Desert, the boat sped at its maximum velocity, three hundred miles an hour. He slowed it to a hundred mph as he brought it slanting down through the rain and the white-hot bolts. At the same time, he had the headlights and blacklight scopes on. He leveled out at five feet above the surface of the desert. Snick gasped when a monolithic rock formation loomed before them. He twisted the wheel savagely and slowed the craft down simultaneously. The side of the fuselage nearly scraped against the rock. Past it, he kept on slowing until he was moving at fifty miles an hour.

Far behind them, shining dimly at different altitudes, wavery in the heavy rain, were the searchlights of a dozen gank aircraft.

Extract from a tape made by Wednesday's World Councillor, Ji Nefzawi Ibson, and sent via secret couriers to the other World Councillors.

USE DESCRAMBLER CODE #1489C.

ERASE THIS COMMUNICATION AFTER ASSIMI-LATION.

Re: the enemies of the Commonwealth of Earth, Jefferson Cervantes Caird alias William St. George Duncan et alia (see Index) and Panthea Pao Snick, alias Jenny Ko Chandler et alia (see Index).

Various eminent and loyalty-tested historians have stated that history ended with the founding of the New Era. Mere chronicling of thoroughly mundane events replaced history. Though such statements should not be taken entirely seriously, they are true in several respects. The most significant is that the New Era has given all people the Good Life (as it's called) but has removed any surprises.

Paradoxically, progress is still with us but change is not.

Actually, change does exist, though it is so slow that it is unperceived and unfelt by the individual citizen.

Racism, sexism, nationalism, poverty, pollution and economic insecurity have been eliminated. The conflict and prejudices among races that existed in the pre-New Era and the early days of the New Era have disappeared. Caucasian, Mongolian, Negro, Amerindian, and Australian aborigine have melted together and become one more or less brown race. However, more than just variety of skin color has vanished. Much of the "color" of everyday life is also gone, though other factors beside racial difference have contributed even more to this loss.

I tend to agree with the historians and sociologists who have stated the above. But such loss of "color" in everyday life cannot be avoided. A price must be paid for every purchase. For every advantage there is a disadvantage.

These are cliches and truisms, but I do not apologize for them. History is a series of embodied variations of cliches and truisms. The names of people, events, and places change, and the effects of war, trade, science, and technology on history vary. (Fortunately, Earth has had no wars for 2000 obyears.) But mostly, it's a recycling powered by greed or idealism, mostly by greed. Both greed and idealism have been and are fueled by the desire for power, whatever the proponents of both claim.

What I'm leading up to is The Hero in History. You're all well educated, have one or more doctor's degrees. Thus, I don't have to spell out to you the role of The Hero (male or female) in mythology, legend, and history. All eras except ours have had a multitude of heroes. The New Era has been remarkably lacking in these. The only prominent one, whose name every citizen knows, is Jerry Pao Nel. He led the doomed rebellion of the Martian colonists against the Commonwealth of Earth. He has been the subject of innumerable dramas, and we have allowed these to be displayed because they are a cathartic for the rebellious and resentful feelings of the citizenry. This latitude is in accordance with the secret rule for governing the citizens of the New Era. That is, let the people have all the freedom they wish—within a certain range. Keep a long leash on them. Don't pull them up short until they go too far. If at all possible, don't let the citizens see the iron hand in the velvet glove.

This rule is for their own good.

I speak of heroes because the New Era now has another. To be exact, two.

These are the male outlaw, Jefferson Cervantes Caird, now known as William St. George Duncan, and the female outlaw, born Panthea Pao Snick, whose latest false ID is Jenny Ko Chandler.

Allow me to briefly review the lives and careers of these two before I go on to my thesis of them as folk-heroes and then to the dangers they pose to the Commonwealth of Earth. We regard these two as outlaws, daybreakers, murderers, and subversives; in short, villains. But many citizens will assuredly make them heroes just as the common people of ancient England and Switzerland made heroes of Robin Hood and William Tell, and the people of ancient China made a hero of Sung Chuang and his band. Or, in the ancient nation of the U.S.A., John Dillinger and Jesse James.

Caird-Duncan, as he is hereafter usually referred to, and Snick combine the political nature of Hood, Tell, and Sung and the anti-social semipsychopathic-economic nature of Dillinger and James.

I am repeating some of the biodata of these two only to make my points re their becoming criminals and this potential impact upon us, that is, on history. Let us hope that they soon become just that—history.

The parents of Jefferson Cervantes Caird, now alias Duncan, were Doctor Hogan Rondeau Caird, doctor of medicine and of biochemistry, and Doctor Alice Gan Cervantes, Ph.D., molecular biologist. They were born in Manhattan State, as was their son, an only child. Doctor Alice Gan Cervantes was the daughter of the famous biochemist, Dr. Gilbert Ching Immerman. Immerman was also the grandfather of Dr. Hogan Rondeau Caird, Jefferson's father. Thus, Immerman was both the great-grandfather and grandfather of Jefferson Cervantes Caird.

As you well know, the organic department did not discover until very recently that Immerman had, when young, developed in his laboratory what we now refer to as the "elixir" or ASF. That is, age-slowing factor. When administered to a person, it slows down aging by a factor of seven. An infant who would naturally live to 100 subyears, if given this at birth, will live to 700 subyears. But since the dayworld system already extends his lifespan to 700 obyears, the infant will now live to 4900 obyears.

If the infant were, hypothetically, living every day, he would survive to the age of 700 obyears. Or 700 subyears, since in his case, obyears and subyears would be the same. During his lifetime, the earth would have circled the sun 700 times.

Immerman, you might say, was the New Era's Doktor Faustus. He had in his hands a gift for humankind that would be a boon or a curse, depending on the viewpoint. For the individual, it would be a gift from God, if I may be forgiven for using a superstitious phrase. God knows that there are still far too many citizens who believe in God. But many also believe in astrology, fortune-telling, ghosts, angels, demons, witchcraft, and gambling.

For society, it could be a curse. We (by we, I mean past and present World Councillors) have kept Earth's population growth rate to zero. In fact, as you know but the public does not, we have managed to reduce the population from the ten billion existing a thousand obyears ago to the present two billion. But the populace (and this includes all but the very highest government officials) believe that the present population is ten billion. We have done this with the highest of ethical values in mind, for the good of the people and for the good of Earth.

For the good of Earth is the same as for the good of the people. Never will we allow this planet to become stripped and polluted again so that humankind faces extinction—as it did in the early twenty-first century A.D.

As I said, Immerman could have made his elixir or ASF public, or could have repressed it. Instead, he decided to use it not only for himself but for his wife and children. His wife was sworn to secrecy re the ASF as were his children when they became adults. Eventually, ASF was given to the extended family and then to others. These formed the nucleus of a secret society the members of whom referred to themselves as "immers." After a time, this group, ever expanding, became a quasi-political body. They also spawned other secret groups which were controlled by the immers but knew nothing of the ASF or its origins.

From what we have found out since the Caird-Duncan and Snick affair, we know that Immerman decided that he must disappear. He was staying visibly younger than his contemporaries, and he had to appear to die before assuming a new identity. (His wife had died in an accident.)

He arranged the reproduction of his body, growing it in his laboratory (government-owned but administered by him). And he arranged the "accident" which partly destroyed the duplicate's body, which was identified as his.

Though an intense investigation is now being conducted to ferret out the insertion of false data in the data banks and the false ID he used, we have gotten nowhere so far. Probably, we will not succeed. As I have pointed out in previous reports, the control of data and close surveillance of citizens by the government gives us great power. But our control of data is a two-edged sword. We use it to monitor trade, traffic, materials flow, and protection of citizens from themselves and from others. But criminals have used data banks for their own purposes. These false insertions of data have usually been detected, but there surely must be some cases that have been quite successful. Just how many, we cannot, of course, know.

Immerman disappeared and became, in effect, just another citizen. But he still controlled the immer organization. Then he abandoned this ID, probably through another "death," and became David Jimson Ananda. This was in that area anciently known as

Albania, now part of the Southeast European Department. You know how he arose from a block-leader in Tirana to World Councillor. His tremendous ingenuity is shown by the fact that his biodata were minutely scrutinized during his rise in administrative positions, yet, though false, escaped detection.

It was after he was established in his World Councillorship that he secretly set up the override circuits on the news-channel communications circuits. We still do not know how he did this nor have we as yet traced the override circuit to its site of origin. Though we can now prevent its transmitting of messages, we must find its initial source. Present speculation is that it is located in one of the seven thousand communications satellites. If so, then it was planted by space technicians, and all who could possibly be involved are being subjected to TM.

However, a scan has shown that three possible candidates have died during the time period that the override mechanism could have been placed in a satellite. One or more of these might have been responsible. If so, we're out of luck. We also wonder how many of the three deaths are valid, and these are being intensely investigated.

Just why Immerman-Ananda set up the override is not known. It must have been part of some contingency plan or, perhaps, though this seems incredible, he had plans for becoming world dictator.

Whatever the reason, he certainly did not expect anyone to force the location and use of the override from him and use it for that person's purpose. That person being his own descendant, Jefferson Cervantes Caird, alias Duncan et al.

At some time, probably when Jefferson Caird was eighteen, he was told about the immers and the ASF. He swore the oath, made doubly binding because, if he betrayed the immers, he also betrayed his beloved parents. Besides, from what we know of Caird's personality, he was thrilled by the idea and eager to play an active part. After graduating from South Manhattan State College, he entered the Manhattan Academy of Organics and graduated with many honors. His doctoral thesis was on the psychological profile and brain chemistry of daybreakers. Given hindsight, we can see how ominous this was for the Commonwealth.

The immers had long been planting their members in various important government bureaus. As an organic, Caird was in a position to know when danger of detection threatened the immers and to take measures to warn them. We do not know exactly when he accepted the role of courier for the immers. Those intertemporal messages which had to be delivered verbally or via hand-carried tapes were entrusted to Caird. He became a daybreaker. To do so, he had to adopt a different ID for each day. False biodata for each ID were inserted into the databanks by a procedure the organics still have not determined.

It was during this early period that Caird's peculiar ability, *one* of his peculiar abilities, was revealed to him and to the higher administrators among the immers.

At first, he was merely assuming a separate ID for each day. Then it became apparent that Caird was not just acting. He had *become* each persona. Thus, though the persona for each day varied significantly from each other, and from the original Caird, he *was* each one. He *was* on Wednesday, Tingle, data banker; on Thursday, Dunski, fencing instructor; on Friday, Repp, TV actor-writer-producer; on Saturday, Ohm, a weedie and part-time bartender; on Sunday, Father Tom Zurvan, a half-mad street-preacher; on Monday, Isharashvili, a Central Park ranger.

Yet an estimated one percent of him retained the Caird persona. This was enough for him to maintain a tenuous continuity with all of his personae and to carry out his courier role.

Caird's parents both died, apparently drowned at sea off Long Island while yachting. This was during a particularly cloudy and stormy day. The satellites could not observe them, and the location signal from their yacht ceased operating. The boat was sunk, but their bloated bodies were recovered a week later. These may have been laboratory-grown reproductions. For some reason we have not been able to discover—Caird apparently also does not know it—his parents had to "disappear." Perhaps they have popped up elsewhere with false IDs or they may have actually died.

While he was still at the Academy, Caird got married and was licensed to have one child. She now lives in Manhattan and teaches history. She has been TMed and proved innocent of any knowledge of ASF and the immers.

The *second* of Caird's peculiar talents, in this case, a *unique* talent, is his inborn or self-taught resistance to the so-called truth drug, TM. Somehow, he is able to resist the effects of TM. He can lie when exposed to it in spray form or when it is injected. Though unconscious after being subjected to TM, he can still lie. Even the electronic devices which monitor such sure indicators of prevarication and mental stress as skinfield potential and blood chemistry and brainwave and eye-movement changes are deceived.

Caird-Duncan seems able not only to lie to others when he's under TM, but also to himself.

Panthea Pao Snick was the daughter of organic officers in Manhattan. She took up her parents' profession and became a detective-major shortly before the events occurred which brought her and Caird together. Her record was excellent, and her superiors recognized her high ability as a detective. That she was given one of the very rare temporal visas demonstrates her superiors' great regard for her.

Snick's assignment was to track down a female daybreaker named Doubleday. You know the story of what happened after that. It's a complicated one, but, during the course of events, Caird (and his personae) became a danger to the immers. Snick was captured by the immers, and Caird objected to her being killed.

Immerman himself, that is, David Jimson Ananda, flew from Zurich to Manhattan to take personal charge of the situation. He seems to have lacked any family feeling because he condemned his own grandson to death. But Caird escaped and rescued Snick.

Meantime, Caird had been heading toward a mental breakdown. All of his personae were trying to take control and dispossess the others. While fleeing both the organics and the immers, Caird became temporarily catatonic and was arrested by the organics.

After questioning Snick, the organics arrested and questioned under TM some of the immers. A Wednesday citizen, Colonel Paz, revealed all that he knew. Of course, he did not know any more than we did that Ananda was in reality Immerman, nor did he know that Ananda was in Manhattan. But the organics were able to scoop up a number of lesser-rank immers, and their testimony plus Paz's revealed to us the existence of the immer society.

Regretfully, we were forced to gorgonize Snick and consign the body to a warehouse in the New Jersey wilderness. She knew too much and was too sympathetic with her rescuer, Caird, to be trusted to keep silence. The main factor in determining to keep her quiet was the ASF. The public must not know about ASF. It would demand it if it knew about it, and its long-term effects would be deleterious to society as a whole. We found ourselves in the ironic position of having to agree with Immerman on that. But we, the World Council, agreed that we would share ASF among us and those of our children who could be trusted.

Now, due to Caird's message and printouts of the ASF formula, distributed worldwide among the citizens, we are facing a very difficult situation. Should we admit that the ASF formula is valid? Or should we deny it and claim that it is useless, a criminal's hoax, and possibly dangerous? Or should we give in to the storm of demand by the citizens and let them have ASF? Or what they believe is ASF. It could be a preparation of harmless ingredients which would satisfy them that they are getting something which will allow them to live seven times longer. By the time they find out that their age is not being slowed down, ten subyears at least, i.e., seventy obyears, will have passed. We can blame Caird for that.

While we debated what to do with Caird, he broke out of a supposedly escape-proof building.

Caird is elusive and slippery, the very model of a trickster. This quality, too, will appear to the people to be admirable and will add lustre to his role of rebel-hero.

It seems that he had again changed his persona before fleeing Manhattan into the wilds of New Jersey. This was the persona he called William St. George Duncan.

He fell in with outlaws, people who had become daybreakers for various criminal reasons. They holed up in ancient tunnels beneath a warehouse. This was the very building in which we had stored the stoned Snick. He found and destoned her. During this time, to throw us off the trail forever, he managed to grow his duplicate in a government-owned laboratory near the warehouse. This he cleverly palmed off as his corpse, presumably killed during a struggle with an organic officer. Caird also killed the officer.

Caird, Snick, and a companion (see Index re Padre Cabtab) made their way to Los Angeles State. There they made contact with a subsidiary underground organization. This had various names, but I shall use just one as a label, OMC. That is, Old Man Coyote. Except possibly for the very highest officials in OMC, none of its members knew about the immers or ASF. OMC was just a tool for the immers.

Caird, Snick, and Cabtab were located finally by World Councillor Ananda, that is, Immerman. He tried to have them killed and then abducted them, for some reason, to his secret apartment on the 125th level of the La Brea Tower Complex. Even the Los Angeles organic generals of each day did not know of this covert residence of the World Councillor.

Somehow, the three prisoners broke loose. Padre Cabtab was slain, but Snick and Caird-Duncan killed all but two of their captors. These were Immerman-Ananda and an accomplice, Carebara. Caird-Duncan used TM on his grandfather and extracted from him various data. This included the clandestine override circuits Immerman-Ananda had arranged many subyears ago. Having initiated the mechanisms which would broadcast his rebellious messages re video and automatic printout, Caird-Duncan then called

36

the nearest organic precinct station. He told the officer in charge that a murder had been committed in the apartment. This puzzled the officer because his call-up of the registry of that floor showed that the apartment suite was unoccupied. However, the few interim organics available were dispatched to the site.

Caird-Duncan and Snick had left the apartment via the roof-hatchway of the hangar room before the organics arrived and burned open the only door to the suite. Caird-Duncan apparently notified the organic officer of the murders because he wanted us to get our hands on a still-alive Immerman-Ananda. He must have expected that we would TM his grandfather and then be forced to reveal to the world the tremendous deception wrought by a World Councillor.

He should have known better. The truth behind this plot is being hushed up as much as possible. In any event, General Kowatt was apprised that Carebara and Immerman-Ananda must die in the hospital reserved for organics, or shortly afterwards. He will be well rewarded for his discretion and prompt carrying out of orders.

The "murders" of World Councillor Ananda and Carebara have been announced (Wednesday). Caird-Duncan and Snick are blamed for their deaths. So far as the organic department can determine, there is no public suspicion that the news-channel stories re the deaths are anything but as reported. The ID of Ananda as Immerman will not be disclosed for reasons I do not have to explain.

The search for Caird-Duncan and Snick continues. We have no idea, at the moment, where they are. After they committed the amazing megacrimes of destoning all the citizens of Los Angeles at the same time, then destroying its electric power distribution center, and then, a few hours later, successfully destroying the thermionic converter and distributor for the entire West Coast, they managed to get away and hide.

They have created a vast amount of confusion, chaos, and major inconvenience for the citizens of these political departments. World-wide publicity re these events has been unavoidable.

Caird-Duncan and Snick must be captured—very soon. No doubt, they plan more attacks against the Commonwealth and hope to stir up an unstoppable storm of dissension, perhaps even rebellion. I recommend that the two arch-criminals be killed when they are located if circumstances permit. If no civilian witnesses are present, Caird and Snick must be terminated immediately. If civilian witnesses are present and the two criminals submit to arrest peacefully, then the two should be taken to the nearest precinct station. A trusted general will be authorized by us to take charge of the personnel and to arrange a "killed while attempting to escape" report.

END OF COMMUNICATION.

ERASE AFTER ASSIMILATION.

Duncan was seldom taken off guard. That Panthea Snick would attack him was unthinkable.

He had located the entrance of a cave in the side of a mountain. The airboat moved out of the driving rain through the ten-foot wide mouth into a hollow. After about forty feet, the downward slope of the rock roof forced the boat to scrape against the floor. But it squeezed through the low and narrow hole into another chamber. There he turned it until it was against a sidewall.

Their flashlights lit up a hollow shaped like the inside of a box that had been stepped on by a giant. The stone floor was littered with old bones, mostly of deer and rabbit. A faint catlike odor suggested that panthers had once laired here. He and Snick removed from the rear storage compartment the lantern taken from the gank office, two inflatable mattresses, and two snapout blankets. While they were arranging these on the floor near the boat, he said, "We'll sleep as long as we wish, and . . ."

"Oh, no, we won't!" she said.

The lantern filled the hollow with a light such as a fish in a bowl might swim in. Snick had stripped off her uniform and stood in her utilitarian underwear, a light purple T-shirt and bikini panties. Her straight dark sleek hair shone like a seal's fur, and her dark brown eyes seemed to glow. Almost—it was his imagination, of course—the delicate high-cheekboned skull beneath the smooth bronze flesh seemed to flash forth. It was a beautiful skull, if skulls could be said to be beautiful.

She raised her arms and pulled the T-shirt off. Her breasts were small perfect globes with huge rose-red nipples. Then she pulled away the velcro ends of her panties and revealed the unusually thick pubic hair, dark and shining.

She leaped at Duncan like a panther. He went back under her attack, not resisting, and fell onto the inflated mattress with her on top of him. Though he was fully dressed, he did not take long getting his clothes off with her help.

"I never expected . . ." he said.

"Shut up!"

Her mouth closed on his lips.

Afterward, lying with her head on his chest, his right arm about her, he thought about why she had, literally, jumped him. She had never said or done anything to make him think that she cared for him in any way sexually. His own attitude toward her had been somewhat shadowy. At first, he had thought he was in love with her. For all he knew, that might have been because he had loved her in his previous personae. He did not remember them. But her bloodthirstiness had somewhat repelled him and he had decided that he could not love her. As if a mental decision had anything to do with an emotional decision. But his response to her now had been more than a desire to expend his lust. He had melted with her into that ecstatic feeling that only love, not lust, could give.

Both of them had been so filled with frenzy because of what they had done today that sex was the only thing that could burn away the high charge in their nerves.

That that had not succeeded, that they were still highly, deeply charged, soon became evident. Snick began kissing him everywhere, and it was not until they coupled four more times that they were utterly empty. They finally lay quietly, though breathing hard, covered with sweat.

After a while, Duncan went out into the rain and stood in it, wincing at the cold water but feeling happy and cleansed. After a moment, Snick joined him. The lightning bolts nearby lit them fitfully. She yelled her exultation and grabbed him again. They sank to the cold hard ground and proved that they were not as empty as they had thought.

The lightning, he thought, is not as wild as we are.

Shivering, they went back into the cave. With towels taken from the storage compartment, they rubbed themselves dry. They smeared their knees, rubbed raw on the rocky ground, with an ointment from the first-aid kit. Then they ate voraciously, she talking merrily most of the time. That was a switch. Usually, he did the talking.

"We showed them, the bastards!" she said. "And we'll show them some more! They won't ever forget us!"

"That's for tomorrow," he said. He crawled onto the mattress and wrapped himself up in the very thin but warm blanket. "Do you want to get in with me?"

"I can't sleep when somebody else is in the bed," she said.

She bent down and kissed him lightly and went to her own mattress. She must have fallen asleep almost at once, though he thought he heard her mumble, ". . . all the way up theirs."

That was the difficult thing to understand about her. She hated those who had framed her and would not hesitate to kill those directly responsible if she had the chance. But she was not a genuine revolutionary. To her, the living-one-day-a-week and governmental systems were not wrong. She just wanted to rip out the bowels of the corrupt officials who had spit at her loyalty and faith to the system.

That did not matter, he told himself. What she was doing

was for the cause of revolution, and she might help bring about the breakup of the dayworld.

Late that morning, stiff and sore, he got out of bed. Snick slept, her head sidewise on the pillow, mouth open. He got a can out of storage, tore off the lid attached to it, and watched the water within the can blacken and boil. Then he went outside while he drank the coffee. When he returned, Snick was awake but not out of bed. He opened a can and handed it to her. She sat up while drinking it, the blanket over her shoulders. When she was finished, she said, "Now?"

"It's stopped raining, but the cloud cover is heavy and blacker in the west than the east. Looks like another thunderstorm coming. If it does, we move out. We'll have about ten miles of open ground before we get to the forest. We'll be O.K. while we're exposed unless a patrol flies by."

She agreed that that seemed feasible. Nor did she argue when he proposed that they return to the La Brea Complex Tower.

"We can take to the wilds and maybe not get caught for a long time," he said. "But we won't be doing anything to bother *them*. They won't expect us to go back to the same place from which we fled."

"Then we play it by ear?"

He did not reply. Her question was rhetorical.

They whiled away the time by exercising for an hour. By then the wind, relatively mild when he had awakened, was whistling outside the mouth of the cave. In another hour, the rain drove into the opening. Thunder boomed, its sound amplified by the echo-chamber effect of the cave. Lightning struck nearby, and a tree, riven, toppled with a crash only faintly heard.

"I doubt the patrols will even be out," he said.

They were in luck unless the lightning hit them.

The observation satellites would have been set by now to detect the e-m field of any airboats the size of Duncan's. Their locations and courses would be matched with those of authorized craft. The moment the detection equipment noticed an unauthorized boat, it would transmit this to the nearest gank stations. While the organic boats swarmed out to intercept the suspicious craft, the satellite would continue tracking it.

However, Duncan and Snick were safe during the storm. The electrical disturbances would thwart the detectors.

Sometimes, Duncan believed that he was one of those rare persons whose "personal magnetism" attracted tychenons. These were the wave-particles postulated by such nonscientists as astrologers and metaphysicians and named after Tyche, the ancient Greek goddess of Chance and Fortune. Tychenons were supposed to collect around certain individuals like iron filings on a magnet and thus increase the probability of good fortune or good luck for them. It was sheer superstition, of course.

Nevertheless, his luck had been very good. So far.

A thousand obyears ago, all this area had been barren desert. It had taken three hundred obyears for the New Era to pulverize the rock and make new soil, seed it with worms and other forms of soil-building life, and plant trees. Riverbeds had been dug, and water brought down from the mountains. Now, where once had been thousands of square miles of dry and lifeless land, trees and bushes greened the eye.

It was under these trees that the airboat moved in a more or less straight line toward Los Angeles State.

By three that afternoon, Duncan parked the craft under the branches of a large conifer on the slope of a mountain. They cut branches and piled them over the boat, leaving a tight path to it. A little way up the slope was an overhanging ledge with a recess beneath it, the shadows of which would hide them. Here they would stay until tomorrow when it was near dawn.

Meanwhile, they had a good view of the towers of L.A. and the water and air traffic.

They spent part of the day sitting in the boat's cockpits and watching the news channels on the auxiliary screens. The newsheads had lost their professional cool, though they were trying very hard to restrain their agitation and indignation. They reported that the two criminals (sometimes they called them supercriminals), Duncan and Snick, were responsible for the attacks against the Organic Commonwealth of Earth and the West Coast States and Los Angeles State in particular.

Equipment had been flown in late Tuesday morning by nuclear-powered dirigibles and giant airboats from San Diego State and Sacramento State. The replacements had been installed by late Tuesday afternoon. But power had not been available until the destroyed equipment at the thermionic center had been replaced. Not until 11:00 P.M. had power been restored to the West Coast.

At 10:00 P.M. this Wednesday morning, order had been restored in Los Angeles. The destoned of all days except Wednesday had been sent back into their cylinders. The citizens had been shocked, confused, and panicky when they found themselves destoned all at once and in a dark city. Los Angeles had been literally a madhouse, and its citizens had gone through the worst experience of their lives. The great majority had been unable to leave their apartments. The electrically operated locks on the doors would not open. The dwellings, designed to hold only the tenants of one day at a time, had been jammed with people who did not have the slightest idea of what was occurring.

The cutoff of air-conditioning had stopped the inflow of fresh air into the apartments. The apartments were now filled with additional people who had rapidly burned up the available oxygen. The ganks had been forced to cut out the locks in the doors to release the tenants. This had been a very slow procedure, though all the city workers had been pressed into service. There were still not enough proguns available to speed up the cutting, but organics and workers from San Diego and Santa Barbara had been flown in with guns.

Even so, it had been a genuine hell, and the cases of mental breakdown reported were in the hundreds.

The city was still in turmoil. Though the citizens had been

told to report to work, they were too shaken to conduct business as usual.

Every ten minutes, the newsheads told the viewers that they should ignore the lies on the printouts issued by the infamous and sociopathic criminals, Duncan and Snick. They should destroy these at once.

"Fat chance of that," Duncan said. "They'll be too curious not to read them."

The newsheads also reported that the criminals were still at large. But their arrests would occur soon. Meantime, all citizens should keep watch for the two. If a citizen observed them, he was not to attempt to restrain them. Duncan and Snick were armed and dangerous and murderers. The citizens who saw them should notify the organics, who would take over from there.

There were also short reports on the deaths of David Jimson Ananda, the World Councillor, and the others who had been massacred in Ananda's apartment on the 125th level.

"They've killed him!" Duncan said softly. He was not surprised. But how much had they gotten out of him by TM before they had murdered him?

So far, the newsheads had said nothing about why a World Councillor whose residence was in Zurich, Switzerland, had come unannounced to Los Angeles.

"There you are," Duncan said. "The whole city is open to us. It'll be a long time before the locks are all replaced. We can walk into any apartment."

"With the ganks and the citizens knowing what we look like?"

Their screens were displaying the icons of himself and her while their biodata were being displayed in the lower part.

"We'll find a place to hide quickly. Damn quickly!"

Late that afternoon, they were sitting side by side on their mattresses under the ledge. They had been silent for some time, during which he had been summoning his nerve to speak about what had occupied his mind much of the day.

He said, "I'm not shy, Thea. I've been wondering . . . I might as well get it out . . . I have to know."

"Know what?" she said. She had swiveled around on her buttocks to look at him. He turned his head to look at her face. Her expression showed that she might be anticipating his question.

"Do you love me?"

She winced, but at least she did not laugh.

"I don't know. I . . . What is love?"

"It may be difficult to define love," he said. "However, most humans know when they're in love."

She was sitting beside him on her mattress. Now, she stood up and got in front of him, then squatted.

"I admire and respect you greatly," she said. "Probably more than any man I've ever known, and I've known many. I trust you completely, and I would never betray you. Would I sacrifice my life for yours? I don't know. If willingness to give up your life for the beloved's is the true test of love, then . . . I just don't know. I'll place my life in danger for you. In fact, I've done that many times and will undoubtedly do it again."

She was silent for a moment. A bluejay's raucous scream came from somewhere near, and he could see a hawk wheeling on the wind.

"You're certainly more than just satisfactory in bed. But there's more to love, real love, than that. You know that. Would I want to live with you for the rest of my life and bear our child?"

Again, she was silent. She chewed on her lip, then said, "I don't think so. I'm certainly not obsessed with the idea, and I'm realistic enough to know that a normal domestic life as wife and mother would . . . well, if it didn't drive me up the wall, it would make me unhappy. But . . ."

He waited a few seconds, then said, "But what?"

She shrugged. "I just don't know. Being in love means being crazy about somebody else, possessed, I think. I know that that feeling usually goes away after a long companionship and is replaced by a quiet sort of love. Being comfortable with your partner, missing him when he's gone for a while, so on. Just now . . . I'm not possessed. What about you?"

"I could be happy."

"Are you possessed?"

"I don't think that's part of love."

She rose, turned, and looked out over the valley.

"I do," she said. "But I'm not crazy about you in the way I said. The idea of living with you all my life doesn't thrill me, it's not something I can't bear to live without."

She turned swiftly to look down at him.

"I hope I haven't hurt you. But I wouldn't be honest if I said I did love you in the way you mean. To tell the truth, Duncan, if I'm in love with anything, it's my work. I mean the work that I had until those reptiles took it away from me. That was what I loved, that was what really made me happy. I've lived off and on with men, but it never worked out. They interfered . . . they wore thin."

"I won't speak of this again," he said.

She squatted down again before him and held his big hand between her small hands.

"I owe you my life. That still doesn't make me love you in the way you want."

"Friends?" he said.

"We're more than just that."

"O.K.," he said. "We're more than just that. That's good enough for me. The subject won't come up again . . . unless you wish to bring it up."

She rose, turned, and walked out into the forest.

He felt very rejected, though he really had no right to do so. Right? What did that mean?

At that moment, the face of a child drifted across his mental wallscreen. It was the same face that had flashed before him not long ago. Now, he recognized it as his when he was about five years old. The first time he had seen the face, it had seemed to be that of a ten year old and he had not been certain that it was his. The features were definitely his own but now those of an infant of five. The face was very sad.

He shook his head after the face had faded away.

What the hell did the hallucination, or whatever it was, mean?

Was it the beginning of a mental breakdown?

He did not know, and there was nothing he could do about it.

Thursday, an hour before daybreak, the airboat slipped from the forest into the eastern waters of the basin. Submerged until the surface was level with its pilot's chin, the boat moved slowly toward the La Brea Tower Complex. The sky was still cloudy but was expected to be clear a few hours after dawn. Duncan saw no gank airboats, but he did pass several large surface craft bringing in goods from the freighters anchored in the harbor outside the basin. The transfer craft were on their way to the docks at the bases of the towers. There they would unload their cargoes.

He slowed the boat as it approached a dock. This was formed of two breakwaters running out from the base of the tower and a curved one half-guarding the opening. The boat slipped into the smooth water where dozens of small sailboats and powercraft and two big yachts were anchored. Above it was the overhang of the second level of the tower. He guided the boat between two yachts and to a floating landing dock. Beyond was the entrance, an arch forty feet wide and twilight lit.

No one was here in this place reserved for the upper class citizens who could afford such expensive craft and dock fees.

While the water bumped the side of the boat against the landing, Snick scrambled out. Duncan verbally programmed the boat, then got out. Its canopies open, the boat sank beneath the water. It would stop when it touched bottom, fifty feet or so, and would turn its power off.

They stood there for a moment, both in organic uniforms, looking like two officers who had every right to be there.

The entrance at the base of the tower was a huge archway beyond which was a big gymnasium. They passed through its bleak walls into a long and towering hall. Doors along this gave access to large rooms. The few that were open showed conference chambers, a large number of stoner cylinders to be used for emergency stayovers or accidents, dining rooms, a chess room, and a handball court. When they got to a suite of offices, Duncan went into the nearest, Snick close behind him. But she said, "Someone's coming!"

He spun around. Snick's hand was on the butt of her gun, still in its holster. He heard a man's voice. A few seconds later, a woman's voice.

He said, softly, "We could hide in here, but they might be heading here. Better to step out as if we're ganks searching for the fugitives."

"They might be ganks, too."

He shrugged, and he walked out the door into the hallway. The woman stopped talking, gasped, and put her hand on her chest. The man looked startled.

"You scared me!" the woman said. "Popping out like that!"

"Anything wrong, officers?" the man said.

Both had halted.

"I'd like your IDs, please," Duncan said.

"Hey!" the man said. "We just came down to go sailing! It's our day off so we're getting an early start!"

Duncan held out his right hand, his left poised above his gun. "It's necessary to see your IDs."

"Do you know who *we are?*" the man said loudly. His face was red.

"IDs, please," Snick said.

"They don't know," the woman said. "They must have a good reason. Go ahead, Manny, cooperate."

She lifted the five-pointed starshape hanging from a necklace around her neck and held it out to Duncan. The man, his face even more flushed, opened and closed his mouth several times, then removed his starshape. Like many citizens, they wore breastpieces in which the ID card formed the center.

"I want to see your IDs, too!" the man said. "It's my right, you know!"

"Of course," Duncan said smoothly. "After we've checked you out."

The man was about his own height though older and rather beefy. The woman was several inches taller than Snick. Since both wore loose-fitting robes, that difference in size between the women did not matter much. If he and Snick had to do so, they could wear the robes.

While Snick stayed with the two, Duncan went back into the office. He found a slot on the wall and voice-activated the screen above it. He asked for a printout, took out the man's card, and put the woman's into the slot. A moment later, with the printouts in his right hand, he went back into the hall. Going to Snick, he said, quietly, "I think we're in luck."

Albert Park Lair and Genevre Tomata Kingsley were executives in DIET, the Department of Import-Export Transportation. DIET was concerned mainly with the traffic of food and manufactured goods into and out of Los Angeles. Lair was First Assistant to the First Director of DIET. Kingsley was head of the Statistics Flow Section of DIET.

51

They were man and wife and lived in a suite on the 125th level. Their only child was twenty subyears old and was a student at the Berkeley College of Economics in San Francisco State.

"Do you have house servants?" Duncan said.

"Yes," Kingsley said.

"Are they in your apartment today?"

Kingsley, her voice quavering, said, "No."

Duncan returned the necklaces and the ID cards to Lair and Kingsley. Then he and Snick herded Lair and Kingsley into the chessroom. These stood in one corner, looking nervous by now. Their captors were in another corner talking quietly.

"This place is the Foremast Club," Duncan said, "reserved, I suppose, for the elite."

The man glared and said, "I demand that you account for your abominable behavior and ID yourselves!"

"We're going straight up to your apartment," Duncan said. "If we run across anyone you know, you'll act normally. Don't try to warn anybody. You'll both be killed."

Lair's face got red again, and he opened his mouth but could not get the words out. He sounded as if he were choking. Kingsley gasped and became even paler.

"You're not ganks!" Lair finally said.

"Not another word," Duncan said, "unless you're greeted by someone."

"You can't get away with this!" Lair said. "I'll . . ."

Duncan slammed his fist into Lair's stomach. Lair bent over, clutching himself, and he gurgled. When he stood up, he snarled soundlessly, but he went along with the others down the hallway quietly. He was trembling, and so was Kingsley.

They got to the elevator reserved for the 125th-floor dwellers and went into it. So far, so good, Duncan thought. There would be no stops until they got to the top level unless the elevator was halted for some reason by the organics. He could think of no cause for that, but there might be ganks at the top end of the shaft. And there were.

52

He saw them as he stepped out of the cage after telling Snick to hold the two inside until he checked the hallway out. They were two, a male and a female, in patroller uniforms. Their holster straps were velcro-closed, and they did not seem to be in a hurry.

He half-turned and spoke softly enough so that the ganks, a hundred feet away, could not hear him.

"Tweedledee and Tweedledum coming," he said. "Routine, apparently. Come on out. Drill these two if they cause any trouble. I'll take care of T and T."

Snick spoke to Lair and Kingsley. "Act like your lives depend on your acting, which they do."

The ganks had slowed down when they saw Duncan. He turned back to face them as the others left the cage. He smiled tightly at them and fell in with Snick behind their prisoners. Lair's and Kingsley's necks and backs were very stiff; they moved like robots.

"No winks, no facial expressions, nothing to attract their attention," he said.

The two were very frightened and close to panic. They might scream for help or grab the ganks or just start running. Then they had passed the ganks, who looked at the two captives and nodded their heads in greeting. Did Lair and Kingsley know them by sight? Would the failure of the two to return the greeting puzzle—or even alert—the ganks?

Duncan nodded at them and walked on. He felt his back prickle when he was by them. It was as if a phantom hand had painted a target on his back, the bull's-eye on his spine.

Though he wanted to turn his head to look behind him, he did not. He noted that the apartment entrance-doors all had holes with blackened edges where the locks had been burned out. The wallscreens on the wide and lofty-ceilinged corridor displayed many designs and landscapes and, here and there, historic scenes from TV dramas. These had been programmed by today's tenants as hallway decorations. Tomorrow, the displays would be different.

Not until Lair and Kingsley stopped before their apartment door did Duncan look back. The ganks were gone. They might, however, recall later that they had seen two people on the 125th level who looked just like the archcriminals.

Lair had inserted his fingers in the hole in the door to move it back into its wall recess. Snick said, "You told me your servants wouldn't be in your apartment today. You'd better not be lying."

Kingsley turned her head. "I'm not stupid."

The door slid aside. Snick entered first, drawing her gun. Duncan gestured to the couple to precede him. He looked up and down the corridor before stepping inside and sliding the door to shut it. No one was in the hallway.

The foyer was spacious and had a thick carpet with ancient American Indian designs. Thursday's occupants, Lair and Kingsley, liked this. But if Friday's did not, they could rearrange the carpet patterns and designs to suit themselves. Some work with the wallscreens and a command, and the lines and colors would change to Friday's tastes.

Duncan had the two stand in the foyer while Snick searched the suite. Presently, a square glowed in the foyer wall, and her face, smiling, appeared. "Come on in. Everything seems to be O.K."

They entered a living room, very large by the ordinary citizens' standards. Its walls were gray, the displays having been turned off. Lair and Kingsley, at Duncan's order, sat down side by side on a sofa. Snick entered the room from the dining room. "You can look for yourself if you want to, but there are two bedrooms, big PP's, two bathrooms, a small gym, the stoner room, a child's room with two beds and a crib—there are five children in stoners—a playroom, a game room, and a huge kitchen. Nothing as big as Ananda's, but they're not World Councillors."

Duncan spoke to the two on the sofa. "You expecting company today? Have any appointments outside of this apartment? Is there anyone who might be expecting a call from you? Or might call you?"

They both shook their heads.

"You don't go shopping today? Nobody will deliver your groceries?"

Kingsley said, huskily, "No. Today's the final one of our three-day weekend. Could I have a drink of water?"

Duncan nodded, and he looked at Snick. She accompanied the woman to the bathroom. There was silence for a moment while Lair tried to outstare Duncan and failed. Then he said, "What's going on? You're not real ganks, that's obvious."

Instead of replying, Duncan voice-activated a wallstrip and asked for Channel 28. Two squares, each three feet wide, glowed. The left one showed the newshead giving the Thursday morning world and local news. The right square displayed the icons of Duncan and Snick and their biodata overlaid with fainter white words: REWARD FOR INFORMATION LEADING TO THEIR ARREST—30,000 CREDITS.

Lair's eyes widened, and he became pale.

"You . . . !"

Duncan nodded and said, "Yes, we are."

He was going to reassure them that they would not be harmed if they cooperated. His mouth stayed open. That child's face, his face, had risen from the bottom of his mind like a ghost through a floor. It had been sad. Now it was twisted with . . . what? Grief? Horror?

Then the face faded out.

"Something wrong?" Snick said.

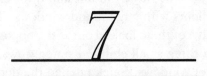

7

"I'm all right," he said. "I just had a thought . . . it's gone now. Maybe it'll come back."

Why did he not tell her about the face?

He had no idea what it meant, and she certainly could not help him with it. Moreover, she might wonder about his fitness in this struggle for survival. If the recurring face was the symptom of a mental breakdown—God, he hoped it was not!—she would not only have to be on guard against their pursuers but worry about him. That might take the edge off a very keen knife, Snick.

Should that hallucination—if it was such—become more frequent to the point where it interfered seriously with his thinking and behavior, he would tell her about it. Until then, it was best that she not have to concern herself with one more problem.

He spoke to the two "hosts." "You. Let's go to the stoner room. But give me your ID cards, first."

They rose from the sofa. Kingsley said, "What are you going

to do to us?" Lair said, "You'll pay for this! We're not just nobodies, you know!"

"Bluster," Duncan said. "Sheer bluster. Give me your cards."

They went silently but pale and shaking. Snick preceded the two; Duncan brought up the rear. They entered a room containing fourteen upright gray cylinders and three casket-like cases. All of them had doors with large round windows. The faces of the occupants in twelve of them looked out at the opposite wall through the glass and the three small children stared upward at the ceiling through the stoner windows. Snick opened the doors of the empty cylinders, and gestured at Kingsley and Lair to go into them.

The woman looked relieved. She was not going to be killed. The man shouted out of his cylinder just before Snick closed its door, "You stinking scum! I'll be there when you're stoned forever, and I'll . . ."

Snick set the dials at the bases of the cylinders. Immediately, the two were statues, their molecular motion slowed down, their bodies cold and hard. The faces and the eyes were those of the dead. But when power was reapplied, they would be alive and warm and the eyes would take in light, not the darkness.

Duncan went back to the living room, where he picked up the ID cards from the sofa. Snick was searching through the personal possessions (PP) closet of their hosts. He went into the kitchen. Its back wall was against the back wall of another suite. The dial of his gun set at BURN, CR (close range), he cut through the wall to a depth of four inches. By the time that Snick, attracted by the stench of disintegrating material, came into the kitchen, he had outlined a potential exit. There would be another inch of wood and plastic to penetrate before the square could be kicked into the next room. This would undoubtedly be the kitchen of the suite behind that of their hosts.

Snick did not ask him what he was doing. She knew that he was making sure that, if they were attacked by ganks through the front door, they had a way out through the back.

"Probably a waste of power," he said. "But every rabbit has an escape route in its burrow."

"Brer Rabbit had more than one."

"We're not Brer Rabbit any more. We're Brer Wolf."

Duncan spoke to a wallscreen and activated a display of Data Information Channel 231.

First, he asked for the location of supply locations in the La Brea Tower Complex, where spray cans of paint were stored. This information was apparently not available to the general public. No reason was given, only the display: DATA REQUEST DE-NIED.

He swore softly, stood a few seconds frowning, then inserted Lair's ID card in the slot and repeated his request. He was given the desired display. Lair, an official of the Department of Import-Export Transportation, was authorized to receive such data.

The spraycans were stored on the 6th level in the east sector.

Duncan asked if there were any cans containing F-bond sprays. These were generally applied to bond metal to metal or metal to plastic. There were such cans, and at the moment there were 12,000 in stock, one-quarter of which contained black F-bond liquid. A moment later, a printout of the arrangement of the rooms and the security measures of the supply store was in the box.

Snick, who was getting breakfast, said, "Spraycans?"

"On just about every corner of every street in every city in the world sits a pole with a TV monitor," he said.

"Tell me something I don't know."

"Spray F-bond on the monitor screens, and they're blind. Moreover, the paint can't be rubbed off or dissolved. Any screen with F-bond on it has to be replaced."

"Who's going to do it?" she said. "Isn't this another case of belling the cat?"

"I'll set the example."

"And get arrested immediately."

"I'm fed up with running and with fighting only in self-defense!" he said, glaring, his cheeks flushed.

"Take it easy," she said. "If you went to a street corner, a dozen, and sprayed the monitors, it'd only be a nuisance to the ganks."

"It could become a stone thrown in the water. The ripples would spread out. Others might copycat me. Then there'd be a lot of thrown stones, and the ripples would intersect and become a storm."

Snick placed two trays full of food on the kitchen table. She said, "Sit down. Eat. You're going to run out of fuel."

"I will. In a minute."

He stopped to face her. His hands opened and closed like the wings of a big eagle just before takeoff.

"The government does its best to keep each day as isolated as possible from the other. But there's a certain amount of unavoidable and legal communication among these. Mostly among official departments and factories. And there's a lot of harmless communication between the days by the ordinary citizens. Like leaving messages for the next day or the previous day. Usually, this has to do with one day failing to keep its apartment clean and tidy enough.

"At least half of the world has gotten the printouts of the messages we sent on the override. The other half is going to find out about them. Also, you can bet that the immers and their auxiliary groups aren't the only subversive organizations in the world. Others will get the messages, and they'll want to act. If, for instance, we could fire them up with a single reported incident of sabotage, spraying the monitors, for example, then they might do the same. And there are a lot of malcontents out there who might follow them or think up their own ways of expressing their unhappiness with the government and the separation of days. Especially if the government insists that ASF doesn't exist."

He stood scowling at her, his fists still working.

"I don't need lectures," she said. "I get the idea."

"Sorry. Was I too intense? We can't do much unless we

have help, an organization with people whose tentacles are deep into the government."

She laughed, and she said, "You make them sound like octopuses."

"The government's an octopus. We need counter-octopuses. There's OMC . . ."

"Which tried to kill us when we became a danger to it."

"Yes, but my grandfather admitted to us that he was its head. He's dead now. Either OMC is so scared it's disbanded, or someone else has taken over. And that person may see the situation's changed, be willing to take us back in."

"Not likely."

"But possible," Duncan said. "It's the only organization we know about. So . . ."

"So?"

"Here's what I think we should do."

Snick listened without interrupting until he was finished. She shrugged and said, "What else can we do? For the moment, anyway."

Thursday went smoothly though Duncan and Snick were not entirely at ease. Despite what Lair and Kingsley had said, it was possible a friend or someone at their offices might call them. Duncan and Snick watched the news between exercising, napping, and eating. They were mainly interested in the progress of the search for them. There was none, though the newsheads and official organic bulletins made it seem that there was.

The next day, shortly after midnight, they greeted Friday's couple as they stepped out of their cylinders. Duncan and Snick rode roughshod over their protests. After using the can of TM he had taken from the University Tower precinct station, Duncan questioned them. They revealed that today was one of their days off from work. Also like Thursday's tenants, they had planned to go sailing. Later, they were going to meet friends for a live show at a theater on the 123rd level.

Duncan forced them to make calls cancelling their appointments. After that, the couple were put into their stoners and gorgonized.

While eating supper, Duncan said, "Thea, I don't think we can pull it off by staying in this apartment. What if tomorrow's tenants don't have a day off? They have a child, and so do some of the others. What if they have to attend school? It won't do any good for their parents to leave a message saying the kids are sick. The authorities will send a doctor at once to check up on them."

"I've been thinking about that, too," she said. "So, why don't we move into Ananda's apartment?"

He stared at her for a minute, then grinned. "That's the kind of bold thinking I like! That's the last place in the world they'd expect us to go!"

His plate still half-filled, he rose and went to the wallscreen. The diagram of the 125th level appeared in response to his request. Ananda's suite was still marked as UNOCCUPIED. It was near the emergency public staircase leading to the roof access structure behind which he and Snick had hidden for a while. They would have to walk almost half a mile along the corridors to get to it. There would be monitor screens along the way and, possibly, ganks.

They assumed that every monitor in L.A.—on the West Coast, too—had been set to recognize them automatically. The ganks, of course, had familiarized themselves with their icons. And the citizens would have seen them often on the news channels. By then, he and Snick had gotten into all of the personal possessions closets by using the ID cards of the tenants. These had been removed from the necks of the stonees and destoned in the kitchen stoner box used for gorgonized food supplies. They took out the wigs, a currently fashionable wear for both men and women, and selected two. They put long robes over their uniforms and hats with wide brims on their heads. Then they practiced changing their walking gaits. Snick bent her knees somewhat and reduced the swing of her arms. She also humped over a little. He made his gait a little stiff-legged and kept his elbows closer to his body while swinging his arms.

After watching each other walk up and down the living room and the hall leading from it, they made some minor adjustments. These included decreasing the length of their strides. Duncan raised his chin more, and Snick cocked her head slightly to the left. She also applied lipstick to make her mouth seem larger. Both stuffed a little cotton under their upper lips.

At 4:30 P.M., carrying shoulderbags which held gank helmets and other items, they left the apartment. A number of people were in the corridor, returning from their offices. Duncan stiffened when he saw four ganks in the direction he and Snick had to take. But these quick-stepped past Duncan and Snick as if they had urgent and serious business elsewhere.

Fifteen minutes later, Duncan and Snick were outside the door of Ananda's apartment. The hole in it had been covered with a tape on which a quick-drying cement had been sprayed. Across the doorway, their ends glued to the wall, were two wide green ribbons on which were white letters: ORGANICS DEPT AREA.

Those three words were enough for the law-abiding citizens. They did not have to be told that unauthorized entrance was forbidden.

Glancing at the seals and the sign, Duncan and Snick walked on. The monitor at the far end of the corridor would film them as they pushed open the doors leading to the public staircase. That would mean nothing unless the monitor had been rigged to transmit an alarm to gank HQ if anyone did use that exit. Very few people would use it, and a gank seeing them do so might wonder about it. But there was no reason, as far as Duncan knew, why the monitor should notify the HQ computer if citizens did open those doors.

They climbed up the very wide staircase to the access structure. This had no monitor screens inside, enabling them to strip off their outer clothes and wigs without being observed. After donning the helmets, they stuffed their shoulderbags with the clothes and wigs. A medium wind flowed around them as they left the structure. Light clouds scudded eastward high above them. No one else was on the rooftop. They walked to the hatchway cover over the hangar room of Ananda's suite. Like the door to the suite, it was sealed with green crisscross ribbons and a sign: ORGANIC DEPT AREA.

It was necessary to cut the ribbons of the seal to open the hatchway cover. Snick drilled through the locking mechanism with a narrow beam from her gun. Duncan knelt and inserted a thin knife blade into the juncture of rooftop floor and hatch edge. The hatch was of thin and light but hard plastic. Prying, he managed to shove the cover back far enough to get his fingers in the opening. Snick helped him shove, and the cover slid back into the floor recess. They opened the hatchway just enough to get through it. Snick hung from the edge with extended arms and dropped to the floor below.

All of this activity would be recorded by the monitor satellites. It did not matter unless it was set to trigger off an alarm if suspicious behavior was filmed at that area. That could be the situation. But Duncan and Snick had to chance it.

Snick placed the ladder against the hatchway edge. The upper end of the ladder was just below that. When Duncan had gotten onto the ladder, he dug his knife into the lower part of the cover near the edge and pushed. The cover slid shut. He went down the ladder and joined Snick. Their guns in hand, they prowled through every room. There was plenty of evidence of the fight during their escape. These included dried blood stains and the chalked outlines of the corpses Duncan and Snick had left behind when they had fled.

They had everything they needed to live in these commodious rooms. Since they might be surprised by organics returning to the suite for some reason, they had to be always alert. Snick slept while Duncan stood guard and vice versa. Neither, however, allowed overanxiety to prey on them. They ate well, exercised hard and often in the well-equipped gymnasium, talked much, though Duncan did most of the talking, and watched the news channels and the educational and entertainment shows. They knew that they had to be out of Ananda's place before Wednesday. On that day, Lair and Kingsley would come out of the stoners with a tale that would electrify the ganks. These, knowing that the archcriminals were in the tower (or had been) would be searching intensively for them.

There had been nothing on the news about the discovery of the airboat that Duncan had sent to the bottom of the dock. That did not mean much, though. The organics would have good reason not to inform the public about it. They could be watching the site in case the two criminals came back to use it again.

Tuesday, early afternoon, he had all the news channels on in Ananda's study. The newsheads of every day had given much of their time to Duncan's and Snick's feats because each day had to have explained to it in detail what these two had done. As Duncan expected, along with the history of Duncan and Snick, time was given to interviews with officials. These claimed that everything in Duncan's messages was a lie. That the world population was only two billion, not the ten billion counted by the government, was obviously absurd and could be easily disproved.

"By the same methods they used in the censuses," Duncan said to Snick. "The government controls the data banks. Any information from it is shaped by the government."

Most of the newshead comments were directed at the claim that the formula in the printouts could increase the life span by a factor of seven. However, to prove to the public that the formula was not valid, the government biologists were going to use the "elixir" or ASF in experiments on fruit flies. These had short enough lives that the use of the formula and its long-range effects or lack thereof could be scientifically demonstrated.

"Extended longevity," Duncan said. "The opportunity to live seven times longer is something the people will fight for. If a false report is issued, it'll be up to us to raise hell about it. It won't end until the government has to prove without a tinge of doubt that ASF is no good. It can't do that."

On the actual count of every five minutes, the three-dimensional images of Duncan and Snick and their biodata were displayed on all channels.

"Armed and dangerous," a newshead said. "Psychopathic killers and completely alienated from society. Wanted for daybreaking, antigovernment activities, assault and battery, possessing false ID cards, resisting arrest, destroying government property, attempted murder, murder, and many other crimes.

"FLASH! We have just been informed that the reward for the identification and location of these criminals has been raised to forty thousand credits. But any citizen who does see them must on no account attempt to apprehend the criminals. Just report their sighting and location immediately to the organic department. I repeat, make no effort to detain the criminals. The government is anxious that no more innocent citizens be murdered."

"Innocent!" Snick shouted.

Few things shook her, but unjust accusations against her broke through that cool attitude and exposed the white-hot lava that burned deep in her. He did not blame her for erupting. She had been the very model of the organic. She had believed thoroughly in her role of law-keeper and had never deviated from the gank ethics as stated in the department's rules and regulations tapes. She had been offered bribes three times in her career and had resisted all without the slightest hesitation or regret.

"I'd like to kill those bastards!" Snick said. "Burn them down!"

"You may get your chance," Duncan said. He waved at the squares displaying the news channels. "Meanwhile . . ."

His close attention to the news was based on what, realistically, was probably a hope as thin as a cirrus cloud. Neither he nor Snick had any idea what it would be. But if they saw it, they would recognize it. Perhaps.

He had no sooner sat down again than he leaped up, his face seeming to radiate, his finger pointing at Channel 8. "There! That's it, by God!"

Snick also rose swiftly. "What?"

"Not what! Who!"

All the channels had from time to time shown their interviewers questioning the citizen on the street. They were brushed off quite often with a "No comment." But there were some who were eager to voice their opinions pro or con. One of these was now speaking, her face momentarily filling the screen. Across it glowed in orange her name and ID number.

Donna Lee Cloyd was a pretty woman of middle height, dark-skinned and having blonde hair and blue eyes the lightness of which might be due to depigmentation. Her robe was not the same as when Duncan had last seen her, though her canary-yellow high-heeled shoes were.

"The face! The mark on her forehead!" Duncan said.

Snick frowned, then smiled.

"The woman who handed us the note shortly after we arrived in L.A.," she said, "the OMC messenger."

Donna Lee Cloyd's forehead bore a tattoo, a small black right-handed swastika, the symbol of the original Guatama sect.

"I don't believe a word of that outrageous lying message," she was saying, her face very serious. "I hope the ganks, I mean, the organics, catch those vicious psychopathic murderers and bring them to justice."

"Thank you, citizen," the interviewer said.

Cloyd's face disappeared, and a man's replaced it. By then, Duncan had told the screen to back up the recording tape and freeze her face. He wrote down her ID number on the pad on the coffee table in front of the sofa. Then he summoned up the tower directory and wrote down her address.

"She's sure covering up," Snick said. "You'd think she loved the government and hated our guts."

"Wouldn't you put on an act?" Duncan said.

Only a few weeks ago, as Duncan, Padre Cabtab, and Snick had left the immigration station to go to the La Brea Tower Complex, the woman had come up to them. She had looked as if she meant to speak to them. Instead, she had slipped a note into Duncan's hand and left swiftly. The note had instructed them to meet someone unnamed at 9:00 P.M. at The Snorter. This was a neighborhood tavern close to their quarters on the twentieth level near the west rim of the west block area in the tower. The unnamed person would recognize them and make contact.

Cloyd was a courier for the subversive group, then named OMC, which had given the three their IDs and arranged for their apartments. They had never seen her again. Not until now.

Her address was an apartment, 364 Tripitaka Street, 12th level. Profession: Part-time data organizer/researcher, freelancer, authorized to work in any nongovernment department. GS 0.5. That is, half-subsidized by the national government.

"She lives in a weedie section," Snick said.

"Californians would say it's a bloney section," Duncan said. "Bloney, from abalone."

"A weedie," she said, unable to keep disgust from her tone.

"Hey, they're just people who prefer not to work full time so they can be rich with their personal time," Duncan said.

"Parasites," she said. "What if everybody wanted just to work now and then or not at all?"

"The point is that only a small minority do. Forget it. It's irrelevant to what we have to do."

Having seen the name of Barry Gardner Cloyd next to Donna's in the directory, he checked it. Barry was Donna's husband and shared her apartment. He was, when he worked, a waiter at a high-class restaurant patronized by upper-level government officials and technicians. Though he was, like Donna, listed as a religionist, he was allowed to work in the restaurant because it was privately owned.

"A good source of information for a subversive," Duncan said. "Food and booze thaw out the customers' security-frozen lips."

"I doubt he did anything with what he overheard," she said. She was scornful of the organization to which she and Duncan had belonged very briefly. He did not blame her for that since it had tried to kill them when it believed that they were a danger to it. But he thought that, if they could penetrate deeper into it, get close to the leader, they might be able to use it. Immerman (Ananda) had organized the group which called itself, among other names, PUPA and OMC. But he was dead. Therefore someone else had taken it over. Unless OMC had been disbanded when its leader died. However, Immerman was not the local chief, and that person might still be running the group.

There was only one way to find out.

He explained to Snick what he wanted to do while he pointed to the big wall display of the 125th and 12th level maps.

"The private elevator we came up on with Lair and Kingsley is to the left as you go out the door. But if you go right, you come to the public bank of elevators. We take a public elevator to the 12th level. We get out near Blue Moon Plaza. We go down Eight-Ways Causeway for four blocks, then turn onto Tripitaka Street. We have to pass by four corners with street monitors."

"And any number of ganks looking for us."

"Yes, but it'll just be routine. They must still think we're out in the woods."

Snick shrugged. "You have to eat the apple to find out if it's poisoned. Or give it to someone else to take a bite for you, and there's no one else."

71

Their shoulderbags were packed and ready to go. They picked them up and Duncan started to deactivate the wallscreens. He stopped, then said, "Wait! I want to see this."

"The talk show on 28?" Snick said.

"Yes."

The subject was the murder of Ananda.

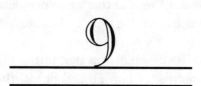

The criminologist, a professor from University Tower according to the white subtitles, said, "What I don't understand, among other things, is how the alleged outlaws managed to get into the World Councillor's apartment. From the brief reports I've seen, there was no sign of forced entry except those made by the organics when they responded to the call from the man calling himself Caird, among other things. And how could only three people, though heavily armed, kill all the armed bodyguards?

"Moreover, how could the alleged outlaws know that the Councillor was in that apartment? According to the news reports and what I've been told by the organics, the Councillor's apartment was not listed in the city directory. No one knew that the Councillor had an apartment there. Also . . . ."

The host said, "Pardon me, Professor Shinn. One question at a time. Major Hafiz, would you care to answer the first question? That is, how did the criminals get into the Councillor's apartment?"

Major Hafiz said, "I can't answer that at this moment. But I'm sure . . ."

Professor Shinn said, "And how were the criminals, the *alleged* criminals, able to override all electronic safeguards and transmit those TV messages?"

Host: "Please, Professor Shinn. No interruptions."

Duncan said, "I'm glad that some people are not just swallowing wholemeal everything the authorities tell them. Maybe there'll be many like that Shinn."

So far, the government was permitting free speech by citizens about the motives of himself and Snick. But if it did clamp down because too many were asking questions like Shinn's, then it would cause a storm of protest. Moreover, the outraged citizens would wonder just why the government had deprived them of their constitutional rights.

The government had a sticky mess on its hands, but he did not feel sorry for it.

Dressed in their uniforms, they went out by the way in which they had entered and closed the hatch. The sun was bright; the satellites would be recording their movements until they went into the access house. After that, the monitors on the staircase and in the halls and streets would be filming them. That meant nothing unless organics had been posted to watch all the monitorings made everywhere on the West Coast. He doubted that that had happened. There was not nearly enough personnel to do that, and those available would be going over the films made of the deserts and forests over a very large area.

When the ganks found out that he and Snick had been in the tower, they would probably rerun all the monitor tapes in this area. By then, it would be too late.

As soon as they were in the access house, they changed into wigs, hats, and robes. These were not the ones they had used when leaving the apartment on Thursday. Ananda's apartment had yielded a variety of costumes and wigs from his closets and those of his male and female servants. Now, dressed quite differently, the two went down the steps until they came to the 10th level. Here they went through the doors and stepped into the flow of afternoon traffic.

Except for the top and bottom floors of the tower, all were laid out in the same pattern inside its mile-diameter. Seen from above, each of 123 levels looked like an archer's target. The bull's-eye was the great central plaza. The causeways were the circles. Four straight avenues starting at the perimeter cut through the circles and met at the central plaza. Both the straight and the circular throughways intersected smaller plazas containing stores and shops, gymnasiums, ice-skating rinks, bowling alleys, "live" theaters, neighborhood taverns and townhalls.

Duncan and Snick had emerged from the staircase onto the junction of Eight-Ways Causeway, the outer perimeter thorough-fare, and Blue Moon Street, which cut across the tower on an east-west axis. They walked to the sidewalk, filled with other pedestrians. The street itself was crowded with bicycles, tricycles, and a few electric-driven cars. A gank patrol car passed them, its two occupants scanning the passersby from behind large octagonal dark glasses. Duncan and Snick walked slowly, taking good but not obvious care to shield themselves as much as possible. They stayed near the fronts of the apartments and matched their paces to those walking on the outer side of the sidewalk.

The patrol car drove on, its occupants seemingly unaware that they had passed the two fugitives.

The sky-blue ceiling of the 10th level was flecked with sluggish white clouds. A simulacrum of the sun moved above the clouds; its position matched that of the real sun outside the tower. In all the levels, except the top and bottom, there was a sun in the daytime and a moon at night (if there was a moon in the outside heavens). An optical illusion assured that the sun was in the correct position in the "sky" no matter where you stood, at the east or west end of the street or in the central plaza. The air was always 75°F. and moving at three miles an hour.

Cuts of conversation came to him as the swifter walkers passed him.

". . . said Ananda was like Caliph Harun al-Rashid, he'd go among the L.A. citizens like he was just one of us . . . disguised . . . wanted to know what your average Jilljoe was thinking . . . who the hell was Harun al-Rashid?"

"You never saw *The Arabian Nights* series? Where you been all your life?"

". . . ganks're not answering some questions. They're ducking them."

". . . if they're really holding out on us about this ASF, there'll be hell to pay, and . . ."

". . . so many personae it's confusing. If he's nuts, then he's not to blame."

". . . guy's lying. Only two billion? What kind of shit is he trying to pull?"

". . . got to admire them. Ever heard of anybody else ever get away so long with giving the finger to the gummint?"

"Seven times as long? If it's true, it must be, all that has to be done is labtest it, then no way the government's going to hold out on us, the assholes."

". . . slime, real stinking slime. Those two murderers ought to be locked up forever with no TV, and . . ."

Moving slowly, as if they were innocent citizens out for a stroll, Duncan and Snick kept on until they came to a plaza. Here they entered a large department store and went into a doorway above which flashed: S & S. This was a public restroom which, at the moment, had only a few men and women in it. They entered separate stalls and stripped off their hats, wigs, and robes. After pulling different ones from the handbags, they put these on. The previously worn items stuffed into the handbag, they walked out of the store. A walk of several blocks brought them to a public elevator bank. Duncan pressed the button for the 12th level. The doors opened, and they went into a cage in which they were the only passengers. The citizens of one level seldom went to another.

Emerging on the 12th level, they walked until they found another store. Here they repeated the same procedure as on the

10th level. A few minutes later, they were on the corner of Nine Sages and Wickenford streets. Here they turned right.

The monitors on top of the traffic signal poles on each corner were ten feet high and consisted of two thin gray squares at right angles to each other. So far, they had not matched up their videos of Duncan and Snick with those in HQ computers. If they had, the two would have been surrounded by ganks before now.

Or, Duncan thought, the ganks had orders to follow them for a certain distance hoping that they could scoop up other subversives also.

Not likely. They would be too eager to grab Duncan and Snick as quickly as possible and whisk them away to the precinct station. Or wherever they had orders to take them. The two had been too quicksilvery, slipping through the fingers that should have held them tight.

Four more street corners and four more double-monitors on each. The two walked along the gentle curve of the street and came near their destination. Ordinarily, since this was a residential district, there would have been few people on the sidewalks. But many were out talking excitedly to their neighbors, gesticulating vigorously, some with printouts fluttering in their hands. Duncan would just as soon that they did not see him and Snick go into the Cloyds' apartment. However, there was nothing to do but proceed as if they had legitimate business here.

Like almost all apartments, the street front of the Cloyds' was one great display. Duncan paused long enough to study it. What the tenants put on the outside screens of their homes often revealed their psyches. The many-colored and swiftly moving and changing icons and abstract forms seemed to be basically religious. In the background was a lightning-shot and dark thundercloud beyond which the top edge of the sun shone. The cloud swelled and filled up the wall, rushing at the viewer, dim whirling images in it. Then the lightning bolts became so many and so bright that the figures were clearly illuminated before fading into blackness again.

One was Buddha, the conventional sitting Mongolian Buddha, which, soaring through the air, altered into a young and good-looking Hindu prince, Siddhartha. It collided and merged with an angel, pale-skinned and winged, then became an elongated body, the wings becoming lightning streaks. Out of its mouth spurted a dark-skinned Asiatic Indian-looking woman who shot out of her mouth a Christ-like man, who expelled from his bearded lips an Arab—Mohammed?—who ejected from his wide-open mouth an ancient forest Amerind—Hiawatha?—who vomited a coyote, who spat a creature half-man, half-coyote—Old Man Coyote of Amerind myth?—who urped a huge white rabbit—Owasso of the Ojibway Indians?—whose huge mouth hurled out a giant black spider—Nandi, the trickster spider of Africa?

The metamorphoses seemed to go on and on but eventually became a baby wrapped in flames. Then the cycle started over again with the Buddha.

Snick clutched Duncan's arm and said, "My God! Buddha's face! It's yours!"

It certainly resembled his. But it was gone too quickly for him to be sure.

"They must've programmed your face onto that man today," Snick said. "That means they're for you; they admire you."

"Dumb," he said. "A passing gank might note the resemblance."

"No, it goes too fast to see unless you're really looking hard at it."

He pressed the doorbell with a knuckle.

A man's voice came from the door-monitor overhead.

"Who is it, please?"

Those within could see him and Snick. Duncan looked up and said, "We need to see you . . . Citizen Cloyd?"

"We're engaged at the moment in a rather private business. Who are you?"

Duncan opened his mouth to tell him that he had business,

too, and it was most urgent. A woman's voice cried out, "Barry, it's him! It's the woman, too!"

The man said, "Who?" After several seconds, he said, "My God! You're right! But what . . . .?"

The voice of another woman, loud and shaking, said, "No! Don't let them in! Send them away until . . ."

The sound was turned off.

10

The door slid back into the wall recess swiftly. Duncan stepped into the living room, Snick close behind him. The Cloyds were standing by a sofa and staring at them. A woman with long black hair was running down the hall. She lunged through a doorway to her right. That, Duncan knew, would open into the stoner room.

Duncan ran past the Cloyds down the hallway and through the doorway. His fear that she would be using a wallscreen to call the organics was unfounded. Smiling twistedly, she walked toward him.

"I panicked," she said. "I didn't want you to know I was here. I'm . . ."

". . . OMC?" Duncan said.

She stopped, her eyes widening slightly. "Yes, though it was OMC and then PUPA and is now something else. How'd you know?"

"Guessed. This damned cell-system the OMC has . . . never more than one contact at a time, nobody knowing more than one other member."

He went out into the hall and waited for her to come out and precede him. On returning to the living room, he found that the Cloyds were sitting on the sofa and Snick was standing by the exit-door. Her hand was inside her robe, ready to snatch out her gun. Picking up the woman's handbag, which she had abandoned in her haste, he dumped the contents out onto the coffee table.

She said, "What do you . . . ?" and closed her mouth.

The pile, except for one item, was what he expected to find in a female citizen's bag. Certainly, the small spraycan of TM was not. It was illegal for anyone but members of the organic department to have them and even this was under restricted conditions.

Duncan, holding the can, said, "Did you intend to use this on the Cloyds?"

The woman nodded and said, "It's a security measure we take whenever there's a possible need for it. With the present situation . . ."

She waved her hand to indicate that everything was a mess just now.

"What's your name and ID number?"

"Oh, no, I can't tell you that!" she said. "It'd be too dangerous!"

Duncan spoke to the Cloyds. "What name does she use when she's dealing with you? And is she your only contact?"

Donna Cloyd spoke before her husband could get his mouth open. "Codename FOX. And, yes, she's our only direct contact."

She hesitated, and Duncan brandished the can of TM. "You might as well tell me the whole truth."

She shrugged. "Oh, well, you'll get it out of us anyway. Though you don't have to be so belligerent about it, you know. We're on your side. Everybody in this apartment, all the days except Friday, is OMC. We leave messages for each other when we get orders to do so."

Duncan gestured at Snick. "FOX, give her your ID card."

The woman wailed, "You're getting me into deep trouble!"

"Give."

Very pale, shaking, and slow with reluctance, the woman removed the fake-gold necklace at the end of which her card hung. Snick took the blue-colored oblong and inserted it in a wall slot. The name, Harper Sheppard Jaccoud, and the ID number appeared at the top of the screen. Her icon turned slowly, revealing full-face, quarter-profile, half-profile, and back. Then the icon, still revolving, shrank, and half the screen was filled with her biodata.

She resided on the 14th level and worked full-time, six hours, as a laboratory technician for a biochemistry research department, privately owned but partly government subsidized. She was unmarried and childless. As of ten subweeks ago, she was living with a man, Johnson Chu Goldstein, an airboat mechanic.

"Goldstein?" Duncan said. "He's OMC, too?"

"I proposed him as a candidate," Jaccoud said. "But I was told that he drank too much, was too loose-lipped. I don't think that was the real reason he was rejected. He doesn't drink *that* much."

"Maybe," Snick said, "he is an OMC, but the higher-ups didn't want you to know that."

Jaccoud looked shocked. She sat down on the sofa beside the Cloyds.

"You've all seen the news, of course," Duncan said. "What you don't know is that World Councillor Ananda was the head of OMC and God only knows how many more underground organizations. He's dead, but the ganks must've TMed him before he died. Unless he was in too deep a coma. I hope so. In any event, someone's taken his place as head of the OMC—unless that person's identity was revealed by Ananda. I'm taking a chance that it wasn't. So, what I'm going to do, I'm going to work my way up the ladder of the hierarchy until I find that person."

He pointed at Jaccoud. "You're the second rung."

"That's crazy!" she said. "Impossible, too! I don't know

who my upper contact is. Except for just once, I never saw her. I'd get coded messages via TV that would seem to the uninitiated to be harmless conversation."

"The exception?" Duncan said.

"I was summoned to meet her just once. It was in a warehouse, shortly after I was recruited for the OMC."

"Recruited by whom?" Duncan said.

Jaccoud turned her head to look at Donna Cloyd, seated next to her. "She did it. She is my first cousin. I've known her since we were little children. She's the one who talked me into this."

"Damn!" Donna said. "You weren't supposed . . ."

Jaccoud interrupted. "What's the difference? They're going to TM me." She looked at Duncan. "Right?"

He nodded and said, "That's why you better not lie to us. Now, describe your contact."

He was not surprised when she had finished talking. His sole experience in a meeting with an upper-echelon OMC person was like hers except that it had taken place in a gymnasium. That mysterious being had been hooded, masked, heavily robed, and speaking through a voice distorter.

There was silence for a moment. Then Jaccoud said, "Oh, hell, you'll get it out of me anyway when you TM me! I shouldn't have done it! I knew it was forbidden, and it was dangerous and dumb! Pure stupidity! But I was just too curious! I couldn't help myself! I followed her after she left the gym!"

Duncan smiled. "That *was* stupid. It was also dangerous. If she'd found out what you did, you'd be dead now."

He had suspected that she had shadowed her contact when she referred to the masked person as a woman.

"Oh, God, you're not going to tell them?" Jaccoud said.

"We'll keep that secret among ourselves," Duncan said. He looked at the Cloyds. "Right?"

Barry Cloyd tugged at a corner of his thick black moustache

and said, "Double-right. Since we know that, we're in as much danger from them as FOX . . . Jaccoud is."

Harper Jaccoud said, weakly, "I'm very sorry."

Duncan said, "You followed her. What's her name and address and ID number? Or don't you know?"

Jaccoud sighed deeply and said, "I know." After a pause, she gave the information slowly and painfully, as if she were hauling up each word separately from her throat with ropes made of barbed wire.

Jaccoud had sneaked after the contact and observed her from behind a pile of boxes. In a dark corner, the woman had removed her disguise, stuffed it into a shoulderbag, and walked out of the warehouse. Jaccoud, fearful yet driven with the kind of indiscreet nosiness that killed the cat, had trailed the woman at a distance. She had taken the elevator to the prestigious 125th level. Jaccoud waited until the level indicator showed where the cage had stopped. Then she had taken another cage and gotten off of it just in time to see the back of the woman as she went around a corner at the end of a very long corridor. After Jaccoud had raced to that corner, she had peeked around it. Her heart, she said, was squeezing out buckets of fear. She saw the woman go into a door. After it was closed, Jaccoud had walked up to it and noted the address.

On returning to her apartment, she had called up the tower directory and matched the address with that day's occupant.

"You won't tell her I followed her, will you?"

"No need," Duncan said.

The woman was Lin Cozumel Erlend, a detective-captain of the 2nd precinct of the 111th level.

"Finding out that she was an organic scared me even more. Was she a bona-fide OMC? Or a gank infiltrator? I couldn't report her to a superior because she was my superior. Even if I'd had somebody else to report to I couldn't do it. I'd disobeyed orders."

"We'll find out if she's bona fide or a plant," Duncan said. "I doubt she's a fake. You and the Cloyds and who knows how many more would've been scooped up long ago if she wasn't a genuine OMC."

He gestured at Snick. She walked up to Jaccoud with the can of TM in her right hand. Jaccoud shrank back and said, "I told you the truth. Is that really necessary?"

"I think you did tell the truth," he said. "But we have to check you out."

Snick, holding the can out at arm's length, pressed the button on its top with a finger. The violet-colored spray struck Jaccoud in the face. A few seconds later, she was unconscious. The questioning took half an hour, but Duncan did not learn much more than she had told him. He was satisfied, however, that she was not a plant.

Then it was the Cloyds' turn. They revealed no more than they had told him, and they were also sincere members of OMC. Proving that was not necessary, Barry Cloyd had said. After all, they had been TMed several times by their contact and also by the other OMCs who lived in this apartment. Duncan had acknowledged that but insisted that they be questioned again.

"People have been known to change their loyalties for one reason or another. Or you could have been exposed and then forced to act as an agent for the ganks. I don't think so, but I have to make sure. I didn't come this far by trusting anybody. Except my partner."

He was not surprised when Jaccoud and the Cloyds, after regaining consciousness, insisted that they TM him and Snick.

"I'd let you do it under ordinary circumstances," he said. "But you *know* who we are. You've seen us often enough on TV. I don't want to waste time being questioned by you."

He asked them if they would be able to get fake IDs for him and Snick.

"Along with wigs, makeup, a fake beard, and thumbprint slipovers in case we have to ID ourselves with those."

Barry Cloyd leaped up from the sofa. "You're planning on

going out into the streets again? You have a good place to hide *here*! Why take more chances?"

"We'll use this place," Duncan said. "But I'm hiding from now on only when it's absolutely necessary. Whenever we see a chance to attack, we'll attack."

Barry Cloyd let himself down hard onto the sofa. "They'll get you sooner or later, probably sooner! Which means they'll get us, too!"

Duncan did not tell him that he was immune to TM. The fewer who knew that, the better. Of course, if Snick were captured, she, not being immune, would spill everything.

"This OMC is no longer a penny-ante organization," he said. "It's in the big time, and we're going for broke. You're all in it, like it or not."

"You're not our superior!" Donna Cloyd said. The right-handed swastika on her forehead was even darker because of the paleness of her skin.

"I'm taking over," he said, and he placed his left hand on the butt of his progun. "Any argument?"

Jaccoud and the Cloyds were silent.

"I repeat, can you get us the IDs and the other stuff?"

Harper Jaccoud nodded, and she said, "It'll be chancy, especially just now. But it can be done. I can't get it for you today. You'll have to wait until next Tuesday."

Duncan did not want to sit in the apartment for an obweek. Taking Snick aside, he spoke softly to her.

"Only one of us can go after Erlend. The other will have to stay here and keep an eye on these three. I don't want them trying to warn Erlend."

"Why should they?" she said.

"I don't know why, but who knows what's going on in their minds?"

She said, "We could TM them again and ask them if they would warn her."

"Just asking them if they would notify her might plant a suggestion that they do so. TM sometimes has some tricky effects. Besides, I don't want to push them too far and make them hostile."

"The Cloyds seem to admire you greatly. Otherwise, they wouldn't have put your face on the Buddha in the display on the front of their apartment."

"But what about Jaccoud?"

She frowned, then said, "O.K. You go to Erlend's. I'll stay. That's what you want to do, isn't it?"

He nodded. "Give me the TM."

11

Duncan was alone in the elevator as it rose toward the 125th level. Though he looked serene, even happy—he was whistling a current tune, *Come One, Come All*—he was keenly conscious of the monitors he had passed and had yet to pass. These included the monitor in the elevator cage, installed for the safety of the passengers, of course.

So far, the tychenons that he liked to think clustered about him had given him luck. His wig and colorful robe had helped him, as had his cotton-stuffed upper lip and his non-Duncanian gait.

He had not called from the Cloyds' apartment because her screen would automatically display the origin number of the call. Since he had no ID card he could use safely, he could not phone her from a public booth. If he had had one, he could not blank out the video portion to conceal his face without making her suspicious.

The cage stopped. He stepped out into Blue Dolphin Hall,

125th level. This looked like all other corridors except for the difference in the displays on the apartment fronts. He walked down Blue Dolphin Hall, turned, strode down another hallway, turned, and soon was before the door of 1236 Piggutt Hall. The only observers in the corridor were the monitors at each end of it. He punched the doorbell, noting at the same time that the lock mechanism of the door had been replaced. A few seconds passed before a woman's voice came from overhead. She had taken a little time to check him before replying.

"What can I do for you?"

"Are you Captain Erlend?"

"Yes. Who are you?"

Her voice was tight.

"OMC," Duncan said. "PUPA. WABASSO."

The last was the current name of the organization which Duncan would always think of as OMC. Jaccoud had provided him with that.

There was a long silence. Erlend must be shocked.

"Anyone with you?" she said.

"No one," Duncan said, "as you see."

Another long silence. He said, "It's not good for me to stand out here."

The door began sliding back. Someone was talking inside —a newshead. He stepped forward, waiting for it to give him enough room for his body to pass through. It stopped with just enough space for his shoulders. Erlend, a tall redhead in a house-robe, was standing in the middle of the living room. Her right arm dangled, a progun in her hand pointing at the floor. She was evidently not sure about him and was prepared for anything. Or so she thought.

She said, "Door! Close!" as he passed through the doorway.

As it began sliding shut, he brought his left hand from behind his back. She said, "Stop there. Put your hands . . ." The violet beam from his gun, which was set for medium stunning at close range, struck Erlend in the chest. She had swung her gun up toward him, but she fell backward, her knees buckling, and the beam from her gun struck an upper corner of the room. The gun fell, the beam ceasing when her finger quit pressing the trigger.

He went to her crumpled form and felt her pulse. It was throbbing slowly and irregularly. Her skin was pale, and her eyes were open. After putting her weapon in the belt under his robe, he lifted Erlend and placed her on a sofa.

The newshead, a handsome man with a very deep voice, probably computer-enhanced, was saying, ". . . authorized to announce that the Commonwealth has decided it's in the best interests of the people to be informed of the latest discovery concerning the outlaw Jefferson Cervantes Caird, alias William St. George Duncan, alias many other IDs. The outlaw Caird has a unique talent in that he can lie while under the influence of TM! It's not known at present whether this hitherto-unknown ability is a mutant talent or the effects of an anti-TM drug unknown to science!

"One of the grave implications of this ability to lie under TM is that the outlaw Caird, a.k.a. Duncan, cannot be dealt with according to established legal procedures. At the moment, the World Court is studying this new development, and . . ."

Duncan lowered the decibel level. He wondered why it had taken the government so long to disclose his singular ability. Then he turned to the business at hand.

He waited half an hour until Erlend had regained consciousness, her pulse had become regular, and she had regained color. He gave her a drink of water. She was silent during this but started to protest when he took the can of TM from his shoulderbag. She fell to her side on the sofa as the spray struck her face and the inside of her mouth. He straightened her out on the sofa again and began his questioning.

His interrogation had to be simple and easily understood. When under TM, the subject was as literal-minded—almost—as a computer. TM subjects never volunteered information. This had to be extracted step by step, and the questions sometimes had to be rephrased.

He knew that she was the person she claimed to be. He had taken her ID card while she was unconscious the first time and had used it to call up her biodata. He got the story from her about her recruitment into the OMC and some of her activities since then. This took time. Then he asked her about her knowledge of Immerman-Ananda. She had no idea that Immerman was now Ananda, and, in fact, had never heard of Immerman. Nor did she know about the ASF, the age-slowing factor, until Duncan's messages had appeared via the override on TV.

He then said, "What is the name of your immediate superior in the organization known as OMC, PUPA, and WABASSO?"

"I don't know."

"Have you ever seen your immediate supervisor?"

"Yes."

"Describe the physical appearance of your immediate superiors."

As he had expected, the person had been robed, masked, and gloved, and had spoken through a voice distorter.

Further inquiry revealed that Erlend had met the person six times. These conferences had been in six different places with no one else nearby.

"Has your supervisor ever made contact with you through other means?"

"Yes."

"What means were they?"

"Wallscreen."

All screen communications displayed the name and ID number of the caller. But that could not be in this case.

He asked Erlend if she had any theory about how her superior had evaded this regulation.

"Yes."

"What is this theory?"

Erlend's face twisted as if she were wrapping the flesh inside it around a thought. Simple description came easy. Anything approaching abstractness did not. After about twenty seconds, she was able to grasp the elusiveness slipping around in her.

It seemed to her that her superior did not transmit TV messages entirely through legal circuitry. The superior had inserted a catch-me-if-you-can circuit or matrix in the data bank base. The messages were routed from the transmitting point to her home. The data bank must have a hidden instruction not to register the message in the credit-debit files. And they would be erased after transmission. These were brief, coded, and consisted of the location and time for the meeting place.

"When was the last time you received a message from your superior?" Duncan said. He gave her the date of today and the week and the present time in case she was confused about it.

"Today, at seven in the evening," she said.

"What was the message?"

"HC-1928. MP. TD. 10:30P. 4L. 1149E. FLOAT CL. 3D OP."

Replying to his questions, she said that she did not know what HC-1928 meant. Duncan thought that the code was probably used by the caller for his or her filing system. MP meant Meeting Place. TD stood for Today. 4L was the 4th level of this tower. 10:30P was the time for the meeting tonight. 1149 was the address number. E was East.

Erlend had called up the tower directory to display all thoroughfares on the 4th level beginning with FLOAT. 1149 East Floating Cloud Avenue was a warehouse. 3D OP meant that Erlend was to enter the door marked 3 and that it would be locked.

"How do you indicate that you have received the message?" Duncan said.

"I say, 'Functioning.' "

His next queries were about the status of the search for him and Snick.

As of when she had left the precinct station for home, she replied, the department believed that the criminals were still out in the wilderness. The hunt was very intensive; many organics from most of the western states had been transferred to that assignment. Each day would continue the hunt until the two were found.

Were the monitors in L.A. set up to recognize Duncan and Snick?

They were.

Had sniffers also been attached to the monitors?

No.

"Why not?" Duncan said.

There were not nearly enough available to be attached to every monitor. Besides, the work and time required to do this would be staggering. It would take seventy consecutive days to install them. However, all patrols were to be equipped with them.

"When will all have them?"

"In three obweeks."

That was a relief. A sniffer was as keen as a bloodhound's nose. Set to recognize the body odor of an individual, it could detect one molecule of that person in a million other molecules. Even saturating himself with perfume would not fool it.

He considered the enigma of Erlend's superior. Was that person the same one who had met him in a gymnasium? At that time, Duncan had been using the ID, though not the persona, of Andrew Vishnu Beewolf. He had thought about how the masked person had arranged the meeting. He must have set up a momentary blanking out of the monitors in the street leading to the gymnasium. That would have to be done so that his entrance to the building would not be recorded. He could not walk through the street and into the gym in a mask. He must have changed into the concealing garb after going into the room where Duncan, as Beewolf, had later joined him or her. He—if it was a male—must also have had the monitors briefly turned off when Duncan had come into the building.

That indicated that the OMC official had access to the monitor controls. He had used them illegally but must be able to control or oversee any investigation into the cause of the shutoff. If there was any investigation. The monitors, Duncan knew, were seldom checked unless they set off an alarm or someone was being shadowed via the monitors.

Anyone able to shut the monitors down and conceal that from the organics must be an organic official. One who was high up in the hierarchy.

Tonight, when that person met Erlend, he would have to arrange for a certain sequence of temporary shutoffs. That meant that Duncan, who intended to go in Erlend's place, would also not be filmed. And the OMC official would not be able to observe anyone else on the street outside the warehouse.

He had one more question. What did Erlend know about the attempt to kill him, Snick, and Padre Cabtab?

She answered readily enough even though she indicted herself. She had been ordered by her superior to send two men disguised as ganks to murder the three. Though she had not asked her superior why these three OMC members should be killed, she had been told the reason. The organics were getting too hot on their trail. Their mouths must be shut forever before they were captured and told everything about the organization.

When Erlend regained consciousness, she sat up blinking rapidly. After she had drunk the glass of water he handed her, she said, weakly, "Well?"

Instead of replying, he removed his wig, the cotton stuffing under his upper lip, and the plastic inserts in his nostrils. She did not recognize him for several seconds. The she put one hand on a breast and said, "My God!"

"I'd be mildly distressed if I had to kill you," he said. "But I'd do it anyway. You did not hesitate to arrange for my death."

"I was under orders," she said. "I'd have been killed if I'd disobeyed."

She paused, then said, "I suppose you're going to kill me."

"Why should I do that? Unless you try something fancy. Then I will. Things are going to change, Erlend. This Mickey-

Mouse outfit will become a raging lion. I'm its new chief regardless of what you or your superior say or do. If you two balk, you go out feet first. If your superior isn't the head of OMC, then I go up the ladder until I find the guiding light."

"You're crazy!"

"If I have to be."

Despite her protests and threats, she was forced at gunpoint into the stoner room. After removing her ID card, he shut the cylinder door and dialed the power to ON. Her face was stopped halfway in a grimace as if she had seen the Gorgon.

12

His progun set at STUN, Duncan shot the masked person in the back of the head. The figure fell forward against the pile of boxes from behind which it had been watching for Erlend. Its hooded head bumped on the hard floor. Duncan came from behind the two rows of stacked boxes. He turned the limp body over on its back. After removing the mask, he saw the face of a dark-haired and dark-skinned man. The epicanthic folds over his eyes were larger than the norm; his nose was snub. He looked as if he were approximately thirty-five subyears old.

Knowing that the man would be out for at least four minutes, Duncan took his necklace and attached ID card from him. He also pulled the man's gun from its holster, noting that he wore civilian clothes under the robe. The card, inserted in a slot in the nearest wallscreen, activated the display of a slowly revolving 3-D icon and the biodata. He was Detective-Colonel Kieth Alan Simmons. (Duncan briefly wondered why he spelled his first name as Kieth.)

Simmons was Tuesday's chief organic officer for the La Brea

Tower Complex. His residence was on the 125th level, of course. He was married and had a full quota of children, both under twelve. His subannual salary was 64,000 credits.

One item surprised Duncan. Simmons's first wife had been Detective-Captain Lin Cozumel Erlend. Duncan knew from his reading of Erlend's biodata that she had been divorced from a Simmons. It had meant nothing then. He laughed softly. Erlend had never known that the mysterious stranger, her superior, was her own husband. Simmons must have been laughing behind his mask during their clandestine meetings.

Duncan returned to the body, replaced the ID card, and dragged Simmons deeper into the aisle formed by two rows of large stacked boxes. A minute later, Simmons opened his eyes and turned his head to both sides. Then, still looking confused, he stared at Duncan. Duncan held the can of TM in his left hand, ready to spray it again if Simmons tried to attack him. With the other hand, he removed his wig.

Simmons' eyes widened.

"You recognize me?" Duncan said.

Simmons swallowed and said, hoarsely, "Caird! Duncan! How did you . . . ?"

"Find you? I have my methods."

"Where is . . . she?"

"Erlend? She's in a stoner just now."

"She told you?"

"I used TM," Duncan said. "None of the people who told me what I wanted to know could help it. So, forget about punishing them. How's your head?"

"It hurts. But it's not bad."

"I gave you the minimum power," Duncan said. "Are the monitors on in here? Don't lie. You'll be in as much danger as I."

"They're on, but they're getting a feed-in of an empty room."

"I believe you," Duncan said, "but I'll check it out anyway."

He brought the can out from behind his back swiftly to

within an inch of Simmons's face. The spray shot out. Simmons passed out with his head twisted away from Duncan. After straightening Simmons's head, Duncan placed Simmons's shoulderbag under his head. He regretted that he could not question Simmons in a more private and secure place. But he could not take him to the Cloyds' or Erlend's apartment. Here was where he had to get the information he needed.

He placed his shoulderbag by Simmons and sat down on it. The first question of the many he had would be about the operation of the roundabout circuit Simmons used to call Erlend.

Duncan opened his mouth to speak. Simmons's fist struck him hard on his chin.

For a few seconds, as Simmons rolled over and rose to a half-crouch, then leaped on Duncan, who was lying flat on his back, Duncan was confused. He might have been more so, but Simmons had not yet gotten his full strength back. The blow did not knock Duncan out, and Simmons was not as fast getting up from the floor as he would normally have been. Acting on the reflexes of a long-trained fighter, Duncan's left foot shot out. The instep slammed into Simmons's crotch. He yelled with pain and fell to one side, clutching his groin. Duncan scrambled to his feet, though not as swiftly as he would have if he had not been weakened by the chinblow. He kicked Simmons's lower jaw once and his ribs twice. Though not unconscious, Simmons was limp. His jaw was open; his eyes, glazed. He did not seem to be feeling pain.

Duncan had recovered from Simmons's fistblow, but he was still mentally stunned. He could not understand why the TM had not taken effect. Simmons had obviously been faking unconsciousness. Yet, the same can of TM had worked on Jaccoud and Erlend. For some reason, Simmons was immune to the spray. Duncan felt as if he had been running a race and was winning it until he smashed into a glass wall.

As far as he knew, he was the only person in the world naturally invulnerable to the truth drug. Of course, it was possible that there were others. But the ability would have to be very rare, and the chances of his running into another with it were extremely low.

Shaking his head as if he could not believe what had happened, he looked through the man's shoulderbag. Among the items he found were a small can of TM and a handcuff-band dispenser. He rolled Simmons over on his face, put his wrists together behind his back, and wrapped the long sticky band to secure his wrists together. Then he propped Simmons up with his back against the bottom box of a pile.

Simmons coughed, grimaced with pain, and opened his dark-brown eyes.

Duncan tenderly rubbed his sore jaw and said, "You've been injected with some kind of anti-TM."

He put it as a statement of fact, not a question.

"Yes," Simmons said. "And I almost got you."

Duncan took two steps forward but not close enough to be within reach of Simmons's boots. Looking down, he said, "I'm not your enemy unless you persist in being mine. I TMed you because there was no other way to get the truth out of you. Now it looks as if I'm stymied unless you cooperate."

Simmons glared at him.

"You know I can resist the effects of TM?" Duncan said. "I can lie while unconscious?"

Simmons nodded.

"Then you're in no danger if I'm caught. I won't betray you. Only you know I'm here, and only I know your ID. If I'm TMed, I can deny knowing anything about you. In any event, you're going to tell me everything."

Simmons said, "Why should I?"

"If you won't tell me who your immediate superior is, you'll die. Now and here. I mean it. I may as well tell you that I plan to take over the OMC. It's been a quiescent and futile organization, but it's not going to be so anymore."

Simmons snarled, and he said, "You don't know what we have in mind!"

"True. But I intend to find out what it is, if anything. However, it's going to be a lot harder than I'd thought. You have anti-TM, and therefore your superior must have it. But those in rank below you don't have it. Why is that?"

He was thinking while he waited for Simmons to reply. Only an obweek ago, he had used TM on his grandfather, Gilbert Immerman, alias the World Councillor David Ananda. Immerman had not been able to resist the TM. Yet he was the head of OMC and probably many other similar subversive groups. Why had he not been injected with anti-TM?

Simmons spoke then. He was no fool; he did not want to die.

"Very well. The anti-TM, we call it A-TM, was developed in a Manhattan laboratory by an allied group. Probably the one you belonged to when you were Caird. A package arrived here late last Tuesday. It was supposed to be given out only to the very highest officials of the OMC of every day. I didn't know anything then about Ananda, nor that he was in the La Brea Tower. Apparently, he had not yet been injected, why I don't know. Maybe his A-TM had been sent to Zurich through a secret route, but he was in L.A. on the emergency concerning you and Snick. Anyway, it was obvious that he had not yet been injected. Otherwise, you wouldn't have been able to use TM on him.

"Ironic, isn't it? If he had not waited, he would have been immune. And you'd never have gotten out of him how to send your messages via the override-circuit device."

"I suppose," Duncan said, "you don't know who your superior is. He's always been masked and robed when you met him?"

"Until this morning," Simmons said. "He revealed his ID after we'd both been injected with the A-TM. He said we didn't have to worry about interrogation any longer."

"There are other methods to make a man talk," Duncan said.

"They're illegal."

Duncan smiled. "Sure. Who is this person?"

Simmons's facial muscles seemed to congeal. He said, "He . . ."

"It's hard to conquer old habits," Duncan said. "But you can do it."

He looked at his wristwatch. It was 10:39. By 11:30, most of the city would be getting ready to go into its stoners. Shortly after midnight, Wednesday's citizens would step out of their cylinders. Meanwhile, Snick and the Cloyds and Jaccoud would be sweating anxiety. Jaccoud had to get back to her apartment before midnight. The Cloyds did not have to worry about being stoned then because Wednesday's tenants were also OMC. But the impatient and edgy Snick might go to Erlend's apartment in search of him, dangerous though that would be. Or she might decide that the ganks had gotten him and get the hell out of L.A. No, she would not do that until she knew what had happened to him.

"I can't take you to him," Simmons said. He straightened out his arms to stretch and winced with pain.

"I understand that. Just tell me what I want to know. What I do after that . . ."

Simmons' face looked as if it were being squeezed in a vise. His mouth opened; but he could not speak. Fear and reluctance plugged up his throat.

"You have to," Duncan said. He pointed the progun at Simmons.

"I'll burn off your toes one by one until you talk. I won't take any pleasure in doing it, but I'll do it. If I have to take off only one toe, I'll have to kill you. You won't be able to make up a story about your mutilations that'll satisfy your superiors. I don't want them to know about this, so I'll just kill you after you've spilled your guts, and you will. Your murder will be another in the list of unsolved cases."

"All right, I'll tell you!" Simmons said shrilly.

Duncan tried not to show his relief. He thought that he was capable of carrying out his threats, but he could not be sure until he had to do it. He certainly did not wish to torture this man even if he had been instrumental in the attempted killing of Duncan and Snick and the slaying of Cabtab.

"He's Eugene Godwin Diszno, today's chief executive of the L.A. Data Bank! God help me!"

"He won't be able to do anything to you, I promise that," Duncan said. "Where does he live?"

He was not surprised at the revelation of Diszno's position. The person who headed the Data Bank had immense power. He would be able to insert false data into the bank with little difficulty and be the least likely to be caught doing it. Mark Twain had once written, "Show me the superstitions of a nation, and I'll control that nation." The truth was that the person who controlled the information flow of a nation controlled that nation. Or, in this case, Los Angeles State. Of course, Diszno had to do what the government ordered, but he could pretty much do what the OMC—or the World Councillor Ananda—wanted and get away with it. Within limits.

Once started, Simmons responded to all of Duncan's questions. Within five minutes, Duncan had all the information he needed. Or, he reminded himself, thought he needed. There might be some questions he should have asked. When he knew these, it would be too late.

He unwrapped the bands around Simmons's wrists but stood back while the man rose stiffly. "I didn't break any ribs, did I?" Duncan said.

"I don't think so."

"Don't forget to preset the feed-in simulations to turn off and erase."

"I am not incompetent!" Simmons said.

"No, but you've got a lot on your mind. Now, remember. You go home, and don't try to alert Diszno."

"For God's sake!" Simmons said. "He'll kill me!"

103

"You're not going to kill Erlend," Duncan said. "You couldn't help yourself. Diszno isn't going to do anything to you or anybody because he can't. I'll make sure he won't."

However, to be certain that Simmons would not warn Diszno, Duncan knocked him out again with another shot from his gun. Simmons was not going to feel well for a while, but he had to be kept out of action for at least twenty minutes. Having stripped the handcuff-band from Simmons, Duncan left. Ten minutes later, he was standing in front of Diszno's apartment on the 125th level. Midnight was ten minutes away, and the corridor wallscreens were flashing orange notices and emitting a soft sirenlike sound.

He stepped into the recess of the doorway, where he was no longer visible. Holding the progun close to his belly, he burned out the lock, then punched out the lock mechanism with the butt of the weapon. It fell inside. The plastic of the door had cooled off by then. He inserted three fingers and pulled. The door slid back with considerable resistance into the wall recess. He stepped inside, gun ready. Though the room lights were on, the walls were gray and soundless. He closed the door and walked through two large rooms before coming to the main hall. Swiftly but cautiously, he went down this, stopping to open all doors slightly and looking within. Diszno and family should be in their cylinders, but he could not take that for granted.

Having satisfied himself that all rooms except the stoner chamber were empty, he went into that. After checking the ID plaques on the bases of the cylinders, he turned the dials of Wednesday's tenants to OFF. Then he turned the dial at the base of Diszno's stoner to POWER ON.

The data banker was very tall and exceptionally broad-shouldered. His dark skin was streaked with pink where curving depigmented lines had been made. His black hair was in a topknot with a long and thick genuine-silver pin stuck through it. A black goatee, heavily waxed, stuck out from his chin. Two heavy earrings, zigzag-shaped to represent lightning, dragged his ear lobes down. Except for a scarlet bikini, he was nude.

He looked very fashionable and very assured. But his jaw dropped and he paled when he saw a man pointing a gun at him. His eyes widened with wonder and fear.

"I'm William St. George Duncan, also known as Jefferson Cervantes Caird. Let's go into the living room and talk."

Stiffly, his head and neck shaking, Diszno preceded Duncan from the room.

13

The time flashing on the wallscreen was 1:10 A.M., Wednesday.

Four people sat in the living room, Eugene Diszno, his wife, named Olga Khan Sarahsdaughter, and the two adult Wednesday tenants, Rajit Belleporte Mayfair and Maya Dibrun Lutter. As soon as Duncan had pried out of Diszno that his wife and the next day's residents were members of OMC, he had destoned them.

He had also gotten Diszno to admit that he was the overall head of the organization in this area. That had not come until Duncan had threatened to burn off Diszno's toes and fingers. By now, Duncan also knew the names of all the higher officials in OMC in L.A. Most of them were gank or data bank executives.

Duncan had told Diszno that he was taking over the OMC.

"You don't like it, I can see," Duncan said. "But the time for lying low and doing little is over. My messages have caused an uproar all over the world, and we must seize the opportunity to make it swell into a rebellion. I'm the one who should naturally lead it, even if I must stay hidden for a while. I have much more experience in active fighting, and my record speaks for itself. I have plans for carrying on the fight. You've admitted that you have none."

"The time isn't ripe!" Diszno said.

"It'll never be riper. It's go-for-broke time. Now, you, all of you, I need your heartfelt agreement that I'll be the head. Your full cooperation, anyway, even if you are resentful that I've taken over and are fearful of the consequences. You have been futting around too long. You've gotten the benefits of the age-slowing factor and now the anti-TM. You must pay for those.

"There's a new setup now. All of the members of OMC must be given the ASF and the A-TM. You've been very selfish in keeping those just for the high echelon, the elitists. You were stupid to do it, anyway. How could a lower-echelon person lie to the ganks if he's caught? He'd eventually betray you. And there's nothing for ensuring loyalty and gratitude like endowing a member with the ASF.

"Now, I've given the formula for the ASF in my message, and you can bet that the citizens are going to get it even if they have to do so illegally. If we can figure out a way to get the information about the anti-TM to the public, we'll do that, too."

"The government controls all the laboratories," Diszno said.

"That didn't stop the immers from making it for their people," Duncan said. "The basis of ASF is a mutated true-breeding bacteria. It can be cultured in any kitchen and then easily injected. The problem is getting the ASF to enough people so that they can give it to others. But that's going to occur without the OMC doing much about it. There'll be lots of people all over the world who'll steal from the labs if they have to and mutate the bacteria and culture them. The idea that they can extend their lives by seven is going to make people wild to get ASF. The government will fight against it, but it'll have to give in eventually. If it doesn't, it'll fall."

"And we'll be martyrs," Diszno's wife, Olga Sarahsdaughter, said.

108

"Maybe not. It's possible, but we can't back away because we might be martyrs."

Duncan had made his points several times. Now, he went on to practical matters. How soon could Diszno get IDs for him and Snick?

Though reluctant to do it, Diszno said that Maya Lutter could arrange that immediately. However, the physical paraphernalia that went with the IDs would take a while. Possibly, they could be delivered by evening of today. Diszno and Sarahsdaughter would stay destoned today, but Mayfair and Maya Lutter had to go to their offices. They had no viable excuse for calling in and staying home. But they would be able to arrange for the physical paraphernalia. Diszno would set up the insertion of false data since he could do it from the apartment, and he could do it even if today was not his legal day.

He also arranged for Duncan to make an untraceable call to the apartment in which Duncan had left Snick and the Cloyds. Duncan had not wanted to reveal the residence. But he knew that he had to go back to it.

A good-looking redhead answered his call to the Cloyds' apartment. He recognized her as Lucia Shoremoor Claving, one of Wednesday's two tenants. As he had expected, she was fully informed of the situation up to the time he had left the apartment. She gestured, and the Cloyds and Snick came into view. Snick looked very relieved to see him. Then she became angry.

"Why in hell didn't you tell me what's going on? We were very worried. In fact, Donna and Barry were in a panic. I was getting close to one, too."

"I doubt that," Duncan said.

"Well, I was worried, anyway."

"I couldn't call you safely until now," Duncan said. "Anyway, it's all going well—so far. I'll explain when I get there."

Donna Cloyd, now standing by Snick, said, "Is everything *really* O.K.?"

"Yes. About seven tonight, destone all the OMC people in

the apartment. Tell them what's been happening. I'll fill in the details. The situation has greatly changed—for the better. Relax. I'll be there about eight."

"I missed out on the excitement, didn't I?" Snick said.

"What I did required that only one person do it," Duncan said. "Two might've been too much. Fade-out now."

After the call, he put in his shoulderbag the ampoules containing the ASF and anti-TM, enough for every OMC member in the Cloyds' apartment. He also had printouts of the formulae for both. At seven that evening, Diszno left for a place the location of which he did not tell Duncan. Duncan did not argue with him about being given the address of the place. Diszno was probably right in insisting that security demanded that only he know about it. At 7:31, Diszno returned and handed to Duncan a small sack. It contained two flesh-colored slip-ons for Duncan's and Snick's thumbs. When—or if—they had to validate credit transactions with their ID cards, they would press their thumbs on the recording plate. The outer surface of Duncan's slip-on bore the prints of a bloney named Makro who lived on the same level as the Cloyds. The other matched the print of Julep Chu Hart, a bloney who lived with Makro. Having spent some time during the day studying Makro's biodata, Duncan was by now familiar with it. When Snick got the slip-on, she would memorize Hart's biodata.

"You're lucky," Diszno said. "Makro and Hart apparently panicked when your override messages came over the screens. They must have thought that all was up and they were going to be swept up by the ganks. They just disappeared. I think they took off for the wilderness, the fools. However, they were being considered as too unstable, and so . . ."

Diszno bit his lip. Duncan said, "You were going to get rid of them, weren't you? Just like you got rid of Ibrahim Azimoff, the agent who operated that candy and drug store. Just like you tried to get rid of Snick and me."

"It was necessary for security reasons," Diszno said. "You understand that."

"I don't hold it against you," Duncan said. "But, from now on, if anybody is thought to be a security risk, I want to be told about it. I want to be sure that the suspect is indeed a danger to us. And there are other ways to handle them. They don't have to be killed."

"You're soft."

"Try me, and find out," Duncan said.

"If the rank and file know that they won't be killed if they try to betray us, they'll not be deterred," Diszno said. His face was red, and he looked indignant.

"They don't have to know they won't be killed," Duncan said. "Let them think they will. But they can be stoned and buried some place."

"What's the difference between that and being killed?" Diszno said. He made no effort to stifle his sneering expression.

"They have a chance of being found and destoned some day."

"What if that day is soon? Then they tell all to the ganks."

Diszno had a good point, but Duncan was not going to kill except in self-defense. What he did not say, of course, was that Diszno might be one of those whom Duncan would have to get rid of. He did not trust the man. He was sure that Diszno resented his taking over and that, if he had a good opportunity, he would dispose of him.

The history of revolutionaries was heavily threaded with internecine power struggles. Diszno was just repeating history, that is, the pattern of human behavior.

He thought, How do I know that? I don't remember what Caird knew or, indeed, what any of my personae except the one I now have knew. But, sometimes, memories I should not have do come through. Leak through. So, I am not entirely walled off from the previous personae.

That face, his face as a child of five, drifted across the screen of his mind. At the same time—and it had never happened before—a big hand seemed to reach inside him, grab his intestines, and yank them upward. It was so localized and so painful that it reminded him of that show in the Paul Bunyan series he had seen a few weeks ago. The gigantic lumberjack, confronted by an elephant-sized bear, had thrust his hand down the bear's gullet, seized its guts, and pulled the bear inside out.

"What's wrong?" Diszno said.

He straightened up, his face smoothing out as the pain faded.

"Nothing."

"Nothing!" Diszno said. "You looked as if someone had kicked you in the belly."

"O.K., something," he said. "It was just a spasm. It couldn't be something I ate. I haven't eaten for a long time. Forget it."

Diszno frowned but did not say anything. He was probably hoping that he could take advantage of this weakness—whatever it was—in Duncan. Probably? Undoubtedly! He would like to see Duncan drop dead.

The face was gone—for a while. He did not know what its popping up now and then meant. Perhaps it was the forerunner of another mental breakdown. If it was, he was not going to worry about it. To become obsessed with it was to hasten the breakdown, if there was in actuality going to be one. The reoccurring face might just be a symptom of an incomplete severing of his present self from the previous selves. A symptom of a minor mental malady, a slight malfunctioning.

Or was this kind of thinking just whistling in the dark?

He did not think about this the rest of the evening. He was too busy working with Diszno and the other three. By eight o'clock that evening, he was ringing the doorbell of the Cloyds' apartment. A moment later, he was talking to Snick, the Cloyds, and Wednesday's tenants.

14

Thursday, Duncan and Snick worked hard, stopping only to eat and exercise and use the bathroom. With the information gotten from Diszno, they made contact with forty-eight chiefs of allied subversive groups in many parts of the world. Diszno would, as Snick said, be having a fit if he knew how many hidden routes of communication they were using. He had told them how to set them up, but he had advised that they should not be activated except in cases of extreme urgency. He did not see that there were any such at present.

"You don't know if the organics are watching those on the other end and are monitoring them," he said. "One slip, and we're all doomed."

The first thing Duncan did after verifying his ID was to send the ASF and A-TM formulae. Then he told the receivers what their use was. Some of the receivers knew all about the age-slowing factor, but only one had been given the anti-TM.

Duncan told them that he was now the overall chief, the

supreme head of all the underground organizations. He ordered them to disseminate both the ASF and the A-TM throughout their membership. Moreover, they were to use any reasonably safe means to leave printouts of the formulae where they would be found by the public. He left the means up to their ingenuity.

"That way, we can get the people themselves to spread this data and cause trouble for the government," he said.

Not everybody personally answered his call at first. Many did call him back and talk to him. A few never replied. All he talked to were shocked when told that he was Caird alias Duncan.

He did not spend much time with each person. Having established his ID and having outlined briefly his plans, he then sent a long printed message.

"How do you know they'll take action on them?" Snick said.

"I don't, and I have no way to enforce their being carried out. Enough of them will do something."

Snick was all for what he was doing. But like him, she knew that sooner or later someone was going to be caught. That person could lie because he had anti-TM. But there were other ways to find the truth, even if they were illegal, and the ganks knew all of them.

Friday's tenants were non-OMC, so Duncan and Snick spent that day in the stoners. They jammed themselves into the Cloyds' cylinders and squeezed themselves against the other occupant until they were in a fetal position. Then the power turned them to a hard substance. Saturday, they came out of the cylinders with that day's tenants and with the Cloyds. Donna and Barry stayed unstoned most of the day because they were so delighted with daybreaking. Duncan, however, used them to help him in his message transmissions. Lemuel Ziko Shurber and Sarah-John Pangolin Tan, Saturday's people, were gone to work most of the day.

The doorlock on the apartment had been replaced on Friday. According to the news, the entire population would have locks by the end of next Monday.

The Cloyds did their work for Duncan in separate rooms, she in the kitchen, and he in the bedroom. Donna, being an Original Buddhist, insisted on taking an hour off to chant for a half-hour before the Primal Circle. This was a twelve-angled rim of mahogany, twelve inches across, set upright on a dresser. Embedded inside the rim was a series of electronic devices which transmitted a hologram of Buddha in the lotus position in the center of a black field. As Donna chanted the Fire Sermon in the ancient long-dead Pali language, the Buddha slowly became smaller, seeming to recede. After fifteen minutes, it disappeared. She continued chanting into the Nothingness, as she called it, until the Buddha reappeared in the seeming distance and then became large.

Barry Cloyd was a Disciple of the Fine-Tuners of God cult. This believed that the worshipper could fine-tune himself until he resonated with the basic vibration of the universe—whatever that meant. To attain this state he combined his prayers with the operation of a theremin. This was an electronic instrument with two antennas. When Barry's hands moved within the electrical capacitance field emitted by the antennas, a musical humming, they controlled the tone and pitch. By doing this, Barry became one with the cosmic vibrations and worked his way through them until he was in tune with the universe and God.

Duncan would have been alarmed about having such irrational people in the OMC if he had not known his now-dead colleague, Padre Cabtab. The bush-priest had believed in a religion even wilder than those of the Cloyds. Yet he had been quite rational and competent in all other respects.

Saturday's tenants, Shurber and Tan, came home from work at 4:30. Shurber, looking around at the many glowing wallscreen sections, said "You only have one news channel on?"

"Yes, and I haven't been paying much attention to it," Duncan said. He waved his hand to indicate the sections, each with its separate secret channel. "I've been talking to our colleagues all over the world."

Shurber shook his head. "I just can't get used to the idea. I expect the ganks to come storming in at any moment."

Duncan shrugged and said, "Could be. But if they do detect these transmissions, they'll do it only by accident."

"Which could happen," Shurber said. "Or one of those persons you're talking to could be an infiltrator."

Duncan did not think that this was very likely. All members of the subversive groups had been interrogated before the anti-TM had been introduced.

"Anyway," Shurber said, "Sarah-John and I are furious. About 3:30 we saw on the news that the government is suspending the results of the referendum until the current emergency is over. I knew they'd find some excuse for overturning it!"

Duncan did not have to ask him what referendum he was referring to. Several obweeks ago, the citizens of selected cities had been permitted to vote for a referendum asking for less surveillance of the people by the government. A slight majority favoring this had won. Thus, it was mandatory by law that the issue be put to the vote on a world-wide basis. Even if the majority were for less monitoring, the details of this would have to be worked out by the representatives of the winners. Then the program would have to be submitted to another global vote.

Duncan knew that a victory by the citizens would be a small one. The government would have logic and common sense on its side when it refused to turn off satellite surveillance. The eyes-in-the-sky were absolutely necessary to regulate the flow of commercial traffic, observe weather conditions, and notify the authorities of accidents or criminal activities. All this was for the public good. There was no way that the satellites could do this and also not record what every citizen in the open was doing.

However, tower cities were a different situation from the horizontal cities. Many citizens did not see why almost every square foot of the streets in a tower should be in view of a monitor. It might be for their good, but they resented it. These irked citizens proposed that the monitors be turned off and only used when a report of an accident or a crime or of domestic strife brought the organics or medical personnel to the particular area.

This would be a small concession for the government. Especially when it could claim that the street monitors were not operating but could keep them on anyway. When the citizens' supervisory committees toured the organic stations to ensure that the law was being kept, they would find that the monitors were not on. When the committee left, the monitors would resume their watching.

However, the search for Duncan and Snick and the recent out-of-hand demonstrations and minor riots reported on the news channels justified complete surveillance. From the government's viewpoint, anyway, and it was this that would determine policy.

"The word is there's going to be a demonstration tonight in various parts of the city," Shurber said. "The nearest one will start at the Blue Moon Plaza. Sarah-John and I'd like to be there. But the ganks . . ."

Snick cut in. ". . . will be there, and you don't want to chance being picked up by them."

The Cloyds had entered the room in time to hear the last of the conversation. Barry said, "We sure can't go."

Snick looked at Duncan. "I'm so tired of being shut in."

"No," he said. "You'd be taking too big a chance if you went."

"Hey," Donna said, "you two must be telepathic. You seem to be able to read each other's minds. Is that because you've been together so long?"

"In some respects, especially in taking action, we think alike," Snick said. "But there are plenty of times when I don't know what the hell he's thinking. He acts like an extrovert, but, basically, he's an introvert."

Duncan shrugged and spoke to a screen section. This was transmitting the final work for today. At the other end, a house in Singapore, the head of the local subversives would be getting a printout of the program of changes the revolutionaries would demand. The biggest and most radical item was the call to abandon the New Era dayworld system of living. It was no longer vital that the population be divided into seven days. There were only two billion citizens, not ten billion as the government falsely claimed. It was past time for mankind to return to the day-by-day living it once had. But the manifesto stated that what was good about the New Era would be kept. There must be no reversion to what was bad in the pre-New Era.

Lemuel Shurber waited until Duncan had turned off the last instruction-transmission. He said, "Sarah-John and I have to shop for groceries. We won't be long."

"Don't go near the Blue Moon Plaza," Duncan said.

"Never intended to," Shurber said. A moment later, he and his wife left. The door slid shut behind them.

"I think," Donna said, "that we should go back into the stoners. Dinner with all of you would be nice, but feeding all of us is a financial strain on them. We'll see you on Tuesday."

Duncan did not try to detain them, though he would miss their merry conversation. He watched them go hand in hand down the hall. Then he turned to Snick and said, "At least, we can watch the demonstrations tonight. We'll see if the trouble we've stirred up results in more than just a parade."

"You mean if the young people have the guts to use those spraycans on the monitors? And maybe even the ganks?"

Saturday's chief had sent a message telling them that a small number of youths had stolen these cans from a warehouse. They were talking big about covering the screens of the street monitors with the black spray. Until the screens were replaced, the monitors would be blind. The chief had said that one of the OMC was a member of the group and had suggested the idea. The juveniles were all for it, but it might turn out that they would be content with just boasting.

On the other hand, if they did back up their bragging, they might inspire other people in L.A. to imitate them. They would be arrested, if caught, and would be punished. Being young, they were not as likely to consider the consequences as the older and more conservative people.

The doorbell rang. Duncan and Snick froze for a fraction of a second. The Cloyds, just about to enter the stoner room door, stopped. The wallscreens throughout the apartment were flashing orange letters: DOORBELL ACT. The ringing was loud and steady and, hence, not being done by Shurber and Tan. One of them would have followed proper procedure and inserted his ID card into the slot outside. This would have unlocked the door, but they would also have waited for those inside to look at the doorway monitor screen. Duncan activated this. A short man and a tall woman, Mutt and Jeff, were looking up at the monitor. Both wore scarlet-slashed purple jumpsuits, the work-uniforms of the Sanitary and Disposal Department of the State of Los Angeles. Their epaulets bore the golden brooms of the Household Engineers Section. The dustpan-shaped badges symbolized that they were inspectors.

Duncan spoke sharply to the Cloyds, who were coming back down the hall from the stoner room. "You'll have to take over. Pretend you're today's tenants."

Barry, looking at the images of the strangers on the wall above the doorway, said, "What in hell do they want?"

"I don't know," Duncan said. "Some housekeeping offense, I suppose. Unless they're ganks trying to get in here and take us without any public fuss."

The Cloyds paled, but Donna's voice was firm. "Why can't we just pretend we're not home?"

"Citizens Shurber and Tan," the woman's voice said. "Please let us in. We're here to check out a cross-temporal complaint made by Sunday's tenants. Sunday's organic department left the message for us. We have a warrant for inspection, and here are our IDs."

The icon and official ID of the woman appeared on the door monitor. She was Corporal-Inspector Rani Isu Williams, and she had the proper authority.

She had been smiling, but now, looking grim and her voice

119

hard, she said, "We know that you have been using extra power and are home. Open up!"

"Oh, Christ!" Donna said.

Duncan swore softly. Though the transmissions he had been making were undetectible, the amount of power over and above that required for normal household use was being registered. Normally, payment via ID card would have been sufficient. It was not very likely that the power department would call that excess usage to the attention of the ganks. But if the inspectors were not admitted, they would report that denial to the ganks. And the ganks might come around with a warrant or set up a special surveillance unit to watch this place.

It was possible that they just might be organics in disguise. Then he thought, Or assassins sent by Diszno.

That possibility was not too far out to reject.

Snick, without being told to do so, had deactivated all screens in the apartment except for the news channels and the personalized wall decorations. Duncan said, fiercely, "Donna, Barry! One of you answer right away! Tell them you were taking a nap. Then let them in!"

Snick was now by the stoner room door. Her gun was in her hand.

"What if they know what Shurber and Tan look like?" Donna said.

"Maybe they won't," he said. "No reason for them to check that out. Answer them!"

Before he reached the hall, he heard Donna. "Sorry! We were taking a little snooze. Had a big party last night!"

Duncan got into the stoner room just as the street door began to slide back.

15

He quietly activated a screen so that he could hear and see the people in the living room. The woman, Williams, was saying that the department had to take action after it had received three interday complaints from Sunday. These were (1) failure of Saturday to put all of its possessions in its personal-possessions closet before becoming stoned; (2) dirt found by Sunday, left by Saturday, along the base of the kitchen wall, northeast corner; (3) a sack of garbage left under the disposal chute, which garbage had not been stoned; (4) failure to replace dirty bedsheets with clean ones. The reprimands left for Saturday by Sunday had not been replied to with apologies. Instead, Saturday had left an insulting and obscene message for Sunday. To wit (but not so witty): Blow it out your asses, hemorrhoid brains.

Donna said, "The bums! Why do they live in the bloney area if they're so damn tidy?"

"There are certain minimum standards of which you must

be aware," the female inspector said. "We're authorized to validate or invalidate the complaints and to make an on-spot inspection."

"But it's a long way from midnight now," Barry Cloyd said. "You can't cite us for untidiness if we haven't had a chance to clean up before then."

"Our orders are to report the general cleanliness during the time of inspection," Williams said. "That's required by Ordinance Number 6-C5, subsection 3D." The short man, Sebta, had said nothing. His jaw worked on a stick of gum.

"This is harassment," Barry said.

Despite the serious situation, Duncan grinned. The Cloyds were so indignant because they were not actually responsible for Saturday's housekeeping, yet they had to take the blame.

"You may report us if you wish," Williams said indifferently. Doubtless, she was used to far stronger and more personal accusations.

Snick spoke very quietly. "Do we hide in Friday's stoners again?"

"Forget it," Duncan said. "We just can't take the chance."

"Good, I didn't want to. But how in hell can we avoid them?"

Duncan told her his plan. She said, "That's just as risky as going into a stoner." She smiled. "But we'll be able to fight."

"Don't you wish we'll have to."

By then the tall brunette, Williams, and the short man, Sebta, dark-skinned and with a purple-dyed beard, were at work. Sebta carried a camera and followed Williams while she spoke into a hand-carried microphone. The light from Sebta's camera beamed on the junction of the screenwalls and carpet while Williams commented on the cleanliness or lack thereof of the area in the camera's view. They went around the living room, then looked under the *siayl* (shape-it-as-you-like) furniture. Williams, down on the floor, said, "Aha!" She reached under a sofa and pulled out a dirty sock.

"That's not ours!" Donna said.

"Whose is it?" Williams said.

"How would I know?" Donna said. "It could be Sunday's, the schmucks!"

Williams dropped the sock into the evidence bag hanging from her belt.

The inspectors and the Cloyds moved into the hall. Williams said, "Open the PP."

Fortunately, the personal-possessions closet door had been left open. If it had been locked, the Cloyds would have been unable to produce the ID card to unlock it.

Duncan and Snick waited behind the half-closed stoner room door. The inspectors could go next to the bedroom or go straight to the kitchen or enter the stoner room. After a few words about a neater arrangement of the items on the shelves, Williams led the others into the bedroom. Duncan, watching them, was pleased when the Cloyds stood in the doorway. They were partially blocking the view of the hall from Williams and Sebta. Then Donna pulled the door towards her, shutting off the inspectors' view even more. Barry made some frantic gestures, which Duncan interpreted as meaning that he and Snick should get out now.

They were acting more coolly under pressure than he would have given them credit for. One of them, maybe both, had figured out that Duncan and Snick were probably watching them through the wallscreens.

Duncan de-activated the screens so that the inspectors would not know that they had been watched. Then he went into the hall, Snick closely following him, and sped to the living room. There he got down behind a sofa. It was near a wall and the most distant piece of furniture from the hallway entrance and the apartment exit-door. He did not want to go outside and attract the attention of the neighbors. Weighed against that was the need to intercept Shurber and Tan before they walked in with the groceries. If, however, he did that, he might attract even more notice. The neighbors might wonder why Tan and Shurber did not enter the house and dispose of the groceries before they walked away from the apartment.

He muttered, "Man, my life has depended upon a lot of very fragile things."

"What?" Snick said.

"Never mind."

Now that he did not dare to activate the wallscreens, he could no longer follow the inspectors' course. Presently, though, Donna said loudly, "I hope everything was all right in the bedroom? Where do we go next?"

"At least minimum," Williams said, sounding disappointed. She did not answer Donna's second question.

Snick said, "I got to see where they're going." She was up from her couch and halfway to the right corner of the hall entrance before Duncan could say anything to her.

He rose up from behind the sofa so that he could see her. Her head was stuck around the corner. Then she withdrew it and came back to him.

"They're in the stoner room."

"Oh, hell!" he said.

In reply to her puzzled expression, he said, "I didn't think about it before. If they notice that both Tuesday and Saturday are not in their cylinders, they'll be suspicious. Probably arrest the Cloyds."

"I thought you thought of that," she said.

At that moment, the front door began sliding back. Though its motion was silent, the increased light and the voices of neighbors in the street caused Duncan to look around the end of the sofa. Here came Shurber and Tan, she pulling behind her a collapsible two-wheeled cart full of paper sacks. Duncan jumped up, waving one hand and a fingertip of the other on his lips. Snick also came out from behind the sofa, mouthing silently and jabbing a finger at the hallway.

Tan had been about to say something. Her zebra-lipsticked

lips remained open, but no sound issued. Duncan strode to them while they looked wonderingly at him. Close to them, he said, "Inspectors! Give me the cart! And get out! Don't come back until about half an hour! Call first! Don't ID yourselves when you do!"

Tan and Shurber walked out. Duncan trundled the cart to behind the sofa. Snick, who had been watching the hall to make sure that the inspectors did not see them from the kitchen, went back to the sofa. The door began sliding back. One of the two who had just left had had the presence of mind to insert his ID card and voice-activate the door-closing mechanism from outside.

Now on the floor with Snick and the cart, Duncan said, "That was close!"

Snick did not reply. She knew it had been tight.

He waited for five minutes before the faint voices suddenly got louder. The group was now in the hall. The Cloyds were talking at a high volume so that Duncan and Snick could get some bearing on their location. They were doing this even though they might not know if Duncan and Snick were still in the apartment.

Duncan said, "Thea, crawl over to the wall and turn on the interior monitor again. Set it for the kitchen and stoner room. And stay there, be ready to turn it off and get back here."

The small command-section, voice-shifted by Snick to the lowest part of the wall, was split into four parts. Each one displayed the room from a screen in the middle of a wall. The inspectors were in the stoner room. It took them several minutes to check the wall bases before glancing at the stoners. They were probably looking for dust on those, though Saturday's occupants were responsible for only their own cylinders.

Duncan was relieved when Williams passed by Tuesday's cylinders and did not look at them. Her main concern was Saturday's, and she went around these two swiftly. Then she asked the Cloyds to voice-sign her recorder to acknowledge that she and Sebta had completed their inspection.

All should be well now, he thought, unless someone at the department HQ should get the idea of comparing the voice-frequencies of the signers to those of Shurber and Tan. No, that trouble would not be taken unless the ganks were behind this visit.

But it was possible that Williams and Sebta were ganks. They might know by now that the Cloyds were not whom they pretended to be. And Williams could have noted the empty Tuesday stoners before Snick had set up the wall monitor. Perhaps, the two "inspectors" were going outside to make their report to the ganks stationed outside. Then, a large force would storm into the apartment. No. Shurber and Tan would have seen these and warned him and Snick.

Williams and Sebta did not know that there were two hidden people here. If they were suspicious, they could just pull their guns from beneath their uniforms and arrest the Cloyds.

Williams said, "The department will notify you of any action to be taken." She jerked her head at Sebta to follow her, and they walked out of the stoner room door. Duncan signaled to Snick to turn off the wall-displays. She did so and crawled swiftly back to him. A minute later, the inspectors had left the apartment.

As soon as the door closed entirely, Duncan rose from behind the sofa. Donna screamed and clutched Barry. He turned and saw Duncan and Snick. "My God, you scared us! We didn't know you were still here!"

Duncan told them what had happened. "Tan and Shurber should be back within fifteen minutes. But they're to call first."

"I was about to crap in my pants," Donna said. "I was certain they'd see our empty stoners! What about a drink? I can sure use one!"

By the time Tan and Shurber returned to the apartment, the Cloyds were deep into their cups. Duncan and Snick were tempted to join them, but they had long ago agreed to limit themselves to one drink a day. They did not want to be intoxicated if they were ever caught off guard.

Shurber and Tan were so shaken that they tried to catch up with the Cloyds' glugg-glugging. Dinner was late. Afterwards, all sat in the living room. Duncan and Snick were the only ones who looked alert. This was despite the excitement on the news channels. The anti-government demonstrations were being covered on many levels of every tower. Donna Cloyd watched these for a few minutes, then said that she was too sleepy. Instead of going to bed, she would enter her cylinder now.

"Then I'll be doubly stoned when I wake up," she said, and she laughed.

"Good idea," Barry said. The Cloyds walked down the hall with their arms around each other to keep from falling over.

According to the newsheads, political demonstrations were taking place in other California states. None of these had been licensed by the organics department. The ganks were going to have a hard time, Duncan thought. But that means that they'll give the protesters a harder time.

The news channels switched around to various meetings, finally zooming in on the one most promising violence. This was in the Blue Moon Plaza, which was not far from the apartment.

Twenty-two wallscreen sections showed the plaza from as many different views. The demonstrators, mostly young men and women, were massed in the middle of the plaza and surrounding the huge many-tiered fountain in the center. Their yelling roared from the screens, causing Duncan to lower the sound volume somewhat.

"We want more freedom!"

"Break up the eyes in the sky!"

"Down with living once a week! Up with the natural way to live!"

"Clean out corruption in the government!"

"Piss on the tyrants!"

"Up against the wall, pigs!"

"Give the people ASF now!"

"We're not scum! Give us the ASF, too!"

"Eat shit, Big Brother!"

And, as the sound detectors beamed in on individuals, "Hurray for Duncan and Snick!"

"Pardon Duncan and Snick! Let them tell the true story!"

"We're tired of government lies! Give us the truth!"

Many in the mob were waving printouts. Duncan could not read these but suspected that they were the two messages he had broadcast only two weeks ago but which now seemed a long time ago. And then he heard a portable transmitter blasting out a part of his messages.

". . . THE GOVERNMENT RESISTS, REVOLT!"

The crowd was surging, changing shape. Tentacles formed by groups reached out, then contracted.

A newshead said, "The illegal gathering in the Blue Moon Plaza is estimated to amount to a thousand. The official estimate of the total number of demonstrators, all unlicensed and hence breaking the law, totals approximately fifty thousand. That is a very small number compared to the total population of Los Angeles State, twenty million. Though the Great Organic Commonwealth Charter of Rights and Responsibilities gives the people the right to demonstrate for political, social, and economic reasons, it also stipulates that local organic departments must issue licenses of permission for such demonstrations. But this tiny minority of subversives and malcontents . . ."

The avenues radiating from the plaza were clogged with ganks. Their proguns were still holstered, but they carried electric stun-sticks, cattle prods, and tear gas grenades. Two enormous water-pressure tanks were stationed at the junctions of thoroughfares and plaza, their cannons pointing toward the mob. Outside the ragged circle of protestors were many patrol cars, now fitted with rotary steam-powered guns which could shoot low-powered sponge bullets.

Some of the screens showed a host of gank airboats landing on the rooftops and in the ports of precinct stations at various levels of the towers. They had been brought in from other California states.

Now the organic general bellowed through his bullhorn.

"This is the last warning! You will immediately disband and

128

disperse! Go at once to your residences! Otherwise, you will be arrested! I repeat . . . !"

"How about that?" Shurber said. "Not one, not a single one, is leaving! They're all staying! Listen to them!"

A newshead was saying, ". . . in San Francisco State. The reports of fighting with the organics have been confirmed. The organic department representative there states that an undetermined number of demonstrators have been arrested. There have been some casualties, no deaths, though, and when the situation clears up, we shall specify the exact numbers . . ."

The general's voice roared over the shrieks, yells, and chants in Blue Moon Plaza. "Officers! Arrest the felons! If they resist, use proper procedures to restrain them!"

"God, I'd like to be there!" Snick said. "I'd show them!"

The first ganks to try to make arrests without the use of excessive force, as defined by the department, were bowled over as the crowd surged against them. The ganks behind these began ramming the prods into those who advanced against them. The general's bullhorn issued orders, but they could scarcely be heard above the uproar. Then the watertanks spouted their red-dyed water over the officers' heads and into the center of the mob. Many were knocked down, screaming, and pushed hard into the ranks of their comrades on the edges of the swarm.

A momentary depression was made in the center, but those swept down were up again. Then the tanks moved in closer, their sprouts knocking down some ganks, too. Abruptly, the entire mass seemed to be a bright red from head to foot. The water, spreading out on the plaza surface, looked like blood.

"Damn!" Sarah-John Tan said. "They won't be able to wash off the dye. They're marked for at least a week! Poor devils! The ganks'll get them for sure even if they run away!"

Suddenly, the crowd burst through the rings of officers. They were past the patrol cars, which had not begun shooting the sponge bullets because the officers were in the line of fire, too. The protestors boiled out of the plaza, charging the deep ranks of ganks at the junctions of plaza and thoroughfare. Many of these went down. So did many demonstrators. But most of these got up and ran on. The general was standing up in his open car and was blaring at them to halt and submit to arrest. Then someone, it looked like a woman to Duncan, rammed a cattle prod, taken from a gank, against the general's belly. He dropped the bullhorn, doubled up, clasping his belly, and fell out of the big car. He disappeared into the melee.

In a short time, at least three-quarters of the demonstrators had fled down the streets. The rest were either lying motionless on the plaza or were being subdued by the ganks. These were dragged off to the public emergency stoners along the edge of the plaza. But the supply of stoners could not meet the demand, and the ganks quit using them. The ganks wrestled the rest of the protestors to the floor and taped their wrists behind them. A spray of TM in the face of each prisoner knocked them out.

"Not bad for a beginning," Duncan said. "Relative to the entire population, the demonstrators were few. But as time goes by, the mobs'll get bigger and more violent. I hope so, anyway."

Sarah-John said, "For God's sake! My husband has passed out! How in hell could he with all that going on?"

She rose unsteadily from her chair. "He never could drink much. Maybe I better get him to bed."

She pulled Shurber up from his chair.

"Watch this!" Duncan said. "I don't believe it! The demonstrators are coming back! This is better than I'd thought it'd be!"

Here came the red-dyed horde, running as fast as they could out of the avenues down which they had fled and toward the ganks. Though the ganks were surprised, they gathered in disciplined ranks in the center of the plaza, thus reversing the original situation. The patrol cars moved back, half-turning, and then forward so that the fixed sponge guns on the hoods pointed at the streets. The tank turrets of the watertanks revolved toward the advancing mass.

The protestors now had cans in their hands. Duncan supposed that they had had them when the demonstration began, but they had kept them under their clothes. Perhaps they had not had the courage to use them then. But now the young citizens were as red with rage and defiance as the dye on their skin and robes. While the majority charged the organics, many climbed the monitor posts and sprayed a black liquid on the screens. Others shot their sprays into the faces of the officers.

The general had managed to climb back into his command car with his bullhorn. He was bellowing something. Duncan could not understand the words, which were drowned out by the hellish din.

The mob was also spurting the black bond-spray on the wallscreens of the buildings around the plaza and on the portable cameras of the TV news crews. Many of the screens Duncan was watching went dark.

"Black them all out!" Duncan cried as he rose to his feet. "Give it to them, the swine! Show them you're not a bunch of sheep!"

Snick also rose from her chair. She cheered.

The lights went out.

16

Duncan said, "What the . . . ?"

He looked at the luminous face of his wristwatch. Exactly 7:11.

Sarah-John Tan's voice came from down the hall. "Oh no! The power's gone off again!"

Duncan spoke the words to reactivate the wallscreens. They did not spring into glow. Nor did the front door open in response to the spoken code.

"I don't suppose," he said, "there's a flashlight or candles in today's PP?"

"Don't bother asking Sarah-John," Snick said. "I've checked out everything in their closet. They don't have any."

The air seemed to be dying. It pressed thick and warm on him. He moved toward the wall, touched it with the fingers of his outstretched hand, and began to move along the wall. Then he bumped into Snick.

Sarah-John Tan had groped her way to the living room. Guided by Snick's voice, she found the sofa. Duncan by now was also on the sofa. He smelled her perfume and the underlying odor of her nervous sweat.

She said, "Lem's passed out on the bed, the lucky son of a bitch."

"I wonder what could have happened?" Snick said. "We didn't mess up the power plant this time. Another subversive group we don't know anything about?"

"I doubt it," Duncan said. "Maybe it's an accident."

He did not believe that. Perhaps, he thought, the government did it. With power off and the only light available coming from the gank vehicles, the demonstrators will be helpless. They'll be busted up easily, run away. Turning the electric power off seems like a very drastic measure, but the government is capable of doing it. It won't take the blame, though. It'll put the responsibility on something or someone else.

Sarah-John, sounding as if she were close to panic, said, "It was terrible the last time. We woke up on Wednesday and thought at first it was Tuesday again. But when all the other days stepped out of their stoners, we knew something was very wrong. We couldn't get out of the apartment for a long time. The ganks had to burn out the locks. We were told we'd have to evacuate the city. The streets were jampacked, of course, and . . ."

"That was then," Snick said. "We know all about it."

"You weren't in that godawful mess," Sarah-John said.

"I don't think the power'll be off very long," Duncan said. "Let's just wait and see, be calm, take it easy."

"It's too bad the lock was replaced," Snick said. "It may take hours before the ganks get here to burn it out. We may have to do it ourselves, and how can we explain that to them?"

"It may not take nearly that long," Duncan said. "The situation's different now. Only today's citizens are destoned, so there'll be only one-seventh the number there was then. There's only one-seventh using up the oxygen, too, so the air should last longer. And there are a hell of a lot more ganks present than then. We'll wait."

He could almost hear Snick fidgeting. She was action personified and loathed sitting until something happened. If events were going to be launched, she wanted to be the launcher. On the other hand, her inborn impatience had been tempered by a stern discipline and long experience as an organic officer. She would not do anything rash unless the situation forced it.

An hour passed very slowly. The seconds seemed to seep down through the increasingly warmer and heavier air and settle over them like tiny dead insects. The four talked fitfully with long silences between the sentences, which became more and more short and jerky. Duncan finally rose from the sofa. "We'll have to burn out the doorlock."

Shurber's voice came then from down the hallway.

"What the hell is going on?"

Tan got up and groped her way from the living room.

"Don't panic, Lem!" she cried. "The power's off again!"

Shurber's voice became shrill. "Not *again*!"

Presently, Tan and Shurber groped and stumbled into the living room. He cursed when the situation was explained to him but was silent after that.

It seemed to Duncan that his theory that the government had cut the power was wrong. Surely, the demonstrators had long ago been dispersed or run down and arrested. Where would they hide? The doors of their apartments were locked, and they could not get into them. They could not claim that they were innocent citizens who had been in the streets when the power went off. The red dye would reveal their guilt.

Unless, he thought, the government was really going to shove it all the way up the asses of the citizens. It would make them suffer so much that they would resent—hate—the persons seemingly responsible for the blackout. These would not have caused it, but the government was going to blame them. He and Snick were going to be named as the culprits.

What would the government's story be? That Duncan and Snick, the psychopathic outlaws, crazed subversives, had once more attacked the Baldwin Hills plant and destroyed the converter-generators? No. It could not do that if it planned to turn the power on again soon. More likely, the government would state that the outlaws had somehow managed to insert a shutdown command into the system. And it had taken the engineers a long time to trace the command down and cancel it.

He was dry and very thirsty. The water did not run in the faucets, but he and Snick had groped into today's PP kitchen cabinet and found the bottles of fruit juice that Tan and Shurber had gotten at the grocery market. All four had managed to empty these bottles. That would normally have been more than enough. But now he felt as if the air were no longer a pile of dead insects. They were very much alive and were sucking his body fluids out.

He felt along the wall toward the doorway. He would find the area in which the locking mechanism was and burn it out. To hell with the consequences. He had to get out before he died of desiccation or oxygen starvation, whichever came first. He had just pulled his gun out of his belt when he was startled by a rapid and hard knocking on the door. He put his ear to the wood and heard, faintly, "Organic department! Knock if you hear me!"

Duncan rapped the door with the butt of his gun, then applied his ear again to the wood.

"Stand back! We're burning out the locks!"

A dim red spot appeared on the door at the area of the enclosed lock mechanism. The spot became larger, and Duncan caught a whiff of smoke. A violet beam shot through a small thin hole, then followed a curve. The beam disappeared. There was a loud bang, and the cutout section flew inward, hitting the floor, its edges still smoking. The odor of burning wood filled the room. Another beam, that of a flashlight, shone through the hole, making the darkness into a twilight outside the circle of its light. A voice amplified by a bullhorn entered through the hole.

Duncan strode toward the hall, guiding himself by the light. He said, "Thea, follow me! Tan, Shurber, you stay here!"

They got to the bedroom doorway just in time. The door slid inward, and a loud male voice said, "Stay inside for now! We don't want the streets crowded. We have work to do."

"Thank you, Officer," Tan said.

Duncan and Snick waited for a minute, then came to the doorway. Tan and Shurber were standing in it and breathing deeply. But the street air was almost as dense and warm as that in the apartment.

The headlights and searchlights of two organic patrol cars illuminated the street. These were parked a few apartments away. The faces of tenants looking out from the doorways were pale in the beams. Four ganks were burning through the locks.

A half-hour passed. The lights of the patrol cars and the violet beams of the proton guns were by now far down the street. People came out of their apartments. Their talking was quiet at first but became a babble in a short time, the chatter of adults mixed with the crying of infants and screeching of children.

Sarah-John Tan said, "It's scary. How are we going to find out what's happening if there's no TV?"

From birth, she had been surrounded with light and with the moving pictures on the walls. Their absence was making her shaky. Duncan and Snick had been conditioned to an iconless environment during their flight through New Jersey. They had been so busy trying to survive that they had not had withdrawal symptoms.

Fifteen minutes later, maintenance and repair department workers brought portable torches. These were being placed every two hundred feet. They gave a feeble light in the area of the apartment since it was almost exactly halfway between two torches. But that was better than none, and it seemed to cheer up the people in the street.

Duncan and Snick withdrew into the living room. Tan and Shurber stayed in the doorway.

Duncan said, "Unless they get the power back on soon, the city will have to be evacuated. The air isn't going to last."

"I'd imagine that the entrances to the roof and the base of the tower have been opened," Snick said. "That should help."

"Probably. But it won't be enough. I think that the citizens will have to be moved out of the tower. Or, at least, to the perimeters, where the air might be fresh enough."

"You mean we can't stay here?"

"We can try to. Maybe, if all those people leave, there might be air enough."

"It's certainly not fresh enough now."

"We can go with the crowd, but that's taking a big chance. If the ganks are on their toes, they'll know that now's a good time to get us. However . . ."

The authorities had enough to do, perhaps more than they could handle. Would they even think about ordering the ganks in the field to keep an eye out for the fugitives? Probably not. On the other hand, it just might happen that a gank would recognize them.

A few minutes afterwards, an M & R worker on an electric tricycle rode slowly by. Duncan heard the bellowing of her bullhorn long before she got to the apartment.

"Attention, citizens! Attention, citizens! All tenants! All tenants! Go immediately to the eastern end of the street! There is no cause for panic! Move to the eastern end of the street!

"Attention, all citizens! Move to the eastern end of the street! This is an order of the governor! Do not panic! Go to the east end of the street! The east end! This is an order of the governor! You will be evacuated via the emergency stairway! Attention, all citizens . . . !"

Her voice receded westward. The people in the street, after some hesitation, began walking toward the ordered destination. They were joined by others coming from the west. Presently, several buses jammed with passengers rolled by. Duncan could not see to the end of the street, but he imagined that the crowds would soon be one huge mass. The ganks were not going to find it easy to handle all these, direct them up or down the stairway, move them swiftly enough but not too swiftly, and quell the citizens' panic. Just how the sick in the hospitals would be gotten out, he did not know. But that was not his problem.

Sarah-John said, "What should we do? Stay here or go with them?"

"We're staying," Duncan said. "It's up to you, but I think you should go."

"We'll see you later," she said. She and Shurber stepped out into the street and merged with the molasses-slow and increasingly more numerous crowd. After a few minutes, however, the street was empty. Then the same woman rode by, repeating her evacuation orders.

After she had gone, Duncan said, "There should be enough air for just us two. It doesn't seem to be getting any hotter."

A half-hour went by while they sat down in the doorway, breathing the slightly fresher air, ready to scramble inside if workers or ganks came by. Both were very sleepy, but they could not go to bed. It was too hot and too hard to breathe in there. Besides, something ominous was happening. They felt it in their unconscious, in their nerves. This blackout was unexplained, and they would not relax until they knew what had caused it. Perhaps not then.

They rose as they saw lights illuminating the area beyond the curve of the street. A moment later, the headlights of two patrol cars shone brightly. Duncan crouched down and stuck his head out beyond the doorway far enough to see with one eye. When he withdrew it, he said, "Two gank vehicles, parked on each side of the street to our right. Their spotlights are on the doorways just by them. One man in each car operating the spotlight. Two men from each car have entered an apartment. Each one of the two was carrying some device. It was hard to see what the device was, but I think they're using sniffers."

"I have to see," Snick said. She crouched down but looked

both ways before moving back into the apartment. "There's activity at the other side, too. The curve blocks my view, but I think there are cars there. Probably doing the same thing as those ganks."

It seemed highly probable that they were looking for him and Snick. Who else could it be? How did they know that he and Snick were in this area? If some citizen had seen him, or more likely *thought* he had seen him but was not sure, he would have notified the organics. But why were they searching for the outlaws now? Why not sooner? Answer (if there were any): The snitch must have seen him hours ago. However, he had only recently reported the sighting because he had not been sure about it. As recently, say, as just before the blackout. He could not have done it after the power was off.

Yes, he could if he went to a precinct station or a gank to deliver his information personally. But he would have had to live close to a station or have seen a gank passing by. He would not have ventured outside in the dark.

But . . . the informer must have been outside his apartment when he remembered seeing Duncan. Or perhaps in a store which had no doors with locks.

Did it matter how it had happened? It was happening, and that was the important aspect.

It did matter that the ganks did not know exactly where he was. Otherwise, they would have been in full force in the street outside the apartment, ready to storm it. In fact, if they thought that he was in this neighborhood, they would be crowding the streets in their search. Perhaps they only knew that he was on this level or in this tower.

He looked around the doorway edge again. A gank was standing by each car and directing its searchlight on the doors of the residences into which their colleagues had gone.

Duncan stepped back and spoke softly. "If they can catch us while there're no citizens around, they can do what they want to. Kill us or arrest us and get us unobserved to the nearest precinct station."

"Which do you think?" Snick said.

"I think they'd like to find out all about our activities and whom we've associated with. But, if we're alive, we might become very embarrassing to the government, plus a rally-around-the-flag for the discontented and the radical. If I were the World Council, I'd want us dead."

"Most assuredly," Snick said. "Let's take as many down with us as we can."

Duncan grinned. The ancient Vikings who despised dying in any situation but battle had nothing on her. If there were a Valhalla, the Valkyries would have to carry her off to it even if she was a woman.

Snick started to say something else, but he held his hand up for silence. A faint noise, a murmur as of many voices, had come through the doorway. She came closer to him to hear it.

"What's that?"

He looked around the corner again, Snick squeezing between his body and the doorway side to look also. The two ganks by the cars had their backs to them. Presently, the lights around the curve became brighter. A patrol car, headlights blazing, appeared. As it rounded the curve, several ganks on foot, their weapons in their hands, came into sight. Behind them, marching in an undisciplined manner, came the first of the parade, obviously demonstrators under arrest. They were shouting slogans, some of which Duncan could hear in the din.

"Let us live every day!"

"Down with the government!"

"A fair trial for Caird and Snick!"

"Up the revolution!"

"Give us immortality, too!"

"Off the pigs!"

"They've rounded them up and are herding them to the staircases," Duncan said. "Or maybe they're going to put them in some theater and lock them up until they have time to deal with them individually."

The ganks in the apartments looked out the doorway. Their curiosity satisfied, they went back into the apartments. A minute later, they left them and entered the apartments next door.

"We try to join the crowd?" Snick said.

"No. They'll be sniffed, you can bet on that."

Soon, the last of the hundred or so demonstrators disappeared around the curve. The patrol cars and foot ganks making the rear guard also went around the curve. The two officers who had been standing by the cars got into them and drove them a few yards closer to the doorway in which Duncan and Snick stood. They started to watch the doorways on which their searchlights were centered. Then, hearing more crowd-noise to the west, they turned to look in that direction.

Duncan and Snick ran out into the street, the sounds of their feet muffled by the noise from the mob. This was, however, decreasing, indicating that the demonstrators were being herded along a street at the end of this one. When twenty feet away from the ganks, Duncan and Snick fired their proguns, set on maximum stun. Struck in the backs of their necks, the ganks fell heavily and did not move thereafter.

Duncan entered the apartment doorway on his left. Snick took the doorway of the apartment across the street. Duncan could see the front room, well illuminated by the searchlight. The hall was less bright but far from dark. When he heard voices coming from the stoner room, he slowed down.

17

The door of the stoner room was partly swung open. Looking through the opening between the door and the wall, he saw two ganks standing before a cylinder. The woman was directing a flashlight beam on the open door. A progun was in her other hand. The man held a cylindrical and shiny gray sniffer by the handles on its top. His eyes were fixed on the glowing display screen mounted on the machine.

There was enough light so that Duncan could see that only two stoners had not been opened. They were looking for an outlaw hiding in a stoner or for a whiff of molecules indicating that the outlaw had been in the stoner.

The woman said, "We're taking too much time. The orders were to just make a quick sweep."

"This is about as quick as we can be and still be efficient," the man growled. He stood up and moved to the next cylinder. With one hand, he pulled on the door handle while the woman, poised to one side, pointed her flashlight and gun at the inside of the cylinder.

"This is crap," the man said. "They wouldn't be stupid enough to stay here. Not while the power's off. Anyway, how the hell do they know they're in the tower?"

Duncan stepped in and shot the woman in the back. She crumpled soundlessly at the touch of the violet beam. Before she had hit the floor, Duncan stunned the man. The flashlight, gun, and sniffer fell almost inaudibly onto the thick rug. The man slumped face-first into the cylinder doorway.

When Duncan got back to the street, he saw Snick coming toward him. "Easy, no trouble," she said. Each lifted up a gank by the armpits and dragged them into the living room of the apartment from which Duncan had just come. After they had dropped the bodies against the wall, out of sight of anyone looking through the doorway, Duncan said, "We know the uniforms at Tan's apartment fit us. We'll put those on."

Carrying flashlights taken from the unconscious officers, they ran to the residence of Tan and Shurber and to the Cloyds' cylinders. The uniforms and helmets had been cached on the bottoms of the stoners. As quickly as they could, sweating, breathing the thick stale air, they exchanged their clothes. Then they ran back to one of the patrol cars, a roofless and doorless vehicle.

Duncan turned the car around so that it faced westward. He drove off, leaving the other car behind him, its lights still on. He intended to use the stairway by the elevator banks past the Blue Moon Plaza. That, he thought, should be much less crowded than the emergency stairways at the tower perimeter. He did not know just when the deserted patrol car and the stunned ganks would be found. But he calculated that he had at least twenty minutes before that happened. His and Snick's scent would inevitably be detected by the sniffers. The ganks would search all neighborhood residences. They would quickly find the outlaws' odors to be especially heavy in Tan's and Shurber's apartment. When power was restored, and that could be any minute now, all those in the apartment would be degorgonized. That would be the end for the OMC members even if they had been injected with anti-TM. By one means or another, the ganks would get the truth out of them.

Duncan felt sorry for his colleagues, but he could do nothing for them. He wished he could at least warn Erlend, Simmons, and Diszno that the ganks might track them down. However, he and Snick would be lucky if they saved their own asses.

Snick's muttered exclamation shifted his thoughts.

"Oh, oh!"

Her hand closed on the butt of the gun on her lap.

About two hundred feet ahead of them, four electrically powered tricycles, two in the lead illuminated by the two behind them, had rounded the corner of an intersection. They were heading toward Duncan and Snick. But the vehicles passed them, horns honking in greeting. Duncan honked back. Snick waved.

Ahead was the Blue Moon Plaza, the great square lined by many stores, some theaters, a sports arena, a gymnasium, a grade and high school and a junior college, a hospital, a precinct station, a superblock administrative office, and several warehouses.

Big portable lights were spaced along the edge of the square and around the now-dry fountain. These illuminated a crowd of perhaps two hundred citizens near the fountain and several large groups of organics. A very large armored vehicle with a watercannon sprouting from its turret was at the far end of the crowd. Patrol cars filled with ganks ringed the mob. The beams of the watertank and the cars blazed on the twisted faces and shaking fists of the prisoners. Though Duncan was too far from them to hear their words, he knew that these were insulting or defiant.

Duncan turned the car to go up the avenue that crossed the street at right angles. He did not want to cross that square. There were too many ganks there. Though they might assume that he and Snick were fellow officers, one of them might recognize him and Snick. The lights were too bright there.

He would go up the avenue and take a street running past

the square. This would lead him directly to the elevator banks and the adjacent staircases.

He said, "Oh, damn!"

Up the street were the many lights of a cavalcade, a swarm of organic cars and tricycles and two very large headlights above the others. Another watertank. The lights showed a dark mass behind the lead vehicles. More prisoners.

There was no room for his car to pass through. He would have to stop it as near to the apartment fronts as he could get it and wait for the mass to flow by his vehicle.

That was not to be. A voice amplified by a bullhorn spoke from the front of the crowd. "This is Colonel Peckapore speaking! Turn around! Go to the plaza!"

Duncan, keenly aware of the spotlights now centering on his and Snick's faces, stopped the car. He backed it up in a half-circle and then started back along the way from which they had come.

"Peckapore apparently doesn't care what our supposed mission is," Duncan said. "He's requisitioning all the personnel he can get."

"Want to make a run for it?"

"No. We'll ride it out, slip away the first chance we get."

Since he had not been ordered to station the car at a particular place, Duncan drove along the edge of the plaza to a place near the watertank. The car was pointed to the west, toward the staircases.

They got out of the car and stood by it, their guns in their hands. The cavalcade rolled into the plaza. There was a lot of shouting and some confusion for a while. The newly arrived group of prisoners was hustled with bellowed orders and cattle prods to a place alongside the fountain. Now there were two masses of arrestees, each separated from the other by the fountain. These did not hold their ranks as commanded but surged back and forth, expanding and contracting and forming pseudopods like two gigantic amoebae.

Over the cries, screams, and shouts soared the voice of Colonel Peckapore via his bullhorn, turned to full decibel level.

"You will cease this resistance and this noise at once! Be quiet and do exactly as you're ordered or I will have you all subjected to stun beams!"

While he was bellowing, a captain stormed up to Duncan and Snick. "What the hell are you two doing just standing there? Get in there and help restrain the prisoners!"

"We had no orders to assist," Duncan said. "We were just told to come here."

"Jesus Christ!" the captain said. Her face was bent with anger. "Where the hell's your initiative?"

The lights came on then. For a moment, there was a comparative silence. Peckapore quit shouting, and the prisoners stopped yelling. Then, as the surprise faded away, the noise began again. The captain seemed startled, though not so much by the reappearance of the lights. Duncan and Snick had started to move away when she said, "Hold it! Come here, you two!"

Duncan, turning back toward her, said, "What is it, captain?"

She went up close to him. Her eyes narrowed, she looked intently at him and then at Snick. Alarm sliced the anger from her face. She reached for the gun in her holster, at the same time shouting, "You're under . . ."

The violet beam from Snick's gun caught her in the chest, and she fell backwards, her loose weapon ringing on the hard floor.

Duncan whirled to look beyond the watertank, the bulk of which partly hid him and Snick. No one seemed to have seen the shooting, but it would not be long until someone spotted the captain's body. He leaped to her, hoisted her over his shoulder, strode to the car, and dumped her onto the floor below the back seat. Snick leaped into the driver's seat. As soon as Duncan had run around and scrambled into the seat beside her, she pressed the accelerator.

Electrically driven, the vehicle did not have a high acceleration, but she gave it all it had. Two ganks on tricycles were coming into the plaza from the west. They had evidently seen him throw the captain into the car. They stopped their vehicles and got off. Duncan shot one of them with his gun, which he had reset to MAX BURN. Snick, steering with one hand, shot the other. The ganks fell backwards, their guns dropping to the floor. Thin smoke rose from their scorched chests. The car sped past the sprawled bodies and then was on the avenue. By now it had reached its top velocity, thirty-five miles an hour.

"They must've radioed in," Snick said.

"I'm not sure. They only had time to draw their guns. They looked pretty surprised."

He doubted that the two they had beamed were dead. They had been close to the end of the full-power range of the proguns. But they would be badly wounded.

The huge round columns enclosing the elevator banks and the staircases were visible a few minutes before they got to them. The car had to turn off the avenue onto a street and go two blocks. Duncan smiled when he saw that the street monitors in the last two junctions had been sprayed with black bond-paint. The monitors on this junction had also been blinded by the demonstrators. That gave him and Snick an edge. Though the power was on, these monitors could not now view the outlaws.

However, two ganks were stationed by the two columns enclosing the elevator shafts and the staircases. These reacted only as they would if they saw two fellow officers approaching in a car. They fell, struck by beams from guns set back onto MAX STUN. The nearby monitor screens would transmit no pictures of the shooting to HQ. They, too, were covered with black paint.

He and Snick got out of the vehicle and dragged the three bodies through the open door of an apartment across the street from the columns. The captain and a gank went into empty stoners. The third one was jammed into an occupied cylinder. Then, panting and sweating, Duncan and Snick went to the staircase entrance.

Now that power was restored, the dispossessed citizens would be returning to their apartments. This would be a long and somewhat confused process and would require that most of those searching for the outlaws would have to assist. However, it would not be long before the ganks they had left in the apartments near the Cloyds' would be staggering out. Also, those under the captain's command would be wondering what had happened to her.

The indicator lights above the elevator doors were flashing the level numbers. They must be bringing up the citizens now, though it would be a long time before those who had left the 112th level could use them. The number of people who had gone down the staircases was probably large. Very few would want to climb back up to the higher levels.

They started swiftly down the stairs, one hand sliding along the banister. The steps were twenty feet wide, and went straight down to the landing. There they turned and ran down the next. By now the wallscreens had been activated, though for only one channel.

The newshead had been replaced by an organic major, Prewett. While he spoke, a section beside him displayed the icons of Duncan and Snick. Below these: BE ALERT FOR THESE CRIMINALS. REPORT OBSERVATION OF THESE TO THE NEAREST ORGANIC OFFICER OR PRECINCT STATION. DO NOT ATTEMPT TO APPREHEND. THEY ARE ARMED AND DANGEROUS.

Major Prewett's voice paced them as they hurtled down the steps.

"Full power has been restored to the La Brea Tower Complex. All citizens will return to their residences as directed by the organic officers. Please be calm. Order is being restored.

"The two wanted criminals, Jefferson Cervantes Caird, a.k.a. William St. George Duncan, a.k.a. Andrew Vishnu Beewolf, and Panthea Pao Snick, a.k.a. Jenny Ko Chandler, have been sighted on the 112th level. For the moment, they are still at large. The reward for any information leading to their capture or death has been raised to 75,000 credits.

"Full power has been restored to the La Brea Tower Complex. All citizens . . ."

149

Duncan thought, the ganks do not know yet that we're in uniform. Otherwise, they would be broadcasting that data.

By the time he and Snick, panting, had reached the 12th level, the situation had changed.

". . . have assaulted and overcome a number of organic officers and donned the uniforms of two. The criminals are now posing as organic officers. We urge . . ."

A third section sprang into glow, showing Duncan and Snick in patroller uniforms. The operators must have worked fast to simulate these.

Immediately thereafter, he and Snick had to slow down. A mass of men, women, and children were trudging up the steps, jamming them from wall to wall. Though many of them must have seen the displays, no one of the mob recognized them or seemed to do so. It was possible that, if any did, he obeyed the order not to attempt to apprehend the criminals. On the other hand, thought Duncan, that reward would surely have overwhelmed fear. The person who first cried out their names and so was responsible for their capture would earn 75,000 credits. Duncan reassured himself that the weary and flustered citizens had not matched the icons with the ganks who suddenly appeared.

Then he and Snick were forcing their way downward along the wall. Even though most people tried to let them by, the press of bodies made for slow going. But it had its advantages. He saw the helmets of two ganks going upstairs. They were near the banister, and, if they saw his and Snick's helmets, they did not think anything of it.

After ten minutes of pushing, they had only gotten down three levels. Then the mass suddenly decreased. For one flight there was only a score or so coming up, latecomers. Then, there were none.

When they reached the second level landing, they looked down around the corner. Leaning against the end of the banister on the first level were two ganks.

18

Duncan and Snick retreated to the gigantic sliding doors which gave entrance to the second level. They glanced through the big windows and ducked back out of sight. Two ganks were standing near it, talking, their tricycles a few feet from them.

"They must've stationed officers at every staircase exit on every level," Snick said.

"If so, they just did it," Duncan said.

He did not know why the two ganks on the first level had gone inside the doors. What mattered was that they had. He frowned and quirked the right corner of his mouth. The monitors must be on, but whoever at HQ was watching this staircase was not reporting on the appearance of the criminals. Or perhaps someone at HQ had set the monitors to fail as he and Snick went from level to level. That meant that some high OMC official was protecting them as well as he could. Diszno? Simmons? It would not be so dangerous to do so if no one was watching the operator. There would be just a momentary blanking out for each level.

If that was happening and it was not just a malfunction, then the operator must be getting uneasy. He must know that Duncan and Snick were blocked by the ganks outside the door on this level and the two ganks at the foot of the staircase. He could blank out the monitors only so long.

Duncan told Snick what he thought was happening. She said, "Let's take the bastards on the first level."

He looked down over the banister. The ganks, a man and a woman, were sitting down on the lowest step. They must be tired—like everyone else in this tower, including me and Snick, Duncan thought. They were resting for a moment, secure in the faith that the monitors would detect the criminals if they came down the steps. They would have plenty of warning if that happened. Which they perhaps did not think was a probable event.

When Duncan and Snick were halfway down the stairs, the woman rose from the steps, stretched, and yawned, then turned toward her companion. Her mouth opened just as Duncan's beam touched her chest. The man toppled over when Snick's beam hit him, his shoulder against the banister rail. Then he slumped forward.

They reset the dials on MAX BURN and looked through the big windows. The layout of the first level was essentially the same as the other levels. The perimeter avenue was very broad, and a relatively narrow residential street ended in it. There were people out in front of their apartments, no doubt talking about their ordeal. So far, no explanation of the blackout other than a malfunction had been given. There were no ganks in sight, and the vehicles of the unconscious officers were parked nearby.

Duncan and Snick activated the doors to slide back into the recesses just far enough for them to pass through singly. Then they closed the doors. They mounted upon the tricycle seats and prepared to drive away. At that moment, they heard the wailings of organic sirens. Before they could decide what to do, a patrol car with lights flashing, followed by four officers on tricycles, came out of a street to their left. Duncan said, "Wait! Just maybe they're not after us!"

He was glad he had decided not to make a run for it. The group sped on around the curve of the avenue. He said, "Let's go!" and their tricycles followed in the wake of the group. He turned on his vehicle's siren and lights; Snick, hers. When the group turned down a street, he and Snick continued on their way until they neared an exit, which was their planned destination.

They parked the tricycles outside a large cubicle, entered it, and went down a flight of steps. At the bottom, they took a hallway that led to the elite yachting club they had entered the night they had fled the rooftop. No one was around, though the monitors were surely active. Unless, he thought, their unknown benefactor was still closing down monitors for them. There had to be such a person. Otherwise, the shooting of the two ganks on the first level would have brought a host down on them.

When they came out of the archway leading to the docks, the same archway they had used before, they stepped into night. The clear sky was starfull, and the other towers and the spanning bridges blazed with bright light. The air was cool. Water slapped against the side of the tower under the docks. The boats in the slips bobbed. The scene had changed considerably, however. Parked between the base of the tower and the docks were over fifty organic airboats.

The officers who had flown them in from other towers had been summoned to help in the criminal hunt and the exodus of the citizens.

He had planned to dive down after the airboat he had submerged and bring it up. That was a cold, wet, and difficult task he had not looked forward to. Now, he did not have to do it, thanks to the ganks.

First, though, even though it would take much time, he and Snick would have to voice-set the programs of all the craft. They worked furiously, but in an hour had programmed only thirty.

Duncan, sweating, said, "That's enough. Some ganks might be going back to their HQ's earlier than others."

"Why not destroy the others?" Snick said.

"I'd like to. But if a patrol boat happened to see all those cannon beams, it might come over to investigate."

He jerked a thumb to indicate the lights of a surface craft about half a mile away.

Now and then, an airboat had also flown over the basin though none was in sight just now.

"I'll watch," she said. "If a patrol boat shows up, I'll tell you to quit firing."

He hesitated. An airboat or waterboat could come around the curve of the tower and see the violet beams. But, what the hell, he meant to do a deed far more chancy and dangerous than this. He was burning with a rage that demanded more and more fuel. He said, "O.K." and he climbed into the cockpit of the four-seater he had selected to take them away from the tower. Its cannon-batteries had a full charge. After lifting it, he took it to the most distant point of the parking area. Then he turned it around, and he brought it to ground level. After setting the MAX PWR dial, he moved the boat forward until the bulbous nose of the cannon was a few inches from the craft first destined for destruction. The beam spat out and cut the boat in half. He thrust his boat forward, its sharp edge knocking the two parts of the parked boat apart. One after the other, while he listened for Snick's voice over the radio, he severed nineteen boats. The work was done in two minutes.

Snick came running and clambered into the seat next to his. She was laughing softly. After closing the canopy, she said, "Man, that was fun!"

Duncan, not smiling, nodded his head. He lifted the airboat out over the water just beyond the docks. "Here goes," he said. He spoke the codeword, Eris, to transmit the radio signal to the programs in the thirty boats. They rose from the ground and turned toward the directions set for them. Their navigation lights began flashing.

His boat lowered into the water until the surface was level with his chin. Just as it began moving toward the west, the thirty programmed boats took off, accelerating at full power. Ten went northward, headed toward the Hollywood Hills against which they would smash. Ten sped westward and would keep going across the Basin and out into the Pacific Ocean until their fuel gave out—unless they rammed into the freighters anchored beyond the Basin. The remaining ten shot eastward, their flight to end when they struck the mountains.

He enjoyed his vision of the consternation and bewilderment the sudden appearance of the thirty boats on the organic tower radars would cause. No air or surface craft was to move in the L.A. area unless the traffic operators on top of the hills were notified. They would be even more upset when the boats crashed.

Having observed that the vessels had a common point of origin, the La Brea Tower, the operators would notify the organics. Those within the tower would hasten down to the docks, and others would be dispatched in airboats to the docks. Here came some now, their lights arcing from the rooftops of the towers and the middle ports of several other towers. They zipped overhead, not seeing his boat, its lights out, most of its hull under the water.

"If I cannot overthrow the gods on high, I will at least make an uproar in Acheron," Duncan muttered.

"What?" Snick said.

"Nothing."

He did not know where that thought, surely a quotation from ancient literature, came. Certainly, he had not learned the phrase since he had escaped from the Manhattan rehabilitation institution.

Another leak from one of his former personae.

Ahead was the Baldwin Hills central power-distribution tower. Lights blazed from its rooftop reflecting from a gigantic silvery dirigible and several enormous airboats. He was too far away to see the cables stretched beneath the aircraft, but he was sure that they were there. The news channels had mentioned several times that an auxiliary converter/distributor was to be installed in the building. If the power should ever be interrupted again, the auxiliary would take over. The newsheads had assured the viewers that this was extremely unlikely to happen. The security measures now used would prevent Duncan's and Snick's exploit from ever being repeated.

The archway through which he and Snick had plunged to destroy the CD (converter/distributor) was closed. But Duncan did not intend to try to use that entrance.

Instead, he brought the boat up alongside the side of the tower, its hull almost touching the hard black metal. By now the canopy had slid into the hull, and the wind of his ascent struck his face. Just before he reached the rooftop, he moved the boat out and then turned it to face the tower. He came over the edge, still rising, and then shot the boat sidewise along the dirigible, his cannon piercing the craft's skin and severing rings and girders and the gas cells within the hull. The magnificent vessel fell nose first, the enormously heavy converter at the end of the cables below it pulling it irresistibly into the opening. There it stuck, its body pointing straight upward. By that time, Duncan had sliced the three Titan airboats in half, and the parts attached to the cables plummeted down into the opening, which was one-third of the rooftop.

The workers on the rooftop had scattered when the dirigible fell. There were ganks among them, but they were too busy getting out of the way to shoot their handguns.

Down into the opening, Duncan took the boat. Galleries in the great shaft shot by dizzyingly. The workers in them stared open-mouthed at him. Then he was by the CD, a Brobdingnagian cylinder that had half-fallen onto its side and smashed many of the lower galleries. The energy indicator of his instrument panel flared bright red as he stopped the boat. He was pressed downward into the seat as the Gernhardt motor strove to decelerate quickly enough before the boat crashed into the floor.

The bottom of the hull struck and bounced. His neck made little snapping noises, and his head seemed to be driven into his shoulders. The energy indicator became a pale red again, and its displayed digits decreased to 12. Ahead was a large hallway down which two ganks, guns in hand, were running toward him. His cannon beam shot between them, and they dived into the nearest doorways. He launched the boat down the hallway, turning its nose quickly to the right, then to the left several times as it moved on a line straight ahead. The violet beam burned through the walls, and the ganks in the doorways were no longer there when he passed them.

The boat sped down the hall, turned to the left, and zipped down another hall. Another turn, another hall. A woman coming down it screamed and hugged the wall. A beam from Snick's gun stunned the woman as they hurtled past her. Another turn, and they were in the hall that led to the entrance through which he and Snick had come only obweeks ago. This time, they were attacking from the opposite direction.

As before, he stopped the boat at the lofty doorway to the towering chamber wherein had sat the converter he had destroyed with his cannon. The boat turned, its nose pointing toward the new converter. The violet beams melted the shell and the equipment inside it while the engineers, workers, and ganks ran. Before he was done, the ganks on the galleries above were firing at him. But they were too high up for their beams to angle near him. They struck the floor and drilled smoking holes in it.

Duncan did not know how long it took him to destroy the converter. Perhaps thirty or forty seconds. But he knew when he had accomplished his task. The lights were out. He wheeled the boat around and flew it a foot above the floor. Before he got to where he thought the hall junction should be, he turned on the headlights. They shone against the smoke but penetrated far enough for him to see about twenty feet ahead. In a short time, he was near the great shaft in which lay the wreckage of the auxiliary converter and the Titan boats. He doused the lights and activated the radar. Guided by this but moving slowly, he went into the shaft. Even more slowly, he rose until he was near the nose of the dirigible. Hidden by its bulk, his craft slid upward between the vast crumpled wreck and the shaft wall. Flashlights stabbed here and there on the galleries, some fastening on his boat but losing track as it swiftly accelerated. Light filtered down from above from the portable lights the work crew had been using in addition to the tower rooftop lights. When the boat was near the top of the shaft, Duncan slowed it. Still concealed by the upper part of the dirigible, it slipped over the edge and descended close to the wall.

Snick closed the canopy when the boat was halfway down the side of the tower. A minute later, the boat was submerged to its canopy. There were many craft in the air and the water now, lights flashing and, of course, their radar and infrared detectors scanning everywhere. Duncan slowed the boat to a crawl and lowered it two inches or so more. The journey back to the La Brea Tower was a sloth's progress, but they got to its base without incident. He waited until there were no gank vessels close on the western side. Then, the canopy open, the boat rose close to the wall.

No illumination seemed to be coming from the rooftop. If there were any gank craft there, they did not have their lights on. He stopped the boat partly below the top of the wall. After he and Snick had made sure that no one was there, he piloted the boat onto the rooftop. Snick turned her flashlight off and on to guide him. They landed near the hatchway lid and got out. Within a few seconds they had slid the hangar door back and flown down into the room, her flashlight showing the way. It was just as they had left it, a partially repaired airboat in a corner of the enormous chamber.

After Snick had put the ladder up against the edge of the

hatchway, Duncan climbed it and pulled the lid shut. Flashlights showing the way, they went into all the rooms to make sure that they were unoccupied. Then they looked into the numerous pantries and refrigerators for food. There were more than enough canned goods, including fruit juices, and slow-decay supplies to last them for days. Not that they planned to stay here any longer than necessary.

They ate and drank by the flashlight beams while they talked merrily of their exploits. Then they went to the huge bedroom in which his grandfather slept during his infrequent visits to Los Angeles. If the power had been on, they could have depolarized the windows, but these were as black as the night outside. There was an advantage to the opaqueness. If they could not see out, those outside could not see in.

Duncan yawned mightily and stretched. "The fire's gone out. I'm going to sleep now. I'm not even going to wash my face."

"Which you couldn't do, anyway," she said. "The pumps won't be working. The toilet's going to be a hell of a stinking mess until power's restored."

"We'll keep the door closed," he said. "Anyway, there are a lot of toilets here."

He started to take off his jacket.

The next he knew, he was looking up from the floor. Bright flashlights blinded him.

A man's voice—it seemed familiar—said, "We finally found you."

19

Extracts from a secret report to the World Council by Gunther Geronimo Zagak, Field Marshal, Organics Department, North American Ministering Organ (governmental unit comprising what once was Canada and the U.S.A.): ". . . thus making it mandatory to declare martial law in the South California subprovince."

". . . intense investigation revealed that the suspected treasonous organization was on higher levels than the computized probabilities. It was learned that Diszno, Tuesday, General of the Organics Department of Los Angeles State, ID No. TLA–x/4529Y, was the chief of the subversive group calling itself OMC, PUPA, and other frequently changing titles. We suspect organic participation by various personnel, some probably highly placed, in other days, too. The officers sent to the general's apartment to destone him discovered that he was absent. He was, however, found in an airboat, preparing to flee. Ordered to surrender, he fired upon the officers, wounding one and killing one. The return fire killed him

161

immediately, though we would have preferred that he be taken alive for interrogation."

". . . would have detected Diszno and the others in the apartment where Duncan and Snick took refuge if the power failures had not delayed the tracing of various illegal circuits."

". . . apparent that General Diszno, or perhaps others not yet identified, aided Caird and Snick during their operations in the La Brea Tower Complex. The failure of the tower monitors to identify the two outlaws was caused, we firmly believe, by one or more organic officers who criminally and treasonably operated the monitors in such a way that detector-alarms were not activated. An intensive investigation re this matter is being conducted, and we are certain that the culprits will not escape the organic net this time."

". . . regrettably admit that . . . no idea where the criminals Caird and Snick are at this moment. Their continual elusiveness and successful attacks point out the weaknesses in our security systems. But part of their success can be attributed to the extraordinary audacity and wiliness of Caird-Duncan and Snick-Chandler. It is, if you will permit a rather nonfactual item in this report, as if Robin Hood and William Tell had teamed up against society. Or as if Stenka Razin and Lu K'uei had become partners. A previous report-analysis of the situation (erasure ordered) compared Caird-Duncan to certain figures of ancient mythology. These included the American Indian trickster-heroes, Old Man Coyote and Wabasso, The Great White Hare. Despite the exaggerations inherent in this comparison, or perhaps because of them, Caird-Duncan and Snick-Chandler are becoming folk-heroes among the less law-abiding and more thoughtless citizens."

". . . the major factor in their ability to hide and to venture forth to attack is due to the weaknesses in our system. For a thousand obyears, discontent and crime have been very minor elements in society. The New Era has come as close to Utopia as is possible for a society composed of human beings. From infancy on, the citizens have been conditioned against violence and rebellion, and their freedom from poverty and the cornucopia of good housing, plenty of food, free education and mental and medical care, and their access to democratic principles and procedures has made the dayworld system a heaven as compared to the hells in which pre-New Era citizens lived. Though a minority of citizens have complained about the close monitoring by the government, the majority have seemed to accept it. They understand that a society cannot achieve New Era desiderata unless it is being monitored."

". . . complacency. The organics department expects immediate obedience by the citizens to the laws and to the commands of its officers. A violent rebellion is not expected because there is no logical reason or cause for it. However, I suggest you review the MIND AND SPIRIT OF HOMO SAPIENS tape-series by the famous psychicist, Doctor Bella Jinrick Fordswanter. She stresses what she idiomatically terms 'the inborn orneriness of humankind,' the irrational inclination to 'kick against the pricks.' Just as a validated ten percent of the population consists of 'born leaders,' an estimated three percent consists of 'born rebels.' Of the latter, half have criminal tendencies. Scientists have conducted a genetic analysis of a certain percentage of born leaders and born rebels but have failed to identify any genetic complex or any environmental factors whatsoever as responsible for these character features."

". . . too lenient and permissive. The government policy of using a long leash on the citizens and only pulling back when the principles and procedures of the New Era are in grave danger must be changed. The people must be made to realize that a stricter control of their actions is for the general good.

". . . surprised. Even I, a field marshal for twenty subyears, did not suspect that the world population was two billion, not the ten billion figure which is to be found in all educational tapes and in subannual government reports. I accept, of course, the wisdom of the World Councillors in keeping these figures from everybody except themselves and, of course, the small but elite body of government statisticians. This manipulation of data had been for the general good, obviously done to forestall any demand for the breakup of the New Era and return to day-by-day living."

"But now the higher officials have been informed that Caird-Duncan's accusation of lying by the government re this matter is true. The higher officials have obviously been told the truth so that they will not feel betrayed when the truth finally comes out. It will eventually come out because there is a growing tide of demand among the populace that Caird-Duncan's accusation be validated or invalidated. I myself do not know how the data manipulation can be continued if a body of disinterested scientists and common citizens are allowed to track down the data re population size. This seems inevitable."

". . . as you know, the citizens of every day in the aforesaid apartment have been questioned. All were revealed to be members of the subversive organization except the couple in Friday. It was evident during interrogation of the other days residing in this apartment that they had an ability to lie under TM. This ability was much like that of Caird-Duncan in kind though not in degree. Certain measures the exact description of which is not necessary forced the suspects to confess that they had been injected with a newly invented anti-TM. (See Report No. OD–HS 7392–C for the details. Erasure ordered.) This revelation has greatly concerned the organic departments of all days. In fact, it has greatly *troubled* the department. It makes investigation and interrogation much less certain and conclusive. It also brings up the question of how wide-spread the dissemination of the anti-TM has been, or, as it is now officially initialed, A-TM."

". . . do not know if the Los Angeles and Manhattan subversives are part of a worldwide organization, loosely allied to others, or completely independent. This question is being intensely investigated on a global and everyday basis."

20

Duncan sat up, his mind-fuzziness gone, his body throbbing with readiness for action. He started to reach toward his holstered gun but stopped. He would be shot before he could touch the weapon.

Snick's voice said, "What happened?" She sounded as if desert dust had been poured into her throat. His own mouth was also very dry, and he had a mild headache.

The same voice said, "Your guns were removed while you were unconscious. You don't need them, anyway."

Squinting into the dazzle, Duncan turned his head to his left and to the right. He counted five beams, and there might be other people in the darkness.

A man moved into the circle of light. He was of medium height, not over six feet, very broad-shouldered, and he was in an organic officer's uniform. The gold-colored falcon on his left chest shone dully. Duncan, recognizing the broad, high-cheekboned face and the prominent epicanthic folds, said, "Colonel Kieth Alan Simmons!"

"The same," Simmons said. "I'm your friend. We're taking you elsewhere. Keep quiet. Obey orders. Here are your guns. The powerpaks have been removed."

Duncan was handed his weapon by a woman who stepped out into the arena of light. He saw Snick, close by, take her gun from a man.

"Just how did you catch up with us?" Duncan said.

"You wouldn't have gotten this far if I hadn't been bypassing the monitor screens when you two left your apartment," Simmons said. "But no talking now. Explanations later."

Snick looked at Duncan. He shrugged, indicating that, for now, they could only do what the colonel demanded. Not that he needed to tell her that.

They left the apartment a minute later. Duncan had expected that they would use the door to the corridor. But they went through the suite to the hangar room. The hatchway cover was fully open, and an airboat was hovering a few inches from the floor of the hangar. It was a twelve-seater, so large that its sides must have scraped the edges of the opening as it descended into the hangar. Duncan and Snick got into it. Four ganks were seated behind them, and Simmons and two others, including the pilot, were in front of them.

The craft rose slowly until it cleared the hatchway. It poised near the edge while two ganks got out and closed the cover. The rooftop was jammed with refugees and bright here and there with large emergency lamps. There were many ganks there keeping order. The nearest looked at the boat, but they would consider it just part of the exodus.

The boat lifted and turned toward the north.

Nobody spoke during the entire trip. The pilot took the boat at an altitude of a thousand feet northward through the heavy traffic. When the craft had left the L.A. basin behind, it ascended to two thousand feet. The pilot turned on the automatic then, and the boat proceeded according to the Valley traffic control. It picked up velocity, going four hundred miles an hour, the limit of its Gernhardt motors. Before it got to Santa Barbara, it began lowering. The pilot cut off automatic and steered downward toward the heavy woods east of the Santa Barbara Tower area. He went over several hills at almost treetop level, then dropped the boat into a small valley. It alighted before a very large log cabin at the base of the hill. The cabin and the surrounding area were well lit. Two barns and a corral were near the cabin. A wide brook ran near the front door.

Still silent, all entered the cabin. The front room was large and had a stone fireplace with a blazing wood fire at one end. Two of the walls were TV screens, blank at the moment. A stairway ran up to an open second floor. The couple who greeted them were in their seventies and were, it became obvious, servants. They brought in drinks and sandwiches while Duncan and Snick were in the bathroom. When Duncan came out, he was told to sit on a sofa near the fireplace. Snick joined him. Both asked for iced tea and were served. Having downed one glass quickly, each asked for another and were given it.

Standing, a glass of bourbon in his hand, Colonel Simmons said, "Now, we may talk. But I'll do most of it."

Three of the ganks had gone elsewhere, but the others sat in chairs not very far away. Having been told by the colonel that they should go into their stoners, the two elderly servants had also left.

Simmons said, "You two may be the wiliest people this Earth has ever known. Certainly, you're among the slipperiest and, God knows, the most personally destructive. But I figured out you just might come back to the very place nobody would think you'd have the chutzpah to go to. Who else would have the balls to do that? So, I set up mass-capacitance battery-operated detectors there, disguised them as furniture items. When you two did come here after that incredible feat . . ."

He paused, smiled, and broke into loud laughter. When he

had recovered from the fit, he said, "The detectors transmitted a radio alarm. They also released gas from containers I'd set up, disguised, too. The rest you know."

"What I don't know is a lot," Duncan said. "Just what are you up to? Why are we here? Something happened to force your hand, didn't it?"

"You two, especially you, Duncan, are to play a larger role in coming events, events we'll cause, than you ever envisioned. You're through running away. That's all behind you. I've decided it's time to take the initiative. Not by attacking and destroying pieces of equipment and inconveniencing people, though you did do far more than that. I'll start by telling you that I've been the real chief of all the undergrounds in L.A. and elsewhere, too. Diszno outranked me in the organics department, but I was his OMC commander. When Diszno was killed, I knew it wouldn't be long before I'd be tracked down. So, I decided to take action. You're my main weapon."

He glanced at the wallscreen. "It's 1:02 a.m. The devil is having a ball in L.A. just now. But we'll take advantage of all that confusion. Now . . . would you two like to get some sleep?"

Duncan said, "Can't we at least get some idea of what you have in mind for us?"

Simmons was smiling, but his voice was a trifle harder.

"You two are my honored guests. But I'd like you to do what I say. You'll see the reason for that later. My people and I have a lot of work to do, and I'd feel better if you were taking it easy just now, recovering from your ordeal, let's say. This is an R & R place for high organic officials. But there won't be anybody coming here for a week, at least. All vacations have been cancelled. The other days will get that message, you can bet on that. You'll have to trust me."

"We can't do anything else anyway," Duncan said. "But . . . how about the servants for the rest of the week? How about our guards?"

"Quit worrying about details. They're all taken care of."

Simmons beckoned with his finger, and three ganks stood up and approached Duncan and Snick.

"Court, Chang and Ashwin," Simmons said. "They're your humble servants. Anything you want, ask them for it. Ashwin will also answer any questions, that is, except those which might threaten security. You understand that, of course?"

He left the cabin with three other ganks. Ashwin, a rather thin dark man with a toothbrush moustache and an overdeveloped jaw and chin, led them to a room on the second story. This had twin beds and an adjoining bathroom. Before bidding them good-night, Ashwin produced two proton guns and several powerpaks from an over-the-shoulder bag.

"The chief said you were to have these. One, to show his trust in you. Two, in case there should be a raid. That's extremely improbable, but you never know."

He bowed and was out of the room, closing the door behind him.

"The room's probably monitored," Snick said.

"It makes no difference. Say whatever you want to say."

"I don't feel like talking, though I've got a lot of questions troubling me," she said. "It can wait until tomorrow . . . when we get out of bed."

Ten minutes later, they were asleep.

Sunday's sky was sunny. Duncan, awake shortly before noon, went downstairs. Snick was already eating breakfast, or lunch, at a table with Ashwin and two women. The latter, who had been among the ganks that picked him up the day before, were introduced as Rani and Jiang. Duncan did not talk while eating. Snick, as usual, seldom said anything. The others, however, talked animatedly about a new miniseries.

While sipping his coffee, Duncan said, "I'd like to get the setup here. And I'd like to see the news and get any information you might have which hasn't been released to the public."

"The chief said you were to be given all the data you want except for certain security items," Ashwin said.

169

Through an open window came the snorting and whinnying of horses and some male and female voices. A crow cawed from somewhere. The beautiful song of a cardinal came from nearby. A mental image of a house in a city flashed through his mind. The house had a grassy front yard and a garden in the backyard. Birds of all kinds, robins, cardinals, bluejays, finches, hummingbirds, were in the yards. A hawk soared far away looking for pigeons or rabbits. The sky and the sun were real, not the sterile world of the tower with its artificial sky and sun and where the only birds were caged in the plazas and the only vegetation were the dwarf trees in the plazas.

That house? Where was it?

"There's not much to tell about this place," Ashwin said. "It's a horse ranch for high organic officials' rest and recreation. The servants and handlers aren't going to be curious about us being here Sunday. Now and then, the organic high officials break day for reasons we don't have to give the help. They know there's an emergency right now, so they accept the fact we're not Sunday people."

He rose, saying, "We'll watch the news now. Not just that restricted to the area. News from all over the globe and from various days."

The local news was chiefly concerned with the blackout of Los Angeles State. The newshead stated that it was believed that the archcriminals, Duncan and Snick, were responsible. Details of the blackout would be available in the near future. The general of L.A.'s Saturday organics would undoubtedly be replaced, and an investigation into the competency of L.A.'s Saturday governor would be initiated.

The rest of the news was about local events. Every ten minutes, though, a separate screen section displayed the images and biodata of the two criminals. The reward for their capture was now 120,000 credits.

Ashwin then activated showings of various tapes from different days and different parts of the world. There had been demonstrations in a number of cities and a dozen riots in cities in the ministering organs of China, South Africa, West Europe, Russia, Brazil, and Australia.

"Simmons must have quite an organization," Duncan said. "It would take a lot of pull and personpower to get those tapes."

"You're perceptive enough," was all Ashwin would say. But he looked smug.

Duncan was pleased. His messages were causing the storm he had hoped they would. How could that be kept raging? How to prevent the agitation from just dying out?

There was only one answer. Not he but the people would have to do that. One man could not destroy the world or save it. The people would have to keep up the fury until it burned away the rotten foundations.

The weakness in this semirevolt—that was all it was, so far, a half-assed revolution—was that it lacked a monolithic organization powerful enough to come out into the open. It also needed a single-minded leader who could coordinate the organization. Perhaps, that impulse that sometimes seized the mass-unconscious might bring victory. The great body of the people had, now and then in pre-New Era days, been possessed by a demon that made them act in unison. Driven to rage like a many-headed but one-souled entity, they had unpedestaled tyrants and ripped governments to rags.

That afternoon, accompanied by Ashwin and another man, he and Snick took a long walk through the forest. Afterwards, Ashwin offered them horses to ride. Though neither had ever been on a horse and probably would never again, they mounted the gentle beasts and rode for an hour up and down a long winding path through the woods on the other side of the ranch. Ashwin gave them instructions while they rode.

Shortly after they had finished dinner, Ashwin came down the big wooden staircase. He stopped before their table and said, "The colonel will see you now. Follow me, please."

He led them back up the steps and down the hall to a door

before which stood two armed ganks. Ashwin knocked on the door; Simmons's deep voice told them to enter. He was seated behind a large mahogany desk on which were baskets full of small differently colored spheres—"tapes"—and piles of printouts. He rose as they came in. His smile radiated glee and confidence, an immense satisfaction with something. His prominent deeply cleft chin seemed to be projecting light as if it were a transmitting antenna.

"I've good news for you two," he said. "I *hope* you'll think it's good news. If you agree to go, we leave tonight for Zurich."

21

"Zurich?" Duncan said. "The world capital?"

"Yes," Simmons replied, smiling, his eyes fixed on Duncan's face as if he were trying hard to drill through to his thoughts. "State of Switzerland. Where the World Council has just issued its list of nominees to replace Ananda."

"I didn't see that on the news," Snick said.

"It hasn't been announced yet."

Duncan was no longer surprised about Simmons's access to nonpublic information. He said, "Why? I mean, why do you want us to go there?"

"Sit down, please."

Simmons leaned back in his chair, his hands behind his head. "You've eluded the organics and gotten away with your attacks because of your audacity," he said. "*L'audace, toujours l'audace*. You know what that means?"

Duncan and Snick shook their heads.

"Audacity, always audacity. It's a great phrase from a great

173

language, French, unfortunately now as dead as Latin. But the Gallic spirit lives on. Audacity, always audacity. You two embody that spirit. But you've been running too long, and it's time that you . . . we . . . made an attack, a strategic move, that will have a greater effect than even your blacking-out of Los Angeles twice in a row, by God! After all, what you did there has only nuisance value, though I think the L.A. citizens regard it as much more than just a nuisance."

He put his hands on the desk and leaned forward.

"Here's what I propose."

Duncan and Snick listened without interrupting until Simmons was finished, though they had to restrain themselves.

"There," Simmons said. "What do you think of that? *L'audace*, right?"

"Or suicidal recklessness," Snick said. "Don't get me wrong. I agree with you in principle. But it's a make-or-break move. Does it really have any chance to work out successfully?"

"We can't know, of course, until we've done it," Simmons said. "What do you think, Duncan?"

"If the whole business is set up the way you've laid it out for us," Duncan said, "it could end up a great victory for us. Could, I say. It's disadvantage . . . well, I hate to deliver myself . . . Snick, too . . . into the hands of the enemy. There are so many things that could go wrong. On the other hand, you can say that about any venture."

"The risks are big, I admit that," Simmons said. "But that's never stopped you in the past. Besides, at this stage of the game, what else is there to do?"

"It would be a tremendous surprise," Duncan said. "It would take them off-guard, unbalance them."

He looked at Snick. She said, "Duncan and I need to talk about this for a little while. Alone."

Simmons stood up. "Of course. I expected you to thrash this out between yourselves. You can use this room. I promise you it won't be monitored."

174

He walked out, Ashwin behind him. When the door was closed, Duncan said, "There are plenty of safeguards in the plan, and the ganks won't dare to shoot us. We'll be in full public view."

"*If* Simmons can do what he claims he can do," she said. "But what bothers me is what's in this for Simmons? Why is he doing it? He'll be in as much danger as us."

Snick was right to be suspicious. Duncan had also wondered about Simmons's motives.

"Power," he said. "If we come out on top, he'll have great power. He must be extremely ambitious to dare this. The rewards he thinks he'll get outweigh the peril."

"Or he could be a true revolutionary," Snick said.

"Yes. But even those are not driven solely by high ideals. They want to shatter the power of the government they're rebelling against and most of the time that government needs to be overthrown. But deep down, in the unconscious, is a hunger for power."

"What about us?" Snick said. "Does this apply to us, too?"

He laughed, and he said, "I don't think so. I've never had any ambitions to rule others. But who knows what's down there where the mindless beast rules? Anyway, Simmons's motives don't really count just now. What does is what happens when we go to Zurich."

"We are going?"

"I am," he said.

"Then I'm going, too. Only . . ."

"Only what?"

"A long time ago, I saw a show about the French Revolution. The main character, I think his name was Danton, was the great leader of the revolt. Everybody in France was scared to death of him. He was responsible for sending thousands to the guillotine. Eventually, he, too, was condemned, and his head was chopped off. During his trial he said, . . . just a minute. Let me think. Oh, yes. He said, 'The Revolution is like Satan—it eats its own children.' "

Duncan did not reply. The child's face, his own, was burning like a meteorite in his mind. And, like the falling star, its disappearance left a blackness, but this one was formed of horror and despair.

"What's the matter?" Snick said.

"All those heads rolling into the baskets," he said. "It doesn't matter. History doesn't necessarily repeat itself."

"Human nature does," she said. "But you're right. We can't refuse to act just because of what's happened to others. We're not they."

He went to the door and opened it. Ashwin was standing watch down the hall. "Tell Simmons we're ready," he said.

A moment later, the colonel, followed by Ashwin, strode into the room. He was smiling as if he expected a very positive acceptance of his proposal.

"We're in," Duncan said. "All the way."

"Good! It's like Julius Caesar crossing the Rubicon River," Simmons said. "The die is cast. The bridges are burned behind us. It's die or be conquered."

Snick said, "He conquered. But he later came to a bad end."

"*Et tu, Brute*," Simmons said, still smiling. "Despite all his canniness and cynicism, he trusted some people he shouldn't have. I won't be making his mistakes."

No, Duncan thought, you'll be making your own.

"I'll give you the details you'll need," Simmons said. "By the time we leave at midnight, you'll have just about everything in the way of data and equipment you'll need."

An hour later, Duncan went to his bedroom and lay down. He closed his eyes and tried to summon up from his mental depths all that he knew of Jefferson Cervantes Caird. Simmons had told him that he would be taken to Zurich under the guise of the colonel's personal servant. During the voyage, he had only to keep quiet and follow the established procedures for intratemporal-zone visitors. He might as well, he thought, start to think of himself as Caird, not as Duncan.

However, he had been so many other personae. Bob Tingle,

Jim Dunski, Wyatt Repp, Charlie Ohm, Father Tom Zurvan, Will Isharashvili, and William St. George Duncan. These were not just assumed identities. He had *become* these people. The short interim IDs of David Grim and Andrew Beewolf were just names associated with fake biodata, play-acting roles. Now, to become again Jefferson Cervantes Caird, he had to work back through Duncan and the others to the natal, the original, Caird.

That was not an easy task. Probably no one else in the world, except a multiple-personality psychopath, had so many personae. He was the only one who could make these at will, become them. But peeling them off, as he soon found, was a different matter.

After a while, he gave up his struggles to get past the Duncan, the most recent. He was breathing hard. His exotic and sometimes surrealistic mental techniques had been useless. Duncan was stuck in the womb of his mind.

All his previous selves were still untouched. They did speak in powerful though tiny voices. Supposed to be dead and buried, they insisted on resurrection and unrolled a little the stones before their cave-tombs. They were all superjesuses or, from another viewpoint, superdraculas. No, not super because they did not come from above. They resided deep below and thus were subjesuses or subdraculas.

He would be again named Caird, but he was, in reality, still Duncan. And the full reblooming of Caird's memories and psyche were not his to nurture. The voices of his ancestors, whom he had made himself, were liable to speak now and then. They threw him off somewhat from the destiny he drove himself toward, just as that child's face did. They made him a self-distorting parabola, a twisted trajectory. Along the curve of his mind rode sine waves interspersed with square waves. The voices caused psychic lightning, which, in turn, caused power surges and drops. Duncan's fingers, it might be said, were not always on his mental rheostat. The fingers of the others were trying to grab it.

He sighed, wondering at the same time if all of the sigh was his alone. He did not know just how closely or loosely those others

177

were monitoring him nor what thoughts and actions were Duncan's only.

He did feel good, though, when he went down to the main room and Snick greeted him as "Jeff." That name alone seemed to be the first step toward regaining his first identity. It was as if a door in a dark room had been cracked open and let in a shaving of light. His mood was further brightened when he saw the new tapes displayed on a screen for the passengers. Some of these were for the public news channels; some, the tapes made by the organics department and only for the eyes of the higher authorities.

The news channels were from thirty or so metropolises all over the world and from each of the days. Though slanted toward the government's position and doubtless censored, they still showed that there was considerable unrest and turmoil everywhere. Caird noted, however, that some of the demonstrations were by people in support of the government, and there were several incidents when these attacked the protestors. He was not surprised. Many citizens did not even want to think about breaking up the old ways. It made them more than uncomfortable; it made them fearful and angry.

The gank tapes showed considerably more of the mobs than the news channels. Some of them, though, were lectures by high organic officials on how to control the demonstrations and how to harass their leaders. They also gave statistics on the number of demonstrators and computer probabilities on the success of government endeavors to quell these. What most interested Caird was the estimate on the number of citizens making and using the illegal age-slowing elixir. This was based on the number of burglaries and raids on biochemical laboratories and the arrests of people selling the elixir. Selling was not an accurate word. The dealers were trading the elixir for gifts purchased through the ID-credit cards of the buyers. In some cases, there had been no trades. Those possessing the elixir had just given it away.

22

At 10:32, the group of fifteen flew away from the ranch in a large airboat. It headed northwestward toward Armada Field, one hundred and twenty miles away. The sky was heavily overcast, though there were a few breaks where stars shone thinly through the mists. The boat, on automatic control, sped just above the treetops, rising with the hills, dipping into the valleys. The visible light beams were off; infrared and radar bathed the way ahead.

The passengers were silent, protected from the wind by the canopy but not protected from the hurricane of thoughts, of apprehension and tension. Their inner voices were loud.

At 10:53, the lights reflected from the sky became stronger. The boat shot over a hill crest, and Armada Field lay on the plains below. It sprawled out like an iridescent octopus. Water towers, control towers, rockets and scramjet launchers broke the horizontality. There was no fence around the enormous field. Why put up one when there were no enemies to guard against? There had been no wars for over two thousand obyears, and the sensors would detect any unauthorized intruders larger than an opossum.

Simmons had not given any details about how he was using the field. He had not explained the procedures used to get across to the field and the transportation of the group from there to Zurich. Caird supposed that the orders had been "cut" through data inserted into the organic-department banks. These may have been quite legitimate, though Simmons's unstated purpose was anything but that.

A screen in front of the pilot lit up. He said something in a low voice into the microphone curving up from his helmet. The automatic control off, he brought the boat in. It slowed and then settled down in a marked parking space. The struts came down and gripped the pavement with their round spongy ends. The canopy slid back. The side doors were opened. The passengers began climbing out. Each carried a large shoulderbag packed with heavy contents.

Two people were waiting for them outside. One was a tall woman in a gank uniform and a long green cloak. She and Simmons spoke briefly while the others went into the building. There were only three others in the room, flight clerks. Their voices rang hollowly in the huge chamber.

Simmons went to talk to them. The others in the party, after placing their large knapsacks on the floor, sat down or paced back and forth and went to the restrooms.

Caird, looking through the big window on the portside of the building, saw another aircraft land. Two men and two women got out of it. Long before they entered the building, their knapsacks rising higher than their heads, Caird recognized two of them, Barry and Donna Cloyd. Each was holding a large box in one arm.

He was as surprised and as cheered as if he had unexpectedly run into old friends. Donna, smiling, put her box on the floor and rushed toward him. She embraced Caird and kissed him on his cheek, then tried to put her arms around Snick. Snick was smiling, but she retreated from the embrace and bowed to Donna. Donna said, "What the hell, Thea. Don't be so cold!"

Barry had also placed his box on the floor. He hugged Caird and grabbed Snick before she could push him away. There was not much she could do about it except submit more or less gracefully.

Before Caird could ask them any questions, Simmons announced that they were going to leave. He led them out of the room and along a wide high-ceilinged hall and into another big room. At the end of a ramp leading to a door were a man and a woman in pilots' uniforms. They welcomed them and led them down a narrow space, through a lock, and into a large craft. Ten minutes later, the craft backed away from the bridge, turned silently except for the creaking of the fuselage—very flexible, that—and taxied up a ramp into a catapult. After making sure that everybody was belted and the seats tilted back far enough—the passengers were almost prone—the warning buzz sounded. The chief pilot's voice told them to prepare for launching. The buzzer sounded again. Orange lights flashed on the walls and the screens. The pilot gave the countdown. At zero, the passengers were pressed backward deep into their cushions. Their blood drained toward the lower part of their bodies. Caird came close to blacking out, and then he felt almost weightless. That was a psychological and false feeling. The Gernhardt motors were on, and the craft was zooming upward, lifted and hurled onward by the interplay of the craft's magnetic equipment with that of Earth's field. A minute later, the scramjets cut in. The fuselage trembled and did not cease doing that until near the end of the flight.

When the altitude was 60,000 feet, the buzzer sounded. Lights flashed again. The chief pilot said that they could tilt up their seats somewhat. They could not loosen or remove the web belts.

By now, the passengers were inside themselves, worrying about the immediate future, wondering if everything would go as well as Simmons predicted. They were projecting a dozen possible scenarios, all of them doom-laden. At least, Caird supposed they were. He certainly was. He did not know what was going on in Snick's usually unreadable mind. Probably images of being cornered and of shooting her way out, happy visions for her. She was probably the only one aboard enjoying the prospect of conflict with the authorities. Unless Simmons also had his bright images of success, but they would not be Snick's bloody scenes.

The boat shook as the scramjets, in reverse, slowed it down. Ten minutes later, the jets were cut off, and the Gernhardt generators took over. The passengers were allowed to get up, stretch, and walk around. A few minutes later, they got back into place. The seats were tilted all the way up now, but they had to rebelt themselves. They had passed into full daylight twenty minutes ago. As they came over the valley of the Linth past the mountains, the time was 11:35 a.m., Monday. The sky was clear, and the ground temperature in the city was 71°F. Lake Zurich sparkled blue and was colorful with white, red, green, and blue sails. Caird had seen tapes showing the freshwater dolphins which populated the lake. Their ancestors had been brought here a thousand obyears ago. They were recognized as sentients and had the same civil rights as humans though they were not allowed to vote. Their chief, however, representing the porpoise council, dealt with a representative of the Nonhuman Interface Department. There were seven human representatives, one for each day, since the porpoises did not have to adhere to the once-a-week schedule.

The city was still located at the northwestern end of the lake. It had no suburbs; the rest of the lakeshore was a public park overseen by rangers. Just at the edge of the city proper was an all-green, many-windowed round tower eighty stories high and a mile and a half in diameter. It was topped by a gigantic pagoda-like structure which bore, at its peak, a rotating globe of Earth. This moved in synchronization with the turning of the planet on its axis. Within the building were the offices and apartments of the administrations for each day of the state of Switzerland and of the world government. It also enclosed all the stores, restaurants, and transportation facilities for the tenants. The city proper, that outside the tower, consisted of small office and apartment buildings, none higher than three stories, and residential houses. These were the famous round houses with doomed roofs that Caird had seen in so many educational tapes. The decorative chimneys on their two sides and the windows, looking so much like eyes above mouths, reminded him of the Neill illustrations of the houses in the land of Oz.

The business of the nontower City of Zurich was mostly tourist trade. Hundreds of thousands of people went there every year. The biggest attraction, aside from touring the tower, was the stoned body of Sin Tzu, son of Wang Shen, the founder of the New Era. It stood on a pedestal in a park near the edge of the lake.

23

The landing field was ten miles from the city and inland from the lake. Part of a mountain had been disintegrated to make room for it. Next to the field was the railroad terminus where tourists, unstoned and stoned, were discharged. The stoned went to a warehouse to wait for their day of reanimation. The unstoned traveled on buses to the city. The field itself was mainly reserved for aircraft on government business. The boat landed near a large round building made of glittering green artificial stone. Since all IDs and the flight plan had been cleared, the passengers were able to land without any questions. The lobby held a lot of people, most of them in uniforms of one department or the other, all talking animatedly.

Caird and the others got into one of the lines at the far end of the room and inserted their ID cards into the slots. The officials of the Tourist Bureau watched the display on the screens, though they did not seem to concentrate on their work.

The procedure went swiftly. Nobody in Simmons's group

had to place their right thumb on the plate for fingerprint comparison with the displayed ID. His ID and rank carried enough weight so that normal procedures could be eliminated.

The TB officers waved them on through, and the group followed Colonel Simmons. They emerged at the opposite side of the building where a bus chartered for his group waited for them. It moved out slowly and silently and soon merged into the traffic on the main highway to Zurich. There were not as many cars as Caird had expected, but the bicycle strips alongside the highway were full of two-wheelers.

The bus left the highway on a ramp and rolled into a side-street. This wound through the park until it came to a parking lot near a large open space. In the center of this was a bronze pedestal on which stood the gorgonized body of Sin Tzu. There were benches for many people scattered through the area and many wagoncarts at which popcorn, sandwiches, ice cream, orgasmo, and drinks were sold. Shortly after the bus discharged its passengers, another bus halted near theirs. A TV crew got out of it. Caird knew that this had been summoned by Simmons through channels which only Simmons knew. That the inevitable organic officer was not with it showed Simmons's foresight. The media people had been ordered there by seemingly legitimate authority.

He had to admire Simmons. The colonel was willing to put his head in the lion's mouth though it was very probable that it would be bitten off. *L'audace, toujours l'audace.*

Simmons was also willing to endanger the heads of other people. That could not be avoided. Would he, Caird, do the same with others if he had such an opportunity? Of course he would.

The head of the TV crew, a tall slender brunette, spoke to Simmons. During the intense exchange, the brunette looked both puzzled and upset. Finally, after some more words from Simmons, none of which Caird could hear, she nodded. She wheeled and walked away and spoke to her crew. They raised their eyebrows and some seemed to be protesting, but they followed Simmons and his group toward the center of the park. The tourists and the loungers drifted toward them, knowing something was up but not what. There were many children among them. Quite a few adults had cameras. These would be recording the event. The ganks, when they came, would try to confiscate all the citizens' cameras, but they would probably not succeed unless they arrested everybody. In any event, they could not blank out the viewers' memories. The ganks would try to keep them from talking about what they had seen. Some would be scared enough to be silent. Others would talk because they had been forbidden to do so.

The two groups halted when Simmons stopped in front of the body of Sin Tzu. The TV people, each holding a small square camera, spread out to catch the action from all sides. Three of them kept the increasing crowd from intruding upon the area around the monument. This was to be taboo ground, though they probably did not know why. The onlookers, well-conditioned to obey the orders of the media, stayed within the invisible bounds. They were both observing and taking part in a ritual. This one, however, was also a mystery. Thus, it was like a religious ceremony of which the viewer does not know the true meaning but which, for that very reason, is much more enthralling.

Sin Tzu, stoned for eternity or for long enough to pass for it, stood on a tall bronze pedestal. He was in the green robes, also stoned, of the Supreme World Councillor, a title no one had held since him. He faced outwards, his back to the city, his open eyes on the mountains across the lake. His features were "pure" Mongolian, seldom seen now because of the intensive hybridization encouraged by the government. But a grandfather had been Scots; a grandmother, Punjabi. His bare head and hands had been painted with lifelike colors to cover the gray of the stoned. His straight sleek hair was black; his eyes, black; his skin, light gold. One hand, extended, held on its palm a large globe representing Earth, its one side bearing raised letters: PAX. On all four sides of the pedestal were bronze plaques with only his name in English and Loglan letters and in Chinese characters.

Supersonic transmitters placed within the tops of the four corners of the pedestal kept pigeons from roosting on him.

Simmons looked up at Sin Tzu for a moment, then turned away. Perhaps he was thinking that he would some day rank with Sin Tzu. Simmons's gorgonized body would be standing on a pedestal while tourists gawked and exclaimed around him and ate popcorn and eggrolls, and music, as now, was welling from a distant merry-go-round.

Caird, while also contemplating Sin Tzu, had been opening his shoulderbag, now placed on the paving near the base of the pedestal. The others of his group were doing the same. He pulled out what looked like a very long rope but was a chain of stoned metal covered with brown material to insulate against the coldness of the links. Attached to one end of the chain was a very thin belt of the same insulated metal. He placed the belt around his waist and tightened it until it hurt him. Then he pushed one end of the belt into a snap-lock and twirled the tiny dial over the lock.

Now, only one person who knew the combination could unlock the belt.

Working swiftly, he threw the free end of the chain up and over the top of the pedestal. Someone on the other side picked the chain up and cast it over the pedestal, and Caird threw the chain back and up. He also helped wrap the chains of others around the feet of Sin Tzu's body. In two minutes, all the chains had been coiled around the ankles of Sin Tzu, and the free ends were thrust into snaplocks on belts and the dials over each secured end had been spun.

The entire group was chained to the corpse of the founder of the New Era.

The cameras of the TV crew and of the spectators had been recording every move.

Simmons had planted some of his people among the crowd. These would be filming with microcameras disguised as buttons or ornaments.

Now, Simmons, facing the tower, shouted, "Attention, citizens! Attention, citizens! I am Colonel Kieth Alan Simmons of Tuesday's Organic Department of Los Angeles State, North American Ministering Organ! This woman"—he pointed at Snick—"is the fugitive and alleged criminal, Panthea Pao Snick! This man" —he pointed at Caird—"is also a fugitive and alleged criminal! You have seen his face and biodata on the screen many times! He is Jefferson Cervantes Caird!"

He paused briefly. From far away came the wailings of sirens. They were on organic surface-vehicles speeding this way, closer than the sound level indicated because the wind was blowing inland from the lake. Airboats, orange lights flashing, were swooping down from the tower. A dozen others were coming in from the precinct stations of the city proper.

Simmons bellowed, "You know how the government, the World Councillors and all their henchpeople, has been lying to you! Manipulating you, the citizens, for the benefit of themselves! You have seen Caird's messages exposing the plot to keep from you the age-slowing elixir but to use it for the high officials so that they could live seven times longer than you, the abused citizens of the misnamed Commonwealth of Earth!"

The first airboat to arrive was settling down on the edge of the paved area around the body of Sin Tzu. It held six ganks whose bulb-nosed guns were in their hands.

Caird felt very excited but very cold. Was his skin as pale as all of the group, except for red-faced Simmons?

Now, another airboat was close to touching the ground on the opposite side of the circle.

Some spectators were walking away. The others seemed unable to rip themselves loose from what they knew was quickly going to be a troubled place. Those who had cameras were still recording.

"We have chained ourselves to Sin Tzu and will remain here until our demands and our cause, your cause, are vindicated!" Simmons shouted. "We do it as a protest against the fraud, corruption, and heinously illegal activities of the government! We do it even though we know we will be arrested! We want this event to be public, and we demand that our trial be public, that the whole world gets an opportunity to see it! We petition that the public closely monitor the trial and protest if the government ignores our rights! We ask that . . ."

An organic general, splendid in bright green uniform, gold braid, epaulets, and a plumed helmet, strode up to Caird. His long narrow face was set in anger, and his skin was as pale as that of the chained. The progun in his hand pointed at Simmons. He shouted, "Colonel Simmons, I arrest you in the name of the Commonwealth and the World Council! You will desist from and cease your subversive speech! You others"—he waved his free hand— "are also under arrest under the same charges: conspiracy to subvert the government, daybreaking, flight to avoid arrest, resisting arrest, sabotage, dissemination of illegal and subversive pseudodata, inciting to riot, inflammatory and false statements against the constituted authority, illegal use of databanks, insertion of false data in the banks, and . . ."

He paused to catch his breath and also to emphasize the final charge.

". . . murder!"

Caird thought, He didn't even mention the blackouts of L.A. But he or others will get to it.

Two more airboats had touched ground. At least twenty organic vehicles were present, and more were coming. The ganks were already demanding that those citizens who had cameras surrender them.

Simmons paid no attention to the general. He kept on repeating his message. By then, however, the loud voices of the ganks and the citizens being rousted tended to drown him out. One brave photographer in the front row around the circle was still busy taking pictures. No gank had gotten to him yet. Then he stopped, removed the tape, a small sphere, from the camera, and put it in his pocket. He dropped the camera, turned, and walked into the swirling and noisy mob.

The organic general, scarlet-faced, boomed, "You will cease talking!"

Simmons broke off his speech to say, just as loudly, "You have not read me my rights!"

"Organics don't have their rights read to them!" the general yelled. "They know them!"

"*We're* not ganks!" Caird said. "You haven't read us our rights!"

"Silence! I demand silence!" the general shouted.

He pressed on the button of his proton gun. The bulb at its top shot a very pale violet light against Simmons's chin. He staggered backward and struck the base of the pedestal, then slumped unconscious, half-upright, against it.

"Organic brutality!" Caird yelled. "Citizens, I testify that all that Colonel Simmons has told you is true! Furthermore, I can add to the data he's presented! I will tell you of many things that the government has unlawfully done, all adverse to your rights and welfare!"

The general pointed the gun at Caird and squeezed the trigger.

24

Caird awoke with a head- and jaw-ache and a dull pain in all of his muscles. The pain was not continuous; it pulsed, a square wave. He was lying on his back on an unpadded table, his head on a thin pillow. A scanning mechanism, its round blank end looking like the eye of God—a rather moronic God—moved back and forth on tracks above him. Ganks stood around the table, watching him and the doctor in her white-and-red uniform. One of them was the general who had stunned him. The only other civilian was a short broad man, about sixty subyears old, with the biggest nose Caird had ever seen.

The doctor said, "You have a headache." It was a statement, not a question. She pressed a syringe against his bare upper right arm. Within a few seconds, the pains receded like a tide waning.

He lifted his arms, then felt around his waist. The belt and the chains were gone. They could not be cut with a maser or proton beam, which meant that they had used a frequency-scanner to determine the combination of the locks.

The wallscreens, of course, were recording everything in the room, and three ganks were using cameras.

The man with the big nose pushed his way through the others to the table. He took Caird's hand in big cool hands and said, "I'm your attorney, Citizen Caird. Nels Lupescu Bearss, of the firm Shin, Nguma, and Bearss, and I come high. But I've volunteered to represent you, and I'm not charging you one credit. The World Council has accepted me as your representative, as they damn well better do."

His voice was deep, resonant, and flowing.

"Thanks," Caird said. "What about the others?"

"Each has his own lawyer."

"Are they all good ones?"

Bearss let loose of Caird's hand. He smiled wryly, shrugged his shoulders, and said, "Well . . ."

The doctor had been looking at the panel-insert on a wallscreen. This was displaying the probings of the machine moving above Caird. She said, "He can be taken to the cell now."

"Aren't you even going to bother to ask me how I feel?" Caird said.

The doctor looked surprised. She pointed at the screen and said, "Why?"

Bearss raised his nose and looked along it at her. "Why, indeed? We need no personal interest here, no compassion or tenderness, heh? Let the machine speak! Lo, having spoke, let it be the divine word! Does God have any loose connections, any malfunctions? Does God care? Does God thunder down from Mount Sinai via display?"

The doctor's face became red. She said, "It's been double-checked."

"That's enough of this nonsense!" the general said loudly. "Take him to his cell!"

"I have a right to confer with my attorney," Caird said.

"All your rights will be scrupulously respected!"

Two ganks took hold of Caird's shoulders and raised him

to a sitting position. When he got to his feet, he found that, though the pain was gone, he was weak. Nevertheless, he said, "I can walk without help." He laughed softly. "And I'm in no condition to run away. Again."

Bearss walked closely behind Caird as the group walked down the hall past many closed doors. Caird knew that the wall-screens were monitoring everything in the hall. He would not be out of sight of the cameras for a second except in the bathroom. And he was not sure that he would not be observed in it. There would be many other means for making sure that he did not escape, but it did not matter. He had not come here to try to break free later.

He called back over his shoulder. "Citizen Bearss, you're my lawyer for today? Do you know who's my lawyer tomorrow?"

"I am. I've been given a temporal pass because of the gravity of your alleged crimes. So have the lawyers for your colleagues."

"It'll be a new experience for you," Caird said. "Living every day."

"I look forward to it."

Near the end of the hall, the group halted. A captain went ahead of the group and spoke a codeword to the door. Caird could not hear the word. The door slid to the right into a recess in the wall. Feeling very tired, Caird walked into a large room. Partitions in a corner, open at the top, formed the bathroom walls. There was the usual prison cell sparse furniture, including exercise equipment, but there was no stoner-cylinder. The general spoke of this for the benefit of the public TV viewers, noting that the practice of stoning a prisoner except for certain intervals was not being used here. The prisoner would be given the privilege of consulting with his attorney whenever he felt like doing so, night or day. The general also pointed out all seventy channels, including the news channels available to the prisoner. The law required that the prisoner see these if he wished. While this was going on, Caird sat down in a chair. Then the general spoke directly to the prisoner.

"Citizen Jefferson Cervantes Caird, Prisoner ID Number

ISB–NN–9462–X, have you any complaint to make regarding your arrest and incarceration treatment so far?"

"Yes," Caird said. "It was both unnecessary and brutal to knock me out with a proton beam."

"It was deemed necessary under WCIC–6 to render you unconscious," the general said. "You may register your complaints with your attorney, and these will be considered in the appropriate court at the appropriate time."

He strode out, and all but Bearss followed him. The door slid shut. The lawyer took hold of his huge nose with one hand and squeezed it several times. Perhaps, thought Caird, he was trying to pump courage and confidence from it through a conduit to his brain.

"We don't have much time. Your trial starts tomorrow, ob-tomorrow, at noon. It could be over by five that evening. It would be if this were an ordinary criminal case. The authorities may want to string it out to cover all seven days. Of course, they may just intend to have it over with quickly and show the tapes of the trial on the channels for the remaining days. But I think the bigshots want to get an idea of the public reaction first before they convict you. You've stirred up a storm, my friend."

He chuckled and said, "Never saw anything like it in mod-ern history."

"You talk as if the verdict is a printout already."

"Oh, you'll be found guilty, no doubt of that. I'll fight against that the best I can, and I'm good, very good. But the evidence . . ."

He frowned, and he squeezed his nose again. Was he hoping that he would find it smaller than the previous time? Or was he unconsciously trying to compress it? Or did he like to call attention to it; was he, Cyrano de Bergerac-like, proud of it?

He hitched himself forward, pulling the chair with him.

"The prosecuting attorney has informed me of certain mat-ters which she's legally obliged to reveal. She says that the gov-ernment is rigidly determined that the trial will not be made into a public forum. The defendants will not have an opportunity to make speeches of any kind. You won't be able to accuse the government of fraud, corruption, or conspiracy against the people.

"You'll be allowed only to plead guilty or innocent to a few specific charges. You and your colleagues are undoubtedly guilty in these cases and will be found guilty. You and Snick, for instance, will be charged with false insertion of data and daybreaking. You will also be charged with the attacks against the power centers of L.A. and the thermionic centers and of causing great inconvenience and distress and suffering for the citizens of Los Angeles and South California. Your reasons for committing these crimes will not be raised during the trial."

"You can't do anything about their gagging us?" Caird said.

"Oh, I'll object, and I'll appeal! But I won't get anywhere. I'll be informed by the judges that the reasons for your crimes are irrelevant during legal process. The reasons are properly relevant only to the therapy the psychicists in the rehabilitation institution will give you."

"Then the sentence is predetermined?"

"In that you won't be sentenced to immediate gorgonization, yes. Whether or not the psychicists will find you unrehabilitable . . . I was not told. Theoretically, of course, the results of the therapy won't be known until you've had it. It may well be that the government doesn't consider it necessary to stone you and leave you to the future to deal with you. That is, if therapeutic techniques are invented which could heal you, then . . ."

"I know that," Caird said. "But what about the TV messages I sent accusing the government of lying to the people, the frauds it committed? If these aren't brought up, the public will wonder why they weren't."

Bearss pumped his nose and looked thoughtful. Whatever was going on in his head, he evidently found it painful.

"The messages won't be in the indictments. But the government intends to clear up that matter. You didn't have a chance to know about it, of course, but a statement has already been

197

released on the news channels. You can see them on replays if you ask for them. The government claims that it has just uncovered the truth about World Councillor Ananda, born as Gilbert Ching Immerman. The whole sordid and vicious story, sordid and vicious are its words, has been revealed. Your connections and activities as a member of the immers has also been revealed. But you won't be charged with any of these. Thus, any testimony you might have that might be damaging to the government will not be put on public record."

"So much for Simmons's plan," Caird said. "But what's it going to do about the ASF? That's something the public isn't going to let loose without a hell of a struggle."

"The government has admitted that it was in error about that. The ASF has been found to be what you claimed it was. Therefore, ASF will be given to any citizen who wants it. You can bet your life that no one is going to refuse it. A lot of citizens resent not having it when they were younger, and they blame the immers for keeping ASF to themselves. I understand—the prosecuting attorney told me this—that you've lost a lot of sympathy from the public because you were part of the elitist conspiracy to keep it from the public."

"There was a good reason for that," Caird said.

"Try justifying it to those who feel cheated. You can include me among them. My life span is going to be lengthened, but it'd have been lengthened much more if I'd had ASF when I was twenty-one."

"Feeling that way, maybe you shouldn't be my lawyer."

"I'm a professional," Bearss said. "Anyway, you won't be charged with concealing ASF and keeping it from use for the public good. So, I'm not involved with that particular element of this case. It's the public that'll be condemning you for that, not the government."

"Then the revolution is a lost cause?"

Bearss smiled as if he took pleasure in answering. "No, it's not. You started something that may have lost momentum in certain respects. But the people are still aroused. You see, the Council has also admitted that the world population is, in fact, as you claimed, only two billion, not ten billion. The head of the Bureau of Population Data and some of his higher officials have been charged with conspiracy to deceive the government and the people with false data."

"For God's sake!" Caird said. "Things have been happening fast!"

"Much faster than they should given the normal slowness of events," Bearss said. He smiled wickedly. "Obviously, it's . . ."

"A setup!" Caird said.

Bearss looked a trifle annoyed at having been interrupted.

"What can I do? If I accuse the government of this, I'll be put on trial while I'm theoretically trying the government. I won't be able to prove a thing, and I'll end up as a rehab."

Bearss shrugged. "I'm a cynic. All lawyers are cynics. It wasn't the practice of law that made me a cynic. I was born one. Only cynics go into law."

After a short silence, Caird said, "Snick was framed by the government—or maybe by Ananda alone—to keep her mouth shut and cover up fraud by the government. That won't be brought up during her trial, of course."

"If she insists on telling about it despite the court's orders not to, she'll be taken back to her cell."

"But the public will be viewing the entire trial procedures. They'll hear her initial objections."

"Not more than a few words. The sound will be turned off, and the public won't hear more than the beginning of her protests. That's legal, since the court will deem her statements irrelevant. She'll be taken away and kept in her room until she agrees to stick to only what the court says is relevant. If she refuses, the trial will go on without her. She'll still have the right to watch the trial on TV, but she won't be able to testify."

"The others? Simmons? The Cloyds?"

"The same. Charged with conspiracy to subvert the government and illegal flight from Los Angeles to Zurich. The filming of the chaining of the conspirators to Sin Tzu's monument, by the way, has been displayed worldwide. The government has freely permitted it. It's smart. It knew that the public was going to see it illegally, and it wanted to avoid accusations of free speech-and-viewing suppression."

Caird shook his head in wonder. "The murder charges against us have been dropped?"

"The government doesn't need them to convict you. It's also afraid that it might not be able to prevent testimony which would reveal that it itself isn't innocent. Murder is the most serious charge on the books, and it might be difficult to insist on irrelevancy in this matter."

"Do you advise that I plead guilty immediately?"

25

"Well," Bearss said slowly. "Your case is unique and unusually difficult. Difficult for the government, that is. Your ability to resist TM is well-known. It's claimed that you can lie when under it even though you're unconscious."

"True," Caird said.

"The court knows this has been established, but you'll have to be TMed again to establish that you have not lost that ability. I'll insist, as is our right, that the test be witnessed by myself and several others, scientists whom I know, or rather believe, to be objective. The test will be filmed, of course. That puts the government in a quandary. To prove you're lying, it'll have to ask you certain questions about certain items. These have to be events which the government knows did exist. For example, you did attack the power centers. You'll admit this. There's no sense in your lying about them.

"You'll also be asked if certain things happened which did not happen. You'll deny that these did happen.

"You won't be questioned about anything which happened in your previous personae. The repetition of the TM test will establish that you do not remember these. Or, at least, very little of them and nothing legally significant.

"It won't question you about any period of your life except that starting with your escape from the Manhattan institution. That period of time after you had created the persona you thought of as Duncan."

Bearss pulled the chair closer. His nose was only a few inches from Caird's. His smile looked like the half-moon.

"Heretofore, the report on the TM interrogation has always been the basis of conviction. If the TM showed that the prisoner was innocent, the court automatically decreed the innocence and release of the prisoner. If the TM showed that the prisoner was guilty, the opposite was decreed.

"But, for the first time, a person has been accused of crimes who can deny his guilt even if he's guilty. I'll be presenting that to the court, and they know I will. They have to be working on that problem right now. I'll insist that your case is unprecedented. Therefore, new precedents will have to be decided upon, and these will become law. Your case will be delayed until these are settled."

"Will that do me any good in the long run?" Caird said. "Won't they have to revert to the ancient system of trial by jury? Decide on the basis of evidence?"

"Yes, they will. But it won't matter in the end. There's no doubt that you did steal an organic airboat and destroyed the power centers. The court judges will try to make your admission of guilt while under TM to be sufficient. They'll consider that admission to be enough to conduct the trial very quickly and under present law. But I'll insist that you have the ability to lie when TMed. The fact that you admitted to the destruction will then have no bearing on your guilt or innocence. There must then be a trial even though everybody knows that you are guilty."

Caird said, "I'm going to let you in on a secret if you'll pass it on to the lawyers defending Snick and Simmons and the others."

Bearss hummed, cocked his head, rolled his eyes, and grimaced. Then he said, "All right. I promise."

"I'm not the only one who can lie under TM. My ability is natural. But Simmons, Snick, all those on trial—they've been injected with anti-TM."

Bearss rose from the chair as if he had suddenly been made weightless. "What?!"

"All of us," Caird said. "And that anti-TM is being distributed throughout the OMC and God knows how many other organizations."

Bearss began pacing back and forth, his hand on his nose. "Blackstone preserve us!"

"Who?"

"Blackstone was an ancient English jurist. Never mind. My God! Do you realize the implications of this? Of course you do! You'll all have to be tried according to the ancient rules of trial by jury, by a panel of judges, anyway. And this anti-TM, it's going to become public knowledge some day. The people are going to demand it, and they'll get it lawfully or not. Think what that's going to do to the judicial system!"

Though he had been startled by the news, he did not seem to be displeased. Caird understood his reaction. This development was going to make more work for the lawyers and a demand for more lawyers.

"You know," Bearss said, his hands now rubbing each other, "you'll be a martyr. But you can console yourself knowing that you have begot a revolution. Eventually, the New Era system will have to be abolished. The ASF is going to cause tremendous social, psychological, and population changes. The anti-TM is going to alter our legal and judicial setup considerably. I can foresee a lot of changes, but there'll be many no one'll be able to predict. Not even their godly computers."

"It's not a great consolation," Caird said. "To know you've caused interesting times doesn't salve the sorrow of knowing you won't share in the excitement."

"We must always try to make the best of it," Bearss said. He sat down again. "Now. I think you should plead innocent. Make them work a little and put off the sentencing. Don't you agree?"

"Innocent it is," Caird said.

"Your mental stability, if you'll pardon my using that term, will be entered for consideration by the court. It should moderate the severity of your sentence."

"Nothing doing," Caird said. "That's a copout, a betrayal of all I've fought for. I forbid you to use that excuse."

"Very well, though I believe that you're throwing away your chances to get out lightly. In any event, you'll be going to a rehab unit. The government's reasoning is that, if you're antisocial, you must be a psychopath, or, at least, highly neurotic. Since the government determines whether or not a psychicist's recommendation that a patient be released as cured is to be honored . . ."

He raised his hands, palms up. "You might be in for a long, long time. You might even be judged incurable and, thus, will be gorgonized."

"That may be. Do you know what really burns me? I voluntarily became an immer. But Snick, she was just doing her job, yet she got railroaded because of it. No one but a wimp would've accepted the injustice, and she's anything but that. Of course she became an outlaw! Wouldn't you?"

Bearss gingerly felt the bulbous end of his nose as if he had just discovered a strange growth.

"It's possible that the bench, if it has a conscience, will consider that. But that depends on whether or not the judges know the circumstances of her illegal punishment. They probably haven't been made privy to that data. And there's no way it's going to come out in court."

"If I ever get free," Caird said, "I'm going to make it my life's work to make sure that, one way or another, everybody will learn the truth about her. She'll be redeemed somehow or other!"

"You're an ever-bubbling pisspot," Bearss said. "But when

you get into trouble again, hire me. I admire you, though I don't necessarily condone everything you've done."

He stopped walking. "We're agreed on your plea?"

"You don't have to ask again."

"I'll see you in court tomorrow."

He spoke a codeword to the wall. A pictureless screen glowed into life.

"We're through conferring," he said. "You may TM my client now."

"They'll be here to start the questioning in a few seconds," he said. "It's just a formality to validate . . ."

"I know. I heard you the first time," Caird said.

"I'll be here throughout the procedure to protect you against any hanky-panky. Two supposedly objective psychicists will also be present."

"Remember your promise."

The general, three officers, two psychicists, and the TM specialist entered. Duncan stretched out on the sofa as ordered. The specialist, a middle-aged woman, sprayed the mist in his face. He went down into the blackness with his answers prepared. Any questions they might ask which he had not reviewed in his mind would not matter. Somehow, his unconscious took over and replied as he would if he were awake.

This time, his mind was not as blank as if he had been stoned. He dreamed.

He knew that he was dreaming. He also knew that he was doing what he had not considered doing and did not want to do.

Something, some *thing*, was taking him over. He was helpless to stop it. He, who had always been in supreme control of himself, except for that one time in Manhattan, was governed by an entity or some rebellious part of himself.

Like it or not, and he certainly did not, he was shaping a new persona.

He struggled against the powerful strands that enfolded him as if he were a fly in a spider's web.

The night within became edged with a pale violet light, though there were, in actuality, no edges. It was dawn without a sun unless it could be said that the sun was his brain. The light slowly spread outwards—at the same time, inwards—until the darkness was violet except for a ragged block as dark as basalt in the center which was no center. But the edges of the field became agitated. They were pulsations of a slightly more dark violet, and they flickered into cone shapes, square shapes, and sawtoothed shapes. They were, he knew dimly, his other personae trying to break through. This was when he was consciously trying to shape a new persona, his moment of greatest strength and also his weakest.

Faint voices came up from where there was no up. He recognized them despite their thinness. The original Caird, Tingle, Dunski, Repp, Ohm, Zurvan, and Isharashvili. Last to speak was Duncan. He could not hear what they were saying, but he understood their tones. They were full of rage and frustration and demands that they be allowed to live fully and to possess this body and mind. That was impossible. Only one could live in full ownership and control of this flesh-house born as Caird.

At that moment he thought, I have to kill them all.

The black thing in the center started to bleed color—violet—and to dwindle. It was melting away while the violet field around it became darker and the shapes on the edges swelled, and the voices became stronger. He strove to push back the menacing shapes. The only voice whose words he could make out was that of Duncan, and that was because he was still Duncan. Partly Duncan, anyway. This was the main battle. He became panicky. He realized that if he did not win this fight, he might lose forever. Somehow, those others knew that he was in a very precarious situation and was now very fragile and open.

He gritted his mental teeth. A voice unheard yet powerful rippled the violet field. The shapes on the edges, ever growing, were thrown back, compressed, as if a foot were stepping on them, were whirled around, and then were jammed below the rim of the vision that was not vision.

The voice was not that of God, certainly, but it was like the voice that roared down from Mount Sinai to the trembling Moses. It was one that would not brook nay-saying. It was—whoever he was going to become—speaking like a volcano in full eruption.

The edges were still flickering. The shapes were going away. Darkness was spreading from them, and the flickering was not from the violet but from the slowly oozing outwards—and inwards—of darkness. The black thing in the center was dripping away, a candle burning with spurts of nonlight.

He was losing the battle with himself.

A thought like a ghost floating down the corridor of an ancient castle, an invisible but felt presence, crossed the violet.

His time was short.

That did not mean what it would have meant if he had been in full contact with the exterior world. Time was a concept very difficult to understand here. Yet, it filtered through and brushed across him, the wings of a moth on the face of a sleeper. The touch and the soft residue of moth-powder left behind did not awaken him to the sense of time. It stirred in him the dream of a dream of a dream. The idea of time thrice removed from outer reality.

This had to be done. He did not want it done.

This was being done.

Being . . .

The image in the center, black as the heart of a stone but soft as putty, had quit waning. The flecks of blackness he now saw rotating across the violet—like motes in the eye—were cast back onto the block. A black fire burned through him. The shape—the persona—concealed in that edgeless monolith, was beginning to emerge.

A face crossed both the dark field and the faintly violet block. It was that face which had shot by him before. The child's face. Himself as a very young boy.

It was gone, leaving behind only ripples. It was like a chronon in a cloud chamber except that the face, unlike the time-wave particle itself, could be seen directly.

Ignoring the slowly dying effects, a curtain shaken by a breeze but still flapping, the image of Baker No Wiley, formed from the mass. It would look just like him, like all of the others.

Baker No Wiley? He had never heard that name before.

He was swelling. He was a balloon figure spreading out to block off all the violet light. When he shoved that light out, no rags, no tags, no wisps left, he would be here.

And he, Caird, would be gone.

This was the most painful and hardest act. To give himself up.

Screaming silently, "No! No! No!", he was wrenched and twisted and aflame with pain.

But he—all his personae—could endure hurt and loss, though the amount of tolerance differed. When he had made Duncan, he thought, he must have been thinking of just this necessity. Duncan had a will of vanadium, hard, hard, hard. Still . . .

This was worse than any other time. Then, he had been connected, however spiderweb-weak, with . . . Whom?

The violet light was gone, and now there was the naked and light-brown body of Baker No Wiley before him, the only thing he could see. He dropped with it through illuminationless space, whirling over and over and also rotating around and around. Center, as a concept, was lost. He had no axes, yet he was spinning along all three at once.

The blackness pressed around and on him.

There was light in which his shrieking voice was almost visible.

"No! No! I don't know you! I don't want you!"

Then, nothing. He was stone, one who had seen the Medusa, and was no more conscious than stone.

26

"You've seen all the known records of your life up until now, Jeff," the psychicist said. "Isn't there even the slightest stirring of a memory of any of your previous personae?"

"Not an iota," he said.

He thought of himself as Baker No Wiley. But, since everybody at the rehab center insisted on calling him by his natal name, Jefferson Caird, he answered to it.

He was sitting in a semireclined chair. Above him, the detector machine moved back and forth on its rails. Its sonic, electromagnetic, and laser frequencies probed the top, front, and back of his head and the naked skin on his legs and torso. The psychicist, Doctor Arlene Go-Ling Bruschino, sat facing him. Her gaze flicked from his face to the monitoring display on the wall behind him and back to his face. On the upper part of the wall behind her was a screen which was also registering his expressions. These were on a grid and were being analyzed by the computer. Next to the screen

209

behind him was another which was reading out the interpretation of his facial movements and the frequency changes of his voice.

The machine above also had a sniffer which analyzed the molecules rising from his body. Its computer was alert for any change which might indicate that he was fearful of lying. This was still used though he had proved to her that he could put himself into a "fugue" and make his body emit the particles of the fearing and the lying man. He could turn them off and on almost as swiftly as pressing a button. That had impressed Bruschino, but she could not understand why he was able to do it. She had said that he should not be able to remember how to do it.

"But, Arlene," he had said, "it's true that I have no memories of my former identities. I also am unable to create any new personae. I've tried many times since I came here and have failed. But I have somehow retained some of these powers, including the ability to lie when TMed."

They were now in the big room where he spent several hours each Tuesday. To his left was a big window looking out upon a sprawling meadow which ended in a sudden drop. When he turned his head, he could see parts of the valley below. On its other side reared a steep-sided mountain with fir trees on its lower slope, rock in the middle, and snow on the peak. He had no idea where he was except that he was probably in an upper temperate-zone or lower arctic state. Though he was allowed to mix with the other rehabilitation patients, he could learn nothing from them about their location. Like him, they had been shipped here stoned.

Arlene Bruschino was a middle-aged very pretty, blue-eyed blonde. Her long hair was coiled in a Psyche knot through which was stuck a silvery pin with a large artificial diamond on one end. The neck pendant was a twelve-rayed star in the center of which was her ID card. It was concealed by a silvery boss in the shape of a labyrinth in the middle of which was a minotaur's head, half human, half bull. Any of the twelve tips of the ornament could be inserted into a transmitting-receiving machine to read off or insert data into the card.

She was wearing a white see-through midriff blouse with a high-necked lace collar, a green calf-length skirt, and sandals. From the few answers to his many questions about her personal life, he had learned that she was living with two men. She had said, laughing, that she had a big enough love to encompass more than two males and her two children.

"Yes, and breasts big enough, too," Caird had said.

That had made her laugh even more.

One end of the cruising machine above Caird was pointed toward Arlene. That was registering her own neural and metabolic changes during the therapy. During these sessions, the psychicist needed to know her own subtle responses. But Bruschino was at ease and not filled with fear. The psychicist in Manhattan, Arszenti, had been afraid that she had learned from Caird too much about the government's illegal activities and that the authorities would dispose of her when she was no longer treating Caird. Caird, of course, did not remember that. Arlene, having seen the tapes of Caird and Arszenti, had told him about them. She had not been at all reticent about revealing what she thought was significant. He had asked her what had happened to Arszenti. She had wrinkled her brow and said, "I do not know. But you can be sure that she did not suffer. Otherwise, the tapes would never have been given to me."

"I'm not so sure," he had said.

He again looked through the window. It was early summer out there. Daisies and other flowers the names of which he did not know sprinkled the meadow. Deer browsed along its edges. They were small creatures, brown with large white spots. A large dark bird, too far away to be defined as either a hawk or eagle, soared on an updraft. The snows on the mountain tip were dazzling from the late afternoon sun. At one time, before the coming of this warm era, the snows would have been down to the midline of the mountain. Or so an inmate had told him.

"I don't need the machine to convince me you're telling the truth," she said. "As you know it, anyway."

"So, what do we do now?"

"I sent in my report validating that you are now another persona who IDs himself as Baker No Wiley," Arlene said. "In the normal course of bureaucratic events, the report would be studied by a panel of psychicists and organics. You might even be required to submit to some examinations by other psychicists. But you would then be given a battery of tests and released. These final tests would determine what your trade or profession should be, and you'd be sent somewhere to start life anew."

She leaned forward. Her hand came across the small table between them and floated gently onto his.

"The trouble is that you are like no other patient any rehab center has ever had. You claim that you are now unable to form a new persona. But you can still lie when TMed or injected with other drugs. The government can't be sure you won't revert to a previous persona or create a new one."

She sighed and withdrew her hand.

"However, I have suggested that you be handled just as any other rehab would be."

She flashed a smile.

"I've told them that, in my opinion, you will make a good citizen. But, since you're not a genuine rehab candidate, just a newborn baby who is able to speak his native language fluently, you should go to an English-speaking country. You'd have a wide choice of locations and climates. Of course, you can't get work as an organic, and I wouldn't advise religion as a profession. It doesn't pay, and the government would not believe in your total rehabilitation if you were a religionist."

"That's not an element in my character," Caird said.

"It is, but it's buried," she said. "You once were a street preacher—when you were the persona of Father Tom Zurvan. Anyway, you could go back to college and get a new profession. Your education would be free."

"What's the use of speculating about a new life if there is, as yet, no assurance I'll be freed?"

"Freed? That makes this place sound like a prison. We prefer to say you'll be discharged."

Caird smiled, and he said, "Do you believe that?"

"It's not really a prison. You're not sentenced to a determinate number of years. When you get out depends on you."

"Maybe for others. Not for me."

"That's not true. For one thing, if you were released, you'd be a bright cursor for the government. It could point to you as a prime example of its humane policies."

"The curser who became a cursor," he said.

She smiled, but she said, "Ugh!"

"Sorry. I should have eliminated that deplorable program for puns, I guess."

He had no hard-disk memory of his lives as a subversive, but all the tapes he had seen had given him an excellent diskette memory. He had no desire to do anything but cooperate with society, a government euphemism for itself. That is, it was a euphemism if one of his fellow rehabs, Donna Cloyd, was correct. He saw her now and then in the nutrition hall and on the exercise yard. She claimed to have known him in Los Angeles and to have accompanied him to Zurich. He believed her since he had seen her in the tapes of the chainings at the Sin Tzu monument. She still was not altogether real to him. Though he could touch her, see her sweat, hear her laugh, he regarded her as a TV simulation.

That was one of his problems, perhaps the greatest. Nobody was real. He expected the people here to fade out at any moment. They never did, but his feeling that they would or could do so was always with him.

The only one he had revealed this to was Arlene Bruschino. She had done some work with him on the "alienation," as she called it. Though she had not stressed it, she probably was convinced that he could not be discharged until the "distancing" was solved. That is, until he regained his sense of the hardness and permanence of things and people.

He had told her that, sometimes, he saw her, not as a very

beautiful and desirable woman but as a pattern of atoms. She had a form, but its edges were fuzzy. She was enclosed and protected by an electromagnetic field which, at any moment, could fail. Then she would expand outward and become a bright chaos.

That disturbed him but at the same time was comforting. He could not get close to her or to anybody. He could not be hurt when he saw others as simulations that could be turned off.

Yet, what caused this fugue? To this question, she had suggested that he had rebuilt his persona too many times.

"Analogous to the site of ancient Troy," she had said. "You know about Troy?"

"I remember Homer's works. That's peculiar because I don't remember in what persona I was when I learned about him."

"Troy was only one in a long series of cities on the same site. The first people to live on it were Old Stone Age tribes. Their artifacts were covered over by succeeding occupants. The little hamlets became villages and then towns and then cities. Each was build on top of its predecessor. You're a living Troy. You've built one persona after another, one on top of the other. Only the latest, like the final Troy, is visible, aboveground. But all the others are there beneath that persona you call Baker No Wiley."

"What're you trying to say? The final city was not influenced by those beneath it. As far as I know, anyway."

"No analogy is perfect. Besides, I'm not sure that it wasn't affected. There's such a thing as psychic influence."

"You, a scientist, believe that?"

"I don't believe or disbelieve. It's possible, though not at all proven. However, in your case . . . Suppose that the final Troy, your Troy, was undermined. It has a shaky foundation which an earthquake rocks, and the subterranean tunnels and caves collapse. That makes the effects of the earthquake worse than they would otherwise have been. You . . ."

"I was subjected to an earthquake, in a manner of speaking, when this persona came into being? You notice I say 'came into being.' I feel strongly, though I can't prove it, that I didn't make Baker No Wiley. It was forced on me."

"Who did the forcing? Anyway, you succeeded in making a new self. But you had put too much storm and stress on your self . . . your previous selves. Something went wrong, I don't know what, as yet. May never know."

She leaned forward again and took his hand. It felt cool and soft, but it was too light. He saw it float; it would rise if the arm attached to it did not give it added weight.

"You have played with reality, your basic person, too long and too severely. Now, you have paid the price, and you're out of credits. Your psyche does not want to have much to do with reality. *You* don't want to have much to do with it."

"Maybe it's not reality as we usually know it that I see," Caird said. "There are different levels of it. I see the atomic level. My gaze pierces through the reality I was born to see and perceives the other kind. One of the other kinds."

"You don't really *see* us as a dance of atoms?" she said. "It's just a mental image, isn't it?"

"Most of the time. Sometimes, I see . . . there's a shift, as if my eyes had switched to another state. I see the molecular saraband moving within its electromagnetic field. It's very disconcerting . . . or was. You can get used to anything, well, most things."

"You're not lying, I think. Why should you?"

"Why should I?"

She removed the hand and sat back.

"It's possible that you'd like to be classified as a permanently mentally ill person."

"Why?"

"Because you cannot face reality. Or I should perhaps phrase that cliché differently. You don't want to deal with human beings. Tell me, when you look out the window and see the deer, do you ever see them as atoms?"

"No," he said slowly.

"Have you ever looked into a mirror or at a tape of yourself and seen yourself as a configuration of particles?"

"Not yet."

"It's possible that you feel, unconsciously, that *you* are the configuration, not the people you see. But you reverse the bottom-line psychology because you could not, for some reason, bear that. You project; you see a mirror image of yourself in others. They are not the enclosed atoms. You are."

He shrugged, "It's possible."

"Think about it. Also think about why you consider that possibility so calmly. Many patients would find it upsetting."

"It's my nature," he said, "this persona's, anyway, to look at both sides of an argument. Still, there can be only one truth. All that stuff about there being many truths is nonsense. Truths don't have clones."

"Ah!" she said, sitting up straighter. "What does that mean?"

"What does what mean?"

"That truths don't have clones."

"I really don't know," he said. "It just popped out. But what I said must be true." He laughed. "Unless what I said was a clone of the truth, and I'm wrong. But that's silly, isn't it?"

"Silly?"

He felt vaguely uncomfortable. He knew that when a patient said that his remark was silly, he was getting too close to something he wanted to avoid. At least, that was what Bruschino had told him, and he had read the same comment in one of the tapes on psychics transmitted to his room from the library.

"If it means anything, I don't have the slightest idea what," he said.

Abruptly, she switched to another subject. Or was it linked to the previous in some way she could see but he could not?

She clasped her hands and pressed them against her chest.

She looked as if she had captured a truth, or an intimation of a truth, a rare bird she wanted to warm against her breasts.

"As you know," Arlene Bruschino said, "I've studied the tapes that Doctor Arszenti made when she was treating you in Manhattan. Also . . ."

"Some of the tapes she made. I doubt that you were given all of them. The government . . ."

"Please don't interrupt," she said. "Also, the tapes made when the psychicist treated you starting when you were three and ending when you were six years old. You were a very timid and shy child, almost pathologically so, according to the reports, though I myself think that was far too strong a judgement.

"Then, suddenly, almost overnight, as it were, you became a very gregarious, aggressive, and outgoing child. This was at the edge of five . . ."

"You let me see the tapes," he said. "They didn't stir up any memories. It was like watching a stranger."

"They stirred up something," Bruschino said. "The detectors showed that. But you shut your reaction down. Anyway, your childhood psychicist was thoroughly puzzled by the change in you. Another psychicist did a followup study when you were twenty-two, shortly after your parents died. She reported you as more courageous and aggressive than the median citizen type. But the psychicist who examined you when you applied for entrance to the organics academy liked that."

Her eyes, which had been directed to the screen behind him, now looked at his face. "No perceptible reaction," she said. "But I believe that you are reacting way down there, deep."

She glanced at the wall digital display behind him.

"Five minutes past our time."

They both stood up. He said, "It must be tough dealing with a patient who doesn't have any childhood. And tougher if he doesn't have any adulthood to remember, yet he's not a genuine amnesiac."

"I've never had a tougher," she said. "I'm thankful for you. There are no boring cases, as far as I'm concerned. But some do get a little wearying, and most are not out of the usual. You're a unique. I'm not sure . . ."

He said, "Why the hesitation, Arlene?"

"It could be you're a mental mutant."

"Meaning you have no precedents for treating me?"

"Perhaps. No. You're right. I don't. That makes you a tremendous challenge, and . . ."

"My case will make you famous."

She laughed, and she said, "I'll confess I do think about that. But it's not overpowering me. No, the main thing is that you're unique and quite unexpected. You can't be classified as a schizophrenic. I really don't know yet how to classify you."

"How about really fucked-up?"

She was still laughing when he left the room.

He did not feel like laughing. As soon as the door slid shut behind him, he was out of the sunshine and laughter, her radiance, and closed in by the darkness. The Leviathan had swallowed him. Trapped in its lightness and oppressive stomach, he was being reshaped by its acids.

27

A political revolution, according to the dictionary tape, was the overthrow of a government, form of government, or social system, with another taking its place.

The government of the Commonwealth of Earth had not been overthrown nor had its form changed.

Caird had viewed everything available to him about the "revolution." Though the TV news and the documentary tapes showed only a minute part of the "unrest," they made it evident that at least a large minority of the world's citizens had been and still were actively protesting against the government. If TV displayed a score of petitions, mass demonstrations, riots, and spraying of paint on street monitors by various groups, it refrained from showing a thousand. But the Big G had ridden out the storm, though it was not yet safe in harbor. Other storms boiled on the horizon.

It was also through the tapes that he found out the fates of those with whom he was supposed to have been intimately involved in his crimes. Caird had had no trial because of his precipitous profound psychic disturbance, as the newsheads termed it. The other alleged conspirators had been quickly dealt with, though not as swiftly as the courts had expected. The discovery that the accused had been injected with anti-TM had forced a change in legal procedures. Nevertheless, the overpowering evidence against them had resulted in their convictions. They, like him, were in institutions and subject to death or stoning if they were judged unrehabilitable.

All were strangers, evoking not a flicker of recognition in him. One woman, however, his close colleague in crime, according to what he was told, roused a feeling in his chest and groin that was as close to warmth as he could remember ever having. She was Panthea Pao Snick, short, only five feet and eight inches tall, slender but with a full bosom, dark-skinned, brown-eyed, with hair as black and sleek as a seal's. Its dutch-boy bob was singularly attractive. Her facial bones were exquisite.

Viewing her, he could believe that she was one person who was more than a simulation, a choreography of atoms.

He had told this to Bruschino. She had said, "She may have been your lover. Whether she was or not, you sound as if you had been in love with her."

"I wish she could be transferred here. I feel as if being with her might help me."

"That might not help *her* therapy. In any event, she can't be transferred, especially when you consider what a dangerous mixture you two were."

Then she said, "That's the first time you've looked disappointed. It's faint, but it's there."

A few subdays later, he found that he could also feel anger. Its outward manifestation did not have the heat of the anger he had seen in others here. It was warm enough, however, to please him that he could feel displeasure. He had just sat down by Donna Cloyd in the dining hall and started to eat his salad. She had turned her head toward him and said, "You know, Jeff, I was very angry with you, very disappointed, too. I thought, still think, you were a traitor. I just could not . . ."

"Traitor! What do you mean? Traitor to whom? To you?"

"Yes. You took the coward's way out. You deliberately became a new person just so the government could not prosecute you for your crimes. You abandoned us to our fates. I never would have thought that you'd do such a thing. It just wasn't consonant with your character. But then, what is your character?"

"I'm sorry that you feel that way," he said. "But I don't know what you're talking about! I have no way to know about it or just why you feel the way you do! Besides I don't think I deliberately did it. It was a . . . well, a breakdown. I had no control over it!"

She grimaced. "If you can't remember anything about it, how can you say you didn't do it on purpose? I felt like killing you, I was so angry! Now, though, I ask myself how I can be angry with you when you aren't you? The answer is, I am disgusted and angry with you, anyway!"

"You really believe that I am . . . was . . . a coward, a traitor?"

"What other explanation is there for what you did?"

"I don't really know. But I have this feeling that I had no control over the change. I can't prove it. But I do feel it."

For some reason, tears were trickling down her cheeks. She had reached up and kissed him quickly on his mouth, then walked away. Puzzled, feeling that he had lost something he could not name, he watched her until she went around the corner at the end of the hall. Then came that same anger, though he did not know why he was angry. A feeling that Donna had been unjust with him? It was going to be a grim life if he did not regain the intensity of emotion which Doctor Arlene Bruschino had assured him was normal and desirable. Without it, she had said, he would be a phantom haunting humanity's corridors. Though as he was now he could not be hurt emotionally to any extent, he could also not enjoy existence. He might as well be dead. Well, she amended, not really. As long as he was alive, he could hope that he would some day get back his full humanness with its quota of tedium, pain, and delight.

"When you lifted yourself by your own bootstraps, as it were, by making yourself Baker No Wiley, you ruptured yourself psychically."

"Do I have to keep telling you I'm sure I wouldn't have done that deliberately?"

"Some part of you did. However, to use another analogy, Baron Frankenstein's hand shook or his mathematical calculations were wrong. Result: a monster."

Why so wan, pale persona? he thought. Instead of becoming a butterfly, you dived back into the cocoon, metamorphosed backwards into the pupa.

The age-slowing elixir would increase his lifespan by seven. That meant that he could live an additional three hundred and fifty subyears—perhaps much more. Did he want to exist—it was not living—for that long in a wraithlike state?

Then he thought, I won't live that long unless the authorities are convinced I'm cured and can be released. They'll only give me so much time to do it. If I fail, I'll be gorgonized.

During the time he was living, unless he battled his way out of his present state, he would be, not on Earth or Heaven or Hell, but in that unworld the ancients called Limbo. He felt the weak semblance of a shudder. He was trekking across a desert and could not turn back because there was no place to which he could return. It was a flat and hard desert with no known waterholes, no oases, and not even mirages. No mirages *so far*. A physical mirage was the deceptive appearance of a distant object caused by the bending of light rays in layers of air of varying density. What was far away could seem to be close. Were mental mirages just the opposite? Could what was close seem far away?

The word *miraj* cometed up from the deep and across the dark skies of his mind.

Momentarily, he forgot about that. The ringing from the

wallscreen called his attention to a summons to the exercise yard. But, before he reached it, *miraj* popped up again out of the pandora's box of memory. He did not know where he had learned its meaning or why. It was just there. *Miraj*. Mohammed's ascension to Heaven. What did that have to do with mirage? Nothing, he thought, except the similar sounds to an English-speaker. It was just one of those puns the trickster hindbrain threw gratis into the conscious.

Or was that all? The trickster never did anything at random. All its actions were connected. What was strummed at one place made a symphony throughout the web even if the hearer received the notes one at a time.

Knowing that did not help him see the connection between mirage and *miraj*. Some day . . .

The days passed, one in seven, though they seemed to be one immediately after another. The Earth circled the sun once. An obyear had passed, and he had lived fifty-two days. The seasons rose and dipped like flags in a parade swiftly marching past the reviewing stand and were gone. He would get up one morning and see the first snow, half an inch thick, on the meadow. The next morning, the following Tuesday, it was two inches deep. Two Tuesdays later, it would be six inches deep, and it stayed at that depth for several Tuesdays. Then it shrank quickly. Two days later, it was gone.

Spring was the strike of a light-green cobra. It was not many days before it suddenly became a deep green. Summer was not as fast-forwarded as spring, but it did not last very long. Autumn put on colors to celebrate the death to come, then seemed overnight to be in the mourning of dead yellow, and then was in white again in a few subweeks.

It would be very pleasant, he thought, to watch the seasons appear slowly. In the New Era, they were like events in a TV program. The editor had ruthlessly cut out the real-life continuity.

His own life was a seldom-varying schedule. Now and then, psychicists, anatomists, physiologists, geneticists, and molecular biologists flew in to probe him. By year's end, every cell, every molecule, every organ, every system had been recorded in three axes and at seven angles. Every firing of every neuron and the circuits of single blood cells through his arterial-venous systems had been taped. The trillions of reactions in him, electrical, chemical, and gestalt, were stored for display and study.

He was completely revealed, as naked as a man could be.

He was still a mystery.

One summer day, the third summer since he had been here, Bruschino said, "If you and I don't get you well soon, you're going to be warehoused. We don't have forever, you know."

"Are you trying to scare me into health of mind?" Caird said.

Bruschino looked sad. "No, far from it. It wouldn't work, anyway. I have reported that you're making progress, which is true. You have made some, and I expect you'll make more. But the state regulates the acceptable rate of progress in criminal rehab candidates. You've been given more time than most because of your regression to another persona. Also, you're a folk hero of sorts, and the state would like to publicize you as a completely rehabbed person."

"Wrong word, regression," he said. "I've gone on, ahead, to another persona. A new one. So how could it be regression?"

"This isn't a game," she said. "The state makes the rules and calls the shots. As of this moment, you are not a completely healthy person. You don't seem to be a danger to the state—I've stressed that in my reports. I doubt that you ever will be, though I can't be one hundred percent certain. But you're not healthy. No healthy person sees others as a lucretian dance of atoms contained within an e-m field. You just don't seem to care about anything. You go through the motions. You're astute enough or cunning enough to act as if you had healthy emotions, with others, I mean. You don't pretend when you're with me. But you're not really fooling the others, you know."

"Or myself," Caird said.

"Myself? Or my *self?*"

"Both."

He was as puzzled by that answer as she was.

The following Tuesday, near the end of a relatively fruitless session, Doctor Bruschino paused, then said, "Colonel Simmons has escaped!"

She looked at his face, then up at the emotion-indicators on the wall behind him.

Caird's blood surged with joy. The tingling throughout his body was something that he had never experienced before. It was not a memory of joy. It was the direct *now* emotion, though, a few seconds later, it did call up memories of emotions or emotions of memories, too fleeting and vague for him to identify the occasions on which they had happened.

"My God!" Bruschino said. "A real emotion! You're not faking it, are you?"

"It was spontaneous," Caird said. "You know I reacted too quickly to be faking it."

"I believe you," she said. "Only . . . you don't remember Colonel Simmons?"

"No. I only know what I've seen of him on the tapes."

"Why would you react so strongly to news of a stranger?"

"I'm a prisoner," he said. "I identify with him, empathize with him."

"If that's true, then you're making more progress than I guessed."

She looked pleased.

"Has he been caught yet?" Caird said.

"Not yet. He will be."

"Maybe."

"Simmons got out of a supposedly escape-proof institution. Only three persons have done that in the last five hundred obyears."

"And I was one of them," Caird said. "I don't remember how I did it, of course."

"You won't get out of *here*. No one has ever done it. Not

225

that I'm worried about you trying. You don't have the desire. If you did, you wouldn't have the fire to carry out any plans you might think of."

The tone of her voice and her expression made him think that she wished that he would at least think about escaping. Then he would be on the path to recovery.

"Do you have any details on how Simmons did it?" he said.

"Those would be known only to the organics. Actually, I'm not supposed to know about Simmons. But I have my sources of information, legitimate sources, of course."

"And you're not supposed to tell me about him, either?"

Arlene waved her hand. "I'm free to do anything which might help you recover. Within reason, of course."

"How about helping me escape?"

She laughed, and she said, "I might describe for you the many security systems which make it impossible for you to get out of here. That, I think, would be permissible. It would discourage you, and thus keep you from even trying."

"Would you?"

She narrowed her eyes and leaned forward.

"Are you really interested? I mean, do you feel excited at all when you think of the possibility?"

"Somewhat," he said. "I like it. I've been bored for a long time, and I'm tired of being shut up. But . . ."

"But what?"

"What would I do even if I could get away? All that out there."

He gestured with his left hand to indicate . . . what? He did not know.

"I don't know much about anything out there, and I really don't want to do anything. Yet . . . I might find something."

"You have to find your self, if you'll pardon the clichè," she said. "That must be done here."

"I have a self."

"Sort of."

"Very well," he said, feeling a low-burning anger. "So, just how do I get it to be *not* sort of?"

After looking above and beyond him, no doubt checking the wall indicators, she said, "You've had no sexual intercourse since you came here. You've not even masturbated. Until last Tuesday, you've never had an oneirogenetic erection. That morning, at 3:06, you had a semierection. You were dreaming. What was that about?"

He hesitated, then said, "It was about you."

Her eyes widened very slightly, and her expression hinted at pleasure. It was a momentary change, but it had been there. He was certain of that. Or was it that he wanted her to be pleased?

"Would you describe it?"

"It was spring, and we were on a hill above a meadow. The sun was bright, and the meadow below was filled with animals of various kinds—cattle, some big bulls, deer, does and big antlered bucks, goats, lots of billygoats, sheep, many rams. They were all gamboling. It seemed to be rutting season. I don't know. I only had a vague impression of that. But someone in the woods on the other side of the hill was playing a flute. And you were doing the dance of the seven veils for me. I was lying on my side watching you. There was a basket of bread and cheese and a flagon of wine by me.

"You removed the veils one by one as you danced . . . suggestively. Then, before you could take off the last veil, I stood up and I, ah, seized you and bore you to the ground. But I only had a hard-on not stiff enough to get it all the way in, and the remaining veil was also an obstacle. I asked you to take it off, but you said I'd have to do that. And I couldn't. I never did. Then the dream faded."

"Were you angry? Frustrated? Keenly disappointed?"

"Somewhat angry, as angry as I'm capable of feeling. Frustrated, yes. Disappointed, but not keenly. You know that 'keenly' is something I don't know the meaning of—not emotionally, anyway."

227

"What do you think about my being the woman in your truncated wet dream?"

He crossed his legs, then wondered if he had a Freudian desire to hide his crotch. Why should he? Nothing was happening. Yet, it was. A very slight warmth and swelling. Like a hot-air balloon that was not fully inflated because the burner had run out of fuel. Or, the balloon had a slit in it and the expanded air was escaping.

"Well. You're easily the most attractive woman in this place. No race there. I don't remember any woman I knew before I came here. Of course, I've seen some beauties on TV, and Panthea Snick, as I've told you, gives me a certain hard-to-define warmth. But you're the only woman I really know, and you're *some* woman."

Her cheeks were slightly flushed, perhaps from embarrassment, which he doubted, or from excitement. Whether the latter was caused by the sexual images or from a hope that they were making therapeutic progress, he could not know. Perhaps it was both.

She looked up past him at the wallscreen. He was momentarily irritated. Why did she persist in trying to get to him via a machine? Why didn't she go directly to him? His face and body language were not enough for her?

Arlene Bruschino said, "Think about it, Jeff. The dream came from your unconscious. The question is, whose unconscious? Wiley's? Caird's? Duncan's? Ohm's? Etcetera?"

"From mine . . . my present self. Whose else?"

"Think about it."

He sat for a while, drank some tea, and frowned a lot. Arlene kept looking from his face to the wall behind him and back again. Finally, he said, "I, my new persona, haven't been in existence long enough to have an unconscious. Not a very developed one, anyway. A nearly empty one, say. But this implies that the unconscious, that sea without shores, can be compartmentalized. Let's see. Caird had the original unconscious. It was all his. Then Caird made Tingle, and Tingle had a pipeline to the unconscious. But most of what was Caird's was denied to him. The two were, however, not completely separate. Then Tingle made Dunski. Or did he? Did Caird make all six of his other personae all at once, one after the other? Or did Caird make Tingle, and Tingle make Dunski, and Dunski make Repp and so on?"

He shook his head.

"I don't know."

The doctor said, "Does it make a difference?"

He raised his chin and slowly lowered it.

"It certainly does, Arley. In just what way, I don't know. Anyway, there was some connection between the compartments. Wiley No Baker dissolved all connections whatsoever. Well, not quite. Sometimes, there are flashes, not very bright, but I don't know if these are just memories or the personae speaking up."

"The strange thing," she said, "is that your Wiley persona kept all the memories you needed to function. You didn't have to be taught a language again. You can read and write, and you know the ins and outs of the mores and customs of your society. You did not forget, for instance, how to handle your fork, knife and spoon or your table manners. All this comes from Caird and the others."

"A man can't live if he has only a conscious mind," Caird said. "He also requires an unconscious. Or, let's say he could live without an unconscious mind, but he'd only be a half-man."

He stood up, hands clenched, and glared at her.

"I am a half-man! A dark reflection of a man in a dark mirror!"

"Not as dark as you were when you came here," she said. "The Caird whom I first met would not have been able to get so angry. You are making progress."

He loosened his fists and sat down. She looked at the wall behind him.

"Time's up. I'll see tomorrow."

"I'll see you *before* then," he said as he headed toward the door.

"What do you mean?"

"In my dreams."

28

"I'll dwell on this very briefly," Doctor Bruschino said. "It's relevant to your ability to change personae, though I confess I don't know in what way. Your sudden metamorphosis in personality, if not in persona, at the age of five. The report of the psychicist, Doctor Heuvelmans, concludes that it was the triumph of free will over genetic determinism. The triumph of free will over genetic determinism! He could not deny that you suffered a strange sea change, as he puts it. But he had no explanations, no theories, as to how you did it. He found it very difficult, he said, to believe that an adult could turn his persona inside out. But a five year old—never. Yet, the facts were evident."

Caird said, "I don't have any more idea than he what happened then. I don't even remember when I was five."

"The memory is down there. But, so far, verbal techniques, pharmaceutical means, neural stimulation and tracking, all have failed to activate your infant memory."

She found that meaningful, and perhaps it was. But he never

thought about it except when she brought the subject up. Whatever that childhood event meant, if anything, he was becoming a little more alive every day. The people around him were getting more solid, less ectoplasmic. He was like crystals precipitating in a liquid. The liquid was his inchoate personality; the crystals were the hard facets emerging from the formlessness.

He was starting to come into being.

Suddenly, he had quit being a loner. He struck up conversations with those whom he always ignored or shied away from. These included the patients, nurses, doctors, attendants, and even the ganks. He also managed to overcome Donna Cloyd's distrust of him. Before long, she was convinced that the man she had blamed as a coward was not in Caird's body. Also, that he had not willingly changed his persona.

One day, Bruschino told him, "You're beginning to come into focus."

Two mornings later, as he entered the session room, he was greeted with a faint odor of PH No. 5. He breathed deeply, feeling the warmth in the pit of his stomach and his groin. For a moment, he stood in the doorway while he reveled in the expensive perfume and its effects. Doctor Arlene Bruschino was standing up and smiling. Her only clothing was a thin and semitransparent light-blue material. The perfume confirmed her intention. PH No. 5 contained laboratory-made pheromones that excited men and women alike.

He said, "I don't need it."

She said, "What?" Then, "Oh, that 5! I know you don't need it, but every little bit helps. Besides, you might need a signal."

"This is the first time in a long time for me," he said huskily as he strode toward her. She came out from behind the desk to meet him halfway. They did not get to the couch; they merged on the floor.

After the second time on the couch, they sat up and drank some wine.

"You were wonderful," he said, breathing hard.

"Thank you. I have long experience and enthusiasm, though I think you outmatched me in enthusiasm. But then I've not been deprived."

"It's been hard on me, no pun intended."

She leaned over and kissed his cheek. "You were quite wonderful yourself."

"I hope we're not being taped," he said. "Though, really, I don't give a damn."

"I made sure the monitors were off. At least, those that I know about weren't on. But you can never tell. However, like you, I don't care."

"Is this just therapy or are you attracted to me?" he said.

"It's both. Therapy, in a way, for me, too. Two men are not enough for me. Oh, most of the time, I'm quite contented. But now and then . . ."

"Am I getting close to the end of the therapy?"

"No. Tomorrow, we go back to regular therapy. I thought you were ripe for a woman, and I was certainly ripe for you. I had some fantasies—I hope you don't mind—while I was moaning and groaning. Was I being screwed by Caird only or were eight others involved? Were the multiple orgasms caused by one penis or multiple penises all at the same time?"

"There was enough to go around for a whole platoon." He laughed. "I'm glad I'm one of those patients it's O.K. for the therapist to have sex with."

"So am I. You know, in ancient days, psychicists would have been horrified at the idea of a therapist going to bed with a patient. But we know better now. Some patients improve if they and the therapists have attained a certain symbiosis. Others . . . no go, don't even think of it. Though it's hard not to think about it."

"And tomorrow?"

"Find a woman for yourself. I got you started."

"Well, I'm not finished yet by any means," he said, touching a breast. "Unless my time's up."

"I've cancelled the other appointments. Your time's up when you can't get it up any more. I'm only jesting, of course. You can talk all you want to when you're through with the couch."

The next day, Caird asked a patient, Briony Lodge, to go to bed with him. But that was after a party in the room of a patient during which they watched a TV seminar show. Normally, partners did not do this unless the program was sexually titillating. But the subject that evening was a debate on whether or not the dayworld system should be abolished.

Caird was sitting in a chair alongside Briony. Both were drinking black russians. Though patients were allowed liquor, unless they were alcoholics, they were given a daily quota of an ounce and a half per hour for four hours—if the therapist permitted it. While they were talking, she had put her hand on his arm, then his thigh, and finally his crotch, though she did not leave it there for long. He had put his hand, moth-light, on her thigh and then, cat-heavy, on her crotch. She not only did not object; she squeezed her legs together on his hand. So far, the socially approved procedure had been followed. The man or woman was to make the first signal that he or she was ready. After that, the man or woman would respond if he or she felt interested.

Caird would have suggested to her that they leave the party now and go to his room. He did want to see the program, but he could have it rerun at any time. However, since the hosts had announced that they had arranged for an extra amount of liquor for their guests, as long as they did not leave the party early, he decided to stay if Briony agreed to that. She did, and so they waited until the show came on.

The INTERIM program originated from Moscow, Tuesday, and was hosted by Ivan Skavar Ataturk. She was a tall slim blonde with knobby knees and a reputation as an intellectual. That is, she depended upon her memory to summon up her obscure references, not upon data displays. Her trademark was a silver cattle prod bearing alto-relief images from classical Greek, Chinese, and Slavic mythology. She never applied the end to guests but sometimes brought it close to their legs. They usually went along with the shtick by pretending fear. Tonight, the talk was about the desirability of breaking up the New Era system and the difficulties in doing so.

It was a high-class show, that is, conducted verbally in Loglan. But, since many people were not fluent in this, subtitles in English and Standard Tuesday Russian were displayed.

Her guests were Stanley Wang Dobroski, first assistant to the Chief of the Ecosystems Bureau; Olga Shin Muller, chief of the Overall Engineering Department, European States; Tanya Alvarez Balgladashi, subassistant to the chief of the Civilian Reconstruction Works Bureau, State of Western Siberia; and Engels Bahadur Tbilisi, first secretary of Transportation Planning.

Ataturk, after the introduction of the theme of discussion and of the guests: "Citizen Dobroski, you have been selected at random to give your opinion first. As the head of the Ecosystems Bureau, you must have definite ideas about tonight's subject. I'm sure you have arranged a certain sequence of scenarios for the tasks your bureau will be faced with if the world goes back to living day-by-day."

Dobroski: "Ahem! Ah, yes, ahem . . . of course. We have not finished our study because of lack of time since we are very busy on current projects. But, given the possibility of such a . . . catastrophe is not the right word . . . such a project of almost overwhelming demands . . . ahem . . . requiring vast amounts of planning, credits, materials, and labor . . . well . . . the planning itself, if such a project should ever come about . . . ahem . . . that is enormous and requires a global . . . worldwide . . . data banking on a gargantuan scale."

Displayed in the subtitles, a definition of *gargantuan*.

Dobroski smiled, baring teeth stained with betel juice.

"It will take subyears before the study of the data is finished. The impact on terrestrial ecosystems must be carefully considered. We want no ecological catastrophes such as the ancients criminally perpetrated. And we . . . ahem . . . have to ensure without the slightest doubt that the vast change from vertical lifesystems, you might say, to horizontal lifesystems, does not undo the work of the past few obmillenia.

"So, those no doubt civic-minded but misled citizens clamoring for a return to the system of the ancients must be fully informed of the quite probable damage and injury resulting from the change. They . . ."

Ataturk, brandishing her cattle prod: "Thank you for that warning."

Looking full-face, closeup, into the camera. "That was Citizen Dobroski, Chief of Tuesday's Ecosystems Bureau. It's evident that he is opposed to the reversion to the pre-New Era system."

Dobroski, loudly: "I did not say that. I only . . ."

Ataturk: "Later, Citizen Dobroski. You will get a full hearing. Citizen Muller. As an important person in the Overall Engineering Department . . ."

Muller: "I am head of the department."

Ataturk, smiling: "Which makes you very important. As chief of this highly integral and important department, you are fully aware of the enormous implications of such a breakup of a system that has been operating smoothly for several obmillenia. Would you care to make a few introductory comments?"

Muller: "More than a few. This subject is not to be lightly skimmed over. I've studied the problems, that is, the larger issues . . . haven't had enough time to get down to the thousands of minor problems and their details . . . these quite often reveal that the larger problems are not solvable or force us to use different methods to solve them, the larger problems, I mean . . ."

Ataturk, pointing the prod at Muller: "What is your opinion at the moment? It's understood that you may wish to revise it in the light of data to come."

Facing the center camera again: "INTERIM is about opinions only. No policies are officially voiced here. The comments of the officials during this program do not in the least bind the officials to commit themselves or their offices to such opinions."

Muller: "I agree with my esteemed colleague, Citizen Dobroski. The magnitude of the tasks involved is staggering. The question is, however, one of possibility or impossibility. If impossible, and that remains to be determined . . ."

Ataturk: "But the motto of your department is: NOTHING IMPOSSIBLE."

Muller: "Well, that's, uh, not exactly bullshit. I certainly wouldn't want to apply that pejorative to the highly successful and always achieved goals of the department. But, let's see. NOTHING IMPOSSIBLE applies only to the possible. You wouldn't ask the department to move the Earth out of its orbit, for instance. Or level the Himalayas, though that is within possibility but would be forbiddingly expensive. You see what I mean."

Ataturk: "Yes, I do. But I believe, no disrespect meant, that that is bullshit. Are you telling me that your department, combined with those of your colleagues, cannot fulfill the requirements of, as Citizen Dobroski said, the change from vertical to horizontal lifesystems?"

Muller: "I didn't say that. I merely . . ."

Ataturk: "You certainly did say that."

Muller, rising from her chair and glaring: "I did not! What I said . . ."

Ataturk, stabbing the prod at Muller: "Now, now, don't get your shit hot. Play it cool. Let's be logical, move within the data. You government officials, no disrespect to the system meant, do sometimes get arrogant."

Muller, sitting back, clenching her hands, her face red: "I am not arrogant, and your remark is insulting to the government. You have strayed from the issue. You . . ."

Ataturk: "On the contrary, you've strayed. You're trying to obscure and obfuscate the theme, lead us off the agreed-upon path."

Muller moves her mouth to form a silent word.

Caird spoke to a fellow patient, Pyotr Villanova Abdullah: "What'd she say? That was Russian, wasn't it?"

Abdullah laughed, then said: " *'Ebi tvoju mat.'* Go screw your mother! An old Russian obscenity. I haven't heard that for years!"

Briony Lodge, draining her glass of Wild Turkey: "I can't believe this isn't all rehearsed. Officials know what they're in for, so the government wouldn't allow anybody who'd blow her cool to participate. It's all a show to put over the government propaganda and clown it up so the viewers won't get bored."

The door to the apartment slid open, and one of the hosts, beaming, walked in. He held a box jammed with bottles in his arms.

Sevring Pu Annyati announced, "Hey, everybody! I contrived to get more booze! I got various friends who owe me favors to loan their liquor. I'll be a long time paying them back, but what the hell!"

Despite the babel, Caird kept watching INTERIM. Tbilisi, first secretary of Transportation Planning, maintained that polls, conducted among 34% of the population, showed that 79% of these were against abandoning the present system. Ataturk rejected the results. She claimed that the pollsters had contacted only those citizens whose biodata showed that they were conservative. Hence, all those polled would resist any radical change. Tbilisi denied this, saying that the poll had been taken at random by a computer. She laughed and said that Tbilisi was close to getting the business end of the prod. Her staff had made a random check of 23,000 of those polled. The computer reported that everyone questioned had been conservative. Surely a spot check would have turned up some non-conservatives.

Tbilisi replied that he was shocked to hear this, but he did not believe that Ataturk was correct. However, he would inform the head of the Data Polling Office of her accusation. The data would be re-checked, and a report made on it in due time.

"Due time," Briony said. She had returned to the chair with a glass of gin. "That means, if the public forgets about it, no report will be made."

After many irrelevancies had been dealt with and some horseplay disposed of, the subject was attacked again. In summary, the officials offered several possible approaches. The conclusion was that all agreed that the New Era system had to continue. It just was not possible to destroy it. Not unless, as Ataturk proposed, the regulation of the number of children was removed. Then the construction people needed could be gotten from the new generations. She admitted that that would take a very long time. And it brought up other problems. All these obstacles aside, how could the shift be made?

"I've had enough," Caird said. He stood up and held out his hand to Briony. "What about you?"

"I tuned out long ago."

29

The next ten days showed him that his new persona had developed a strong element of compassion. It had come up out of the deeps like a leviathan, a benevolent Moby Dick, and swallowed him.

If he saw anyone was unhappy, he did his best to comfort them. He worried about them until he felt that they were no longer, as he put it, in the slough of despond. He did as many kindnesses as he could. He spent long hours talking to people who were lonely, and there were more than he could handle. The ganks, too, came into his circle of attention. Rather, he moved into theirs. Despite what the prisoners thought, the ganks were human, and many were lonely or unhappy. He talked to them, joked with them, and even ran little errands for them. He was aware that some of them and many patients regarded him as a suckass because of this.

During a session, Doctor Bruschino said, "You're getting to be quite a character. Some patients are even referring to you as Saint Jeff. Others . . . well, as Saint Nuisance."

"There will always be some who are malicious or, perhaps, just do not understand," he said.

She shook her head. "Frankly, I'm puzzled. In one way, you're a psychicist's delight. In other ways, you're a complete frustration."

"I don't comprehend it myself. But I don't have to do so in order just to be. Being, that's what counts. Doing. Acting. Chute the philosophy!"

"As long as what you're doing is for your good and that of others. But you're too active. You've lost weight."

"I try to eat in moderation. So far, I've been very successful."

"Does your food taste good?"

"Very good. But I have no compulsion to overeat. I feel energetic, very much alive all the time. You should be pleased. I don't feel like a ghost, and I no longer see others as congeries of atoms."

"That could be because you're burning yourself up. When the fuel runs out . . . Probably not, though. However, I'm pleased at your remarkable progress."

There was silence for a while. Caird wished that the session could be ended now. He had too many people he wanted to talk to, people who needed him.

Three minutes passed while she looked steadily at him, frowning slightly. Then she said, "If I could have my way, I'd ask that you be released soon. I think you're ready to return to outside society. I also think you're not going to revert to a revolutionary. You'll make a model citizen, of that I'm absolutely convinced."

She sighed. He waited. Then she said, "If it was entirely up to me, you'd be a free man within a few weeks. Unfortunately, it's not all up to me. There are too many psychicists who want to keep studying you. They think they can analyze you, find out what makes you tick. They're fools, and I've told them so. That doesn't make me very popular with my colleagues, though I don't care about that. My position is very secure. I am, after all, the grand-daughter of a World Councillor.

"In addition to the psychicists, there is the World Council. They have to be very sure about you. If they should agree to let you go, you'll go. If they do release you, they'll use you as a propaganda tool, a showcase. Your freedom will be advertised as evidence of the liberality and compassion of the government. Don't expect a lot of privacy if you are freed. And you'll be the most closely monitored person on earth."

"Then there is a chance I'll get out?"

"A chance. Do you feel any anxiety about getting released?"

"A little, as you well know. Why do you question me when you can see my reaction on screen?"

She laughed. "That's one of the problems about you. Nobody is convinced, least of all me, that the machine can detect your true reactions. It makes the WCs very nervous to think that there is one man on Earth who is unreadable."

"Just one man?"

"One. Though it makes them wonder if there aren't others like you out there. They don't like that. Also, they wonder if, somehow, you could teach others your unique ability, if it is unique."

"Maybe I could have at one time," he said. "Not now. I don't know how it happened, but I'm cut off from that talent. Maybe it was because a part of me was tired of being a psychic chameleon. It wants this to be the last change forever. I think."

"I believe that you believe that. But you're a tricky bastard. Or you were. How do I know that you haven't set up something in your psyche that you now don't know about but which could be keyed in some day?"

"Keyed in?"

"By some stimulus, I don't have any idea what. But you could have something down there that's just waiting for the right codeword, the right situation, whatever. When that happens, out pops another Jack-in-the-box."

"I swear that . . ."

He stopped.

"Exactly. No use your swearing. You wouldn't really know."

He stood up. "Look. The allotted time for this session isn't up, but I have things to do. As far as *I'm* concerned, anyway, I don't need therapy any more. I thank you for your help, which has been splendid. I'd like to see you now and then because I like to talk to you. But the study and the therapy are over."

Her eyes widened; her mouth opened. She did not say anything, however, for a full twenty seconds, as indicated by the wall display.

"By all that's . . . ! You . . . you behave as if you're the doctor and I'm the patient! You can't quit!"

"I'm tired of this dillydallying around and the politics that keep me here. I can't walk out of this place, but I can be uncooperative."

"They'll declare you unrehabilitable, and you'll be stoned."

"I still have the right to appeal—if they follow their own laws. I'll get a good lawyer. I can't pay him, but the state will have to. Any lawyer who isn't scared to death of the state will jump at the chance to get the publicity."

"You really mean it!"

"I do."

She stood up. Her surprise and dismay seemed to roll off her as she rose, as if she was defying some sort of psychic gravity. She was smiling.

"Very well. I'll apply immediately to have you released, and I'll do my best to present a strong case. This is the first time this has ever happened to me. I didn't quite know how to react. But I think you're really cured. Certainly, you're a high case of remission."

"That's all nonsense," he said. "I didn't need curing. I just needed recognition that I wasn't . . . all those other people, any of them. I'm Baker No Wiley, no one else, even if the state insists on IDing me as Jefferson Caird."

"I had to be sure of that first," she said. "I hope that they'll be sure."

"If they're wrong, they'll know how to correct their error."

Three subdays later, Caird received notice via TV and an official printout that he would soon be discharged. Whether his slight shakiness at the news was from joy or fear, he did not know. He told himself, "I'll be happy to get out of this chicken place." He was not, however, as joyful as he had expected to be. It seemed to him that an orphan might feel the same if he were suddenly told that he would have to get out and somehow survive in an adult society.

He asked the doctor if the main reason he had been released was the influence she had used with her grandmother, the World Councillor.

"All the influence in the world would have done no good if all the psychicists involved in your therapy had not recommended your discharge," she said. "Of course, my recommendation carried the most weight."

"But you did ask your grandmother to help get me out?"

"I suppose that even the Old Stone Age people used their connections for their own benefit or for that of somebody else," she said.

"And you used yours?"

She smiled but did not answer.

The Tuesday night that he was scheduled to depart, he was the guest of honor at a large party attended by patients, staff, and some ganks. He got reasonably intoxicated, was told by three women, including Briony, that they loved him, and had to comfort Donna Cloyd. While she was hugging and kissing him, she whispered, "I don't know what's going to happen to me. I just can't feel sincerely that I was a criminal. But if I don't feel true repentance and regret and convince them of it, I'm done for."

"Your anti-TM will enable you to lie. So, lie."

"You lied to get released?"

"No. But I didn't have to."

He did not know if she would take his advice, but that was the best he had to offer. When the hour of midnight got close, he said goodbye to the party, one by one. Bruschino kissed him and said, "Good luck, Saint Jeff."

"Thanks for everything," he said. He stepped into the cylinder. "Maybe I'll see some of you some day."

He doubted that he would, and he felt sad that he would not. Nevertheless, he could do nothing about this situation except feel sorrow. He hoped that he had done some good while here.

The door was closed. His last look was at Doctor Bruschino, Donna Cloyd and Briony Lodge. All were crying. Whatever the cause, crying was good for the weeper. It helped discharge pain.

He awoke the following Tuesday in the Manhattan immigration receiving station, a huge building three blocks square on 12th Avenue and West 34th Street. Just west was the Westway Parkway and the Hudson River Immigration Dock. A few blocks north was the New Lincoln Bridge.

He stepped out of the cylinder into a babel and what seemed to be confusion but was very organized. He was at once taken in hand by two officials. A gank kept the TV news crew behind a rope barrier while Caird was put through the ID process. He was hologrammed, and comparison recordings were taken of his voice, DNA (from a clipped hair), and thumbprint. These were submitted to the computer which verified that the immigrant was indeed Jefferson Cervantes Caird, but whose new ID was No. C*–238319–ST, citizen of Manhattan State, North American Ministering Organ, Organic Commonwealth of Earth. The next step in normal procedure would have been to give him his instructions and the address at which he would temporarily reside. Instead, he was given five minutes to answer questions from the newshead, Wilma Perez Szuchen, a statuesque redhead who spoke in loud and clipped tones.

She asked him how he felt about returning to Manhattan, the state of his birth and residence until several subyears ago.

He replied that he did not remember anything about it, and she damn well knew it.

Szuchen: "You have been released by the commonwealth and certified as thoroughly rehabilitated. But what about your alter egos?"

Caird: "What about them? They are gone, and the only thing I know about them is what I've seen on tapes or what I've been told. They're no more I than you are."

Szuchen, holding the R-T unit close to her mouth: "Then you persist in maintaining that you were a multiple-personality and, therefore, innocent by reason of insanity?"

Caird, moving his head to avoid being jammed in the mouth by the unit: "I was not a multiple-personality according to the scientific definition of that term. I was never insane."

Szuchen: "Would you mind explaining for the benefit of our viewers just what you mean?"

Caird: "Yes, I would."

Szuchen, smiling fixedly, obviously taken aback: "What are your plans for the future?"

Caird: "Plans are never for the past. They're always for the future. I have applied for work as a hospital orderly and expect to get it. Some day, I might go to medical school and try for the M.D. degree. I really don't know about that. It depends."

Szuchen: "Depends on what?"

Caird: "Depends on whether or not I'm harassed by people hung up on what my former personae did."

Szuchen: "Why do you want to be a hospital orderly?"

Caird: "There's a lot of suffering and pain and hopelessness in this world. I would like to help alleviate some of that."

Szuchen: "You want to do good?"

Caird: "Don't we all?"

Szuchen, whose smile became a snarl: "Of course. Don't be a smartass, Citizen Caird. You wish to repay society for all the crimes you've committed?"

247

Caird: "Eat shit, Citizen Szuchen. You persist in talking like an asshole. Are you trying to provoke me? Would you like me to file a complaint against you for harassment? I'd file one against you for stupidity, but that's not a legal cause."

Szuchen: "Citizen Caird, I'm just doing my job."

Caird: "Not very well, in my opinion."

Szuchen: "You act like a troublemaker and a weedie, Citizen Caird. We have reports that you had become a very caring and compassionate person, but your attitude certainly does not bear that out."

Caird: "I have work to do. I don't like to waste it with people who make no attempt to understand me and ask dumb questions. I don't want to be bothered by needle-noses asking me questions about what my body did—my body, not me—just to satisfy their festering curiosities. You undoubtedly know my case history. The government has given that to you. But if you didn't do your homework, that's not my fault. This interview is over."

30

Fifteen minutes later, he walked out of the building onto 12th Avenue. He took a bus down it to West 14th Street and transferred to a bus which took him crosstown to 1st Avenue and East 14th. The streets were filled with bicycles, electrically-driven tricycles, and buses. The only larger vehicles were occasional organic patrol cars. The sight of his natal streets evoked no memories. Carrying his shoulderbag and a small suitcase, he walked on north to the middle of the enormous Stuyvesant Town Building. This, however, was only four stories high. The towering skyscrapers that had distinguished ancient Manhattan had been torn down millenia ago.

Sweating from the hot early summer sun, he entered the complex structure, found the block leaders' central offices, and was directed to his second-floor apartment. He inserted his ID card in the slot of its door, and the door slid open. After drinking a tall glass of water, he inspected the premises. It was as clean as he could expect in a weedie district. He showered, put on a clean blouse and kilts, and went back to the local block leader's office for a formal check-in. Evidently, the secretary had seen the tape of his interview. He did not say anything about it, but he giggled when Caird told him his name. After inserting Caird's card, he read the data on his desk-screen.

He handed the card back, saying, "Heterosexual. What a shame."

"Life is full of disappointments," Caird said, smiling.

"And clichès, too."

"And facetious conversation to bar meaningful communication."

"God, I can't bear that!" the secretary said. "Meaningful communication, I mean. It always leads to trouble!"

"Man is born to trouble as the sparks fly upward."

"Very true. Isn't that from the *Good Morning, Tuesday!* show?"

"I don't know where it's from," Caird said. "Have a super day."

"I'm not off until 4:30. The day will be practically shot."

Caird went down the stairs and down long halls to the west lobby and across the street to the four-blocks-long Acme Memorial Hospital. He checked in at the employment office and was told to report next Tuesday morning for his first training class for orderlies. After that, he found the local block tavern, the Seven Sages, and entered it. Its interior was roomy and dark and had more customers than would be found in a higher-class district at this time of day. Most of the tenants were on minimum-wage guarantee but had part-time jobs. If they earned credits above a certain scale, they lost their own MWG. They managed to keep below the limit. He intended to work full time and so would not be a genuine weedie. Or, as they were sometimes called, *mawgs.*

The drinkers looked at him expressionlessly. They were not sure that he was not a gank in civilian clothing. He slid his card into the slot on the bar and ordered a beer. The bartender looked at the ID and the credit amount displayed. He said, "Hey! Citizen Caird! I saw the interview. Way to go, man."

After sitting for a while and eavesdropping on the customers' conversation, Caird went back to the apartment. He did not feel like spending his time alone that evening. The itch to talk to others was still with him, and he supposed that it would never go away. On the other hand, he was at a loss about just what to do. He called up the schedule of local-area events and noted that there would be a meeting of block leaders at seven. The public was invited. Since he did not know anything about the situation here, he thought he might as well go to that. It was a citizen's duty to attend such. Weedies, however, were noted for ignoring them unless they had some complaint. And then they usually presented it first to their local leader. Let him or her take care of it.

His personal possessions closet was empty of food. After seeing a display of the items available at the local food store, he went down to it and purchased a small amount and a collapsible cart. He pulled the cart and contents, stoned supplies and some fresh fruit and vegetables, to the elevator and down the hall to his apartment. He had just destoned and microwaved his dinner when a loud buzzing and orange letters on the wallscreen told him that he had a call. Thinking that it was probably from a gank checking up on him, he coded in the video-audio. A young, well-dressed woman, good-looking even though she had a long sharp nose, was displayed.

She said, somewhat hesitantly, "Dad?"

"Jefferson Cervantes Caird," he said. "You must . . ."

She looked somewhat familiar. Then he remembered. He had seen her on the tapes at the rehabilitation center. She was Ariel Shadiah Cairdsdaughter, his only child.

"I know your name. I wish I could say I remember you, Ariel, but I don't. I'm sorry."

"I know that," she said. "I'd like to see you, anyway. Now. Could I come to your place?"

"I wouldn't deny you that. But I'm afraid you're going to be very disappointed. Don't hope you can stir up my memory of you. It'd be a waste of effort."

"I'll leave at once. I should be there in about twenty minutes."

According to the ID he asked for after she had cut off the screen, she taught history at East Harlem University. She'd take the East Side subway and get off a block from the Stuyvesant area. He knew that because of the transportation map he had called up on the wallscreen.

He was nervous. Tears had rolled down her cheeks as her image had faded. There was nothing he could do to change the situation, though he could tell her that he loved her. But that love was for humanity itself. He just did not have the love of a father for his daughter. He doubted that he could relearn it—if he indeed had ever had it. To do that, he would have to have a somewhat steady and close contact with her which would build up his love. Since their locations and professions were so different, he and Ariel would probably see very little of each other.

It took a lot of courage for her to visit him. Most people would avoid him if they knew who he was. He was under unremitting surveillance, no doubt of that. The organics had probably implanted a transmitter in his body even if it was illegal to do so. It would be low power, but their detector-amplifiers would pinpoint his exact location at all times. Though he had not noticed anyone shadowing him, he was certain that they would also be using human agents to check on him. One reason he had chosen a weedie area to live in was that most of its citizens did not care if he was thought dangerous by the authorities. In fact, they would enjoy that and admire him. They did not become friends with anyone just because of their social ranking or approval by the ganks.

He supposed that Ariel had been thoroughly investigated and put under TM because she was his daughter. She would have been proved innocent of any participation or knowledge of his criminal activities. But she knew that the authorities would not like it if she renewed contact with him.

What could he do for her? Very little. He would like to help her ease her sorrow at his loss—he was, in a sense, dead to her—but he could only be a friend and a sympathizer.

He destoned a half-quart of lemonade and some ice cubes. While he drank in the living room, he watched the news. His interview by Szuchen was shown, and he tended to agree with her conclusion that he was a bit of a shit.

At the bottom of the screen: THE OPINIONS OF THE REPORTER ARE NOT NECESSARILY OFFICIAL OR THOSE OF THE MANAGEMENT UNLESS SO STATED.

There followed something about nearing the end of the construction of an artificial river system in South Arabia. He started paying attention when there was a newsbreak. The newshead announced that the World Council had received the results of the referendum vote by the population of the commonwealth on the issue of abandoning the New Era system. Contrary to expectations influenced by an unofficial poll, those in favor of breaking up the present system were in the majority. The world population number had been revised, officially stated, "accuratized," to two billion. Of the one billion authorized to vote, fifty million had failed to do so. Those voting for the breakup numbered more than six hundred and thirty-three million, a two-thirds majority.

"The voice of the people has spoken!" the newshead said with more excitement than a professional should project. "Of course, this referendum is only a nonbinding notice to the World Council of what the populace desires. Questioned by the higher representatives of the newsmedia, the chief liaison secretaries of the seven Councillors said that it is too early for comments from that august body."

There was more, but he half-heard it. The revolution had taken a step forward. Despite the campaign by the government to convince the citizens that a changeover was impossible, the majority had refused to accept that conclusion.

The screen lit up with orange, a buzzer sounded, and Ariel's image appeared in a section of the wallscreen reserved for the door monitor display. Caird opened the door for her. Ariel hugged him and wet his chest with her tears. He cried, too, because he sorrowed for her. After she released him, she dried her eyes and face, accepted a glass of lemonade, and sat down.

"This is, unfortunately, a one-way tie," she said. "I realize that the old relationship can't be continued. But you are my father, even if you're a stranger. If we could get to know each other well, we won't at least be strangers."

"I'd very much like that. But a one-way tie is no bond at all. What tied us together originally is forever gone."

"I know that."

More tears trickled down.

They talked for a while, telling each other details of their recent lives. Ariel had married an official in the Department of Physical Services and was very much in love with him. They had petitioned the Department of Reproduction and Child Care for permission to have a baby and expected to get it.

"You may be a grandfather."

"I am delighted," he said. "The baby and I can start off on an equal footing, both brand new."

That caused her to weep again because she and Caird might not be able to do that. But he said that they would be able—perhaps. What she knew about him would help her. She loved the old Caird and he hoped that love would ease gradually into a love for him as he now was.

After a while, they got less tense. They talked of other things, especially of the news about the referendum.

"I didn't expect it'd turn out that way," he said.

"You can take much of the credit for it," she said, smiling. "Just think. My father, the great revolutionist."

"The new me doesn't seem to have any radical enthusiasm for change or any conservative zeal to keep things the way they are. Still, I'm interested in what's going on."

"You should be. You were the catalyst for the revolutionary events. Anyway, as a historian, I study current trends and events and try to extrapolate into possible futures. It could be that the World Council is not now as resistant to a changeover as their official stand indicates. From its viewpoint, certain aspects of the change-over might be desirable. Especially those concerned with the consumption of electrical power."

He raised his eyebrows. "The changeover will result in a need for six times the present need."

"Think about it. The power needed for heat, light, and fuel is small compared to that required for stoning and destoning. The electrical power required for stoning and destoning eats up ninety percent of the power available. The electrical power gotten from solar panels, tidal, deep-sea, and magnetohydrodynamic sources is used for only ten percent of our needs. The stoning power is provided by tapping the heat of the Earth's core.

"But if the world reverts to pre-New Era living, if the stoning-destoning of all the world's citizens is done away with, we'll be up to our ass in excess power. It'll be exceedingly cheap. In fact, the savings should be more than enough to pay for the cost of clearing all that land and building new cities and farms and roads and so on."

"It's a big plus item," he said. "The people should like that. But the other aspects . . . the changeover is still going to involve much hardship, uprooting, sacrifice, a lot of unfairness, confusion, and chaos."

"When the people fully realize just what's going to be required of them," Ariel said, "they'll rebel. If the government overrides them, it'll be swept out of power or, at least, the citizens will try to overthrow it. There may be much bloodshed.

"Take Hoboken, for instance. Manhattan's Wednesday people are slated to move to that area. They'll be living in tents and quonsets while they build the city. For an undetermined time, they'll be, in a sense, dispossessed people and suffering from the physical and psychological traumas the dispossessed can't avoid. You think they'll like leaving their nice orderly lives to go to a wilderness which is below sea level—the dikes're the only thing keeping the sea from drowning them—and be construction work-ers? It'll be a long hard time before they can dwell in good houses and return to their normal routine and professions. When they fully realize what they're in for, they're going to erupt. It'll be the French Revolution plus the Russian Revolution all over again."

"I don't know," he said. "Most citizens are so conditioned against violence for obedience."

"The Old Stone Age savage still lives deep in most people. He bides his time, waits for a chance to break out."

Caird's eyes opened wide as if sprung by a mechanism be-hind them.

Ariel said, "I can almost see the bulb over your head lighting up."

"What if somebody comes up with a viable plan for making the changeover much more smoothly and without unendurable hardships for the citizens who have to relocate? What if . . . ?" His voice petered out.

She laughed and said, "Wouldn't that be something? I can't imagine what this rabbit out of the hat could be, though. Or do you have an idea?"

"No," he said. "Not quite. But something almost clicked in my head. I don't know what. Maybe it'll come back."

They talked about other things for a while and then came long silences. Finally, Ariel said that she had to go. She cried a little when saying goodnight.

He felt some grief after the door had closed behind her, but he did not know exactly why. After all, they would be seeing each other again. If it was impossible to renew their old relationship since he remembered nothing of it, a new one could be built up. If both of them desired that . . . The question was, would they?

Before going to bed, he called up the instruction tape he was supposed to view before reporting for work to the hospital. Having mastered it, he was ready for his duties, simple ones, at first. He would be accompanied for the first subweek by a veteran orderly who would teach him all he should know.

31

At nine o'clock he tidied up the apartment and then lowered the bed. He told the screen to wake him up at a quarter to twelve so that he could enter the stoner, and he passed almost immediately into slumber. He had several dreams, only one of which he remembered on awakening. He lay for a few minutes in bed after the gonging alarm and his own voice had sounded from the wall. He told the wall that he was awake and to shut up.

The dream was a puzzle in meaning, though its origins were evident. While in the rehabilitation institution, he had seen *Zombies Have Nightmares, Too*, a horror-drama about the psychological problems of the living dead of ancient Haiti. It was supposed to be a satire on civil servants, but most viewers had missed that point. The tomb out of which the horde of zombies burst to eat their witch-doctor master stood for bureaucracy, another symbol few people had understood. Caird had dreamed of the final scene and been terrified, but the zombies had been mixed with elements from another show. That was *Babes In Toyland*, a recent remake, one in a long line going back to a pre-New Era classic. The giant toy robot soldiers, accidentally made by the two inept comic-relief characters, merged with the zombies, became them, and they marched out to destroy the Bogeymen led by the evil Barnaby. Caird actually heard the music of *March Of The Wooden Soldiers* while the robots were defeating the evil monsters invading Toyland.

While he was surging up to consciousness, he was aware that he was moaning with terror. One of the horned and furry Bogeymen had escaped the bayonets of the soldiers and was about to seize him in its sharp-clawed paws.

He got out of bed, drank a glass of water, and went into the stoner room. Passing Wednesday's cylinder, he muttered, "Good morning." The diamond-hard face beyond the round transparent window did not, of course, respond.

Just as he closed his cylinder door, he caught something thrown up by the churning lightning-ridden ocean of his mind. He thought, I hope I remember that!

He did. He had no awareness of the six days' oblivion between the moment stoning power came on and the moment that destoning power gave full movement back to the molecules of his body. He was not at all conscious of any interlude. But, though he knew better, he identified stoning with sleep. Hence, his concern that he might not remember the idea that had burst in his brain like a nova.

"I really got something!" he said as he pushed the door open and stepped out. "No one else has thought of it—as far as I know!"

He immediately recorded the idea and then went to bed again. Awakening at six, he exercised for half an hour, after which he prepared and ate his morning meal. A section on the wall in each room glowed orange and emitted a low buzzing while he ate. After his session in the bathroom, from which he emerged clean inside and out, he turned the recorder-alarm off. He was not going to forget its message. The next step was to call up a directory and note the name and number of the civil servant he wanted to talk to. Having done that, he placed his message to the man in the data bank. Sometime today, Robert Hamadhani Munyigumba should read the printout of Caird's idea in his office. Whether he would act on it quickly depended upon the character of Munyigumba and the amount of priority work he had. If Caird did not hear from him this Tuesday, there was next Tuesday.

As he had half-expected, he did not get a callback from Munyigumba at the hospital or his apartment that day. He was busy learning some of the tasks an orderly must master. These included changing sheets, bringing in flowers for the patients, storing supplies, and moving the patients into the stoners in the evening and out in the morning. One of the more interesting and pleasant duties was the ten-minute conversation he was supposed to have with his quota of patients who wanted to talk, and most of them did. He also helped bring in the new admittees and destone them. These had been gorgonized in nearby emergency cylinders when they had gotten sick or been injured.

Just before quitting time, the supervisor who had been observing and instructing him, said, "You may make it, Caird. You seem to have a knack for this profession. You're the first one ever got Citizen Grandjean to laugh. And you were a great comfort to Citizen Blatand. She's really afraid of dying, but she refuses to be stoned and wait until a cure for her kind of cancer is found. Not that she would get it. She'd be too old to destone unless they also discover rejuvenation. Anyway, you were very kind to her. But you don't really believe all that religious bullshit you gave her, do you?"

Caird shrugged. "Why not make her feel better?"

"That's the way to go. If she wants a rabbit's foot for luck, give it to her. Man! She's one hundred and eight subyears old, been on this Earth seven hundred and fifty-six obyears. You'd think she'd be sick of this life. But, no, she wants to hang on until her last sour breath before she goes to heaven."

Caird felt reasonably sure that he would pass without trouble through his probation period. It should not be too long before he got the badge, uniform, and rank of private as a permanent orderly. Then he would receive a good salary, and he would be taken off the MWG. Orderlies, like all service personnel, were paid well and were highly esteemed.

The following Tuesday, he waited until three in the afternoon for Munyigumba's message. When he tried to get through to him, a display told him that the First Assistant to the First Secretary of the OCSSI, the Office of Citizens' Suggestions for Social Improvement, was not available for consultation at this moment. Caird's call would be returned as soon as possible.

As possible did not happen that day. Nor did it the following Tuesday. Shortly before four, Caird put in another call and got the same reply. He had just turned away from the wallscreen when his supervisor, Quintus Mu Williams, came into the orderly room.

"Hey, Caird, guess what? I was in the sergeant's room when I saw a newsbreak. Some guy named Munyigumba, an OCSSI big muckamuck, has submitted an idea for making the changeover possible! It's gone through channels and is being considered by the World Council! There's a lot of excitement about it. The newshead practically had an orgasm!"

Caird grunted as if struck in the solar plexus.

"This Munyigumba," he said, slowly. "He proposed that the people now stoned in the warehouses be unstoned and put to work building the new cities?"

"Yeah!" Williams said, eyes widening, eyebrows rising. "You saw it?"

"No, I didn't."

"Somebody already told you?"

"No. Did Munyigumba also propose that the destoned people taken from the warehouses live every day while working? And that they be given pardons for their contribution to the work?"

"Yeah. But, say, if you didn't see it and nobody told you . . . ?"

"That son of a bitch!" Caird said. "He stole my proposal

and took all the credit! Only . . . maybe I'm jumping the gun. My name wasn't mentioned, was it? Any credit given me?"

"No way," Williams said. "You saying it's your idea?"

"I certainly am."

Williams looked as if he did not believe Caird. That was the attitude of everybody else Caird talked to while trying to prove that he was the originator of the "Munyigumba Concept."

The First Assistant to the First Secretary finally answered Caird's message. He denied having received any communication from Caird. When Caird went through the court to get the records for calls made to Munyigumba, he found that they obviously had been erased. He was not surprised.

He called a press conference and denounced Munyigumba. This was shown briefly on the news. Szuchen, the chief newshead, was as sarcastic about him as she could be without stepping over the libel limits. He expected that. He had made an enemy of her. But it would have made no difference if he had been a friend. She was evidently under orders to discredit him.

A few days later, the newsheads announced that Munyigumba was being transferred to Tuesday's Zurich. He had been given a raise in salary and a new ranking. He would be one of the honored members of the newly formed Think Tank which would plan the disposition of the destoned criminals. It was expected that his contributions to that group would be valuable.

Even the weedies at the Seven Sages tavern joked about his claim, though they were good-natured about it. For a while, some of them called him Citizen Munyigumba. He licked his wounds, which healed rapidly. It would have been nice if he could have gone down in history as the originator of the idea. But what really mattered was that his idea might solve a very big problem.

The authorities, however, were not going to let it go. They were after him, though they would not admit it. While he was halfway through his probation period, he was summoned to the office of Captain Ad Sherwin Lennow, the chief orderly supervisor.

Lennow handed him a printout of a communication from the Manhattan Department of Education. Caird read it, then looked unbelievingly at Lennow.

"They can't be serious. They can't claim I'm unqualified to take orderly training because I don't have a high school education. They say I don't have even a grade school education!"

"There's no record of it," Lennow said. "Checked it out myself before calling you."

"Of course, there isn't!" Caird said heatedly. "You know my biodata. How could there be?"

"I'm sorry. Your work record and geniality index are good, and I hate to lose you. Perhaps that might only be temporary, however. You may not have to go back to school . . ."

"Starting with first grade!"

". . . if you can convince the Department of Education to give you examinations for a high-school degree. If I were you, I'd put in a petition immediately."

"I'm not a troublemaker," Caird said, flapping the printout as if it were a flag blown by a hot and wrathful wind. "I only want to be a good citizen and contribute something worthwhile to society."

"Weeeel," Lennow said, steepling his hands and smiling faintly. "There is that claim that Citizen Munyigumba stole that idea from you. It has been hinted—not by me, I assure you—that your claim indicates mental instability. I myself have paid no attention to the talk."

"Who's saying that?"

"Not for me to say. In any event, it's irrelevant. What matters is that." He pointed at the printout. "I can do nothing but discharge you, though I regret doing so. When you have a high-school degree in your record, I'll be happy to consider employing you again. The seniority you've accumulated during your period of employment will be maintained. If you should return to work here, that is."

Caird could do nothing except get a budder, an ombudsperson, to present his petition to take the examinations. Though he was not sure that he could pass these, since his memory was so selective, he did file his request. A reply was required by law within four subdays after the filing. Eight days passed, however, the Department of Education saying that unusual circumstances had held up the decision. These were not explained, and the budder said that it would not help to demand explanations. They would be forthcoming, though not necessarily true.

On the twelfth subday, late in the afternoon, the petition was denied. Reason: Caird's unique case required that the Manhattan lower legislative house, composed of superblock leaders, would have to pass a law giving him permission. That would have to be voted on by the upper house, consisting of five district leaders.

He went to the office of his ombudsperson, Amazing "Maizie" Grace Haydn. She told him that he could petition the lower house to pass such a "personal situation" law.

"But I scent a government plot to keep you down. I could be wrong. Everything that's happened to you has been legally justified. From what you've told me, I think that everything you do to advance yourself is going to find obstacles. For some reason, the government wants you to stay on MWG, wants to keep you down."

"I can't hurt it," Caird said.

"Not in any way you know. They, however, probably have their reasons, which, of course, they won't tell you."

"I can't just sit around and booze it up or watch TV. I'd go crazy."

"Maybe that's what they want. My opinion is that they'd like to put you away for good. You're an enigma, an unknown quantity. They're just not convinced that you won't change your persona again. And they believe that that persona might be a danger to them."

She smiled and said, "After all, they have precedents to

justify that belief. I'm sorry, I really am. Do you want me to get together with a public defender and draw up a petition to investigate your case?"

He looked at the wallscreens. Ten calls had been on hold when he had first started talking to her. Now there were thirty. Though she was showing no impatience, she had a lot of work to do.

"Maybe later," he said. "I have to think about this."

He stood up and bowed with steepled hands against his chest. "Thank you for what you've done for me."

"My pleasure," she said. "How about dinner tonight at eight?"

32

She certainly was a looker, middle-sized but slim, curly jet-black hair, big and very lively dark eyes, and a smooth depigmented white-jade skin. She was congenial but ambitious. Studying for an M.A. in erodynamics psychology. Why would she be interested in a weedie who had few prospects for rising to a higher class?

She had said it herself. He was an enigma and, hence, fascinating.

"I don't have any hard ties just now," she said. "My roomie moved out at my request."

"I might be a handicap to your career."

She laughed, and she said, "I didn't say I was inviting you to move in with me. Besides, how do you know you'd hobble me?"

"They'll be watching you, and they won't like any continued and close contact you might have with me."

"Let me worry about that."

Dinner was on Maizie and was at a high-class restaurant on 34th Street. He discovered that she sometimes sang here and thus picked up extra credits. When she was younger, she had been a member of an acrobat team. Did he remember seeing her on TV? He shook his head.

She had taken her first two names on becoming twenty. A person could change his name any time he wished as long as the proper authorities were notified. The ID number remained the same. She had chosen Amazing Grace because it was the title of her favorite song and also attracted attention.

"After you asked me for a conference," she said, "I checked into your biodata, though, of course, I had seen a lot about you. One of your personae was Wyatt Bumppo Repp, a TV writer and producer. Do you know that writing is one of the very few professions that does not require a high-school education?"

"No, I didn't."

"I never heard of a writer who didn't have a college education, but there's always a first. You see, the arts somehow slipped through those requirements. You can be a singer, a composer, a musician, a painter, a sculptor, a poet, or a writer and not have a high-school degree. I suppose that, originally, the lawmakers thought that these did not need degrees. You can't teach the arts without a Ph.D., but you can practice them."

"Yet a bartender has to graduate from high school."

"That's the way it is. Unfortunately, you'll have a hard time trying to get into TV writing. If you apply for a job, you can't submit your resume for Repp. You're not Repp. Anyway, you weren't a writer in Tuesday. If you gave some scripts to the channels for consideration, and the muckamucks liked them, they still wouldn't hire you. They'd get the word from the government that you are persona non grata. But . . . are you a good singer? Good enough to get a job?"

"Not near good enough."

"Any artistic talents in any field?"

"None."

She sipped her wine, her eyes narrowed. Then she said, "I

have an idea. I took the liberty of approaching several channel vice-presidents about it, and they said they're interested. But they made it plain without actually saying so that they couldn't hire you. However, they liked the idea of a miniseries based on your life. You've had an enormous amount of publicity, and they don't think the government would put any pressure on them to suppress your story. You'd have no control over it. On the other hand, you'd be paid well for your permission to use it. You might get so much public attention and backing that the legislature would pass the special law you want."

He felt a mingled anger and admiration for her. She had certainly been busy on his behalf. All this must have happened before he had his first appointment with her.

"If I agreed to do that," he said, "the channel could portray me in any fashion it wished. I know what'd happen. Everything I did would be dramatized as the acts of a criminal, and they'd undoubtedly have me show the proper socially acceptable regret and repentance at the end. There'd be nothing in the script that could be thought of as anti-government. Nothing of the government's fraud, corruption, and murder."

"It would be presented so that the viewer would have sympathy for you, identify in some way with you. You'd be shown as sincere but mistaken. And your final persona-change would be shown as your renunciation of your previous personae. It'd be an act of abnegation, the sacrifice made to cut yourself off from your former acts. You'd end up as Good Citizen Caird."

"That I am," he said. "But I don't like what I did misrepresented as just criminal acts. But the government just won't stop hounding me. It won't let me be what it claims it wants me to be and what I want to be."

"It's not that bad," she said. "I mean, the script when it'll be written. I've thought of a great idea. The story will be told from your viewpoint—it'll say so before every episode and be subtitled so now and then during the action. That way, we can get around any government interference. Of course, we'll also be showing the viewpoint of the government, too, but that can be minimized. I . . ."

"*You've* thought of the idea!" he said. "You sound as if you're already working for the channel."

"Oh, I am," she said. "You know how many irons I have in the fire. This is one more. I . . . didn't I tell you? I forgot, so much to say. I'm engaged to work on this project, that's all it is, a project. And I . . ."

He stood up, folded his napkin, and put it on the table.

"You've been using me! That's why you're dining me and and why you practically invited me into your bed. And you an ombudsperson!"

"Hey," she said, looking angry, "I am doing my very best for you as your budder. I never shirk my job and never let anything interfere with it. Don't you forget that! But there's no law says I can't make extra credits or get ahead on anything I want to try. This TV thing is just too good to pass up. Besides, I think I'd be a natural as a script writer. It doesn't take any great talent to be one, you know. Also, don't forget that this will benefit you. It may change your whole life for the better!"

"It certainly will yours," he said. "Thanks for the dinner."

He walked out. Not without some regrets. Since she was an erodynamics engineer, she knew all there was to know about the mechanics of coition. His regrets, however, passed quickly. She did not love him, probably was not even fond of him, and so could not give him the one thing that made all the difference to him.

Ninety subdays later, the two-hour pilot of the seven-segment miniseries, THE MAN WHO SHOOK THE WORLD, appeared. Caird was not caught unawares since it had been advertised for a submonth. He learned that the channel had not needed his permission to portray him. The original Caird, and his succeeding personae, Tingle, Dunski, Repp, Ohm, Zurvan, Isharashvili, and Duncan no longer existed. Their agreement to be depicted did not have to be considered. The final part, dealing with the new Caird, was to be nondramatic. It would be composed of tapes made while he was at the rehab institute, shots of him eating, exercising, and talking to inmates and ganks. Voiceovers by various commentators, psychicists, newsheads, and government officials would accompany these. There were also films of him made since he had returned to Manhattan. He had not been aware that these had been taken, but he was not surprised.

Despite telling himself that he would only be angered and deeply disturbed if he watched the series, he was too curious to ignore it. After it ended, he was glad that he had forced himself to view it. In many ways, he was as ignorant of his own personae as the average citizen. The only method he had for determining when the program deviated from the truth was by comparing the suspected sections to the documentary tapes of these events. Since most of these were short news reports, he had little with which to compare.

He did learn more than he had thought he would. Apparently, the channel had gotten access, with government permission, of course, to many of the official reports. Thus, a re-enactment of his breakout from a supposedly escape-proof institution was shown. According to the statement made before that segment, the scenes were one hundred percent realistic.

"So that's how I did it," he murmured.

Like other viewers, he was thrilled when he, as William St. George Duncan, rescued Panthea Snick from the New Jersey warehouse. And he marveled at his own cleverness when he had sneaked into a laboratory near the outlaws' nest and had arranged to make the duplicate of himself in its vat, then had arranged to leave the dead duplicate in the forest to be found by the ganks. The hunt had been called off for a while; the authorities believed that they had proof that he was dead.

There was, however, nothing about fraud, lying, and corruption among the higher-ups in the hierarchy. The villains were all members of various subversive organizations who had infiltrated positions of authority, including the now-dead World Councillor, David Jimson Ananda.

Parts of the show were tapes run during actual organic conferences when the hunt for Caird was in full cry. He found these interesting. It was the first time that such meetings had been publicly shown. They not only gave an insight into the gank methods and their frustrations while looking for him, they added to the suspense even though the viewer knew what the end would be.

The actor playing Caird looked exactly like him. That was because he was no actor but a computerized simulation modeled on the real person. Snick's role was also played by a simulation.

The final segment did not end as Caird had been told it would. It was a fantasy with eight simulations of himself gathered in one room and talking among themselves. They ended up disagreeing, often quite violently, about what they had started out to do and why their courses had been deflected toward antisocial ends. They finally admitted that they had been deceived. They had thought that they were fighting the government but it had turned out that they were battling other criminals. These were minor officials who wanted higher status and more power and had used illegal ends to attain these.

It was all very convincing, though Caird did not quite believe all of it. He was nagged by the feeling that the original Caird-persona, who supposedly knew what was going on, would have disagreed.

Though the commentators never said anything about the revolutionary end-effects of the acts of Caird and his companions, any intelligent viewer could see the implications. Because of Caird, society would never be the same again. The age-slowing factor, the anti-TM, and the public demand to break up the New Era system of once-a-week living had come about because of Caird. He should be a hero; statues of him should be erected in public places. Or so it seemed.

The series had ended fifteen minutes short of two hours. That that time period had been planned by the producers and the government occurred to Caird after the newsbreak immediately after the final credits.

Szuchen, his old enemy, appeared. She was looking very grave even though it was mandatory that newsheads smile while announcing the worst of catastrophes.

"Citizens, this is a newsflash of the utmost importance! Please stay tuned in! The World Council has just announced that The Changeover will be initiated! It is definitely launched! From this historic moment, Tuesday, at 8:46 D4–W4, Freedom Month, the world has turned about! The Changeover has begun!"

There was much more, including an interview with First Secretary Munyigumba, the man responsible for the idea that had convinced the World Council that Changeover was possible. Caird listened for a minute, then turned the screen off.

As he prepared to get a few hours of sleep before entering the stoner, he thought: Events will reveal if Munyigumba will be, in the end, a hero or a villain. He may be sorry that he stole my idea.

33

The Fifty Subyear Plan came out so quickly from the World Council that Caird knew that the government had considered the Change-over long ago and had drawn up plans for carrying it out. Now that Munyigumba's brilliant idea seemed to have solved or at least alleviated that problem, the World Council had issued plans that had been stored for a long time as classified material in the data banks.

The plans for cutting down of certain forest areas, the laying out of farmlands, the building of roads, waterways, houses, factories, airports, and the hundreds of other items necessary poured out of the computers. Much of the labor and the operation of machines and robots was going to be done by many of those now stoned in the warehouses. Added to them would be all the non-productive and semiproductive citizens and those who volunteered for the projects.

As a citizen who had no job, Caird knew that he would one day be drafted into the work force. The notice to report for in-

273

structions was displayed on the wall one morning when he went into the kitchen just after getting out of bed. Lotus Hiatt Wang, in whose apartment he was now living, was sitting at the table and drinking coffee. She was a store clerk whom he had met when he was purchasing an umbrella. She was tall and dark-haired and had blue eyes (depigmented) and was very pretty. But she tended at times to brood on the neglect of her by her parents. She also needed constant reassurance by him that he loved her. Despite her sometimes irritating and frustrating moods, he was very fond of her.

She was silent when he entered. He sighed, thinking that she had fallen into one of her black moods. But her sorrowful face was not caused by him or her parents. It was the message on a wallscreen. Though she had turned off the buzzer alarm, the letters still waxed and waned bright orange.

While he was reading it, she said, "I knew it. Both of us! We're going to be forced to go into the wilderness! And I don't want to go!"

"We'll be together."

"You and your fucking optimism!" she said. "Pollyanna with a prick!"

"Look at it this way. It's an adventure. A paid vacation with work to keep you from being bored. Think of all the sights, the new people you'll meet. You've complained about how tedious your clerk's job is. You may be operating a big bulldozer. Think of all that power in your hands. Imagine you're flattening out your parents under those big metal treads."

"Honestly," she said, glaring, "you make me sick."

He poured some coffee and sat down at the table. "Only sick people are made sick by other people."

"That's a sick proverb."

He shrugged and patted her hand. He had a lot of compassion to pour out, and Lotus certainly soaked up much of it. Sometimes, though, she shed it like the stoned shed rain. She also resented his staying at home instead of working. He had ceased explaining that it was not his fault. "You can go out and find *something* to do that'll pay off," she always replied.

Nevertheless, on her days off she was usually cheery and fun to be around and as sexy as a Siamese cat in heat—if she did not happen to think of her parents. She liked being the roomie of a famous, if unemployable, man. Even when they went to Central Park for a picnic, he was recognized, and people were always coming up to talk to him. She glowed in the reflected light.

The next Tuesday, he and Wang reported, acknowledging via screen that they had received the notice. They told the screen to make a printout of the acknowledgement in case it should, by a remote chance, not be recorded at the bank of the Department of Extra-Employment. They waited six submonths before they got the notice to report in person at the DEE building on Houston and Womanway. Lotus called her manager at the store to inform him that she would not be able to come into work next morning. He told her that she was supposed to report for instruction at the DEE on her day off. The recently released regulations made that clear. After she transmitted the DEE order, he told her he would call her back. Three hours later, red-faced, he did so. He had been in quite a wrangle with the DEE official. Angrily, he told Lotus that she would have to take time off. Though he had pointed out the regulation to the son of a bitch at DEE, that son of a bitch had calmly said that the department could override regulations if circumstances demanded.

"He wouldn't admit that the DEE had made a mistake," the manager said. "He knows it did, but he just covers himself by saying that there's an override available. Well, I'm calling up the table of departmental regulations, and we'll see if the bastard is lying."

Later, the manager called Lotus and told her that there was no override permission in the instructions issued by the DEE. But he had cooled off, and it would be too much trouble to raise hell about the arrogance and stupidity of the DEE. He might find himself in hot water if he did, though he had legality and right on his side.

Caird and Wang were at the DEE at eight in the morning with about three hundred others. After an hour's delay, they were ushered into a viewing room. The instruction tape they saw could just as easily have been transmitted to their apartment, and no one was there to give answers to any questions.

On the way home on the bus, Caird said, "I can see how smooth the Changeover is going to be. Very well organized, no screw-ups, no tangled lines."

"I told you it would be a mess."

Lotus had not said anything of the sort, but he discreetly did not point that out.

That evening, while he and Lotus were at the Seven Sages, a huge weedie named Quigley steamed up to their table. Legs straddled, eyes red, voice slurred, Quigley said, "You're the great revolutionary, the asshole who's responsible for this."

"For what?" Caird said mildly. "Though I don't admit I'm the revolutionary."

"Don't try that multiple-personality crap on me!" Quigley roared. "If it wasn't for you, I wouldn't have to go to the wilds of Hoboken and work my ass off! I could live the way I want to live. But, no, you screwed things up for me!"

"The government did that, not me."

"Blame it on the government, blame it on the government!"

A few minutes before, Quigley's loud voice at the bar had been doing just that, excoriating the government. Now, suddenly, Caird was the villain.

Before he could protest further, he was knocked backward off his chair by a hard fist against his forehead. He fell hard, half-stunned, unable to move for a moment. Quigley drove the sharp toe of her shoe into his ribs. Lotus screamed and hit the big redhead on the back of her neck with her bottle of beer. That staggered her, but she recovered swiftly and backhanded Lotus across the mouth. After that there was the brawl that always lurked in the wings of a weedie tavern, ready to step into the spotlight. Caird stayed on his back until the ganks came, though he wanted very much to plunge into the melee. He had not struck a blow, but he was arrested along with all the others. Since he offered no resistance, he was allowed to ride in the van with the more peaceable rioters. Quigley and a couple of others were rendered unconscious by stun guns and stoned, then transported to the precinct station. Caird and Lotus got off with a lecture from the judge, a light fine, and a promise to attend psychicist counseling for three days. Quigley spat in the judge's face and tried to attack Caird again. She was stunned again and carted off to the jail.

"Now I'll have to take more time off from work to go to the psychicist," Lotus said as they walked home. "I hope nothing like this happens again."

"I doubt I'm going to be very popular," he said. "There are too many like Quigley. They'll blame whoever's handiest and I'll be handy."

He was right. Whereas he had been a hero of the locals, he now was a scapegoat. Hostile stares and muttered insults were to be a common reception. After a while, he quit going to the Seven Sages and tried another, though Lotus complained about missing the old place and her friends. He got the same treatment there from those who had been drafted into the Hoboken project. Eventually, he did most of his drinking at home, which caused Lotus more unhappiness. Finally, weeping and screaming that he had never loved her, she kicked him out. Her life had been hell since she had started rooming with him. Both statements were distortions of the truth, but he did not argue. He got a bachelor apartment on the West Side.

He saw Lotus a number of times again. He could not avoid it since they had to attend the same instruction sessions, and he had to endure her reproaches after the meeting. If he had truly loved her, she said, he would have resisted her order to leave. He would have argued with and cajoled her and convinced her that he truly loved her. She had been miserable, absolutely wretched, since he had gone. But she did not want him back.

"Then it's best we don't talk to each other," he said. He started to walk away.

"That's right!" she shouted after him. "Reject me, you son of a bitch! You never did love me! I knew it all the time!"

"Why do they blame *me*?" he said to the psychicist, Adrian Koos Hafiz, at the final counselling. "I didn't cause the changeover."

"Oh, yes, you did," Hafiz said. "If it weren't for you, it would never have come about."

"It's evident that the government had planned it all along," Caird said.

"It would not have come about so soon," Doctor Hafiz said, "maybe not for a very long time, if you hadn't catalyzed it."

"You really dislike me, don't you?" Caird said. "You should be angry at the government, not at me. It wasn't I who did it. I'm not the original Caird. I don't even want to be named Caird. I think of myself as Baker No Wiley."

"You can't expect the common citizen to make the distinction."

"How about you?" Caird said. "Have you been inconvenienced by the Changeover?"

"Inconvenienced, hell!" Hafiz said loudly. "I've been ordered to go to Hoboken to be a camp counsellor! Do you know what this means to me and my family? Do you have any idea at all what we have to give up? No, you don't, weedie!"

"I could report you for your nonprofessional attitude, your antagonism, and your insults," Caird said. "But I won't. My condolences."

The Changeover did not move swiftly. Four submonths passed before he was informed that he should report for training as a waiter in a camp mess hall at the Brooklyn Forest Park. The requirement of a high-school degree for this job had been waived.

Each day for four subweeks, he traveled via a DEE bus across Washington Bridge and then north to the training site. According to a plaque at the gateway, this area had been occupied in ancient times by a U.S. Veterans' Hospital. Caird, under close supervision, spent a subweek waiting on diners at a long wooden table in a huge quonset. The diners were robots programmed to act like human eaters. Whoever had set up their behavior was either a joker or had a very cynical view of humans. The human-looking machines were very hungry, unreasonably demanding, and uncouth. They "accidentally" knocked over glasses and pitchers of water and orange juice, dribbled food down the fronts of their shirts, spilled food on the table and the floors, and frequently belched and farted. Their complaints about the slowness and sloppiness of the service were loud.

Why the camp was set up here and not in the Hoboken area, Caird never learned. Nor did he find out why he had to put in eight hours a day for twenty-eight days to learn something he could have mastered in five hours or less.

He had looked forward to waiting on real human beings. But when he did, he discovered that the citizens might as well have been robots. The humans were, thank God, not as flatulent as the robots, but they were as demanding and complained more often and more loudly and were not far behind their mechanical counterparts in slovenliness and bad table manners. At first, he thought that this was because most of the diners were weedies. Then he found out, as time went by, that there were more of the "upper class" there than there were weedies.

The situation got worse when the diners found out that he was Jefferson Caird, the man they blamed for their situation. They found fault with everything he did and were not backward in insulting him. Near the end of the third subweek, he was attacked. A man who had been grousing about the quality of the food (unreasonably, Caird thought) rose from his table, slammed a plate of meat and vegetables into Caird's face, and then punched him in the stomach.

He was not consoled by the immediate arrest and consequent conviction of the attacker. He had to spend two days in a hospital bed. Moreover, except for one orderly, a Robert Gi Snawky, he seemed to be disliked and resented by all the hospital personnel. Snawky told Caird that he had heard that there were openings in the newly created destoning corps. He advised Caird to apply for one. Caird doubted that he would escape the resentment of people in the corps. However, the work would be more interesting than being a waiter.

Caird had talked via screen to his daughter now and then. He told Ariel about his troubles and his wish to be transferred to the destoning corps.

"There was a time when I would've scorned trying to use connections to get a job," he said. "But I'm becoming more realistic. Your husband is fairly high up in the Department of Physical Services. Do you think he could do me any good?"

"He will if he knows what's good for him," Ariel said.

A subweek passed before he heard back from her.

"Great news! Morris used his influence, and he's been promised that your application will be accepted. It'll be in the hands of the general committee, they're all on intertemporal visas because of the need for swift coordination, and a woman Morry knows, he doesn't want anyone to know her name, will see to it that you get into the destoning corps."

The application was accepted, but neither Morris's connections nor the vaunted speed of computers could hasten the glacier-slowness of the bureaucracy. After two submonths, Caird was informed that his application had been accepted. He was to report to a camp in New Jersey three subweeks from the date of notification of acceptance. Since this was too far away for him to travel each day, he took up quarters in it. This turned out to be very near the warehouse in which he, as Duncan, had freed Snick from her enstonement. He did not become aware of that until Ariel told him about it during a Tuesday evening long-distance conversation. After a period of instruction, he worked under direct supervision.

His task was to take the newly destoned person and guide him through the adjustment period. He found that fascinating, though often traumatic.

Only those who were physically healthy and young enough to work were brought out of the cylinders. These were all criminals of various degrees. Some of them had been here for over a thousand obyears, waiting for the invention of psychological techniques or chemical treatments which would ensure their rehabilitation. But they were not going into therapy. Instead, they were going to work for The Organic Commonwealth of Earth. Moreover, they would now be working every day. The government had decided that the destoned workers and their supervisors would no longer be gorgonized six days out of seven.

It was not easy to make some of the destonees understand what had happened. When they finally did, they were told that if they did not wish to participate in Changeover, they would be warehoused again. If they did choose to work, they would be given a pardon at the end of fifteen subyears. After which, if they managed to stay out of trouble, they would become full-fledged citizens.

There were five billion in the warehouses. Of these, there were almost a billion who were healthy, sane, and young enough to qualify as workers. That meant that, even with a slow destoning process, the population of the Earth would be increased by nearly a billion within the next fifteen obyears. Knowing that this number of new people would greatly strain all its resources and be impossible to control, the government was going to destone only about one hundred million. These would mostly be felons convicted for the lighter charges, though there would be among them many who had been stoned for crimes of passion.

"One hundred million crazies!" Caird's boss said. "They'll have to be kept in walled camps with armed guards. Otherwise, they'll just take off into the woods. There's not enough person-power to go after them. Just guarding and taking care of them is going to be a hell of a project!"

That was bad enough, Caird thought. What was worse was

that those who guarded and trained and served the destoned would also become prisoners.

"There'll be barbed wire around the camps," the boss said. "Do you realize there hasn't been a barbed wire camp for a thousand years?"

Many of the destoned were not going to make the grade as workers, Caird knew. They would go back into the cylinders, and others would be released to try their luck.

One of his wards, a Michael Simon Shemp, was a very cynical young man. "Yeah, they promise us we'll go free after we've built all their new cities," he told Caird. "But you wait. When it's done, back we go into the stoners. They'll find some excuse."

"If you believe that, why don't you ask to be stoned again?" Caird said.

"No. Anything's better than that. I think."

Whatever else awaited Shemp and Caird, they were no longer timehoppers. They would see every sunrise and every sunset; they would enjoy the natural slow-motion growth of a flower from seed to stalk to bud to bloom, no gaps between planting and cutting.

34

Part of Caird's job was to observe and evaluate the conduct and attitude of those under his care. If one appeared too dangerous, too intractable, Caird was to report his judgement to the chief organic officer in charge of this section. Caird hated the idea that he might have to send anyone back into the stoner.

Shemp had been selected for destoning because he had been a construction worker. Though he obeyed orders with quickness and a smile and showed no signs of obstreperousness, his biodata indicated that he had a violent temper. He had been convicted because he had killed a gank attempting to arrest him. He had failed to be rehabilitated, and so he had gone into the stoner. Shemp had been twenty-six subyears old then. His sole child, a daughter, had been born when Shemp was twenty-five subyears old. She was still living but was in Wednesday's New Haven, Connecticut-subarea, and was eighty-eight subyears old. Her son was dead, and her grandchild and one great-grandchild also lived in New Haven.

"I'd like to see them," Shemp said.

"You don't have a chance in hell of doing so," Caird said. "Not until you've been discharged as rehabilitated, and you won't even get any therapy until you've completed your work assignment, which'll be years from now."

"Which means never, right?"

"That I can't say. Be realistic. You'd be a stranger to your family. There's no background of long intimacy. Besides, you're a felon. That'd make them uncomfortable."

"I'm going to see them, one way or the other."

"You're going to try to escape?"

Shemp did not reply, but his intention was obvious. Caird, however, did not report the conversation. He was no snitch, though he was supposed to be. He attempted to talk Shemp out of the idea, and it looked as if he had convinced him. At least, Shemp seemed to agree. Then, one morning, Shemp did not appear for roll call. Two hours later, he was brought back from the forest into which he had fled northward. That he had been found so quickly indicated to Caird that a transmitter had been implanted in Shemp. He suspected that all the destonees were carrying transmitters in their bodies. This was illegal, but then he was probably carrying one, too.

A half-hour after his return to the camp, Shemp was thrust, screaming, into a cylinder, stoned, and then trucked back to the warehouse. Caird was called on the carpet by his boss.

"This'll be a black mark on your record," Donald Turek Normandy said. "You should have warned us of his recidivist tendencies."

"How was I to know?" Carid said. "He never said anything to me about wanting to escape. I told him that escape was impossible."

"We know. Shemp was TMed, and when we asked him if he had ever told you that he was going to attempt to escape, he said no. If he'd said yes, you'd be out of a job and probably on trial for conspiracy."

Caird thought back on his conversation with Shemp. It was

a good thing that Shemp had only said that he was going to see his descendants, "one way or the other." People under TM were literal in their replies to the questions.

Normandy said, "You'll get a printout of an official rebuke. But, on the whole, you've got a good record. You get along with the felons, and they seem to like you, though that in itself could be a cause for suspicion. You know how some of these ganks are. Makes no difference now. You're going to Hoboken. The work here is almost finished. You'll continue doing there what you're doing here, unless you fuck up again."

Two submonths later, he got onto the train near the warehouse and rode in a car that floated a few inches above the trackbed while it was shot forward by electromagnetic fields radiating from the line of huge rings surrounding the road. He arrived at the receiving station outside Hoboken within twenty minutes. The scenery had been mostly woods, but once, he passed by a vast clearing where machines and people were busy preparing a new city.

After he was shown his quarters, a cubicle in a monstrously large quonset, he attended the initiation briefing. Nothing brief about this; it lasted three hours. After that and lunch, he was in a group tour of Hoboken and then of the complex of warehouses several miles from it in the western forest.

The city had a population, per day, of 35,000 and consisted mainly of a half-a-mile-square building four stories high and the docks. Though in the New Jersey Forest, the area was under the jurisdiction of Manhattan State. The plans were to expand the city horizontally so that it could house 300,000 citizens. These would be Thursday's occupants of Manhattan State, that day being chosen by lottery. But the immigration was a long way off.

While in one of the gigantic warehouses, Caird noticed a number of other groups being conducted through the many rows of the stoned. His leader took them along the center aisle past the greyish bodies standing side by side like naked soldiers on review. In the center of the assemblage was a great square, and here his group encountered a second group. The two leaders called a break and talked to each other for a while. Caird was standing, somewhat bored, to one side and was looking at the members of the other party. A woman's face zoomed out of the crowd. He quivered as if he had been struck with a dart. She was short and dark and lovely-faced, and had sleek dark hair cut in a dutchboy-bob. Numbly, he walked over to her.

"Pardon me," he said. "Aren't you Panthea Pao Snick?"

She gasped.

"Jeff Caird!"

"Baker No Wiley, really," he said. "But officially I'm Caird."

"Yes, I know. You took me by surprise."

"I don't remember you, not from direct contact," he said. "I've seen you on tapes. I don't know if I should've come over. I haven't the slightest idea how you feel about me. But . . ."

She surprised him by reaching up and pulling down his head and kissing him on the mouth. When she released him, she said, "I thought I'd never see you again."

"You're an adjustment counsellor, too?"

"Yes."

They were silent for a few seconds. What did they have to talk about? He did not share with her their many adventures except at second-hand, as it were. But he felt very attracted to her. If he were capable of a schoolboy's sudden passion, he would think he was falling in love. That was nonsense, however. Still, he was drawn to her as a salmon was pulled upriver to its spawning place by instinct.

He was thinking, reacting, rather, like an adolescent.

Why not? He was, in a sense, only three subyears old.

How was she reacting? What had been, really, their relationship? Had they been lovers?

He asked her where she was stationed. She said that she was in Sector No. 3.

"Coincidence!" he said, smiling. "I'm in the same sector! What's your triangle?"

"Number Six."

"I'm Number Eight, only two over."

He paused, then said, "Could we get together?"

She cocked her head to the left and said, "You want to talk about us? You're curious to find out just what happened?"

"Among other things."

"You look . . . seem . . . different," she said. "Face, voice, gestures, the same. But your tone, your expressions . . . they are softer. And something else . . . what is it?"

He did not reply at once. As if a thick curtain in a midnight-dark room had been raised, revealing bright noon outside, he was dazzled. Time seemed to thicken. It was the chronons suddenly accumulating on him, he thought. Chronons? The wave-particles of time, analogous to photons and gravitons. What a strange concept. Everything is going to go faster from now on. What was a shapeless mass, seemingly shapeless, has been hammered out into a sharp spearhead. He heard footsteps, and now they were running where a moment ago they had been walking.

He rallied, and he fought his way out from the heaviness, which was at the same time a lightness. Water was heavy but brought weightlessness, picking up houses and rushing them away as if they were bubbles. He was simultaneously heavy and light.

"I'm not the same person," he said.

"Who is?"

"Nobody changes like I have."

Snick said, "You were in love with me or seemed to be. You never said so. I suppose you felt that I did not love you. I came close to it, I would have, only . . ."

"Only?"

"You . . . I admired you for your courage and your determination and your trickiness. You slipped through like hot butter every time they tried to squeeze you. You were also open and congenial and sensitive . . . under the circumstances . . . likable. But there were too many times when I sensed that you were not quite with it . . . with me, I mean. I think most people would never have noticed it. I'm rather quick to notice such things. But every time I began to believe that that had gone away, it returned. The remoteness, the wall. At first, I thought maybe it was shallowness. That, I found out, wasn't it. It was . . . you were elsewhere. You probably didn't know it yourself. But I certainly did. And that made a great difference. I don't want a man who's always circling me and sometimes comes near but never closes in."

"I think I can close in, grapple, now," he said. "But I really don't know. Why don't you give me a chance?"

"I will. But it may be too late. If not too late, well, two ships locked together sometimes go down into the sea together. Anyway, it sounds too much like combat."

"It was only a metaphor," he said.

"That's what life is made of. We are metaphors."

"What does that mean?"

She laughed, and she said, "I'm not sure."

"We get through life by making everything similes and metaphors. We never actually touch reality itself."

"How would you know?" she said. "You haven't been here long enough."

"That's true. Maybe."

He heard music from an open door. Someone was running a tape of an example of what the ancients called rock-and-roll. Though the original tape had been found in an excavation and was dated at N.E. 1220, it was the end result of what must have been many retapings. The historians said that the first recording had been made about A.D. 1988. The song was called "Jettison" and had been made by a group called Naked Raygun. Its type of music had been unknown until lately, but the twenty specimens found had been retaped and distributed. Weedies and teenagers liked its hard drive and the anti-establishment lyrics, even if some of them were no longer appropriate. The respectable citizen was made un-easy, if not outright repulsed, by the music.

Caird liked Naked Raygun's version of ancient rock. It throbbed like the compacted heart of the cosmos just before it big-banged, destroying itself so that it could be created again.

Now, rehearing "Jettison," he felt that the chronons were, barnacle-like, piling on even thicker. Through them pierced the thought that his personae had been flotsam and jetsam thrown up from the storms that thundered and boiled deep down in him. Or that he supposed were there.

He was in an incomplete cycle, himself the cycle, in which the curves were just about to meet.

Perhaps this was a wish brought up from the abyss by run-ning into Snick. He had no objective data to confirm his feelings.

By then, the two touring parties had merged into one and the supervisors were taking turns in lecturing.

The group had by now entered the rear section of the ware-house.

"As you know from experience," a supervisor said, "you start with the latest arrivals and work back to the earliest. There are fifty thousand stoned in this building, of whom five thousand have been selected as potential candidates for reconstruction workers."

The woman droned on, telling them what they already knew but were required officially to hear. Caird was near the back of the group, shifting restlessly from one foot to the other, looking around, half-listening. To one side and a little behind him was a row of stone pedestals on which were placed carved bassinets. In each was the body of an infant, and these seemed to range from newborn to six months old. He was somewhat curious because infant mor-tality was so rare. Yet these innocents had had the hard luck to die when not long out of the womb. This row, which extended as far as he could see through the warehouse, was reserved for babies only. The other children he had seen were old enough to be stood up for viewing.

He edged toward the nearest baby, a pink bonnet on its head, its eyes closed, its pale gray color covered with flesh tones, seemingly sleeping.

From that baby, he passed on to the next. Its head was covered with a frilly blue cap, and it, too, looked as if it would awake soon and demand milk or a change of diapers.

He wondered what had caused its death. He bent down to look at the ID plaque sealed into the pedestal top.

He read the name.

Light seemed to fill the warehouse. He was blind from the searing dazzle. He cried out, and then darkness roared in, soundlessly, and he felt, vaguely, that he was falling. But it was as if he were a feather zigzagging downwards in a breeze. He was almost weightless.

The name of the dead and stoned infant was BAKER NO WILEY.

35

He was vaguely aware for a while of the ceiling far far above him and of faces looking down at him and voices coming through a thick filter. He could not hear the words, but he could detect the questioning and concerned tones. These faded. The cycle had joined ends, a positive and a negative wire touching each other. The shock had gone through him and jolted him out of the world of present time and location. He fell swiftly away from the sights and sounds of now. Then they were gone and with them any consciousness of them and of the present.

Now he was terrified and screaming, though he could hear no sound. Now, he was falling. No. He was descending so swiftly that he seemed to be falling. But he felt the . . . muscles? slippery flesh? . . . of a gigantic throat enclosing him. He was being swallowed.

Now he was being chewed up, and this was somehow after he had been digested. He was not only going downwards, he was going backwards. Then he was no longer being chewed. He was in pieces, but these were exploding. They flared as they disintegrated with a light blacker than the blackness through which he was hurtling.

The silence and the darkness became part of him. He was ingested, no longer a separate being, a discrete thing. He was part of the silence and darkness, and they were part of him. But something huge and monstrous was pushing the object composed of himself and his immediate surroundings toward a cliff he sensed but could not see. Then sound and light slew the silence and darkness, and he was now himself, no longer contained in something he thought of as globular.

He was seeing himself on a floor-to-ceiling screen.

There in bed, below him and ahead of him, was Jefferson Cervantes Caird. Five subyears old, the only child of Doctor Hogan Rondeau Caird, biochemist and M.D., whatever those titles meant, and of Doctor Alice Gan Cervantes, molecular biologist, whatever that meant.

According to the wall-display glowing in the darkness of his bedroom, he had awakened at 3:12, Tuesday morning. Last Tuesday evening, he had gone to sleep and been carried to his stoner and gorgonized. Then, this morning, he had been destoned and, still sleeping, put to bed. At this hour, his father and mother would also be sleeping. But he had to get out of bed. He was thirsty and must urinate.

He got out of bed, touching at the same time the top of the head of the big teddy bear on the other pillow to reassure it that he would soon be back. And to reassure himself. He left the bedroom by the twilight illumination coming from the hallway. The hallway became somewhat brighter when he stepped into it. After emptying his bladder, he flushed the noiseless toilet, filled a glass with water, and drank part of it. He was in the hall on his way back to the bedroom when he heard Baker No Wiley calling softly to him from behind the half-open door of the stoner room.

Jeff went to the doorway but did not enter the room. He was frightened by the rigid figures inside the cylinders, people who were dead yet somehow not dead. He seldom went into that king-dom of the cold and the rigid in the daytime, and he had never gone into it after dark except when his father or mother had carried him, sleeping, into it. Sometimes he had very bad dreams in which he awakened in that coffinlike box and could not get out, and the half-dead crowded around the stoner and looked down at him through the window and mouthed silent threats and made gestures showing how they were going to eat him if he came out of the box.

He was horrified because he could not get out of the box, and, if he could, would be torn apart by the stone fingers of the adults and ground to bits in their stone teeth.

He had told his parents and the psychicist about these. He had told only his mother about Baker No Wiley after getting her promise she would tell no one about him. Apparently she had not told the psychicist the name of Baker No Wiley, though it had been impossible, she explained, not to tell the psychicist about his imaginary playmates. Or, as she sometimes called them, mental mirages.

Jeff suspected that she had broken her word and told his father about Wiley's name. Now and then, his father had dropped some hints that he knew it. But he had never admitted that he did, and his mother had denied telling his father about Wiley.

His mother had suggested that name when Jeff had first confided to her that the playmate had appeared one day, stepping out of the stoner room, and he, Jeff, was now looking for a name for him. At that time, his mother had not been so concerned about his "mirages" or his fantasies. Jeff had never asked her where she got the name or what it meant to her, if anything.

Now, Jeff no longer confided much to his mother. He felt that she had betrayed him.

"Baker's not real," his mother had said. "You made him up to compensate for your own excessive shyness and timidity. He's your twin brother—in your imaginings, I mean—but he's somehow bigger and stronger and much more brave than you really are. You act out your fantasies using him as your vicarious champion."

Jeff had not understood what a lot of her words like com-

pensate, excessive, and vicarious, meant. But he had consulted the
dictionary tape and learned them. His mother was right about him.
He was very shy and timid and easily bullied by the boys in his
own class and the older boys and, sometimes, by the girls. When
they called him bad names and taunted him and threatened to hit
him or actually did hit him, he ran away. He did not like school
—in fact, hated it—and he spent all the time he could in his
bedroom. There he watched TV to learn his school lessons or for
entertainment or playing with his "imaginary" companions.

Like the others, Baker had been rather thin when he first
appeared, so thin that the light shone through him. As time went
by, Baker became more solid and opaque. He became as real as
the children at school but a lot more pleasant. Jeff's other "mirage"
companions slowly faded away, and only Baker remained.

Baker was no fantasy. As surely as he knew that he breathed,
Jeff knew that Baker was no figment. Jeff could touch Baker's
flesh, feel its solidity, and feel Baker's breath on his face.

In some ways, Baker was more real than his schoolmates.
Play with him was lots of fun, and the fun was especially great
when Jeff imagined that the bullies were in his bedroom and Baker
was beating the stuffing out of them.

The bullies would have been pummeled bloody by Baker
if Jeff had not called him off. Baker was a hell of a fighter and
afraid of no one and nothing.

Now, Baker stepped out from behind the door and came
into the hall. He seemed to loom above Jeff, and he certainly was
far more muscular.

Baker was, for some reason, in street clothes, not the pa-
jamas, just like Jeff's, that he donned at bedtime. He said, "Let's
play, Jeff. We can do anything we want now. We can even go
outdoors. We got the house to ourselves."

Jeff felt scared. "You mean Dad and Mom are gone?"

"No, silly. I mean our parents are sleeping. We can pretend
we own the apartment and we can do what we want to in it."

Baker put a fingertip to his lips. "But we have to be quiet so we won't wake Dad and Mom up."

"I don't know," Jeff said slowly, though his heart was beating hard with excitement.

"Well, we *might* make too much noise," Baker said. "So let's sneak outdoors and have adventures. There won't be many big people out on the streets now."

"What about the monitors?" Jeff said.

"Who's watching them at this time of the night?" Baker said. "The ganks won't be watching the screens unless they get a call from somebody or an alarm goes off."

"Yeah, maybe," Jeff said. "But if we open the front door, Dad and Mom's alarm will go off."

"No it won't. Dad and Mom don't know we know the codeword to turn it off."

"Yeah, but . . ."

"Fraidy cat! Sissy! Pansy! Gutless!"

"Don't you call me names," Jeff said. "You're my friend, my twin brother. You don't call me names. I don't like it."

"Well, I'm doing it," Baker said, grinning. "I got to get you going, man. I love you, but I ain't too happy with you sometimes. You got to be more like me. How you going to do that if you don't practice being like me?"

"All right," Jeff said. "Only, first, I got to change into street clothes."

Reluctantly and slowly, he put on the clothes. At the same time that he was shaking with fear, he felt very excited. Maybe, just maybe, he could do this, have a real adventure. The only trouble was . . . if he got caught, he'd be punished and Baker would not be touched.

They went down the hall after Jeff had commanded the wallscreen to keep the hall light dimmed. One of his parents might wake up and see the light and get up and investigate.

Halfway down the hall, he heard the voices. They made a

295

murmur the words of which he could make out. He stopped, and he whispered to Baker, "They're awake! We can't go now."

"Don't you wish!" Baker said. "Let's go anyway."

They stepped softly down the hall, Jeff thinking that his heart was going to shatter his breastbone with its battering. Before he got to the bedroom door, which was a few inches open, Baker said, "Let's listen. Maybe we'll find out something. Adults don't tell us much, you know. They think they're so superior and mysterious."

Jeff followed Baker to the doorway. The bedroom was dark. Dad and Mom were talking so softly that Jeff could hear only a word here and there. Then he caught his name. They were talking about him.

He strained to hear more, but their voices were just too low, though they were intense. Why were they awake at this hour and talking about him? Somehow, he got the impression that they were talking about something that had troubled them for a long time and would do so for a long time. They sounded both sad and angry, angry at each other.

Baker whispered in Jeff's ear, though he did not have to whisper. Only Jeff could hear him. "Let's go back to our bedroom. We'll turn on the audio to their bedroom and listen in."

"That wouldn't be nice," Jeff said. "Besides, if they catch us doing that, they'll punish me, not you."

"They won't catch us," Baker said. "Are you going to be a namby-pamby forever?"

"But what if they told the wall to turn off their audio?" Jeff said. "We won't be able to hear them."

"How're we going to find out if we don't try? You do what I tell you, and you won't be a fruitcake. Maybe."

That made Jeff mad. "I'm not what you called me, those bad names. I'm not!"

He hesitated. He was very curious about his parents and why they would be talking about him.

"O.K. I'll do it. But if they catch us, I won't ever play with you again!"

"Sure," Baker said. "Who you going to play with then? You'll be all alone. You won't ever get any place, you'll always be a pansy if you kick me out. Or *I* walk out on *you*. You're plenty disgusting, you know."

As they went back down the hall, Jeff was wondering if he had done something very wrong that he did not know about. As far as he knew, he had been good. He had done nothing to upset them. Except not being brave and refusing to fight kids he knew could beat him up and being tongue-tied when called on to recite in class. He could not help that, and they should not hold that against him.

But you never knew about your father and mother. They got upset about the least little thing. They had rules and regulations that often made no sense to him. Their explanations of these—when they bothered to explain—sounded good to them but nuts to him. Sometimes he thought that adults were no more human than those aliens from outer space on TV.

But then he was not sure that his schoolmates were real Earthpeople.

He went with Baker into their bedroom and sat beside him on the sofa. He said, "What if they turn on the video to our room to see if I'm O.K.?"

"Why would they do that?"

His heart beating even harder, Jeff voice-activated the audio to his parent's bedroom and raised the volume to amplify the sound. He did not want the video on. If he was caught doing that, his punishment would be doubled. Anyway, their room was dark, and he would not be able to see them. But what if they turned the lights on and did you-know-what?

He told Baker that thought. Baker snorted, and he said, "They didn't sound very loving to me."

"No," his mother was saying, "we should never tell him. We must not. The shock would affect him the rest of his life. He's not a strong boy, he's very sensitive, too sensitive. Besides, what if we did tell him and then he told somebody else? We'd be in very bad trouble, and you know that."

"Of course I know that," his father said. "I'm really not stupid, though you talk as if I am. We wouldn't tell him until he was old enough to know that he'd have to keep his mouth shut."

"But why say anything at all?" his mother said. "It's not something he had to know. It won't make him any happier or better."

"It's the truth!"

"Damn you and your *truth*!" his mother said. "We're not dealing with science here. We're talking about our son, about human feelings. What's truth got to do with it? Better he doesn't know it's a lie, a lie meant for his own good, not to mention ours. You know people lie all the time to each other. There are times when the truth should be told, but there are lies that people need. And Jeff needs this one."

"No," his father said. "The truth should always come out. But it should be told discreetly and in the proper circumstances and time."

What? What? Jeff asked himself. His heart seemed to be tearing itself apart, and he was sweating and shaking. What?

He knew from TV dramas that children were sometimes adopted by childless couples. For some reason he did not quite understand, an adopted child was in some sort of peril. Or shame. Something to be dreaded despite what the actors said about love being the most important thing. *Not my flesh and blood!* Someone had said that in a show.

"Let's drop this and get some sleep, for Christ's sake!" his father said. "I've got a tough day tomorrow, EX will be running its final tests. And you've got to meet the MBDA committeeperson, and . . ."

"You always say that or have some excuse," his mother said. "For God's sake, let's talk it out now and come to a *sensible* decision! I can't stand this putting-off, and there's no reason why we should!"

"A *sensible* decision," his father said sarcastically. "What you mean by that is *your* decision. Why can't we wait? Even if we agree to tell him, we can't do it now. It'll be years before we can. So why not wait until the time comes, if it does? When he's eighteen and can also be told about the immers?"

"You know how I am," his mother said. "I can't stand to dodge issues. Procrastination (What was that? Jeff thought) drives me crazy. You're right when you say we can't tell him now. But I'll lie awake nights for years worrying about this if we don't get it settled now."

"You're neurotic."

"At least, I'll admit it."

"What does *that* mean?"

There was more, some of which Jeff did not understand. After a while, they became calmer but no less hard-headed. Though they spoke of other problems, they kept coming back to their main subject of contention. He had to put together the separated items, and then he began to comprehend the subject that was keeping him from sleep. Or he thought he did. His five-year-old mind could not really wrap itself around some of their references.

It was at first a slow leak, then it became a spurt, and then the seawall burst open, and the flood roared in.

Jeff One, as distinguished from himself, Jeff Two.

Jeff One had been their baby, born on the day that Jeff Two had been told was his birthdate.

Jeff One had died when he was two months old.

Neither parent had said outright what or who had caused the infant's death. Jeff Two, listening to the words and feeling the tones of their speech, got the idea that his mother was responsible for the accident. The baby's brain had obviously been damaged, and it had died a few minutes later.

His mother was forty-five subyears old then. His parents had delayed having a child because they were too occupied with their professions and social lives. That was what his mother said, and her voice was nasty when she said it. Then, since she was so old, in terms of child-bearing, and her cryogenized ova had been destroyed in a fire, they had decided that this was their last chance. So Jeff One, a healthy boy, had come into this world via Caesarean section. He would be the first and the last child for Doctor Caird and Doctor Cervantes. Though couples of their high professional rank and excellent genes were allowed to have two children, she had had to get permission because of her age. And that had been gotten only because the doctors had used their influence with some high officials. She would not have been licensed to have a second child.

Jefferson Caird, watching himself and Baker No Wiley on the display screen he had mentally projected, understood this. When he was five, he had known nothing about the procedure, of course. Nor did he know about the immers, then. He also understood now why his mother was unable to inform the authorities that her chronological age was forty-five but her physiological age was only thirty-two. She had become an immer when seventeen and had been injected with ASF then.

The baby, Jeff One, had died. For the first few minutes after stoning the baby, the parents had intended to call the hospital ambulance and the organics, though they knew that nothing could be done for the baby. Then Doctor Caird had an idea. He and his wife wanted a child of their own very much or, at least, had thought so at that time.

His father had destoned the baby and removed some skin cells from him. Then he had stoned these. The death was not reported. Using the immer underground organization, Caird and Cervantes had gotten the stoned body of Jeff One into a warehouse in forested New Jersey. To account for the body, the immers had inserted false data into the data banks.

Jeff One, now named Baker No Wiley, had taken his place among the silent and motionless rows in the warehouse outside Hoboken.

The clone had been grown in the laboratory headed by Doctor Caird, though only he knew that it was a clone. He took care of the records of the pseudo-experiment and the explanation for the end of the experiment and the supposed disposal of the body. Jeff Two had been spirited home to take the place of Jeff One. His father had operated on him to form the artificial navel. The few friends who saw the baby did not notice the age difference.

"I wish to God I hadn't suggested to him that he call his imaginary playmate Baker No Wiley!" his mother said, and she began sobbing. "Why did I do it? He asked me for a name, and it came out so quickly! I knew the moment I said it I'd made a mistake. Now, when I hear him say that name, and sometimes even when he doesn't, I think of our baby out there . . ."

"We have Jeff."

"I know, I know. I love him. But a clone is not the same person as the donor. It has different experiences. Anyway, it isn't the same even if it has the exact same genetic makeup. It's a separate and different person."

"We both know that," his father said. "There's no use rehashing the same story again."

"It's not a story!" she cried. "It's life, reality. It hurts!"

"You haven't adjusted very well," his father said.

"Are you saying I should take therapy? One whiff of TM, and the whole thing comes out. You know that."

"Maybe we made a mistake," Doctor Caird said.

"No! Never! I love Jeff and so do you! But . . ."

Baker No Wiley said, "Hey, Jeff!"

Jeff said, "What?"

He was numbed, unable to move, his brain sluggish, creeping like lava down a gentle slope but cold, cold.

Baker had risen from the sofa and was standing in front of him. He looked grim but also very powerful and brave. Jeff felt as if he should scream and sob and weep, but nothing would come out from him. Baker, however, did not look at all as if he were in pain.

"There's only one way to do it," Baker said.

"What?" Jeff said again.

"Let's play I'm the real person and you're me."

The light on the screen began to fade then. As it died out and just before complete darkness dispossessed the light, Jeff saw Jeff One and Baker No Wiley embrace and merge. It was as if Baker was a T-cell and had engulfed him, Jeff One. He had become both.

By the last of the light, a fast-blackening spark, Jeff thought, I must have lied when my childhood psychicist TMed me. I never told him anything about this. Or it was so deeply buried that not even TM could dig it out of me.

36

"He's a five-year-old boy in a grown man's body," Snick said.

She was watching Jefferson Caird on a screen. He was playing with a big teddy bear, talking to it and also, now and then,
speaking to someone invisible. The children in the huge playroom
were getting used to him and sometimes let him join their games.
But they still did not know what to make of him and never would.
Though they had been told that he was not mentally retarded,
they evidently thought of him as some kind of alien creature. They
had been told not to make slighting remarks to him, but some of
them could not help doing so. And Jeff had to be closely watched.
A five-year-old with the strength and mass of an adult could be
dangerous among small children.

"We'll have to abandon this particular experiment," the
psychicist said.

"But he can't be isolated," Snick said. "He would never
develop normally. What are you going to do with him?"

"I don't know yet," the psychicist said. "He's unique. There's never been a case quite like him."

Snick said, "Surely, you aren't thinking about stoning him? Warehousing him until workable techniques to treat him are developed? If they ever are."

"No. He's too interesting, too challenging. We'll work out the techniques with time. My colleagues and I wouldn't want to lose the chance of studying him."

"That's all?"

"Don't get me wrong," the psychicist said. "Of course, I regard him as a human being with problems that should be solved, not just as an experiment. I'm not cold and detached. He's not a bug, and I'm not an entomologist."

She watched Caird, as, hugging the toy and rocking back and forth, he spoke to the boy only he could see. She had directed the amplifier at him so that his deep voice was audible.

"Now, what we have to do, Jeff . . ."

"This Jeff?" Snick said. "He's himself?"

The psychicist shook her head. "I don't think so. It's puzzling. But he's not an alter ego. I just don't know . . . yet."

"He's escaped again," Snick said.

"What? Oh, I see what you mean. From himself."

"Yes," she said, but she had meant that he had once more eluded the government.

Snick glanced at the wall-display time.

"I have to get back to work. But I'll be back from time to time. Thanks again for allowing me to come here."

"You were in love with him?"

"He's the only man I could have lived with for very long."

"Don't despair," the psychicist said. "He'll develop into a normal adult . . ."

"Which he never was . . ." Snick said.

"But he may become one. Or the adult in him may surface again."

"Which adult?" Snick said.

The psychicist smiled and raised her eyebrows. "Who knows?"

Snick took one last look at Jeff Caird and his teddy bear before stepping out of the room. She was remembering the gibberish he had spoken after he had fallen to the floor in the warehouse. In its midst, two sentences had been clear enough to be understood.

"The dayworld is breaking up. So am I."

37

Twenty-five years had passed since the Changeover had begun, twenty-five years as measured by the circling of the Earth around the sun. Ten years ago, the division of time into subjective and objective had entirely ceased. The New Era calendar of thirteen months in a year had been kept, but people now lived horizontally according to it, not, as in the old days, vertically. Birthdays were now celebrated once a year instead of every seven years.

Many cities had been completed as long ago as fifteen years before the present date. Many cities had only been built as recently as five years ago.

Ariel Cairdsdaughter had been wrong in her predictions that a worldwide and bloody revolution would shatter the government and result in a new one. There had been some rebellions, but these had been quickly and sometimes savagely crushed. On the whole, the citizenry, though often unhappy about its lot, had submitted. And a majority were satisfied with what the "revolution" had accomplished. These were (1) the breakup of the New Era system

307

of living, (2) the giving of ASF, the age-slowing factor, to every person on Earth, the Moon, and the Martian colonies, and (3) the legalization and availability of anti-TM. The people had regained their age-old ability to lie.

One of the demands of the revolutionists had been that the members of the government throughout its hierarchies be closely monitored. This would find corruption and prevent additional corruption. Some small reforms had been made, but the keen watching of officials and the power to remove them by monitoring committees had not been done. There were still sporadic demands by citizens' groups that this be brought about. Little had resulted from this.

Though the World Council and the provincial governors were chosen by popular vote, the World Council selected the candidates who could run for office.

The close monitoring of people by the government was still in full force. It was for the good of the people, the government insisted, and no amount of demonstrations or mass petitions had changed the status quo.

Couples were allowed to have only two children though there was a minority of citizens who continued to agitate for extending the limit to three.

A small minority had not quit asking for the right of religionists to build churches, synagogues, mosques, and temples and to repeal the law forbidding religionists to work for the government.

Panthea Pao Snick, considering the goals achieved and lost, thought about Jeff Caird. If he were the original Caird, she told herself, he would still be out there somewhere fighting to bring about the complete revolution.

Panthea Snick had had seven different jobs during the twenty-five years after the Changeover began. She had lived in three different cities: Trenton, New Jersey; Springfield, Illinois; and her present residence, Denver, Rocky Mountain State. She had been thirty subyears old when the Changeover came and was now 250 obyears old. But the physiological age on her ID card was 33.5 years.

For the past seven years, she had been a planning coordinator in the Department of Reconstruction. This position had required a lot of time outdoors and in the field. Now, though, she was more and more bound to the office. A woman of action, she grew more restless and resentful every day. Since she had more free time, she had been running lists of jobs on her office and home screens. What looked most appealing at the moment was a forest-planting project in the Central Siberian Uplands. The jobs that she actually most wanted were in the Organic Department, and she scanned them even though she knew that she did not have an Albanian's chance of ever getting one.

Thus, the visit from General Anthony Wik Horn, upper staff member of the Internal Affairs Office of the North American Organic Department, did more than just surprise Snick. For one thing, Horn did not make arrangements for the meeting via screen. She appeared at the office early in the morning, breezed past the monitoring secretary without answering her questions, and entered Snick's office. Snick did not protest at this lack of protocol because the woman was a high-ranking organic. The epaulets and bars and badges on her green robe made that evident. For a second, Snick thought that the woman had come to arrest her. But if the general had wanted her for any reason, all she had to do was to send some officers to pick her up. Or just TV her and order her to appear at a precinct station.

Anthony Wik Horn was very tall and curvy. Her waist was startlingly small, though the enormous breasts and flaring hips may have made her waistline look smaller than it was. Snick decided that Horn could only be described by the cliché "statuesque." She was also overpowering in looks and personality. Her voice was unusually deep for a woman's.

Stopping just before the desk and looking down at the diminutive Snick, she steepled her hands on her chest and bowed slightly.

"Detective-General Anthony Wik Horn!" she boomed. "Sit down!"

Snick obeyed, saying, "No need to introduce myself, of course?"

"Of course!"

Horn remained standing though Snick offered her a chair.

"I'm here in person because my superiors think it's best that we don't use TV," she said. "I've been given this job because it was decided that a higher official should deal with this. I hope you'll pardon me, but I've made arrangements to turn off all wallscreens, and this office has been swept for bugs."

Snick looked at the dead gray of the receiving-transmitting strips and shrugged. She did not comment. She waited for Horn to inform her about the reasons for her mission.

Horn smiled, exposing big white teeth. "Your biodata states that you're not very talkative."

Snick saw no reason to comment.

"The records of your sessions at the rehab center also revealed that you were keenly disappointed, highly frustrated, because you were barred from the profession of organic officer."

"Then you also know," Snick said, "that the frustration comes mostly from the injustice done to me. I was framed. I said it then, and I say it now. The government railroaded me. I was a dedicated gank, and I was betrayed by the very people whom I was loyally working for. What would your reaction be if you'd been treated like that?"

"I'd hate the department's guts," Horn said. "No doubt about that. In fact, I was not ordered to bring you the department's proposal. When I heard about it, I volunteered to be the one to contact you. I sympathize very much with you. You got a really rotten deal. Apparently, the department realizes that now. It wishes to make amends."

"Amends?" Snick said. "After all this time?"

Horn lifted her big shoulders and said, "It could've been never. I'm authorized to offer you a full reinstatement in the department. You'll also be given a promotion. You'll be a field colonel. All data re your record as a revolutionary, your illegal gorgonizing, too, will be erased from the biodata on your ID card. We can't erase that data from the permanent organic data banks, but it'll be accessed only by the highest officials and then only if a high need is shown."

Snick held up her hand. "Hold on a moment. *Why* am I being offered all this?"

"I'll be frank," Horn said. "I don't know everything about this case. I don't know all the whys. What I was told is that your record shows you were a highly competent officer. More than that. An extraordinary detective. Also, you showed a tremendous amount of ingenuity and aggressiveness while you were a revolutionary, and . . ."

"I never was a genuine revolutionary," Snick said. "I became one because I was forced to."

"We know that. It's in the rehab psychicist's reports. And . . ."

Snick, narrow-eyed, said, "Is my redemption to be public? Or is it something just confined to the department?"

Horn, looking slightly annoyed, said, "I was getting to that. There'll be no publicity. It's thought best to keep all this quiet, but you'll have no trouble in inner-departmental affairs."

"I want my restoration made public," Snick said.

Horn sat down and sighed as if she knew she was in for a longer session than she had expected.

Snick continued. "I want the people who were directly responsible for framing me punished. And I want it on the news channels and on callup tapes."

"My God!" Horn said. "Your biodata indicated you have the nerve of a monkey triple-bound in brass, and it certainly did not exaggerate! You've suddenly got what you've been lusting for all these years, and you're making demands!"

"I thought you understood me," Snick said. "You don't talk as if you do. I repeat. I want them punished, and I want a public acknowledgement I was framed and an apology from the government."

311

"You're not really in the driver's seat, you know," Horn said.

"I think I am. I don't know why or how I got there, but I am in it."

"Very stubborn, too," Horn said. "O.K. I'm authorized to give you certain concessions. If I say yes to them, I'll be fully backed by my superiors. However, you have to realize . . . may I call you Thea? . . . that the man responsible for stoning you was David Ananda, a.k.a. Gilbert Immerman. He's long dead and so are those who carried out his orders. Dead or stoned."

"If that's true . . ."

"It's true, Thea."

". . . I still want the frame-up disclosed to the public."

Horn frowned slightly. Then she said, "Very well."

"Why this sudden interest in me?" Snick said. "The government doesn't have a conscience, and it never does anything unless it's forced to do so or it's for its benefit."

"I was once a colleague of Jefferson Caird," Horn said. "We were both Tuesday, and I was the organic commissioner for Manhattan."

"What does that have to do with my question?"

Horn said, "We want you to track down Caird."

That startled Snick, though she did not show it.

"I didn't know he was missing."

"As of three years ago," Horn said. She leaned forward and gazed intently into Snick's eyes. "He's not wanted for any crime, not yet anyway. His ID card hasn't been used for three years. That's not a crime, but it is a misdemeanor if a citizen moves to another place and doesn't record the move. He was living in Colorado Springs and studying electronics at Rocky Mountain University. He had gotten his M.S.E. and had registered for the four-year doctorate program. The day before classes began, he disappeared. There was a violent electrical storm that day. He apparently took advantage of it to avoid satellite detection."

"Jeff," Snick murmured. "I didn't have the slightest idea

312

what he was doing. I kept up on his progress for six or seven years. Then I moved. Now and then, well, you know the news media. They made reports on him for a while. But when he ceased to be of much interest, they quit commenting on him. The last I heard, he was doing quite well, though he still had no memory of his life before he was five. And he did not remember anything about his former personae."

"The department has kept a close watch on him, of course," Horn said.

"Of course. Just as they have on me."

Horn leaned back against the chair and said, "We'd like to find him, find out what he's doing. As I said, he's not wanted for any crime—as yet. But there have been some troubles, interference, data insertions, satellite malfunctions, that we suspect . . ."

"That Jeff caused?"

"Yes."

"But you have no proof?"

"No. But he has to be found anyway. He's missing."

Snick's heart beat faster, and something hot and delicious ran through her. Once again, she was the hunter.

However, Caird was the quarry. What would she do if she did find him?

Horn, as if reading her thoughts, said, "You don't have to arrest him. We know how personally involved you were with him. Just report to us when and where you found him. If, however, you feel duty-bound to apprehend him, do so."

"I'm surprised," Snick said. "It's my duty to arrest any criminal, no matter what my relations are to him."

"This is a very special assignment, and it's to be done very quietly. If he's just guilty of failing to report his location, he'll be fined or put in a labor force for six months or possibly both. If he is committing any felonies or has done so, he'll be arrested and given his due trial. There won't be any publicity about either situation. The truth is, the department doesn't want to stir up old memories or make him a martyr again."

"What you suggested he might be doing," Snick said. "That sounds pretty serious."

Horn shrugged and said, "He's innocent until proved guilty. Except for the failure to report a move, of course."

"What if someone killed him and buried his body?"

Horn said, "Oh, we've considered all possibilities. That one is not high on the probability list."

"I'll do it!" Snick said. "Provided, of course, my terms are met."

"They will be. You'll be completely exonerated. Your case'll be made public, and you'll be reinstated in the department and given your new rank. You'll have carte blanche, anything you need to help you. Oh, yes! I forgot to mention that you'll also receive all the credits you would have had if you had stayed employed. They'll be based on the pay of a detective-captain, the rank you held when you were stoned. That'll be quite a large sum."

They're bribing me, Snick thought. They didn't have to do that. There must be another reason why they've hired me to do this job. It can't just be because I'm so good at it. But she did know Caird better than anyone else, far better, and that would be an advantage in the hunt for him. That might be one of their motives for using her.

It was ironic. She had begun this long circuit by trying to catch Caird, had instead run with him, and now she was hunting him again. The ends of the positive and negative wires were about to make contact. Perhaps.

After Horn and Snick had talked about the details of the case for fifteen minutes, Horn stood up. "You call me if you need anything. I'll be your only liaison. I'll say goodbye for time being."

She bowed, turned, halted, and turned back.

"Oh, this is a small point, but it might be of some significance. While Caird was in Colorado Springs, he had a framed photo of you on his wall. He took it with him when he left."

Snick did not trust herself to speak. She felt choked and, at the same time, a hotness in her breast.

Horn said, "Does that mean anything?"

Snick swallowed and said, "I have no idea. I won't know until I find him, will I?"

"Will you?" Horn said. She smiled and turned away again.

Panthea Snick went through the required two months of retraining at an organic academy and a month in the field. Then she was given her promised rank of colonel. During this time, she studied the many tapes sent her by Horn. All of these were of Caird's career as known by the organic department, including the monitorings of him since he had what the psychicists called his "regression to infancy." His conduct since then was exemplary. In fact, he had been such a model citizen, up to the point of his disappearance, that the ganks considered it to be suspicious.

There were six cases of false data insertion in the data banks of Las Vegas and Colorado Springs while Caird was living in the latter city. Though he was suspected of having committed these crimes, the organics could find no evidence that he was responsible.

The department was very upset, however, because the culprit—whoever he was—had gotten through security measures considered to be absolutely impregnable.

Another event far more serious was the simultaneous shutting down of all the monitoring satellites over the Rocky Mountain area. Since these refused to respond to any signals from the ground stations, they could not self-test themselves. Spaceships carrying engineers had to be sent up to troubleshoot the satellites. Though the engineers were able to start them up again, they could not trace the source of the shutdown. It was obvious that transmissions from the Rocky Mountain area had caused the failure. The ganks swarmed over this territory like ants scenting honey. The hunt was even more intensive than that for Caird after he had fled Colorado Springs. (If, indeed, he had ever left the city, Snick thought.)

The search was still continuing, but it was being conducted by routine and occasional unscheduled foot and airboat patrols.

Since the satellite incident, nothing untoward had happened. Snick thought that Caird, or whoever was causing trouble, had just been testing his electronic techniques. He had demonstrated that they worked well and that the methods used and their source of origin could not be determined.

Every type of sensor, visual, infrared, ultraviolet, sonic, and olfactory was used in the searches. Also, knowing that the outlaw might be taking refuge in caverns, the magnetometer maps of the entire area were checked. Not one hollow in the earth in the vast area was overlooked. Those caverns without entrances were personally checked to make sure that none had been plugged up by humans or were concealed by camouflage. This search was long and expensive and succeeded only in finding a few outlaws. None of these could have been responsible for the data insertions or the satellite failures.

Snick still thought that it was very probable that Caird was out there in the wilderness. One night she woke up, startled, hearing a man's voice by her bedside. But it was a dream, and she had heard only the voice, not the words, of the speaker.

Nevertheless, she sat up on the edge of the bed, quivering, a thought as bright as a new ID card shining in her. After some concentrated thinking, she got back under the covers and was asleep in two minutes. The next day, she called up on her apartment wallscreen the latest magnetometer survey of the central Rocky Mountain area. This was ten years old and was the one the ganks used in their search. The previous survey had been made twenty years ago. She summoned that and had the two surveys compared.

The computer instantly found one discrepancy between the two charts. This was a cavern complex halfway up Cloud Peak. It was in the Bighorn Range and was the highest mountain in that area once known as Wyoming.

Snick laughed softly.

Caird had managed to erase that one item of data from the latest survey.

The ganks, relying on this, had not gone to the cavern and probed it.

"Always the trickster!" she said.

38

First, she had to ascertain that a microtransmitter had not been implanted in her. That it was illegal to do that to anyone except convicted felons would not stop them. Even though she had been fully rehabilitated (according to the psychicists), had been restored to the organic department, and her case had been publicized, the department would not fully trust her.

On the other hand, she was a veteran gank, and they would know that she would eventually check on the possibility that a microtransmitter had been placed in her body.

But, knowing that she knew this, the ganks might calculate that she would consider the probability of the illegal action as very low. They could have entered her apartment while she was sleeping, injected a hypnotic, and put the device under her skin. The wound would be covered with artificial epidermis.

She had to make sure that she was not bugged. She went to an organic hospital and was scanned. Not to her surprise, she found that there were two microtransmitters in her. One was halfway up her left forearm; the other under the skin on the back of her neck.

This examination would be reported to General Horn, of course. Horn would steel herself for Snick's fiery indignation and legal suit against the organic department. She would be wondering if her career were in danger. But Snick did nothing, leaving it to the much-relieved Horn to believe that Snick did not care if she was bugged. After all, if Snick was on the up-and-up, why should she resent the signals? They would assure her that she would be located if she were alone in certain situations and needed help from her colleagues.

Horn might also figure that Snick did not want to cause any trouble. Snick did not give a damn what Horn thought. She just wanted to be certain about being bugged.

Having checked the long-range weather predictions (which were not much better than those of two thousand years ago despite the advances of the science of meteorology), Snick made her plans and waited more or less patiently. The rain-and-thunderstorm struck the Rocky Mountain area two days after its scheduled arrival. On the third evening, the boiling clouds sped darkness over Colorado Springs, the wind bent trees, and the lightning turned the clouds into electrical chaos. Snick climbed into the airboat she had requisitioned and had packed with mountain clothes and equipment. The airboat rose into a howling and crackling terror despite the orders from the air control department grounding all craft.

She had smeared a heavy metallic paste over the areas marked with indelible ink on her forearm and the back of her neck. And she disconnected the automatic transmitter placed behind a bulkhead in the stern of the boat.

Riding in a tossing vessel which battled a sidewind and tried to maintain a fifty-foot level above the trees and the now-and-then bare terrain, fitfully dazzled by nearby lightning bolts, her eyes on the instruments and especially on the topographical display, Snick reached Cloud Peak in seven hours. The programmed automatic navigation brought her to the entrance of the cavern complex, dimly seen in the headlight beams. It entered the rough arch in the steep rocky side of the mountain. The wind caught the stern and swung it so that it scraped against the right side of the entrance. Twelve feet inside past the arch, Snick landed the boat.

The headlights showed a hollow about twenty feet wide and thirty deep. Beyond that was the mouth of a tunnel which ran straight for a few feet, then curved and disappeared. It was not wide enough for the craft. She got out and, carrying a flashlight, walked down the tunnel. The roof varied from two to three feet above her head, and the walls were sometimes almost close enough to brush her shoulders. Then she was faced with two entrances. On her right was a hole large enough for her to crawl through without bumping her head or squeezing her sides. The flashlight showed that it ran straight ahead into darkness. The left hole was narrow but crawlable and seemed to open into a larger space.

Though both tunnels could be booby-trapped, Snick entered them. Both ended in piles of rock. If there were continuations of the tunnels beyond the tumbled masses, they were blocked off.

That meant that the entrance or entrances to the cavern complex were elsewhere—if Caird were inside this mountain.

She slept the rest of the night in a sleeping bag on an inflated mattress. Her watch alarm woke her up an hour before dawn. It was still raining, but the thunderstorms had passed, and the wind was not as strong. After eating, she took the airboat into the forest. She filled her backpack with food and water and other items and then climbed a pine tree. Halfway up, she found a reasonably comfortable perch and tied herself to it. The next six hours were miserable, but she was a veteran of long, boring, and uncomfortable stakeouts.

At six minutes to ten in the morning, she saw through her binoculars something moving in the brush. This was not the first time. Two deer, a fox, and a bear had attracted her attention. But this was a movement of the pine-needle covered ground. It was between two trees the branches of which interlaced.

She had figured that any underground tunnel Caird made would have an exit not too deep inside the woods. And it would emerge somewhere in a small area just about here.

The trapdoor, covered with needles and branches glued together, rose up. Though the branches between her and the trapdoor hindered her view, she could see a man raise his head from the hole. He looked around cautiously. There were probably sensors at that spot and elsewhere close by to detect anybody aboveground before he came out. Nevertheless, some one beyond the range of the sensors might be looking his way. Having satisfied himself that no one was in the neighborhood, he climbed out and began to lower the camouflaged trapdoor. Snick had untied the rope securing her to the trunk and was already climbing down.

Two minutes later, she came up behind the man, who was wearing a camouflage suit and helmet. He held a combination laser rifle and parabolic sound-detector. On his back was a small cylinder attached to a long flexible hose at the end of which was a smaller cylinder open at one end. This, she was sure, was a sniffer set to catch the molecules of deer odor. He was hoping to bring back the makings of venison for Caird's dinner table.

Snick said, "Freeze!"

The man obeyed. At her next command, he slowly placed the rifle on the ground, then moved ahead several feet. Having picked up the rifle, Snick said, "Turn around."

He did so, his eyes widening slightly but his face impassive, his hands clasped behind his neck.

"Don't try to use that knife hidden under the neck of your jacket," she said. "But I'm not here to arrest you. My name is Panthea Pao Snick. Do you recognize it?"

The man smiled. "I recognized you. I'm Sherban Shi Mason."

Snick said, "Take me to your leader."

She could not help grinning as the man guffawed.

Then she said, "I'm not here to harm you or anybody in Caird's band."

"I believe you. Caird has said more than once that you'd find him some day. Or vice versa."

A few minutes later, they were in the bottom of the shaft to the trapdoor and going slowly in the low and narrow tunnel. This led gently upwards between walls of solid rock. He led, his hands still on the back of his neck despite his protests that she was in no danger from him. Her flashlight brightened the way ahead. Then they were climbing on the metal rungs set on the wall of a shaft. The rifle was slung over her back. Though her handgun was holstered, she had told Mason it would be out before he could try anything. She did not think he would, but she had not lived this long by trusting strangers. Or even long acquaintances.

She had gone first up the ladder, the flashlight held in her teeth. He was to follow her when she got to the top of the rungs. He could run away toward the other end of the tunnel, she said, but he would be shot before he reached the other shaft below the exit.

"I believe you," he said. "Anyway, I've no reason to run."

She pushed up the trapdoor and, with one hand, probed the beam around the rockwalled room. It was empty of people and furnishings. When Mason got to his feet in the room, they proceeded along another narrow tunnel, he in front. Then he opened a door, and light flooded out.

"It's O.K.!" he called. "It's Mason! I'm with Panthea Snick!"

She was startled when a woman's voice spoke behind her. "Your turn to freeze."

The hard bulb of a handgun was jammed into her back.

"Damn!" Snick said softly, and she dropped her gun and locked her hands against the back of her neck.

She had seen no thin lines on the tunnel wall to indicate that a door was there. But there must have been one, and the woman had come through it to get behind her. She was glad that she had not tried to invade this place with intent to kill.

321

Three men and a woman stepped out from behind the door as Snick entered it. With Mason now behind her and the others flanking her, relieved of her gun and hunting knife, she was directed through the tunnel into a very large cavern with stalactites hanging from the ceiling and stalagmites projecting from the uneven floor. Several large lamps gave a dim illumination. They went through some other caverns to the left. There were a few people there, most of them sleeping in bags.

Mason said, "You wouldn't be here, you know . . . excuse me, most probably don't know . . . if it weren't for Caird. He's the one put pressure on the government to exonerate you and to reinstate you in the organic department."

"No," Snick said loudly so that Mason could hear her clearly. "I didn't know that."

"Caird got word to the World Council that he had firm evidence of the dirty dealings of some of their members. He guaranteed to reveal those to the public unless you were reinstated."

"How did he do that?" Snick said. "And how would he get the data to the public?"

Mason did not reply directly to that question.

"One of our group is a computer genius."

Snick noted that their route did not include any places containing the large machine needed to interfere electronically with the satellites. Everything she saw could be quickly bundled up and carried away by their owners. They were obviously ready to move at a minute's notice.

Then they were at the end of a tunnel and before a doorway from which hung a heavy curtain. Mason told her to halt, and he pushed the curtain aside while he entered the room. She glimpsed a well-lit room with rock walls. She sucked in her breath when she saw a large photograph on the wall. Her face, looking straight ahead, was in the frame.

When she had been told that Caird had taken a photograph of her when he had fled Denver, she had considered the implications. Caird, as Baker No Wiley, had no memory of her. But he

322

had seen the many tapes of him taken in his previous personae. She had appeared in some of them, and he had doubtless then obtained tapes devoted to her. Why?

She could only find one valid answer. Whatever his selves, he was attracted to her. Even a tape summoned up that feeling deeply lodged in him. He must be in love with a picture. But that image resonated with unconscious memories.

Though she was not at all romantic, she was very touched by this and her breast warmed.

His identities, she thought, were like differently shaped and colored beads on a string. The string was the basic person, the primal identity. It continued, smooth and unbroken and always of the same density and material, in the center of every bead. The original Caird was the string. Those others, Tingle, Dunski, Repp, Ohm, Zurvan, Isharashvili, Duncan, and the present Caird, were the beads.

The string had always been a rebel, though a very canny one, a trickster.

Mason pushed through the curtain, muttering, "I've never seen him like this."

He looked at Snick. "Though I might've expected it. You can go in now. Alone."

Though it was not her nature to hesitate, she paused a few seconds before pushing the curtains aside. Then, breathing deeply, she went into the room. The curtains closed behind her with a very slight swish, like a sword cutting through the air.

Caird was the only one in the large but low-ceilinged chamber. Against a far wall was a big silvery cylinder, probably a power supply. Cables tentacled over the floor everywhere. Wallscreens flashed with words, numbers, and formulae and news channels from many places, Zurich, Shanghai, Sydney, Cairo, Chicago, Buenos Aires.

Caird, standing before a workstation but facing her, was smiling. Then he strode toward her, his arms out. He enfolded her in them and kissed her, enmeshing their lips for many seconds.

She had not expected such a warm greeting, but she welcomed it.

When he released her, he said, "I'm assuming too much, I know. I was overcome for a moment."

"You're not a stranger to me," she said. "And even if you don't remember me in the flesh . . ."

"Have you come to stay? I knew you'd always find me one way or the other. But I wasn't sure in what role you'd come. I mean . . ."

"I know what you mean," she said. "I wasn't quite sure, either. But, yes, I've come to stay."